Charlotte Nash began stealing her mother's Jilly Cooper novels at thirteen, and has been enthusiastic for romance ever since. She started writing after medical school, and her enduring stories of courage and love are now published around the world. She writes from a cottage on the east coast of Australia. *On A Starlit Ocean* is her seventh novel.

Visit charlottenash.net for all the books. She loves to hear from readers through:

@CharlotteNash79
AuthorCharlotteNash
@charlottenashauthor

Also by Charlotte Nash:

THE WALKER-BELL SAGA
Ryders Ridge
Iron Junction
Crystal Creek

On A Starlit Ocean

STAND-ALONE NOVELS
The Horseman

CONTEMPORARY FICTION WITH ROMANTIC ELEMENTS
The Paris Wedding
Saving You
Twenty-Six Letters (forthcoming)

On A
Starlit Ocean

Charlotte Nash

FLYING
—NUN—
PUBLICATIONS

Published worldwide in 2020 by Flying Nun Publications, http://flyingnunpublications.com/

ISBN:
978-1-925775-21-1 (paperback – Australian edition)
978-1-925775-22-8 (MOBI eBook – Australian edition)

A catalogue record for this book is available from the National Library of Australia

Cover by Designrans

Chapter 1

Aboard the *Fair Winds*, March 2011

Erin Jacobs watched the island of Great Haven slide over the horizon at seven minutes after dawn. The eastern sky was all spreading apricot and salmon clouds by then, painting the island in a golden rim, the ocean clapping softly against the limping yacht's bow. The soft chugging of the diesel motor fell flat into the sea.

Erin shielded her face from the light, peering ahead. Nothing looked to have changed. Not from the jutting height of Bella's Leap at the island's southmost tip, to the embracing curve of the main beach, to the gulls lazily trailing her mast. And look, there was the same sign on the marker at the head of the channel, reading *Welcome to Great Haven* in faded cursive letters.

Only, everything had changed, hadn't it?

Four years had passed, and she was alone on her boat. Four years since she and her father had sailed away, and she had never intended to come back.

Her heart ached with regret as she steered around an underwater coral crop she knew jutted into the edge of the channel. Her father had taught her to avoid it. He'd taught her all about the waters around Haven.

Erin tried to shake the memory away. That wasn't the reason

she was here now. Her sister Skye – who had never once called since Erin left – had reached her on a bad connection to the satellite phone, and told Erin she needed to come home before the call broke off.

Erin, who'd been between jobs in the Bahamas, had jumped a boat to Florida and then a flight to the Gold Coast where she'd collected her boat (and hastily insufficient provisions), and turned north. Three days later of sailing around the clock, and here she was.

Well, just.

The *Fair Winds* had clearly suffered in neglect. There'd been mould growing in the freezer box, shackles loose on their moorings. And then an hour ago, as soon as she'd met the first famous bluster of the Haven winds, the boom had cracked like a whip and the main halyard – the rope holding up the main sail – had snapped.

Erin had pulled the sail down in the dark and slung it in alternating pieces over the boom. The breakage itself wasn't a disaster; she could move around the boat with her eyes closed, and knew how to limp along on the foresail until she was close enough to start the motor. But she tried and failed not to see the event as an omen.

Her stomach flipped as the island neared, close enough now to pick out the individual palm trees behind the dunes. Her body knew this was home. She loved Haven's deceptive beauty, where the paradise of beaches and forest was set in a stretch of tricky waters, with frequent harsh storms and fierce tides.

Even now, she could see the spray crashing below Bella's Leap. At the top of the cliffs, the peak of Helmut's art studio was just visible on the next point – everyone said he was crazy to live up there with the storms. To the west, the cliffs dropped dramatically into a long main bay. The village was at the western end of the premium white sand, while the eastern end was lined with palm trees – the resort's front to the beach.

Erin frowned.

Wait, something had changed.

The bay should have held a dozen anchored yachts, as it had the day Erin and her father had sailed away. Now, the water was all but empty. She throttled down the motor, her ears straining to hear the powerful engines of the tourist shuttle coming from the mainland. But there was only the whine of wind and the feather-rush of gulls.

Too quiet.

Erin squinted at the resort again, still in the shadow of Bella's Leap. It looked as though a fence ran along the front, a nine-foot, chain-link, keep-out kind of fence.

Erin's chest hollowed. Wait, was the resort *still* closed?

Three years ago, when she'd been racing in the Seychelles, she'd heard on the grapevine that the Great Haven resort had shut down. But that had been deep in the time she hadn't wanted to hear anything of home, and it was old news anyway. Yes it had closed – the same week she and her father had left – but temporarily, for renovations. The new owner had assured the village it would reopen within six months.

Now, as Erin limped into the jetty, the desolation of the shore put a chill in her heart. There were no surf skis on the beach, no catamarans. No toboggan carving a wake across the water. She could see two fishermen down at the far western point, their lines in the ocean. But the jetty itself was empty.

Why hadn't Skye mentioned any of this?

Killing the motor at just the right moment, Erin let the yacht drift into the pier, throwing out the fenders and taking up the stern rope. With one hand on the railing, she jumped for the wooden deck and threw the rope around a hitch, just as the yacht fenders grazed the piers. The *Fair Winds* groaned to a stop.

There. Perfect.

Immediately, a wind gust caught the boom and her mainsail slid in a rush of canvas, landing in the water on the other side of the hull.

Erin swore some delicious curses she'd learned in the Caribbean. She swung herself back up onto the deck and scrambled around to retrieve it. But with the snapped halyard, the sail had gone completely overboard. Not only that, but it had snagged on the railing on the way down, tearing a gash in the fabric. Getting it back on board soaked Erin through, and elicited her most creative swearing. If the quiet hadn't been disturbed, it certainly was now. The air should be blue.

At least there wasn't anyone around to hear.

Only, as she finally hauled the last of the damaged sail on board, Erin's neck prickled. Someone was watching. Spinning a slow circle, she found the jetty still empty, and so were the decks of the few other boats. Not a soul on the beach either. Then she heard bubbles.

"I haven't heard language that bad since my sergeant in boot camp," said a male voice.

Erin spun to see a diver had surfaced a few metres away, and was watching her with an amused expression. His blond hair was slicked against his head, his mask held lazily in his hand. He looked the mocking type.

"You need some help?" he said.

"Nope, thanks very much."

Erin turned away, surveying the damage. The diver

disappeared. But a moment later he emerged at the jetty's ladder, climbed, and began shedding his gear.

"There's a sail repairer down the beach," he said, starting to strip his wetsuit, and shaking water out of his ear. He was built, this guy, solid like a rugby forward. One-and-a-half rugby forwards.

"I know," Erin said, frowning at his unfamiliar face. "Which one of these yachts is yours?"

"That one," he said, pointing across to a small tin motor boat. On the side its name read *Green Dream*.

"You live here?" she asked, feeling an odd qualm. After the unexpected dereliction of the resort, this man felt like an unwelcome invader.

"At the end of the point. Darren Travers." He offered his hand. "Dive services. Repairs, salvage, whatever, I do it."

She shook reluctantly, even though she had no real reason to loathe him except for his smart comments. "Erin Jacobs."

His eyebrow shot up. "Oh, you're Skye's sister?"

Erin felt a peal of nerves. She'd been gone long enough for there to be someone new in the community, someone close enough to Skye to know who her family was.

Then again, at least he hadn't said *Dr Jacobs' daughter?* Because then, she would have confirmation for her worst fears. That she'd left the island with her father four years ago, that he had disappeared, and that she was the only one that knew what had happened.

"I have to go," she said.

Erin ran down the jetty to the beach, then up onto the paved path into town. She took the western fork, skirting around the buildings at the eastern end. All so familiar.

She hesitated outside the small driftwood house, its yard neatly trimmed with no leaf out of place. That was all Skye. But the tinkling windchimes in the paperbark were definitely her mother's.

Erin's mouth was so dry as she knocked.

Skye opened the door in a deep-blue sundress printed with white smiley faces, but her expression was anything but happy. Erin watched as shock, then contempt, pulled her sister's mouth into a string line.

"I never thought you'd actually come," she said.

Erin blinked. "But you asked me to."

Skye folded her arms, blocking the doorway, her dark ponytail swinging. "We had a brief conversation that got cut off, and then I never heard from you. That was over a week ago."

"You said to come home."

"I said to *think* about it."

Erin frowned and glanced around Skye, looking for clues for what was going on. She'd expected this meeting to be awkward, but Skye was acting strangely, as though there was something in the house she didn't want Erin to see.

"Is Mum here?"

"Not right now."

"Is she okay?"

"She's fine, Erin. She's off on one of her hikes around the island. Doing research."

"What for?"

Skye's didn't answer for a long moment. In the silence, Erin could only feel how different they were. Erin was wiry and tanned from a life on boats, her hair always split and bleached. Skye had their mother Anna's Celtic colouring: dark hair and pale skin that scorched in the sun. While both of them could sail, Anna and Skye had always stayed on land under broad hats, while Erin had been the one begging to be out on the water.

Now, Skye's voice turned artificially bright as she said, "Why didn't you call?"

"I tried," Erin said. "No one answered. And then I had problems with the boat."

"The tower's been on the blink." Skye paused. "Wait, what boat?"

"My boat."

"You sailed here? What's wrong with a plane like a normal person?"

Erin took a shallow breath, sensing she had missed something dreadfully important in all this. Used to feeling tiny changes in air pressure at sea, surprise was unusual and unwelcome. "Skye, you asked me to come. I'm here now, so what was so important?"

The moment the words were out of her mouth, Erin regretted them.

Skye drew herself up with indignation. "What's so important? Did you *look* down the main beach? Did you once think, any time since you ran off, about what was happening here? No, of course not. You were too busy leaving us to cope after the funeral. With the resort closed, and the school running out of money, and everything else you never bothered to find out about."

Erin said nothing as the cicadas kicked off droning up in the trees. She wanted to take Skye's hurts away, but she'd been keeping her secrets for so long all she could say was, "I'm sorry I didn't call. But I still don't understand why you did."

Skye huffed a breath. "Look, it wasn't my idea, okay? And

while I do appreciate the apology, we are actually doing quite okay. I don't need you to breeze in after years away. So you feel free to go on to whatever glitzy race meet is on your calendar next."

"It wasn't your idea?"

Skye stepped out of the doorway and pulled the door shut behind her, as if she was about to walk Erin back up the path. Erin caught a waft of perfume. "You're awfully dressed up," she said, "who's that all for?"

Skye hesitated, and suddenly Erin had an idea of what was going on here. Yes, Skye was pissed at her for abandoning the island these last years, but she was also expecting a visitor. Someone she didn't want Erin to see.

"Who's the guy?" Erin said, guessing.

"Well, it's the new resort owner, if you must know," Skye said.

"The new owner?" This should have been good news, but Erin felt a flip in her chest like a silver fish.

"Yes. I told you we were doing just fine."

"But who's the owner?" she asked, bewildered as Skye opened the cottage gate. But then she didn't need the answer, because Erin had caught sight of a man coming down the road towards the house, and her blood shock froze to see him again.

"Tristan," she heard Skye call, her voice joyful and bright, and very far away.

All Erin could think was, *oh biscuits, Tristan.* Tristan Drummond, the man she'd been with for nearly two years before it all ended in a spectacular mess. The same man who'd then gone off and made a pile of cash in business-land. She sometimes caught his name in the yachting news, as an owner of a winning boat. Every time, her stomach would bottom out, even if she was sitting in a harbour in Barbados on the other side of the world. The feeling of unfinished and not entirely pleasant business.

In that moment, she knew that Tristan was the one who had asked Skye to call, and also, that Skye was jealous as hell.

Son of a bitch.

If Tristan had not been walking, Erin wouldn't have recognised him. When they'd been together all those years ago, he'd been an ambitious boy from the island putting himself through business school on the mainland. She'd met up with him after classes, hitching rides with other deckhands in the marina to the university bar. She would always be half-way down a beer when he came rushing in, late from work on some assignment. He'd always been in cargo pants, his hair fit for seagulls, but his posture was always straight as a hoisted mast. She'd heard that he'd cleaned himself up in his final year, but that was after they'd ended, with Tristan declaring he was never coming back to the island again, and Erin secretly thinking that was fine by her. She'd not wished him well as he'd stalked away, still carrying himself in that upright way. *Mast up the arse*, was closer to what she'd thought then.

Now, though, here he was, a transformed man. His haircut was sharp, his suit a casual charcoal that he wore with open shirt. Erin had worked for enough millionaire yacht owners from the Caribbean to Croatia to recognise the expensive tailoring, the soft leather of his shoes. He'd lost youthful roundness to his face and acquired instead a chiselled bone structure, setting off the dark green eyes. He still walked the exact same way, only now it worked with all the other stuff he had going on. He didn't look pretentious anymore. He looked like he owned the island.

Erin wiped her sweating hands on her damp cut-off denims. How was it possible she could race for the line on a few tonnes of boat, against the raging elements, but seeing him again so threw her?

"Erin," he said, as he swept in before them, holding out his hands. She took them awkwardly, then found herself drawn into a flawlessly European double cheek kiss. "I was hoping I'd find you here," he said, his touch lingering as he let her go. "Though I tried Gus's first. You have trouble with your sail?"

"How did you know about that?"

Tristan chuckled and tapped his nose, as if he had a network of spies on the island just waiting to report every arrival. "Oh, I have my ways. How are you, Skye?"

Skye moved in for her own embrace, but Tristan put a steadying hand on Skye's arm. "Can I trouble you to give me a minute with E? I need to talk business, okay?"

Erin caught the mutiny on Skye's face, but her sister could hardly refuse, so she said she'd make tea and went back into the house with a resentful backwards glance, leaving the door open.

"Well, how about this?" he said, once they were alone.

"I know," Erin said, taking a small step back. "You surprised me. I seem to remember you said you were never coming back."

Tristan laughed and shook his head. "I said a lot of things. But I didn't really have a choice this time."

Erin raised her eyebrows.

"The resort. Come on, Erin, you must have known what was going on here."

"Skye never mentioned it."

Tristan's eyebrows popped up. "You didn't know it's been

closed for four years? Oh, I suppose that must have been after you left … and Skye did mention you hadn't been in touch."

Erin looked away. She folded her arms, feeling misled, angry at all the changes that had happened while she'd been away, angry that he of all people knew more than she did. "Why not just call me yourself?"

"I'd rather talk about the opportunity. It's not just a new resort – it's way more than that. I have a special role for you in mind. There are dozens of people I could have, but you were my first choice. You were always the best."

He stepped towards her and took her hand. "Look, I know it's been a long time," he said, squeezing her palm. "But the island's dying, Erin. I plan to save it, and I want you on board."

Erin pulled her hand back. "First choice for what exactly?" she said, suspicious and aware Skye was probably eavesdropping through the window.

"There's a town meeting on Monday night. That's only two days to wait. Come and see what I'm planning. I'm not the developer from out of town pushing my ideas on the locals. I *am* one. And after, we can talk about your role. No obligations. You don't like what I offer? No problem."

"Sorry. Vague promises don't pay bills," Erin said, wary after empty promises of rich owners. "I've got a boat to keep in the water."

"Come on, E. I know you love the island. And I'm deadly serious. If I wasn't, I wouldn't be paying for the village to have a new doctor, would I? The practice is already leased to us, and he flies in Monday. Are you really going to leave Skye and your mum and everyone without hearing what I have in mind?"

Erin's stomach flipped again. *New doctor.* Someone to replace her father.

"Fine. Just until Monday," she said.

"Great." The smile creased his eyes. "Now, will you give Skye my apologies? I need to run back for a meeting. See you Monday."

Erin stayed in the yard a full minute, staring after his straight back as he vanished around the corner. It was hard to imagine that her past with him had ever happened, and she hated that he'd extracted a promise to stay. But he was also right … Erin wouldn't forgive herself if she left behind a chance to help the island.

When she stepped through the cottage door and into the kitchen, she found Skye sitting at the kitchen table with her arms folded and thunderclouds on her face. The special cups were out, and Erin could smell fresh tea from the fancy box that smelled like rose petals, and only came out for special occasions.

"Where's Tristan?" Skye said.

"He has another meeting now."

"I see." Skye rose dumped the tea into the sink, turning over the mugs with unnecessary force. "And what was all the secret talk?"

"I don't know yet. I have to wait until Monday."

This at least seemed to ease Skye's anger. "I suppose you want me to make up the sofa bed."

Erin shook her head, feeling sad in the familiar kitchen. She didn't want to hold this guilt over the secrets she couldn't share, didn't want to be back in Tristan's orbit. Didn't want to be reminded of her father, or know there was a new doctor coming to take over his surgery. Didn't want to witness the animosity Skye held for her. She should never have come.

"It's okay, I'm staying on the boat."

The day had turned into late afternoon by the time Erin had taken her sail to Gus's, and cleaned through the cabin and deck in a muddled fervour. She was bringing up a garbage bag, her sweating hair escaping from its rough bun, when she saw a figure waiting on the jetty.

"I heard you were home."

Erin dropped the bag, her heart beating like a rabbit's. Her mother was dressed in a wide sun-faded hat, hiking shorts and an old t-shirt that had ripped away its edging.

"Mum," she said, stepping off the boat. She hesitated. "I'm sorry, I'm filthy and I smell."

Anna pulled her into a hug anyway. "My, yes, you do!" she said, but didn't seem to care. She seemed delighted to see her eldest daughter, but Erin could only feel a tide of guilt.

Then, Erin noticed the sharp bones at her mother's shoulders. That her hair was full of great waves of silver. She seemed frail, a diminished version of the woman Erin remembered. The tide of guilt ran higher.

"I'm sorry that I … that it's been …" she began.

"You're here now," her mother said, putting out a hand for the garbage bag.

"No, no," Erin said. "I'll take it down later."

She wasn't going to hand her trash across to her mother as the first exchange they'd had in four years.

"Well, you'd better make tea instead then."

They sat on the deck, sipping from their cups, not saying much. The resort's construction fence loomed in the distance, but they didn't talk about it at first. Anna asked instead about Erin's life overseas, and Erin talked mechanically about this race or that. The gulf between the two of them seemed wider than the Mediterranean.

Then her mother said, "You know it closed two months after you left. Sold twice since then. The fence went up two years ago, to stop looting."

"Skye mentioned it," Erin said, but she was stuck on the *after you left*.

"Did she mention there's going to be a new doctor?"

Erin looked down at her cup, nodding because she didn't trust herself to speak. She didn't want her mother to bring this all up.

Anna sighed. "Maybe it will be a good thing," she said, but with a resignation that said she'd seen too much to count on it.

"Maybe," Erin whispered.

Anna stood, leaving her cup on the deck. "I'm so glad you're home, Erin. So glad. Why don't you clean up and come see us up at the house?"

"I don't know that I am home," Erin said quickly. "I'm staying till Monday with this meeting thing, but I don't know how long after that. Besides, I'm not sure Skye wants me up there."

She braced for remonstration, to see pain and hurt, or to have a Skye-style rebuke thrown back. But her mother just nodded slowly. "Well, I'll come down and see you then. Every Monday while you're here."

"Okay."

As Anna left down the jetty, Erin reflected that if she were Skye, Anna might have suggested a visit every day. But Erin had never been like Skye. Erin had been her father's girl, and all of them knew it. And that made her secret all the worse.

Erin snatched up the garbage bag. She felt about as useful as the cast-off things inside it. A sailor unwelcome in her home port, and not much welcome in any others either. But she couldn't go anywhere until her sail was fixed, so that would give her until Monday to come up with a plan.

Chapter 2

On Monday morning, Dr Alexander Bell wasn't sure the window seat had been the best idea. It gave him rather too good a view of how high they were above the water, how tiny the approaching island seemed. Just a smudge of dark green, rimmed with pale sand, in all that endless water. Treacherous water. You only had to look at the way the reefs coloured the sea in deep blues and greens, the way the waves foamed angrily over shallow rocks at the foot of a cliff at the southern end of the island.

Don't look at the rocks.

He dragged his eyes back into the cabin, sucked a deep breath. Tried to release the fingers that he'd dug into the arm rests. He should have just taken the ferry. But his employer had insisted, and Alex hadn't wanted to explain.

"Not a good flyer, darling?"

He glanced across the tiny aisle. A woman stared back at him with a kindly expression. Alex was surprised he hadn't noticed her, what with the fake eyelashes, 70% cocoa tan, bleached blond hair, and the rioting red kaftan. She must be a local.

"Something like that," he said.

"Pretzel?" She offered a half-open packet. "Or maybe," she dropped her voice, "something stronger?" She produced a tiny silver flask from within the kaftan, and shook it with a conspiratorial eyebrow.

Alex smiled. But it wouldn't be a good idea to show up at the surgery with liquor on his breath. He was all about avoiding bad impressions these days. So he shook his head. The woman offered her hand instead.

"Stella Moon, artist's muse," she said, making it sound a serious occupation.

Alex shook around her long fingernails. "Alex Bell, bad flyer."

She laughed. "And what do you do, Alex Bell? You're not a model, are you? Those arms, that jaw, perfect for a charcoal, I think."

Alex blushed. "I'm a doctor," he said. Even as he said it, he felt how unfamiliar the words had become, as if he was newly engaged again and trying out the word *fiancé*. He leaned back in his seat, trying to imagine he wasn't on a small plane hundreds of metres above the ocean. The tiny plane held only fifteen seats, so he could see all the way to the cockpit. And for all the fact they were bound for a tropical island, the passengers looked anything but ready for the beach. Two men in hi-vis gear sat near the front, and behind them a man and a woman, both wearing business suits. In fact, the only one who looked ready for a holiday was Stella.

When he looked back, Stella was eyeing him expectantly, clearly waiting for an answer.

"I said, are you having a nice vacation?" she said, when he asked her to repeat the question.

"I'm actually here to work."

Stella's eyes widened. "But that means *you're* the new island doctor? Oh, how exciting. We haven't had one of those for years. Not since Dr Jacobs. It'll be so nice to have someone at home instead of having to trek across to the mainland all the time. That's where I've just been."

"I'm only here every second week," he said, gripping the seat again as the plane shuddered.

"Oh, that will still be grand," Stella went on, with sure authority. "There's less than a hundred people living here permanently. Once the resort's open again, though, I'm sure you'll be up at all hours, sorting out all the food poisoning from the dinner buffet." She smiled knowingly.

Alex had been relieved about his work arrangement at first: he still had his job on the mainland, working emergency department shifts in the base hospital. Coming out here every second week seemed like an antidote for those long hours. An island paradise was a cure-all, wasn't it?

Only now, glancing out the window again at that endless blue ocean, he wondered at his motivations. Was he just making himself face that part of his life he'd rather forget?

"Looks beautiful," he said, just to say something, and maybe to reassure himself.

Stella laughed. "Oh yes, but she's deceiving, is Haven. Just ask anyone. She keeps her mysteries behind all that beauty. At least, that's what Helmut says. But I'm sure everyone will be grateful to have a doctor again. It was so sad, what happened to Dr Jacobs. If a few people are funny about someone new, don't let it worry you. They'll come around. And you must come up and visit us at the studio."

Alex pulled his eyes away from the ocean again. "What happened to Dr Jacobs?"

Stella hesitated. "He died at sea," she said. "At least, we assume so. One of the many mysteries of the island. But we're almost there, now. Grip my hand if you need to, darling."

But Alex's fingers had already wrapped around the seat rests again as the tiny plane dived down. He closed his eyes. *Died at sea.* He had visions of the waves going up and down around the horizon, of seeing nothing but endless dark blue. If he had doubts about this island before, they were screaming at him now.

As it turned out, the pilot put the wheels down with barely a bounce, and Alex had his legs steady under him again by the time he walked down the steps. Well, almost steady.

The airfield was a single strip of packed grass nestled in the island's limited flat country, separating the faded red roofs of the resort from the bush of the interior. The signs of abandonment were obvious, even from the tarmac. The huge fence contained buildings overgrown with creepers, drained swimming pools and collected sand drifts. But beyond all that, he could see the heads of palm trees nodding in the light breeze.

He sucked a lung full of air. Hot sand. Surf. And the faint tang of diesel. Smells from a former life that used to mean good things.

A woman in a flowing skirt and a white shirt with sleeves rolled to the elbows waved him over. She removed her oversized sunglasses to reveal eyes creased in a mass of smile lines. "Dr Bell?"

"Yes."

"Well, you're much younger than I expected. They usually send the crusty ones over to the island."

Alex looked down at himself. "My crust is in my bag."

She cracked a smile that said he'd passed some kind of test. "I'm Sandy. I'll take you down to the village."

They drove down in an old golf cart whose seats were split from the sun, Alex's bag stuffed into the rear seat. Sandy drove with her foot to the floor, past the fence of the old resort and down the paved road under the palms.

"That's the main beach on the left, and we'll go past the shops in a minute," she said, as they bumped along beside pristine white sand, thatched roofs appearing in the distance. "Beyond is the backpackers' safari tent area, and the village houses are in behind. We prefer to be back from the beach a bit – when the storms come in, things get a bit wild."

As they came to the shops – just a row of four whitewashed huts, one clearly vacant – Sandy hooked a turn into the shoulder and jerked to a stop.

"That one's mine," she said, nodding towards the bakery. Alex leaned out and caught a waft of meat pies and fresh bread. He felt something in his mind snap back in.

"I thought you said you were the receptionist?"

"Oh, I am," she said, pulling out again, and shooting up the right fork in the path. A little down the way, they came to a low white building with wide eaves, *Surgery* painted in classic black letters on the front door. "I used to fill in for Anna – that's Dr Jacobs's wife – when she couldn't do it, so I'm trained in all the systems. But there's not much demand for appointments, and I only do the early shift baking. Not much call for bread at the moment either!"

Alex unfolded his legs from the golf cart and surveyed the surgery. Palm fronds and seed pods had fallen in the yard, and the gardens were overgrowing with succulents. The building looked solid, but neglected, with cobwebs in the corners of the outside windows.

"Sorry we haven't cleaned up out here yet," Sandy was

saying, "but the inside's been gone over completely. I called a practice on the mainland for help with restocking, but you'll have to check the orders I've made."

She fished a key from her pocket and pushed the door open with a fall of fine sand. Alex followed, the cold air inside raising a chill as it met his sun-warmed skin. Quiet. He looked around: the front counter was neat, but the information posters were several years out of date. The waiting area showed two gaps where chairs had been removed. To the left was an open door into a consulting office. He'd expected to find it empty, but instead it felt as though another doctor had just stepped out, even down to the crystal jellybean dish.

Sandy hovered behind him. "We weren't sure what you'd need in here. If there's anything you don't want, let me know and I'll box it up for Anna."

"That was Dr Jacobs's wife?" he asked, running a finger over a potted fern, expecting to find it plastic. But it was real. "She's still here?"

"Yes. She and her daughter Skye live right down the path."

Alex raised an eyebrow. "I heard he died."

Sandy's smile fell and she pushed her sunglasses up on her head again. "A few years back. Would you like to see the appointment book?"

Alex pondered as Sandy bustled off to retrieve the book. A small place like this being without a doctor for years was hardly a surprise, but if the last person to sit in this chair had been well-loved and was still being mourned, he'd have expectations to meet. He remembered the attachment of small towns to their doctors from his junior years, when he'd been posted out west.

"Sandy," he said gently, when she came back with a bound red book. "Was Dr Jacobs here a long time?"

"Fifteen years. Came over when his girls were still small," said Sandy, tilting her head with a wistful look. "Very happy family. He worked on the mainland, too, but this was home."

Seeing tears beginning to gather in her eyes, Alex put a hand of apology on her arm and cut off the line of questions. He felt himself being drawn on an investigative bent with Dr Jacobs, and it wasn't time for that. He looked down at the appointment schedule. Well, maybe there was time. No bookings today. Two tomorrow. One on Wednesday.

"Lots of space in case there's walk-ins from the day-trippers," Sandy said. "Now, tomorrow, you've got Greta — she's the safari village owner. She's got blood pressure issues. The other one's a tourist — nice young man from France. Don't know what that's about exactly, but I hear it might be something, you know." She whistled in a fashion that made it clear the problem was likely to be in the nether regions. "And Wednesday," she went on. "I'm keeping a spot open for Helmut. He's the painter who lives up on the cliff. Stella made the appointment, so he probably won't come, but just in case."

Alex looked up. "Wait, *the* Helmut? The artist?"

"The same. You've heard of him?"

"I've seen his work. He donated a painting for a charity auction at the hospital a few years ago."

In fact, Alex could still remember the picture, the image of mist and clouds swirling off a seaside cliff, their shapes suggesting a young woman looking down into the spoiling waves. The image had haunted him, and he'd kept walking down the particular hallway where it had been displayed, trying to dissect what it was about the lines and strokes that had hooked into his mind.

"Yes, he's the talent around here. Keeps to himself though.

Who knows what kind of shenanigans go on up there, with all his ladies. He's probably coming for something you-know-where as well."

Alex thought back to Stella on the plane; when she'd mentioned Helmut, he'd been too preoccupied to register who she meant. He felt the thrill of knowing something about his patients, of being part of their lives. A tight knot that had lodged in his chest eased. For the first time, he thought this might have been the right move after all.

"All right," Alex said. "And I understand someone here is a nurse?"

"Oh. Anna was way back, but she hasn't really wanted to be involved since … you know."

"Any medical experience yourself?"

"Two healthy children raised to adults," Sandy said proudly. "That counts, doesn't it?"

"Definitely," Alex said. "Anyone else? Just in case we have a bad day. Doesn't hurt to have extra hands."

"Oh, well there's Darren. He's a diver, moved here about a year ago. Prefers to be called Travers. He used to be a medic in the army apparently."

Alex's interest piqued. That could be very useful. "Where does he live?"

"Rents one of the seaside cabins, down the end of the point. But he's often away on his boat. Think I saw him this morning, though."

A knock came at the practice door.

"Oooh!" said Sandy. "Now, don't you do a thing, Dr Bell—"

"Alex is fine—"

"—just you sit right here and let me find out who it is."

So, Alex sat at the desk, a small smile on his face at the

enthusiasm of his part-time receptionist, trying to hear voices through the consult door.

The next moment, a knock came, as if they hadn't just been speaking.

"Doctor, this is Skye Jacobs," said Sandy formally, giving Alex a significant eyebrow so that only he could see.

Alex looked around to see a fine-boned woman with dark hair, holding an oversized straw hat. So, this was Dr Jacobs's daughter. He rose. "Thanks, Sandy. Miss Jacobs," he said, offering his hand.

He didn't miss the once-over she gave him. "Skye," she said.

"Alex is fine, if you like."

"I won't keep you," she said quickly. "I just needed to give you a run down on the power situation. Mum insisted."

Alex gestured into his office, and sat down. After a moment, Skye took the patient's chair. He noticed a flint in her now, some kind of hardness that allowed her to come here in her discomfort when her mother clearly hadn't.

"We run generators for the village," she began. "But unless it's really hot weather, we often turn them off overnight to save fuel. It's not that we want to, but with the resort closed we don't have a more reliable power source. Will it cause you problems with your fridges? I know vaccines are kept cold."

"I can ask my employer for a back-up generator."

Skye gave him a nod and stood. "All right, then. I guess I'll see you tonight."

She left so quickly Alex didn't have chance to ask what tonight was. He had begun going through the desk drawers, when another knock came.

"Doctor, seems you have a patient," said Sandy, with a grin.

Alex rose and caught sight of reception where a boy of about twelve with freckles and thin arms stood clutching a huge black dog. The dog's pink tongue was lolling good-naturedly from the side of his mouth.

"This is Tim and Monster," said Sandy.

"Okay, Tim," Alex said. "Can Monster stay outside?"

Tim frowned, and glanced at Sandy, who stage-whispered back to Alex. "*I think Monster's the patient.*"

"Ah, I'm not exactly a vet," Alex said.

"He's limping," Tim said. "And we're supposed to go rock-hopping later. Monster's a born island dog."

Alex laughed. "Come on then, Monster," he said, wincing for Tim as the skinny boy hauled the dog inside the consulting room. Before he followed, Alex leaned in to Sandy.

"I'd better have some disinfectant for the table afterwards. How many dogs are there on the island?"

"Three," Sandy said, dropping her voice. "Not counting the Haven Beast, that is."

"Well, let's see what we can do about a separate consulting room for them. Word of this gets out, they'll all be down here."

Sandy gave him a grin. "There's a storeroom we're not using out back. That'll be perfect."

And then she was off, leaving Alex with Tim and Monster.

Monster had managed to lodge the end of a fishhook deep between the pads of his foot. So Alex, figuring the principles had to be the same, drew up some local anaesthetic and laid out a minor surgical kit. For his own part, Tim was fascinated, and especially impressed when Alex put the tiny surgical drape over Monster's foot. And the dog, despite his devilish appearance, sat calmly and unmoved, only giving Alex a reproachful stare when the needle went in.

"Monster's got a sixth sense," Tim said, as Alex worked.

"That so?"

"Yep. He knows when the ghost is going to appear."

"The ghost?"

"On the Leap."

"Oh, I see," Alex said, trying to concentrate.

Ten minutes and a small incision later, Alex had removed the fish hook, cleaned the wound and fashioned a dressing that he didn't think would last, given the interest with which Monster was sniffing the bandage.

"I think you should bring him back tomorrow and let me look at it again," Alex said, while googling – on the island's slow and intermittent internet connection – to find out if Monster would need a tetanus shot.

Soon, a return appointment was fixed and Monster had bounded out with unlimited energy, dragging Tim with him.

"How shall we write that in the accounts?" asked Sandy.

Alex shrugged. "Gratis. Dogs don't have Medicare numbers anyway."

After that, Sandy showed him to the rear of the surgery, where his room was set up, complete with a queen bed and air-conditioner.

"I put your bag in here. This used to be for the visiting docs, or if someone had to stay overnight. I'll leave you to get settled."

"Wait – Skye said something about seeing me tonight. What's that about?"

"Oh, there's a big meeting about the resort's future at the hall, and we're putting on a dinner afterwards. Be a good place to meet people. You should come down. And have an explore around before then."

"Okay."

Sandy paused on her way to the door. "Just be careful heading up Bella's Leap. The tracks are a bit overgrown."

"Bella's Leap? Is that what Tim was talking about?"

"The cliff at the end of the main beach — can't miss it," she called as she left.

After she was gone, Alex listened to the gentle brush of low hanging gum tree leaves on the roof. He paced back into the clinic, straightening the consulting room, throwing out the paper drapes Monster had sat on and wiping down everything with Chlorhexidine. He checked stocks. Tested a jelly bean. Okay, two jellybeans. Then he slipped out the back door.

Breeze whispered in the sheoaks, and there was a rhythmic shush of waves on the beach. Alex followed the sounds of wind and water across the path, past the bakery and into the dunes. At the crest, he faced the curve of perfect blue ocean that pulled into to the horizon, holding the moored boats and the distant knobs of the smaller Haven islands. Calm. Tranquil. Those would have been the words on the glossy brochure.

Further around the bay he could see the rocky cliff rising high over the water. So, that was Bella's Leap, the same cliff he'd seen from the air, with the waves breaking over its rocks. From here, it didn't look too threatening.

He blew out a breath. He could do this, even if his first patient had been a dog. But he was also aware how alone he was, how far from a mainland hospital. No ambulance. Just him. So, Alex turned away from Bella's Leap and went to look for Travers the medic.

Chapter 3

The sun was going down, dragging streaks of pink and purple into the sea as Erin checked her watch that evening. From the deck of her yacht, she could see the coloured lights around the village hall peeking above the other buildings, could smell the food cooking in the air. She didn't really want to go, but she'd eaten too many frozen and dehydrated meals in the last months to pass up Sandy's stroganoff pies. She'd told Tristan she would come. It wasn't fair not to follow through, and she would have to look for work soon anyway. It wouldn't hurt to hear him out. Would it?

She padded down the jetty, her deck shoes soundless on the boards, two seagulls eyeing her hopefully. She wondered if she'd have a different reception from the town.

Skye was manning the door as she arrived, handing out lucky prize tickets. She spotted Erin sidling through the shadows, waiting for a queue to clear.

"There you are," she said, marching over. "Mum's in the kitchen with Sandy and the rest of the committee. You can help me with these tickets."

So instead of being able to disappear inside, Erin found herself handing out tickets and flyers for the upcoming dance to the villagers, many of whom were as familiar to her as Skye was.

"Erin? Oh my god!" seemed the standard reaction, followed

by hand-holding and statements of how good it was to see her. No one seemed grudging, not to her face. Only, after they'd moved inside, Erin knew they were turning back for a second look, and whispering. At least many of the kids were too young to remember her. Most of them looked puzzled until she explained she was Skye's sister. One kid with freckles and a huge black dog – complete with bandaged paw and a cone around his neck – offered his hand to shake. But Erin was glad when she could tug the ticket stubs off their staple and drop them in the bucket.

"That's it then," she said.

"Not so fast." Skye caught her arm. "Here comes the new doctor."

Erin spied two men approaching the hall along the wooden boardwalk. They were about the same height, but the one on the left was bulkier, and walked with a slight limp. Erin had no trouble recognising him as Travers, the smart-mouth diver she'd met on Saturday morning. The one on the right, though, he was athletic with an easy unhurried stride. When they reached the end of the path and fell under the hall's spotlight, this man looked right at her. Erin glimpsed a gale in the depths of his eyes that stopped her cold. She blinked and that impression of him was gone, but not his attention. His gaze lingered on her as though he didn't have a choice. Erin read it as a challenge: this was the man who'd come to replace her father.

"That's Alex Bell," Skye began. "The new—"

Erin shook Skye off. "I really don't need this."

She shot through the door into the back of the hall, and leaned against the shiplap. It was still the same canary yellow she remembered painting as a teenager. Over her shoulder, she could hear the men chatting to Skye, who was trying to push extra raffle tickets on them.

A warm hand closed on her arm, and she jumped.

"Erin, I am sorry, I scare you."

At once, Erin's chest flooded with relief. "Helmut!"

The painter was just as she remembered him: sun-bleached hair in a nest of curls, beard streaked with Prussian blue and cerulean. Erin had spent many afternoons camped out on the floor of his studio, wrestling with school work and he'd always provided a refuge. Stella had helped with maths. "I didn't expect to see you here," she said.

"But of course. I can always keep selling paintings, but if no one cares about this island, the value ..." He made a diving thumbs-down.

Erin leaned in. "Do you have a clue what this is about?"

"None. But I have an odd feeling, here." He rubbed his round belly with the hand that was missing its little finger.

"I hate waiting," Erin grumbled. "I don't even see Tris—"

But then, Tristan was there. Erin spotted him at the side of the stage, speaking to Greta, the safari tent park owner. They'd rolled in a portable microphone on a trolley, the hall's rickety lectern coaxed onto the flat spot on the stage, on the far right. Tristan strode past it, grabbing the microphone with the confidence of a rock star, and sat on the edge of the stage. Having shed his jacket, and in a delicate blue shirt, he seemed boyish and inviting. A hush blew through the crowd.

"Friends." Tristan grinned. "I love that I can say that. It's not often I get to sit in front of people I hold so dear, to talk about something so exciting. As most of you know, I grew up a few houses that way."

He pointed north, into the heart of the island, going on for a while about how he'd loved growing up here, how he missed his own father, who was now in Sydney for health reasons. Erin tapped her foot, waiting for him to get to the point. She didn't like listening to the liquid confidence of his voice.

"We all know," Tristan finally said, "how much difference the resort makes in the life of the village. We like our community small, but the resort means reliable power, better food supply, and customers in our businesses. We know this is paradise, but we want to share it."

He gave the room a long pause. Erin looked about, impatient, but found no one else fidgeting.

"But we also know," he went on, dropping his voice, "how hard these last years have been. We've been made promises by new owners, only to see it sold again and again. Well, no more. When the opportunity came, I thought, that's what I want Drummond Enterprises to do next. I want to come home, and do something right. So I bought it."

A cheer went up, though everyone already knew this much.

"Funny, how he says *we*," Helmut complained softly. "When he hasn't lived here this many years."

Erin, knowing anyone could level the same criticism at her, said nothing.

Tristan went on. "I know you're being patient with me, that what you really came for is to know what comes next."

Erin checked her watch.

"You'll have to forgive me – I've had to keep the plans quiet for a while. But now I can confirm the rumour I'm sure you've all heard. Yes, I'm reopening the resort."

A murmur stole through the crowd, heads nodding at the confirmation of what they'd hoped.

"But that's not all," Tristan said. "We all know resorts face difficulties, and I don't want ours to be in the same situation again. So, I've made bigger plans. Bolder plans. Not only will the resort reopen, but I'm making it a hub for the region, the home of the new Great Haven Regatta!"

Erin felt an electric jolt. *What?*

"That's right," Tristan was saying. "Haven Resort will be centre-stage for an international yacht race series, of the highest calibre. Our waters are famous for their tricks – golf has Carnoustie and Pebble Beach. Well, sailing will have Great Haven. Right now, the top racing boats are heading north for Hamilton Race Week. But our sponsorship will be world class, the prize money unignorable. They'll all want to stop here first. It will be the premier onshore event of the year."

The hall was suddenly consumed with excited chatter. Erin watched Tristan with an open mouth, hardly believing what she'd heard. How could this be possible? The resort was far from ready to open; such an event had to be a year away at best. If he was offering her a racing crew position, the work was a long way off. This was all a colossal waste of time.

Tristan let the buzz go on for a few minutes, then began taking questions. Most people wanted to know about the resort. It would take nine months, he said, and directed people to the brochures for drawings. Amid the questions, he looked up and found Erin's eyes at the back of the room. A smile creased his lips, which she didn't return.

"You know, I've been talking a long time," he said. "And I don't know about you, but the smell from the kitchen is driving me mad. I've stacks of prospectuses here. I'm going to step away, let you read, have a great meal, and then we'll come back to questions afterwards."

"Clever," murmured Helmet. "Everyone will be much happier when fed."

Erin grunted, but Tristan was now giving her a beckoning nod towards backstage.

She apologised to Helmut. She was going to give Tristan a serve for wasting her time.

She found him in the heavy red curtains to the side of the stage where the air smelled of sandalwood and dust. The smell reminded her of long-ago times when they'd snuck up here to kiss, the velvet curtains brushing on her skin.

"Erin," he said.

He tried to take her hand, but she dodged him. "Is this what you wanted me to stay for?" she said. "Come and crew a racing boat for you next year sometime, if you ever get this regatta up and running?"

"You're angry," he said, but he had a sparkle in his eye, as if he remembered past fights with her fondly.

"Damn right," she said, finally meeting his eyes, needing to see his reaction. "I waited two days for this nothing-show. You could have told me on the phone."

"Erin." He reached for her hand again, a softness in his voice. This time, she let him, not liking the way her breath caught at his touch. "I couldn't tell you all the details because they weren't settled. And crew for me? You give yourself too little credit."

"I don't understand."

"I've watched your career, every day since you left. You're far better than crew. You've raced in every blue-ribbon course around the world. And more, you're an island local. We still need to do a lot of work, organising, attracting sponsorship, but we're going to run pilot races soon. And when it comes time for the big event, I want you on one of my boats. Wearing my colours," he added, more softly.

Erin couldn't speak for a long minute. She could hear the desire in his voice, and it mixed up all the things he was saying. Made her want to trust him, just because they had a history. She had to remember that their relationship was long over, and he was talking about business. That she'd heard enough empty promises from big-talking wealthy men to be cautious.

"Am I being clear enough?" Tristan asked, with a small laugh. "I want you to work for me. Almost as much as I wanted to see you again."

"Tristan?" Skye's voice suddenly cut into their space. Erin pulled her hand back. "Tristan, are you still up there?"

He leant back into the main lights. "Yeah?"

"We've kept a plate for you, and I'm taking a list of questions. I thought you'd want to look at it."

"Gimme a sec." Tristan ducked back into the curtains. "Duty calls. What do you say, Erin?" he asked quickly. "Come work for me."

"It's a lot to take in," she said.

"At least tell me you'll think about it?"

"Okay, I guess."

He grinned as if she'd agreed. "Not too long, though. I'll need an answer by the weekend. So, why don't you go and think it over, and come back with a 'yes' at the dance on Friday."

When he was gone, Erin sat a long time, breathing in the sandalwood, and the fancy cologne Tristan was wearing. If he was serious, it could be an amazing opportunity, but warnings were doing laps in her mind. She'd seen the look in his eye when Skye had called out, that flash of anger that stripped all the light out of his face. Too much a reminder of why they'd broken up.

As she left the hall, she passed a man standing at the ramp rail outside. It was that new doctor, staring off into the ocean. Out there, the full moon threw a pale glow over Bella's Leap, so that it seemed a rocky island hanging in the sky. Erin stopped for just a moment as she looked for Bella, the ghostly woman who sometimes appeared on the cliff. Hearing her footsteps pause, the doctor looked around.

He didn't say anything; they just stood and stared at each other, for a fraction longer than they should have. A moment caught in a moonbeam. For just those seconds, it was as if he sensed what she was thinking: that this wasn't a time for words. It was for running along the beach in the dark, roaming over the island hills, running far, far away from tomorrow.

Erin blinked, and the moment collapsed. She stalked away, no closer to working out what to do.

Chapter 4

By eleven the next morning, Alex was busier than the appointment book would have suggested.

"Oh, everyone's just curious," Sandy said, after the third walk-in patient appeared for a "check-up", which really meant a sticky-beak around the surgery and Alex's room. Sandy had already shooed out one woman who'd brought a vase of cut flowers. Now, he faced Greta on the exam table, who'd actually made an appointment. From her file, she was in her mid-fifties, and had limbs of sinewy muscle that barely filled the smallest adult blood pressure cuff he had.

"How long have you had the blood pressure issue?" he asked, as he pumped the cuff and pressed his stethoscope against her elbow.

"Ten years," she said. "It's the genes – my mother had it too."

"But it's been more problematic these last few years?" he asked, making a note of 145/95.

"More stress," she said. "And worse food. Can't get enough fresh stuff over here. Of course, when the resort opens again, that'll be different."

"Everyone seems excited about that," Alex said, settling his fingers to feel her pulse.

"Too right. Less excited about the Jacobs girl being back

though. Never thought to see her again after this long. I think she'll be gone again soon, though."

"Oh?" Alex asked, feigning indifference as he placed the stethoscope on Greta's lungs. In truth, he'd been unable to keep his eyes off Erin at the meeting last night. Was it just that she'd so obviously cut him dead at the door? Or that she'd stood in the wings the whole night, looking unimpressed with Tristan's smooth delivery? He'd always been drawn to the girl at the edge of the party. Or had it been the look in her eye when she'd passed him outside in the moonlight? She'd looked ready to do damage. Whatever it was, he was curious. More than curious.

"I wouldn't want you to think I'm mean, Alex, but after what happened with her father? The girl's bad luck, that's what. And we don't need that with these plans to get the resort open again."

"Bad luck?"

"Yes. Dr Jacobs was such an experienced sailor. What happened to him doesn't make any sense."

It wasn't the last time he heard such a thing today, but people were cagey about the details. All they would say was that there'd been some kind of accident at sea, and that Erin was involved. Alex was interested, but he had other mines to dodge.

"What about you, Doctor? Have a wife back on the mainland? Kids?"

"No, just me. Married to the job," he said, more than once, a little white lie that avoided him saying *not anymore.*

Only the young backpacker – whose issue turned out to be a swollen lymph node in his groin and not a venereal disease as Sandy had intimated – gave him a break.

By the time the day was over, his social patience was as raw as a butcher's window. He sat on the edge of his bed, the air full of wattle scent from the flowers now on his bedside table. He was meant to be here to get away from all the mental chatter.

On the desk, Sandy had left books – a yellowing diver's guide to the surrounding reefs was on top. Alex flicked past it. Even if he had been in the mood to go diving, he'd have asked Darren Travers for advice before trusting a guide book. The former medic had been instant good company, and happy to lend a hand if Alex ever needed it.

"Just remember, I'm going stale on the emergency stuff," Travers had warned.

"Well, you're the only pair of hands I've got."

They'd stuck around after the town hall meeting, drinking beers, Travers telling him a few war stories, but never once asking Alex about his own past. Alex liked the man for his discretion. Other men might have pushed. And Alex might have told them he came from a well-respected medical family, most of whom lived down south. That his father had been a doctor, that his cousins were all doctors. And then he might have thought he could talk about what had happened with the crash, which he would then regret. But Travers … it was as though he'd sensed all the history, and had the tact not to go there.

Now, Alex flicked over a few ageing paperbacks – a Tom Clancy he'd read before, a Jeffrey Archer he hadn't. And there at the bottom, he found a map of the island. Perfect.

Map in hand, he slipped out the back door and slogged through the sand to the top of the dunes. The sun was coming down over the mainland, a ball of orange flame rolling over grey clouds hugging the horizon. It would be light a good while yet.

He faced down the beach, aligning the map. The village and the old resort were drawn as a collection of dark squares along the main beach. The rest of the island was a large scalloped coastline, full of inland waterways, mountains in the north, and cliffs at the eastern end of the main bay. A homestead was clearly marked in the centre. He frowned at it, wondering who lived there.

Walking tracks were dashed across the terrain, all the way to the far northern point. He squinted at the numbers scratched against landmarks, partly cut off by a bad photocopy. Six hours to the northern point, it said. Too far for an afternoon.

But the cliff at the end of the bay, that was a different story. It looked doable in an hour, there and back. *Bella's Leap*, the map said, and a small square drawn on the next promontory over was marked *The Artist's Den*.

Alex closed the back door, keen to shake off the day. He followed the construction fence until it bent away into the scrub, where the map said there should be a vehicle track to follow up onto the cliffs. But the bushland in front of him presented no such path.

Eventually, after fossicking through the long grass, he found an old trail marker, hidden in a shrub. The resort had been closed so long that the trail had grown over.

Once he was out of the greener zone behind the beach, however, the path came into sharper relief. The cicada drone vibrated in his chest, the smell of eucalypts filling his senses. Half-way up, he paused, looking down along the beach. It was a perfect arc of white sand, the water shimmering with sunset orange. He could see all the way to the village, and out onto the long sandy finger that the point pushed into the ocean.

Beautiful. And calm. He took several minutes to really feel it.

He hiked on and the path levelled out, then the trees retreated, leaving a barren crop of cracked stone. Alex could hear the pounding waves striking the rocks below. The path led onto the exposed shelf, so he inched out, his eyes searching for where the map said the trail would continue around to the next headland, where Helmut's studio was supposed to be. He couldn't find it, not anywhere in the thick shrubs that clung to life all over the rocky crop.

He found himself right at the edge, and staring into that blue oblivion.

The waves breaking on the rocks weren't as big as he'd imagined from the noise. All the hard rock echoed, amplified the sound. Still, it was a long, long way down, straight onto the ribbons of cutting oyster shells. *The sun going down into a dark night.* He shuddered, pulling his eyes up, and rubbed his arms. The next headland was clearly visible from here, and now he spotted the hard line of a roof amidst the trees.

Then, he saw the stone steps.

They were cut into the rock of the cliff, an old wire rope for a handrail set into the stone and rusted in the salt air. The stairway was so steep he couldn't see further than the first three steps.

He stopped, suddenly sure he was being watched.

Someone stood at the edge of the tree line. He only had to take one look at her long, brown limbs, curved with muscle, and the tousled sun-bleached hair to recognise Erin Jacobs. His stomach dipped at the sight of her.

"I wouldn't go down there if I were you," she said.

"Not the path to Helmut's, then?"

"What do you want with Helmut?"

"I like his work." Alex turned away from the stone stairs, approaching her, feeling his heart pound. He offered his hand. "I'm Alex Bell. I'm the visiting—"

"I know who you are," she said.

"Well, I'm just getting to know the place."

They stared at each other, like they had outside the hall.

"You're Erin Jacobs," he said slowly, her name thrilling on his tongue. "I saw you Monday night, dodging Travers at the door."

She narrowed her eyes at him. "How do you figure I was dodging Travers?"

"Because if you were dodging me, you wouldn't have bothered warning me about going down there."

She laughed unexpectedly, her eyes creasing, her amusement bringing a smile to his lips, too.

"Might have figured you'd come up here, with you staring at the Leap the other night," she said.

"Noticed that, huh?"

"Those steps run out half-way down," she said. "The rest broke off in a storm years ago. People think they can jump the rest of the way, but then they get stuck down there. When the tide comes in ..." She ran her fist into her palm.

"Jesus, shouldn't it be signed or something?"

She shrugged. "It was. But metal rusts through in a season, and print fades in the sun. The resort used to do maintenance, but no one in the village is silly enough to do it anymore. The path to Helmut's comes off the trail about twenty metres back. You just missed it."

"But the map says it's here," he said, showing her the dark lines.

"That map was drawn by a teenager with a felt-tip. See here?" She pointed to the edge of the island's outline, where a tiny *SJ* was drawn in slanting letters.

"Skye?"

"Afraid so. School assignment."

She stepped back, rubbing her arms. "At least you made it to the top," she went on. "Most of the tourists get the wiggins and turn back, look at it from a safe distance, over at the studio."

"Because of the ghost?" he said, remembering Tim and Monster. "Bella?"

"Isabella Mason. She lived in the homestead, once. Now she's supposed to appear when the storms roll in."

Pieces clicked together in Alex's mind. "So *that's* who Helmut paints. Is she supposed to have jumped? I mean, it's called *Bella's Leap*."

Erin shrugged. "That's one story." But she didn't quite meet his eyes. Alex felt as though she'd pulled some barrier up between them.

"Have you ever seen her?" he asked.

"Once," she said. "I think. But maybe I imagined it."

She moved towards the edge to peer down on the rocks, stepping towards him. In the narrow space at the cliff top, her closeness was natural. When she looked back at him, her eyes were the colour of the ocean itself, and for just that instant, it felt as if they were alone in a world of endless blue.

"I used to love sailing on nights like this," he said. The words flew out of his mouth before the associations could stop him. Then came the memories, feeling ugly in his heart. He found her staring at him, waiting for what he'd say next. ... *but I screwed it up. ... but that was a long time ago.* Not the kind of thing you said to someone you didn't know, much less an attractive woman. He'd been pausing too long, now. Most women he'd known would have registered the pause, asked him what was wrong, or to go on. But Erin didn't. Instead, a quizzical look wrote itself in her features, though Alex didn't know if it was interest, or if she was working out how much of a crazy person he was.

"I better head back. I'll show you the path," she said.

He followed her into the trees, not wanting her to go yet.

"That's the trail, there," she said, nodding to a vanishing line of sand off the main path. Then she paused, and said, "My yacht's the *Fair Winds*, off the jetty."

Alex was left with only a glimpse of her suntanned shoulders disappearing into the scrub, and the tantalising hint of her invitation.

Erin had her charts spread on the small table in the main cabin when she heard the soft creak of footsteps on the wooden jetty. The sky had gone dark in the portholes and the first moths had snuck inside to bash themselves against the lights. But when the footsteps stopped alongside, she knew instantly who was out there.

Alex Bell, doctor-new.

What the hell had possessed her to tell him her boat? A moment of weakness, that's what. Because he was an attractive man, and she'd been alone for too long. Forgetting that he was the man who was sitting in her father's chair. He was completely not her type. She liked her men unmysterious, not coming with woo-woo moments in the moonlight and clifftops. Growling at herself, she crept up the cabin stairs and stuck her head out.

"I was just working out how to knock," he said.

"Funny," she said. "Never heard that one before."

"Sorry. I'm still recalibrating to human contact, you know, after having a dog for my first patient."

She smiled despite herself. And he did have a cute face. "So that was your work on Monster?"

"Guilty," he said. "I'm hoping the vet board won't come after me, you know, practicing without a licence."

All right, he was a little funny. And not overassuming, still standing on the jetty. He ran his eyes over her yacht, his hands in his pockets, a few feet back as if giving the *Fair Winds* a respectable distance. Erin in turn ran her eyes over the muscled legs under his long board shorts. His chest was certainly broad enough for a mastman, but he was too reluctant for a sailor. Had he been lying about that? He wouldn't be the first man who tried a come on pretending to know his way around a boat. Maybe he was a runner, or worse, a Crossfitter.

"How was Helmut?" she asked.

Alex looked down, sheepish. "I didn't make it. I must admit I spent a while searching around the cliff top, imagining what Helmut must see there when he paints. Then I started correcting the paths on the map, which ended up with me slightly lost down the hill."

"Slightly lost?"

"All right – a lot lost. Fortunately, it wasn't too hard to find my way out again because I could hear the waves, but after that it seemed a bit late. Didn't fancy navigating back by the stars."

Erin laughed at him, until the corner of his mouth lifted in a wry smile. He really was attractive when he did that. "Don't tell Skye about the bad map, she'll be offended," she said. "Are you coming over?"

"I'm thinking about it."

He was thinking about it. Something was a little odd there. Man, the moment he started on with the benefits of his nutritional plan, she was jumping overboard. "I'm looking at charts. Shoes off."

Seeming to finally make up his mind, he stepped out of his

boat shoes and across onto the yacht's deck, moving with the grace of muscle memory. All right, now he looked like a sailor. His eyes tracked over the rigging in an experienced way. "Nice set-up," he said. "You sail it solo?"

Erin forced herself to unfold her arms. "She's rigged that way now. But I can break it back to two hands or more. She races pretty well with a small crew."

"Where's your mainsail?"

"Busted the halyard before I got to the Haven channel, then ripped it when I docked. It's with Gus – he's the chandler up the beach. It's my fault, really," she said, leaning back against the bimny. "I had *Fair Winds* in port too long down south. Didn't get back to her as often as I meant to, what with the racing season."

She caught herself before she said, *Dad would kill me for the lack of maintenance.* She looked away, out over the jetty and towards the last smudge of orange on the sunset horizon, and then pretended to check the time on her watch. Alex sat on the short padded bench.

"How does a chandler make a living on the island?"

"With difficulty these days," Erin said, glad to be distracted. "Random jobs from yachters island hopping and putting in for repairs, and he specialises in restoring antique fittings. There's a small market in it online, but the postage must be brutal."

Alex grunted, and reached up to steady the boom, which was twitching in the breeze. Erin fixed on his hand, the familiar way he touched the boat, the long fingers, smooth and brown. Maybe she should invite him downstairs.

"Gus would be happy about this resort and regatta plan, then?"

"Everyone's happy about it," Erin said, quickly.

Catching her tone, Alex raised his eyebrows. "And yet, you don't sound like one of them. You didn't look too pleased when you were leaving the meeting the other night."

Erin took a breath, wrongfooted, a thousand competing thoughts in her head. Like, why had he noticed what she'd been like? And, what was she supposed to do about Tristan's plan anyway? The resort had been a long string of broken promises, but maybe it could be different this time, if someone who really cared was involved.

But did that person have to be Tristan?

It gave her a terrible headache. Things were so much easier when her gut told her clearly what to do.

"Wow, sounds complicated," Alex said, observing her silence.

Erin shrugged, and even with the beach she would forever think of as home right behind her, she said, "I don't know how much it matters to me. I'm just passing through."

Was that disappointment in his eyes? Then he said, "Are you configured for cruising or racing below decks?"

"Somewhere between. No fancy additions, but I still have cushions on the couch, and a mattress on the bed," Erin said, with a small smile herself.

He ghosted a smile. "I didn't mean that to sound how it did."

"Sure." She was familiar with this routine, all through the racing circuit, and expected events to turn sexy. But a minute later, she realised she'd misread him. Alex wanted to hear her answers.

Sitting under the emerging stars, they discussed the boat, and which races she'd done last, and with what teams. He didn't want to talk about his gym routine, or about himself at all. When she asked about his own sailing, he shrugged.

"All that was years ago, now," he said.

Before Erin knew what had happened, she was telling him about the characters of the village, what it had been like years ago when the resort was open. The waves of people who washed in and out of the island every day, the carnival feel of the summers, and the lazy beach bonfire nights of the winters. The crazy storms that leapt up from the sea and thrashed them every few months, the backpackers and locals shoulder to shoulder under the big pavilion riding it out. Villagers going to the rescue of yachts that had snagged their keels on the reefs, and who worked in the resort as mechanics, gardeners and managers, instead of eking out an existence splitting their weeks with the mainland, as they were now.

Time slipped like a racing hull through a glassy dawn sea as they sat together, nearly touching as the boat swayed under them.

"You know, for just a moment up on that cliff, I thought you were a ghost," he said finally.

Erin turned her eyes on the distant bluff, barely visible against the night sky now, the moon not yet risen overhead.

"You know, Dad always said—"

She stopped herself, and as if the time-spell had broken, she remembered who he was. Who she was. What she had done. And how she was leaning in to him as if none of it mattered.

She stood. "Better turn in. Early start tomorrow."

He stood, clearly confused by her abrupt change of mood. "I must have kept you from dinner."

She watched him step down off the deck, and find his shoes. He gave her a cautious smile before he turned down the jetty. Erin didn't return it. *Don't go there*, she thought as his footsteps faded. That man is a complication you don't need. She sensed it in her reaction every time he turned to look back at her.

She still had to make a decision about Tristan's offer. If she didn't take it, she would need another plan.

She went back below decks to the charts spread out on the table. One was a huge coastal map, showing the state coast, the Great Haven island group a tiny speck. What were her other options, really?

Hamilton Race Week further north was a month away, so she'd left it rather late to get on a crew, especially after being fired from her last one. Hardly a glowing endorsement for a new employer. She could probably call Ivan, who would be enjoying the summer in the Caribbean before breaking for the Block Island Race Week off Rhode Island. The billionaire was one of the best bosses she'd ever had. He'd paid reliably, and had been talking about a serious bid for Sydney to Hobart for several years. But he also liked his crew close, like family. And Erin didn't want that right now.

She pushed the charts away. Suddenly, the endless grind of team sailing, training, and travelling seemed exhausting. And while being home was painful, with all the eyes on her and the reminders and Tristan … the conversation with Alex had reminded her how much she did care about what happened here. Alex himself had nothing to do with it.

She curled into the tight corner of her bunk, rocked to sleep by the gentle waves. Whether she was staying or going, she needed the *Fair Winds* in better shape.

Early the next morning, Erin picked her way across the grass tufts down at the point. The sun was already baking on the dunes, but the point cabins had been built on stilts under the palm trees at the edge of the beach. They enjoyed almost year-round shade, and their out-of-the-way location made them an oddity in the village: most were owned by people who came across for the holidays, or who rented them out. Erin only had to take one look down the row to find the cabin with three wetsuits drying over the railing.

Darren Travers opened the door in a pair of board shorts, his hair only fit for the bedroom, and his eyes scrunched up against the light. "Do you know what time it is?" he said.

"Eight-thirty," said Erin. "Wake up. I need to hire you for a job."

Travers pushed the door open and beckoned her inside. "Wait here."

Erin eyed the thick scar on his shoulder as he trudged into the bowels of his man-cave, before checking out the rest of the living room. Hmm, neater than your average single man. There were no empty bottles in the kitchen, no open food containers on the benches. A single plate was in the drying rack, and on the coffee table were two dive knives lying alongside their sheaths, with a bottle of lemon oil and a cleaning rag. She'd tipped enough men out of bunks over the years not to be worried about how they lived, as long as they did their job. But it was still pleasing to find someone who kept a tidy ship.

When Travers came back, he'd pulled on an old battalion t-shirt and brushed his hair.

"I would have picked you for an early riser," Erin said.

"I got up at dawn for twenty years, so now I sleep in when I want. What's this about a job?"

"I need my hull cleaned, the intakes too. Can you do it?"

"Aw, man, hull cleaning? I'm a salvage and research diver."

"Can you do it or not?"

Travers cracked a smile. "Yeah, I can do it. But not till next week. I've got a grid to finish for the university first."

"Can't you just get up early and fit it in for me?"

Travers affected a hurt expression. "Man, they could have made you a drill sergeant. You got somewhere else to be?"

"Don't know yet."

"Look, Erin, I like your balls. But I love my job and I don't do it half-cocked. You hire me to do something, I'll do the best job you ever saw. So, give me till next week and I promise you that much. If you have to leave before then, that's your call." His smile turned coy. "Although, I'm betting with your sail still in Gus's, you have a few days grace."

"Fine," she said.

She turned, her gaze lingering on his gear, lined up in its orderly rows. She didn't like not being able to force her leaving options open earlier, but she also knew Travers wasn't a man who played games.

"Erin," he said, as she was almost to the door.

"Yeah, what?"

"You okay there?"

She looked around in surprise. He was a big man, bulky in the way of an old bodybuilder, muscle underneath a layer of hard-beer-drinking softness. She would never have picked him to ask such a question.

"Fine," she repeated.

He shrugged. "Had to ask. See ya later."

But she wasn't fine, not really. Last night talking with Alex may have reminded her how much she cared about this place, but also how much she no longer belonged here.

Maybe it would be better to sail away tomorrow and not look back. But she wasn't a coward, and that's what it would be to leave Tristan without an answer, to leave her mother and Skye without a goodbye.

And maybe, to leave Alex Bell the way she had last night.

Chapter 5

On Saturday morning, Alex took the launch back to the mainland, preparing himself for four nights of twelve-hour hospital ED shifts.

Saturday night meant drinking, and that would lead to cases walking in the door around ten. Alex checked his watch, giving Wendy, the triage nurse, a significant glance.

"Two stitch-ups, two head injuries and one MVA," he said, laying down a ten dollar note.

Wendy grinned, shaking her head. "You're going to lose your money, Doc. *Two* MVAs, three stitch-ups, a broken leg and an MI. Plus something you've never seen before. It's full moon. You have to allow for the crazy."

"That full moon stuff is rubbish," Alex said. "I read the research."

Though they'd all have been happier to have a quiet night, it was bad luck to say it. Sailors weren't the only superstitious ones. Even if Alex didn't believe in that stuff, he had to work with people who did.

Wendy was scoffing at him now. "I'll give you rubbish, you young pup. I was working here before you could walk."

"That you were," he said, offering her the proper respect.

"Well, you're a good boy. I'll almost be sad to take your money."

The first case to appear was a young woman, concerned about her early pregnancy, and Alex was happy to reassure her when the Doppler showed a strong heartbeat. Next came two boys around eighteen, caps sideways, one holding his elbow and the other wearing fresh scrapes down his legs and arms. Alex sent the elbow to x-ray, but they couldn't see a fracture. So the kid got a sling and an appointment to come back on Monday.

Alex checked his watch – only nine-thirty. The second night shift doctor, Karen, arrived half an hour later. They stood around the triage desk with Wendy and two other nurses, drinking coffee and listening to the silence of the night.

"Is there a town curfew we don't know about?" Karen asked. "I mean, there's not even any kids. Usually by this point, someone's swallowed a button or got croup or asthma or something."

"This is why I have a bad feeling," Wendy said.

Alex grunted. He could feel it too, the gathering in the air, the wind pressure before a storm.

The mayhem broke at a quarter to twelve. One moment, the ED was nearly empty, the next, it was a chaos of flashing lights, blood, and uniforms. A brawl had gone down at the town tavern: two men had been glassed. Another had a stab wound. Two more had facial injuries from fists.

"How's that evac coming?" Alex called to Wendy, as he checked the status of the stab wound man, who was conscious, his blood pressure holding. The wound was just under his ribcage, but Alex had no idea how deep it was. The man needed surgery, and better imaging than the small hospital could provide. He wondered idly if one of his more successful surgeon family members might be the one to take the case.

"How's the pain?" he asked, listening to the man's chest,

checking if the morphine he'd given was enough. The guy was well over six feet and built like a tanker. A short nod came in return. Alex moved on. Another of the glassing patients had damage to his eye, which would need a specialist. Another's x-ray showed a fractured eye socket.

It wasn't until four am, when the orderly was mopping the floors, that Alex, Karen, Wendy and the nurses caught time for black coffee and a debrief.

"I told you," Wendy said. "Full moon."

Alex handed across the money. He was utterly wiped.

Karen refilled his cup. "Bet you're missing the island lifestyle now, Alex."

Alex smiled, but what flashed in his mind at that moment wasn't the beaches or the palm trees, it was Erin Jacobs, leaning on her boat with those long suntanned legs. Wendy threw a sugar packet at him. "Earth to Alex? I said, how's it going over there on Haven?"

Alex pushed himself up in his seat. He knew better than to say anything about Erin; Wendy would be on to him in a flash. So he reached for the next closet thing.

"Did you know a Dr Jacobs? He had the island practice a few years back, and used to work shifts here, too."

"Jacobs, Jacobs … can't say that I do. But I've only been here three years."

"Name's familiar," Karen said. "I was at the district hospital before … I think I remember seeing that name on referrals."

"Any idea about what happened to him?"

One of the nurses said, "Wasn't he in a car crash or something?"

Alex mulled on this. It didn't fit. A car accident, however horrible, was a sadly common thing. People didn't avoid talking about car crashes. They avoided talking about suicide. Or violent crime. Or maybe he was making too much of it. He was just exhausted. But the kernel of curiosity was still there as he pulled the blinds down against the sunlight in the visiting doctor's flat. He'd seen the look on Erin's face as she'd unwittingly mentioned her father. A look of pain and regret. He'd recognised both, because it was the same way he'd felt when he'd mentioned sailing.

Two days later, Alex washed his face after another twelve-hour stint. The early sun streamed in the locker-room window, but his eyes felt full of fine sand that even three coffees were failing to shift. Alex knew he needed sleep, but Karen was in the middle of a case and they had to hand over before he left. He'd just pulled off his scrub shirt to change when he heard footsteps.

"Alexander Bell? We meet at last."

Alex looked over, bleary-eyed, to see a man in a pinstripe suit standing in the locker-room door. His stomach flipped, wondering if this was a lawyer. But a hairline second later, he registered the familiar features, and his sleep-deprived brain switched gears. He'd seen this man before. At the town meeting.

"You must be Tristan," Alex said, extending his hand to his employer. "Glad we can finally meet in person."

"I know you were at the meeting the other night," Tristan said. "I intended to find us some facetime, but well, there were a lot of questions. I trust everything in the island clinic is satisfactory?"

"Looks like it," Alex said, groping for his shirt. The first item of clothing he pulled from his bag was a pair of gym shorts. Man, he was tired. He paused, trying to remember something he knew was relevant. "Oh, Skye Jacobs mentioned something about generators being turned off at night, so we could use a back-up for the medical fridges."

"Of course."

Finally having found his shirt, Alex paused again. Tristan was waiting expectantly, as though there was an agenda for this conversation Alex had no idea about. "You didn't come all the way over to the mainland just to ask me about the clinic?"

"No, no. Do you have a few minutes to talk?"

Alex checked his watch. "I need to do handover."

"I can wait."

Alex rubbed his forehead, his thoughts so sluggish. "Sorry, Tristan. I just finished my third night on the hop, and I'm well short of sharp. I really need to sleep. Can it wait till I've got some neurons to rub together?"

"Just a few minutes. I think you'll want to hear this. I'll wait in the conference room."

Fifteen minutes later, having been left little choice, Alex found Tristan reclining in one of the boardroom-style chairs and looking out the big window that faced the esplanade. Hearing Alex come in, he pushed himself up. "Nice refurb we did on this room, don't you think? Best telemedicine system money can buy."

"Must admit I haven't used it yet."

Tristan pushed a large takeaway cup across the table. "Only the good stuff. I guessed a double shot with two sugars," he said.

Alex, who never took sugar in coffee and only liked the barest grace of milk, wrapped his hands around the cup anyway.

The room felt so cold; another symptom of needing sleep, he was having trouble regulating his body temperature. He wanted to go, but with his patchy professional history, he didn't want to give his employer reason to dislike him.

"They all speak very highly of you here," Tristan said. "And I have a proposition, if you'll permit me."

Alex raised a questioning eyebrow, wary, and harnessing all his will to concentrate on what Tristan was saying. He'd seen the man on stage at the town meeting – self-assured, friendly, and obviously used to getting his own way. If he was about to ask Alex for a favour, he'd need to be careful, especially because his temper could get the best of him when he was tired.

"As you heard, the island's future is taking an exciting turn. The resort is going to open again, and that means there'll be hundreds more people there every day. Tourists of all demographics. With that scenario, it makes sense to restore the medical practice to full capacity, and to be able to support racing series when it gets going."

Tristan paused, tapping a finger on the table. "Would you be interested in a small changes of terms?"

"You mean, alter our contract?"

"For a permanent arrangement on the island. Give up the night shifts here, live by the beach, fully in control of your own practice."

"And be on-call?" Alex said, the reflex response of any doctor asked to run a solo practice.

Tristan's smile was quick. "The resort will employ a nurse, too. I can guarantee you wouldn't be up more than one night a week."

Alex could feel the flash of anger inside him, his automatic response to anyone who tried to change an agreement. No one could make such a guarantee. He'd thought a long time about this job before he'd taken it. He couldn't process what this change might mean, especially not now.

He blew out his breath, long and slow, letting the anger be there, but not being controlled by it. He deliberately pulled his face into a contemplative expression, part frown, part squint. Wendy teased him about it when he was examining x-ray films. But it was his defence, the way he dealt with things now. It meant he didn't use his fists anymore.

"I'll think about it," he said.

Tristan took a short pausing breath. "I want you to know, if it has any bearing on your answer, that we don't hold your past against you. I believe in second chances, I really do."

Alex jerked, the words slicing through his sleep-deprived haze. Not once in all the negotiations for his position had anyone brought up Alex's professional past. He had been relieved about that. So why was Tristan mentioning it now?

"Okay," Alex said carefully, "I'll let you know when I put some sleep on it."

Tristan stood and Alex felt the primitive thrill in realising he was two inches taller. Tristan adjusted his tie.

"Well, give it some thought. I'll be at the village dance on Friday."

And he walked out before Alex could do it first.

Alex stared after Tristan's departing back, the qualm of his employer holding something over him washing in and out of him like the tide. He'd thought all that was behind him, and now he'd been reminded it was still clear and present. Later, as he tried to lie down and sleep, another picture became lodged in his mind: Tristan and Erin, talking in the back of the stage at the meeting. Tristan being his charming self, but Erin with her arms folded, her back hunched. Alex hadn't thought of it since. They clearly knew each other; probably, they'd grown up together. But now, something about the two of them gave him a discomfort that kept him awake far too long.

Chapter 6

On Thursday morning Erin pushed open the door to Gus's chandlery, hoping to replace a broken cleat block and pick up her mended sail. The chandlery was on the island side of the shop block, one of the original village cabins converted into a store. The inside was more a museum than a business, with bins and baskets covering every shelf. A huge central table remained clear for Gus's sail work, which is where Erin found him, with Radio National turned up to eleven, his glasses down his nose and a slick of glue stuck in the side of his spiky grey hair.

"Gus!" she yelled over the talk-back program.

He waved and hit mute on the radio. "Ready to go, Miss Erin," he said, hauling her neatly packed sail bag from under the counter.

Erin held up the broken cleat. "Got one of these, too?"

Gus squinted. "Not that exact one, but close enough to do you. This way." But as he was fossicking in a bin of parts, he paused to give her a sly look, and said, "So, how's about that new doctor, then?"

Erin's blood thickened. "How about what?"

"Sandy's taken a right shine to him. Thinks he's *attractive*. Word is, Stella's angling for him to pose for her, too."

Erin took the cleat from Gus and pretended to examine it.

"Course, I told her to just be careful, now."

"Why's that?" Erin said, affecting indifference.

"Had a yachty in here on the weekend, needing a part for his motor. Had this nasty cut on his finger from getting the hatch open, so I was telling him Doc Bell was off-island for the week. And he says, that wouldn't be Alex Bell, would it? And I said it would, and what's it to him? And he says they used to be in the same club, up north. Told me all about it. How Doc Bell was thrown out of the club – started a fight with another member. Put him in hospital, apparently. How's that for a story?"

Gus laughed, evidently enjoying it.

"Sounds like idle gossip," Erin said. After all, she was sure half the village were talking about her at this very moment, too. Gossip was a fog on the island, clinging to each new arrival. She told herself it wasn't worth thinking about, but then she still was thinking about it later that afternoon, when Sandy dragged her down to the hall to help decorate for the dance.

Erin was surprised to see her mother opening catering packs of plates and napkins. They'd had tea again on the yacht on Monday, as awkward as the first time. Her mother had talked about the walking trails on the island, and about the book she was researching, but all Erin could feel was the gulf between them. And her mother had made no mention of the dance. Erin wondered now if that had been because her father had always enjoyed dances so much.

Skye kept Erin mercifully busy. "If you're going to be here, at least keep working. This prep isn't going to do itself," her sister complained, catching Erin staring off into space while thinking what else needed fixing on the boat.

Grumbling, Erin picked up the coloured card and scissors, and began cutting out the shape of a cow. "Who picked this farmyard theme, anyway?"

"I did," Skye said pointedly. "The school's doing a term on understanding where food comes from. About time, since most of the children think it comes off a ferry."

Erin tried, but she was useless at cutting out, and eventually Skye took the scissors away, and banished her to bringing down the straw bales. But all she could think was that Tristan had wanted her answer by tomorrow tonight, and she was still torn between the cowardice of leaving, and the pain of staying.

The next day sped past, the village hall transformed by sunset. Erin dreaded the evening, if not for her lack of answer for Tristan, then for the awfulness of the barnyard-themed dance extravaganza. Her mood could not tolerate the upbeat zaniness of the Nutbush and Cotton-Eye Joe dances on endless repeat. She would much rather stay outside on the beach, where the gathering evening enveloped her.

Every blue shade was delicate and soothing, from the ocean's calm expanse, to the azure sky chasing the last of the sun, to the shadows under the dune bushes. The air was perfumed with summer and jasmine, and slipped smooth as coconut oil over her bare shoulders. She could hear the wavelets lapping, the breeze shushing in the dry grass, and in the distance, the excited shrill of children leaking from the hall windows. Life had been like this growing up here, every day.

She'd forgotten how beautiful home was.

When she reached the hall, she poked her head in the side door, surveying Skye's handiwork. Less soothing in here. The four corners were stacked with straw bales, the walls covered in posters and cardboard farm animals – cows, pigs and chickens, including one that Erin decapitated, and that Skye had taped back together. *Milk!* declared one poster, with lots of pictures of jerseys and milking machines. Another was about wheat.

Even with her sister being frosty, Erin had to admit Skye had commitment. The hall was already filling, all the kids in some kind of costume – mostly cowboy hats and broomstick horses. Erin slid onto a straw bale as then the music started up, flooding the hall with the barn dance songs. The kids were soon thumping around to the heel-and-toe polka, while the parents stood on the edges filming and laughing and picking up the smaller ones after falls. Skye was right in the middle of it, making sure the music was cued or striding into the kitchen to check on the food, then emerging a minute later to shepherd in new arrivals. No Tristan yet.

Instead, across the hall Erin spotted Travers, straddling a straw bale, nursing a beer, and failing to be nonchalant in how he was watching Skye.

Erin sidled across and sat beside him. "Enjoying the show?" she asked.

Travers rolled his eyes. "'Just help us move the pig roast,' they said. Next thing, I've been here three hours up ladders, hanging cut-outs of sheep. On the upside, I think I finally understand what a do-si-do is."

"See anything you like?"

Travers narrowed his eyes at her. "And here I thought you might be coming to complain about my work on your hull."

"I was. You missed a spot," Erin said.

"Missed a spot, my butt."

"Fair. I'll admit, it's the best job I've ever seen. You weren't wrong about that."

Travers leaned back, satisfied smile on his face. They watched two more dances in mutual disdain, until finally Tina

Turner began singing "Nutbush City Limits". All the kids squealed.

"Feel free to jump up and join in," Travers said.

"You go ahead," she said, not yet feeling the elation of dances-past.

"Not on your life."

"Shame. That would have been entertaining."

"Which is exactly why I won't be doing it," Travers said, sitting stoically through the frivolity until the song ended, and the kids were herded off the floor towards the kitchen. "So, clean boat, mended sail. You blowing town soon?"

Erin took a breath to answer just as Tristan strode into the hall, a grin on his face. He was wearing a dapper pair of chaps, a check shirt and a huge western belt buckle, clearly at home with full participation. Erin's stomach wobbled like a broken compass.

"Hell," muttered Travers, who'd come in his standard board shorts and singlet. "All yours. I'm gone."

"There you are," Tristan said, "Just the lady I wanted to see. How about a dance?"

Erin glanced around. Her palms were suddenly slick, her answer still not ready and she wasn't in the mood for his enthusiasm.

She got up, but instead of taking his offered lead to the dancefloor, she pulled him to the side door and out into the cool and relative quiet. All the stars had come out.

"What, no dance?" he said. "And I got all dressed up for nothing."

"Tristan, about the job. I know that you wanted an answer tonight—"

"I wanted a dance."

Erin took a slow breath. "Can we be serious for a minute?"

"I'm very serious." His face was so impassive, she couldn't tell if he was joking. Then he broke a small smile. "You know, I can't remember why we split up."

I do, Erin thought. "That was a long time ago," she said quickly, seeing her way out. "Look, if I'm going to stay here, I need details. Start date. Role. Pay. A written contract. A word isn't enough."

"Even mine?"

Especially yours. "I have a boat to keep on the water."

Even as she said it, she thought about Skye and her mother and the village. What would they all say if she turned Tristan down?

"I respect that. Give me a few days to put the formal offer together," he said, a little too close now. "You'll be pleased, I promise. You already know how much I want you to do this."

She took a breath to tell him that if this went ahead – *if* this went ahead – then under no circumstances would they be dating again. But from inside the hall, someone was talking into the microphone, followed by a round of clapping, and then clearly Tristan's name being called through the echo of the PA system. Tristan dropped his shoulders. "Dammit, I forgot the raffle."

He left Erin sitting on the bench under a palm tree, breathing in a Tristan-sized waft of expensive cologne.

Erin wandered around outside the hall, in more of a muddle. She had compelling reasons to leave the island, what with her history with Tristan, and Skye's displeasure. Not to mention the guilt of seeing her mother again. But her funds were running low, and she didn't have many other prospects right now.

And what about Alex?

She flicked the thought away in irritation and kept walking, puzzling out the pros and cons as gusts of evening air blew sea scent through the palms. Bursts of applause leaked out of the hall, and children kept running by shrieking and laughing, playing some variant of Red Rover under the spotlights. She watched them, sadly, remembering the exhilaration of staying up late, the sweets, and the raw freedom of nighttime beach games.

She wasn't a kid anymore; she had adult-sized problems, ones that couldn't be cured with a dance. She needed a sign. So when the "Macarena" started up inside, she rolled her eyes. Well, that was a vote for going: Great Haven and its hokey dance was too far from the steel drums and relaxed sophistication of a Caribbean rum bar. Only the smell of the spit-roasted pork had her stomach growling. She couldn't possibly leave without trying that.

She followed the smell to the annex where she could see into the hall, and hear the kitchen chatter through the window.

She spotted her mother in the hall, standing by one of the straw bales, a sad half-smile on her lips, as if she was trying very hard to enjoy herself, but just couldn't make it happen, even for something as ridiculous as dancing the Macarena.

Erin's stomach twisted: another sign to go. She was about to slip away when she spotted Tristan approaching her mother. The next moment, he'd drawn her into the crowd, taking her through the dance steps. And while Anna protested, clearly embarrassed, Tristan persisted. He put his hat on her head, and then suddenly Anna was dancing with the rest of them, a little stiff, but for the moment her old self.

Erin released a breath she didn't know she'd been holding. It was the first time she'd seen joy on her mother's face since she'd left four years ago. Erin silently relented in her attitude to Tristan, and leaned back against the wall. Maybe he really had changed. Maybe she was giving him too little credit.

"Did you see? Anna's up dancing," said a voice from the kitchen window, clear even over the clink of dishes.

"Who with?" came another woman's voice.

"Tristan Drummond, if you please!"

The other woman clucked her tongue. "That boy's a treasure. What would we do if he hadn't come back?"

"You know, he used to see that Erin Jacobs."

Erin stilled, her skin prickling at her own name.

"Are you sure?" the other woman was asking.

"Oh yes, years ago. When he was at university on the mainland. Erin was always racing here and there. My daughter was on the same campus. She used to see them in the college."

"I had no idea. What happened?"

"Must have realised he could do better. I mean, look at where he is now! Never thought I'd see her come back, though. Anna must be finding it so difficult."

"They never did find him, did they?"

"No. But it was all very odd. They had that huge argument before they left on that trip. Then the next thing, he's missing and she's the only one who knows what happened. Her story never made much sense."

Erin's body had petrified now, every emotion a hard crystal against her heart. She wanted to scream at these women, but she could barely make her lungs move.

"Skye is just lovely, though, isn't she?" the first woman went on. "Real community spirit. She does so much for the school."

"Desperately wants a bub of her own."

The first woman laughed. "Might need the husband first."

"I think she's working on that. Would be a good pairing, don't you think? Tristan would be a gorgeous father."

"Speaking of gorgeous, how about that new doctor."

"Stunner," said the second woman. "But … bit reserved, don't you think? Not like Dr Jacobs was. I don't give him long here, like all of them."

"You know, I could have sworn I saw him leaving Erin's boat the other—oh, put that bag out, will you?"

One of them stepped towards the door. A hot burst of adrenaline broke Erin's freeze. Moving like a spooked animal, she ducked underneath the windows and ran down the other side of the hall. The music had stopped again, and the scrapes of tables being dragged over the floor chased her all the way.

She rounded the corner near the beach and ran straight into Travers carrying a plate overflowing with cracking pork and roast potatoes.

"Where are you going so fast?" he said, around a mouthful of roast. "Looking for Alex?"

At the mention of his name, Erin pulled up. "Why?"

"Said he was looking for you. Man, that's good pork."

Erin felt a qualm. "Looking for me, why?"

Travers frowned. "In the way that a man looks for a girl he likes to talk to. How dense are you, Erin Jacobs?"

Erin didn't answer him. She was distracted by how Travers could eat so fast and speak at the same time. He was balancing a plate of pavlova underneath his main meal.

"Can I have your plate?" she asked. No way was she going back in.

"Hell, no," he said. "I have set up props, I have carried chairs and tables, and I can take no more of the soundtrack. I saw them loading up the 'Grease Megamix'. If anyone wants me, I'll be in my cabin with a beer."

"What about doing a little run back inside to get me one?"

Travers turned away. "They start playing Metallica, you come get me."

Erin watched him go. She didn't want to make another appearance for the gossipers, but she was starving. She was still hanging at the corner when Alex stepped out of the exit, also carrying a plate.

She ducked around the corner, expecting him to take the inland path and head back to the clinic. But he didn't. He came right towards the beach. He passed her position and kept going, down through the dunes.

Erin pulled off her shoes. The sand was cool under her feet, only the barest hint of the trapped afternoon sun in the thickest drifts. Alex's form became a wash of greys and blues as he left the lit path and climbed the dunes. Erin gave him time to crest the hill before she followed, crouching beside the saltbush at the top. He'd gone down onto the hard sand now, walking towards the old resort, his feet barely making dents under the moonlight.

When he reached the jetty, he paused and looked towards her yacht, still moored off the western side, all its lights off. Erin felt her heart thudding as he stared at her boat. Would she follow if he went down there?

When he appeared to give up and keep going up the beach, Erin silently slipped out from behind the bush and slid down through the soft sand. Where the hell was he going now? Well, she wasn't going to find out.

She tiptoed down the jetty, heading for her yacht and another packet meal. She only made it a third of the way down the boards.

"I thought that was you."

She froze and spun. He must have come back down the beach, as silent as she had been. The jetty's spotlight threw shadows across his body.

"Were you following me?" he asked.

"No," she lied. "I was just coming back here."

"I see." He sounded disappointed again.

And then she smelled the roast. "What exactly do you have there?" she asked.

He showed her the two foil covered plates. "Oh, just dinner for two. I thought when I didn't see you up at the hall that you'd be down here. I was happy to share."

It was almost enough to forgive anything, but she couldn't quite forget the shade Gus had thrown on him. "And where exactly were you heading, having given up on me?"

"Ah … that's a little secret."

Erin wavered. "I don't really like secrets."

"That's okay … I haven't really given up on you. Come on."

Chapter 7

He led up the beach, to where the dunes met the resort's chain-link fence, then followed it east. Erin had a feeling of being back in time, to when she'd gone exploring the island as a teenager. But the resort had always been open, then. It had always had lights, and activity. Now it was all black shapes lanced with shafts of moonlight caught on glass or concrete. It made her sad.

Alex finally stopped where the fence dived inward around a large palm tree. He reached for a corner of the fence wire and pulled it open. "Ladies first."

"We shouldn't go in there," she said.

"Trust me, there's no one here," he said. He ducked through the hole, and held it open for her. "But I'm taking the food with me."

"Cheater," Erin said, as she stepped through the gap.

It took a moment to orient herself. She'd known the resort blindfolded when she lived on the island — its long row of beachside rooms, the pools, the huge central restaurant and entertainment spaces. The other guest rooms were in rows behind. But with the island slowly reclaiming the buildings, the resort was eerie, all the familiar features hidden under vines and shadows.

Alex touched her shoulder. "This way," he said.

She followed under an overpass, the walkway between two wings of the beachfront rooms. They skirted a pool, empty but for drifts of fallen leaves, beyond which Alex picked his way to a stairway in the back of the old recreation wing, now wearing a coat of jasmine. He lit his phone's flashlight as he went in.

Erin's heartbeat thumped as they climbed, sand crunching under her shoes. They reached the first floor, once the resort's main restaurant. The glass windows out onto the beach were still intact, but the carpet had been stripped, and light fittings hung limp from the ceiling. Alex caught her hand. "Watch the step."

Her fingers tingled at the touch. She leapt across a pile of boards stacked in front of the stairs. On the next floor was a bar, now empty of chairs and tables, all the taps gone, but still smelling faintly of sour beer.

"One more," Alex said, leading through a much narrower doorway into the roof stairs. Up and up Erin went in the dark, until Alex pushed open the roof door into the deep blue of shadowed moonlight flooding the rooftop terrace. Alex flicked off his light. They were high above anything else in the resort here, open to the sky. In the centre, someone had dragged up two old deck chairs that had once been around the pool.

Erin smiled in the dark at the clandestine hangout, until she caught a narrow sweep of a light, somewhere down in the complex. "Wait – is that a torch?" she whispered.

"Security guard," Alex answered. "Don't worry, he spends most of the night smoking in a chair over by the construction offices. He's at least twenty stone, and probably poorly paid. I put his odds of wanting to climb stairs at extremely limited."

He sat on a deck chair, and held out one of the plates.

"A lot of effort just for somewhere quiet to eat," she said, taking the offering. Man, it smelled good. "And you told me no one was here."

"That I did," he said. "I'd have done worse to spend some time with you."

She laughed softly. "You are a bad man," she said, enjoying herself. It really was like being a kid again.

He gave her an eyebrow, his smile a little devilish in the corners. "I can be," he said. "But I want to show you the other reason I come up here."

"Do I want to know?"

Alex checked his watch and said, "Eat. You'll see."

When they were finished their plates, he stretched out on one of the deck chairs, dropping the back so he faced the sky. He gestured for Erin to do the same. "Should be starting any minute now."

"What?" she said.

Then, a brilliant spark burned across the sky. The trail only scribed the length of Erin's extended palm, but the incandescence of the shooting star pulled a gasp from her throat.

"Keep watching," Alex said.

They kept coming, one after another. Sometimes they would pause for a long silent minute before another cluster began. Erin lost herself in the anticipation, forgetting when and where she was. All she knew was the smell of jasmine and the sky so full of stars. When the shower seemed to be over, she shook her head. "That was—"

"One more, look this way ..."

She turned her head to follow where he was pointing, to the west over the mainland. He kept an eye on his watch. "Three, two, one, now!"

A bright point flared into view a few fingers above the horizon, burning like the brightest jewel in the already sparkling heavens. Erin tracked its arching path, all the way over the main beach, on and on for over a minute, until it finally disappeared right over Bella's Leap.

Alex blew out a long breath. He sounded content.

"What was that last one?" Erin said.

"The International Space Station. Tonight is one of the best nights this year to see it." He paused, then said, "It might sound naff, but I like watching the sky. Meteor showers, satellites, or just the stars turning through the night. Something about it keeps me sane on the bad days."

They lay unmoving, a peaceful bubble around them. Erin considered what he'd said. She thought she understood what he meant. "Because it makes your problems seem small, at least for a moment?"

"Something like that," he said.

Erin thought of all the times she'd served a night watch under the unspoilt night sky. She'd rarely looked up, then. She needed her attention on the boat's instruments. But the sense of the space above had always been there.

"This is what I liked best about living on a boat," Alex said suddenly. "All the sky, all night anchored somewhere with no one else around."

"What did you sail?" Erin asked, her fingers drifting towards the edge of the sun lounge, towards him. She wanted to touch him, to extend this connection she felt between them.

"Forty-two footer, up north," he said quickly. Abruptly he sat up, swinging his legs to the side, and the peaceful bubble wobbled. Erin sat, too, one of her knees slipping between his.

"Sometimes, you can see the waves glowing off Bella's

Leap," she said. "It's a bright blue phosphorescence. People say it looks like the galaxy through a telescope."

"Really?" He turned his head towards Bella's Leap, the twist in his body causing his leg to brush against hers.

"You won't see it from here," Erin said, noting that he hadn't removed the contact. "You have to go up to the cliff top. Or down on the rocks. I took a photo of it once, years ago."

Her mouth was so dry, just from how his skin felt, like smooth warm water.

"Not sure I'd want to be too close, down on the rocks," he said, but softly. His gaze was fixed on her eyes now.

Erin grazed her teeth over her lower lip. She could smell a trace of his aftershave, something spicy and masculine. She imagined reaching for him with the boldness of a boat captain in a new port, hunting for a bunk companion to obliterate the long time at sea, to blot out the bruises on her heart. But he wasn't that man, she realised. There was something else here. He wasn't someone just for tonight.

"What do you see?" he said.

She took a moment to answer, the rumours about him briefly flashing in her mind. "I don't know."

He reached out and cupped her face, drawing her towards him, and then he kissed her softly. Erin didn't need such restraint. The moment she felt his lips on hers, she knew how right this felt. They were soon on the one deck chair, making out like teenagers, not even caring the chair was hard plastic and less than comfortable.

Their make-out turned into companionable as the hour passed. Alex held Erin against him, both of them watching the sky in between kisses and she had no desire to be anywhere else.

"You know you can walk all the way round Bella's Leap to

the east beach over the rocks, as long as you avoid high tide," Erin said eventually, her head resting on his chest. "The tourists used to – everyone wanted to see that beach."

"Why?" he said, and the feel of the word through his skin made her feel as carefree as she had on summer nights here growing up.

"It was in a music video years ago, plus it's the one on all the resort promo brochures. I always thought the wreck was more interesting. It's off the far east headland, always underwater, except at a king low tide."

"Wonder if Travers has been down there."

"Probably," Erin said. "More than one boat's snared a keel on it. The waters around these islands have a reputation for things like that."

"Is it really as bad as everyone says?"

"Yeah, it's tricky. There's lots of little shallow points. Maps are great these days, but throw in the wind and tide conditions, not to mention the storms, and even experienced sailors misjudge it."

"Why here for the storms?"

"Oh, something about being in the right path for fronts off the mainland. Hot air funnels down the range over there, meets moist air from the sea, and we cop it first. Surf can get really big then, especially on the eastern side. There's caves in the cliffs around there."

"Yeah, Travers mentioned that."

Erin turned to face him, playing her fingers through the stubble on his chin, loving the affection he had in his eyes for her. "Did you know Travers before the island?" she asked, curious. "You seem good friends."

Alex shook his head. "No. I went looking for him because

he's an ex-medic. Good to know there's someone around to help, if we ever had an emergency. We just happened to hit it off."

The reminder of who Alex was hit Erin unexpectedly hard. She pushed herself up. His hands lingered on her waist, but she felt suddenly miles away from here. Her eyes sought Bella's Leap, looking for something, anything, to recover the mood from just moments ago. But while the cliff sat quietly in the ocean tonight, the waves barely breaking on the rocks below, the moment was gone.

"You want to tell me more about Bella's ghost story?" Alex whispered.

Erin glanced around. He meant it as a joke, she could tell that. He could sense their connection had slipped, too. She forced herself to smile. "I think we better call it a night."

Alex found sleep hard that night, and the next. Erin had left a pleasant and yet complicated trail in his life. He wanted to see more of her; that much wasn't in question. But he had his own nice carousel of baggage to consider. Things that he wasn't ready to share and be judged. When she'd pulled back, he wondered if somehow she sensed it.

He also had more practical problems: every time he tried to find her over the weekend, some medical issue came up, demanding his attention. Tim brought Monster for a paw check-up, which was healing fine, and the two of them bounded off on some island adventure. Then, when he was about to walk down to the jetty, Sandy brought in two backpackers with severe sunburn. Neither of the pair spoke much English, nor seemed to know about the Australian sun. Resorting to drawing pictures and sign language, Alex wasn't getting far when Sandy dropped in with a French dictionary.

"I'm pretty sure they're speaking Spanish," Alex called after her.

Although, if it was Spanish, it bore no resemblance to the language Alex had once learned for a trip to South America. Finally, he walked them down to the island store, and pointed out the 30+ sunblock.

When he walked back ten minutes later, he looked towards the jetty. Beyond Erin's yacht, dark clouds gathered on the horizon, and the wind had a different smell about it now. Fresh, and a little too cold. He shivered. He knew that smell. Rain was coming.

He figured he should go down to the jetty and offer to help in preparing for the storm, but when he reached the *Fair Winds*, Erin wasn't there. He spun around, checking she wasn't somewhere nearby. There was an odd qualm in his chest. He remembered Travers saying that Erin was planning on leaving soon. Would he wake up tomorrow and find her boat gone from the pier? Would she leave his life as abruptly as she'd ended their night on the rooftop?

He didn't like the idea. He was just striding up the beach again to see if Erin was at Skye's when Sandy appeared, waving like a troubled swimmer from the top of the dunes.

"Patient for you," she said, sounding overly excited. "It's *Helmut*," she added.

"*The* Helmut?"

"Yes, you know he never comes down from his studio. This is quite an honour."

Back at the clinic, Alex found a man waiting in reception. He stood with his hands clasped behind his back, bouncing a little on his toes, as if examining the desk for its best angle. He was barefoot and tanned, with a scraggly beard and hair, his clothes covered in paint.

Alex gestured Helmut to a seat and firmly closed the door on the hovering Sandy, half expecting the woman would be listening at the keyhole.

"Mr Meyer, how can I help?"

"You know who I am, I think?" Helmut said with a challenge in his voice.

Alex nodded slowly. "I know your work, at least a little," he said. "But otherwise I have to tell you I don't know one end of a paintbrush from the other."

Helmut chuckled. "Okay. Then you call me Helmut," he said. He gestured to his daubed shirt. "Painting is my life's work. It is, everything. But now ..." He pressed his fingers to his eyes, drawing them away in despair, as though he couldn't give the problem a name.

Alex guessed. "Your eyesight?"

"Ja. The colours are not the same anymore, and in the far away distance, is all a blur. It is like I have something in my eye, some veil. Everything looks like Monet. And when the sun is on the sea, shining like silver, I cannot look at it anymore."

"Ah." Alex ran through a full examination, testing Helmut's visual acuity, carefully examining the lens and retina, and ruling out neurological issues. He was glad to be fairly sure of the problem.

"I think you're developing cataracts. Do you know what that is?"

"My mother, I think she had this. Clouds in the eyes."

"Right. It usually develops slowly, with the lens in the front part of your eye becoming thicker over time."

Helmut's words came tight with worry. "It will worsen then? My mother – she was nearly blind."

"Gradually, yes," Alex said. "But these days it can be easily treated."

Helmut's attention snapped up. "*You* treat it?"

Alex shook his head. "You'll need to see an eye specialist, on the mainland. I'd recommend that anyway – to be sure this is what we're dealing with."

"I do not like the mainland. You said it will change slowly?"

"Usually. Some things can make it worse. Do you smoke?"

"I give up ten years ago." He sounded incredibly jaded about it. "Stella … she is on me all the time about the cigars."

"Good for you – much better for your health."

Helmut shrugged. "I admit, it ruins the canvases. And I keep Stella happy."

"Do you wear sunglasses? The radiation in sunlight can make cataracts worse."

"Never. I like seeing the light."

"Start. But you'll need to make sure you get the right type. I'll go with you to the shop to see if they have any."

"Maybe next time I come down."

"Okay," Alex said slowly, wondering if that would be months away, and thinking what else he should cover now. "I'd also like to run a test for diabetes."

By the time Alex finished, Helmut seemed eager to return home, and Alex wondered if he'd done too good a job of reassuring him.

Helmut paused before he left. "Thankyou, Dr Bell. May I ask your first name?"

"Alex," he said, offering his hand.

"Ah, Alex, this is a good name," Helmut said, pumping

Alex's hand affectionately. "You visit me next time, ja? Now, I go before the storm."

An hour later when he had closed the clinic, Alex stood again at the crest of the dunes. The dark clouds were rolling in now, the wind whipping the palms and driving sand onto his legs. He could see Erin had moved her yacht away from the jetty, its bow attached to a bright orange moor point, a much better place to ride out the chop. Alex felt great relief that she hadn't sailed away yet; and disappointed that her boat was no longer accessible from the pier. The first raindrops driving ahead of the storm crashed into his forehead, shedding splashes that caught on his eyelashes. The front looked just like one of Helmut's paintings – all swirling greys and blues, the palate of midnight clouds.

In that moment, Alex glanced towards Bella's Leap. A woman was standing on the edge of the cliff, a flowing white gown behind her, staring into the foaming water. Alex's blood chilled. He blinked, and then he could see only mist and spray. And no matter where he paced down the beach, the image was lost in the rain that came down on the headland.

Chapter 8

The storm lasted into the evening. Not long by island standards, and when Erin stuck her head up out of the hatch on Monday morning, damage appeared minimal. One old rotten palm had come down across the beachside path, a few other branches were strewn around, but the sand dunes were intact. She began checking over the *Fair Winds* anyway.

She'd just gone below when she heard what sounded like a man clearing his throat. Erin whirled and came back up to look, heart hammering, wondering if it somehow was Alex, who she'd been unable to shake from her thoughts since Saturday night. But the pier was empty. Then she glanced over the side of the yacht, and her heart sank.

Tristan was sitting in a kayak, in an outfit that looked straight from a Kathmandu catalogue, the oar balanced across his lap. He held up two takeaway coffees. "I was about to knock," he said with a laugh. "Let's have that serious chat."

Erin was mildly conscious she was still in her pyjamas, her eyes full of sleep, and her hair a wild nest. She'd crewed enough boats not to be precious; people had to take it or leave it. But this was Tristan, who came with all those old guarded feelings. "You might let a girl wake up first."

"That's what the coffee's for. You going to throw me a line?"

She tossed a rope over and left him to climb aboard while

she went below to tug on a shirt and pull a brush through her hair. When she re-emerged, Tristan had settled himself on one of the cockpit benches and had put up the collapsible table, leaving plenty of room next to him for her to sit.

"You didn't get that coffee from Sandy's," Erin observed as she slipped into the seat opposite. "Don't let her see you with those cups."

Tristan gave her a devilish smile. "I have a machine in the office. It's easier than walking all the way down to the village."

Erin paused mid-sip. "You have an office? Where?"

"In the old resort, of course. It's just a part of a building we've cleared on the village side, near the airstrip, but I need somewhere to take meetings with the trades foreman."

"I didn't realise work had actually started," she said, thinking again about Alex's secret spot.

He nodded. "Survey's putting down markers now. First contingent of heavy equipment will arrive next week to start demolition."

Erin's first thought was of the peaceful rooftop, lost to the bulldozers. Her second was the memories of her childhood attached to every corner of the place – racing around the pools when they shouldn't have been there, conducting secret scavenger hunts on school holidays. "You're knocking it down?"

"Well, not all of it," Tristan said, seeing her expression. "But the accommodation wings out the back are structurally compromised. And the whole thing is dated – very eighties, very Skase – all those tacky fake gold taps and marble banisters. We need to bring it up to a suitable standard for hosting a big event here. For sophisticated people."

Erin swallowed her coffee – mmm, it was better than

Sandy's, too — sensing this was where she'd need to extricate herself from his plans, and actually look for a job that would keep the *Fair Winds* in keels and biscuits. She was hardly sophisticated. "I know you said we needed to chat, but I can see the resort is months off being ready. I'm used to jobs falling through in this business. I can still get on a crew for the Sydney to Hobart."

He sat back as if offended. "Erin. I promised details, and I meant it. So here it is: come on board as my Racing Director."

Erin blinked. "What?"

"Races don't organise themselves," he said. "I have huge respect for you as a sailor, and you know the waters around Great Haven better than anyone. I have a big sponsor nearly over the line for the regatta, but he'll need convincing to put his money in. So the success of the pilot races is critical. Those start in just a few weeks."

"A few *weeks*?"

"We have to be able to demonstrate what we can do here, and I want you to take the lead."

"But that's too much for one person, and I don't even know where to begin."

"I already have a team working it. Sales, marketing, merchandise, all that. But we need someone who knows sailing. Who knows it *here*. I want you to set the course, and tap your contacts to see what other teams we can tempt to race. They're all heading north after the Sydney to Gold Coast right now, ready for the capturing."

Erin laughed. "You can't be serious. I mean, I have no experience doing something at that level. I'm crew or strategist, nothing like a *director*."

"A hundred-thousand a year says I'm serious," he said, then

grinned when she couldn't speak.

Erin jumped up to pace in the limited floor space, then grabbed her coffee to help her think. No one had ever offered her a salary like that.

Tristan watched her with an amused expression. "I'm not saying that it will be easy, but I think you've got the goods, Miss Jacobs. And when you do all this for me this year, next year in the main regatta, there's something else."

"God, what?" she whispered.

"I'm putting you at the helm of a new racing yacht, as captain. Not only here at Great Haven but in all the eastern seaboard races. What do you say?"

Erin put her coffee down on the galley bench and leaned against the hatch, her stomach tied in knots. For the first time in her life, she wasn't sure she could do something. She looked at the flecks of salt crusted on the hatch seal. *That* was what she knew: the minutia of the yacht, the turns of the race out on the course. Was she really cut out to be an organiser on land? In a room dealing with sponsorship and courses?

The *Fair Winds* gently rocked as she slid back in to her seat. A second later, Tristan had risen and slid in beside her. "It's a lot to take in," he said, gently, "but I've offered this to no one else. If you don't say yes, you'll break my heart all over again."

Erin met his eyes, wary. He seemed sincere, his dark gaze searching her face. He'd used that look when they were together, as if he could understand what she thought just by looking hard enough.

"Tristan," she said. "It's been a long time and I'm not sure about all this yet."

He squeezed her hand. "I'm not rushing. In the business side, yes, but not with you." He leaned in and kissed her gently on the cheek.

"That's not what I meant," she said, frozen, trying to gather the right words. She hadn't wanted anything to start up with him again, romantically or otherwise. But Tristan did seem to have changed. He had always been a man with his foot to the floor. He liked everything fast – cars, boats, even sex. This gentle, patient Tristan was something new. Maybe she could work for him.

"This isn't some awful joke, is it?" she asked.

He chuckled. "I have the contract in my office. Come in tomorrow and meet the team. I'll bring them over on the morning boat."

Later that afternoon, Erin moved her yacht back to the jetty, intending to make a trip to the store for resupply. When she finished tying the stern rope, she looked up and started.

Her mother was walking down the jetty, wearing a long flowing grey dress, her skin so white it was glowing in the sun under the dark cloud of her hair. She looked so like Bella in Helmut's paintings, Erin nearly toppled over.

"Mum," she said. "I was going to come up this time. After I fixed the boat." Even as she said it, Erin heard Skye in her head, saying, *That's the order of priorities in your life.*

"I looked for you at the dance, but you seemed to have things on your mind."

"I'll put the kettle on," Erin said, guiltily ducking below.

They sat around the small table in the cabin, where just a few hours ago Tristan had made Erin such an incredible offer, milling about again in painful small-talk. Her mother's writing project was going well, but she didn't want to go into details while she was still drafting. Yes, the *Fair Winds'* repairs were coming along. Erin could feel a hidden agenda in her mother being here, like a whale rising up beneath the boat. It was in the way she took a breath before asking a question, the way she looked around, searchingly. But Erin never wanted that whale to break the surface.

"I remember when you were that small," her mother said wistfully, when they'd stumbled onto how much the children had enjoyed the dance. "You'd have five kids down the beach after bedtime, digging for pirate treasure, and Skye would be there, torn between having fun and coming to tell on you."

Erin frowned into her tea, embarrassed, and unsettled by this talk of secrets. "I had no idea you knew about that."

"Of course I did. You were both so different and while we were here on Haven, I didn't see any problem with letting you run. It would have been different in Sydney or Melbourne. I'd have been worried about you taking up train surfing, or meth, or whatever the kids are into these days."

"Mum!" Erin exclaimed. Her mother smiled, a cheeky edge in it, and in that smile Erin glimpsed the woman she used to know, who'd been lively and not sad. Before four years ago.

"The worst you could do here was cut yourself on the oyster rocks. And you survived that once or twice." Her mother turned her tea mug, as if searching for a warm place for her hands. She was yet to take a sip.

Suddenly, she said, "Erin, I wanted to talk to you."

Erin's heart stopped, like a running rope trapped in a vice. "About what?"

Her mother glanced out the hatch, then down at the table, letting a pause run like a sucking tide. Erin wanted to fill the silence. She felt the *I need to talk to you, too*, gathering on her tongue.

"About your staying here," her mother said, stopping the tide. "I understand Tristan's made you an offer."

"How do you know about that?"

"How did I ever know about anything? People talk."

Erin sat dumbly, wondering where this was going.

"I know his coming in to save the resort means a lot to so many people. But is this what you want to do? Do you really want to stay here?"

Erin took a breath, a new pain searing around where the guilt lance had already run her through. Was her mother saying that she didn't want Erin on the island? That she couldn't stand to look on her daughter every day and be reminded of her husband?

Erin said, very quietly, "Do you want me to leave?"

"I want you to do what is right for you. You're my brave daughter, Erin. You've always walked into big things that you had to work out how to handle. But that doesn't mean you have to this time. I know you and Tristan had your problems."

Erin had to glance away as tears stung her eyes. She hadn't heard anything after *brave*. If only her mother knew, she wouldn't say these things.

"Mum," she began. "There's something I need to tell you."

Then she couldn't continue. She couldn't make the words leave her mouth. Her mother waited, expectant, her eyes questioning above her thin cheeks, as Erin floundered like a netted fish, caught in the bind of what she'd done and what she'd promised her father.

She couldn't do anything about that. But she could help the island.

"I'm going to do it," she managed finally, feeling an utter

coward. "I'm going to take Tristan's job."

Her mother drew in a long breath, and nodded once. "All right, then."

As her mother walked back along the jetty ten minutes later, her grey dress catching the wind, Erin knew that she'd made the decision out of guilt. And, as her mother predicted, now she had to work out how to handle it. Tristan might want her as an organiser, but she was a sailor at heart.

She ran a critical eye over *Fair Winds*, an idea forming in her mind. The only problem would be having Tristan agree.

Chapter 9

The next morning, Erin's bravado faded with each step towards the old resort. The once-daily ferry was pulling away from the main beach, so Tristan's people would be here now. The idea of meeting them, of doing any of the things Tristan was talking about, filled her stomach with flapping sails. He'd called this morning just after six to make sure she was coming.

She shook the jitters from her hands as she took the left turn at the keep-out fence, heading for the airstrip at the back of the complex, where Tristan said the offices were. At the corner, beside the grassy runway, she found three shipping container modules plastered with construction notices. In the distance, a man in hi-vis and dark shades was fiddling with a surveyor's tripod, but she didn't see anyone else. Behind a gate in the chain-link fence, she could see the resort's old reception building with its door open, but she wasn't sure if she should go in there.

"There you are."

Erin spun to find Tristan ducking under the low hanging branches of a tree inside the fence. He straightened, brushing the shoulders of his polo shirt, which had Drummond Enterprises stitched over the left breast.

"Right on time," he said, hefting a thick sheaf of papers bound with a monster bulldog clip, and opening the gate. "Let's go meet your team."

Erin licked her lips. "I want to talk to you first."

"I know what you're going to say," Tristan said, and held out the papers.

"What's this?"

"Your contract, as promised. Now, let's not keep them waiting."

With a hand on her lower back, he guided her towards the far shipping container. Inside was a long table, the walls covered in nautical maps of the island and satellite photos of the main beach. Four people were already seated, intent on their laptops, but they all scrambled up when Tristan entered.

"Troy, Benny, Kit, Shelly – this is Erin Jacobs, our new Racing Director."

Erin swallowed. All these people were wearing suit jackets, and had neat hair, make-up and—lord, were those fake eyelashes? Erin noted two of them eyeing her denim shorts and striped t-shirt. At least this was just a *hi, how are you*, and she could find something more formal next time. But Tristan was already pulling out a chair, and looking comfortable.

"So, where are we, team?" he said.

They all sank into their chairs and tapped on the laptops while Erin stood awkwardly.

"Omega's on board for a bronze sponsorship, so we're over the top now and into profit on the pilot race," said Kit, or was that Shelly?

"Excellent," Tristan said, smoothly pulling out the chair beside him and patting it for Erin to sit. "What about entries?"

"Still short. It's been hard to attract major media coverage. But if we can land a top-level team, more entries will follow."

"Erin's going to help us with that," Tristan said.

Erin's stomach disappeared—what had he just said? She hadn't brought a pen, so she crammed her hands in her lap, the text of the contract swimming before her. She tried to pay attention, but everything they were saying slipped from her head.

Then Tristan said, "We better have a course for the potential entrants soon. Where are we on that?"

"Proposal's right here," said one of the men, unfurling a chart of the islands as wide as the table, with the course drawn in red. Finally, Erin felt her brain click back on. She leaned over the map, her eyes finding the familiar landmarks.

"We're doing an extended rum-race format," the man went on. "A series of buoys to negotiate. Makes much more interesting television than a flat course just out of the bay. When we do the 3D fly-around, the outer islands provide reference points. It'll be excellent."

"Wait, this is going to be on TV?" Erin asked. Sailing struggled to attract coverage for all but the premier events, and even she had to admit that it wasn't exciting to watch on a screen.

"We have some interest from cable," Tristan said. "One of my companies is developing a next-gen sports visualisation package. We're dangling that as a carrot – being able to show wind and tide, zoom around to where each boat is, put advertising on the water. Try out the new tech, in exchange for covering the day."

"Wow," she said. She pulled the chart towards her, imagining taking the *Fair Winds* out on that marked red line. Another minute later, she had the whole course in her mind, and a frown on her face. "Who put this together?"

"We did, with input from the mapping program," Troy said,

with a defensive note.

"This won't work. We need to change it," she said, tracing the route with her finger. She looked at Tristan. "You're thinking a midday start?"

He nodded, his eyes glittering with interest.

"Well, then the wind will be switching around, so you don't want the first leg to run west like this. Run them south out of the bay, straight towards the smaller islands. And this part here? Can someone tell me the tides on the race date?"

All four people reached for smart phones. "Low's at three," someone said.

Erin punched her finger at a point on the course. "Right. So, you can't run through here. There's rocky outcrops, and you're hoping for million dollar boats. They'll never come back if you bust their keels."

"There's nothing about that on the charts—"

"Charts aren't up to date between those two islands. Take the northern passage, and push them out into the open with a tight turn to come in—" Erin paused, visualising the whole thing in her head "—you'll get a tight turn around the buoy, and if the winds are what I think, you'll get them under spinnakers roaring back inside the calm water. From there, you can dog-leg them across the face of the bay, and finish under full sails so the people on the beach can see."

A tense silence hung over the group, until Tristan chuckled.

"Ladies, gentleman, Erin Jacobs," he said. "This is exactly why we needed you. Now, you'll lock down the exact coordinates for the buoys? And give Kit any notes for writing up the course rules."

Erin sat back, her heart thundering in her ears, relieved she hadn't bombed completely. Maybe she could make it through this first meeting.

Then Tristan stood. "Well, I'll leave you to it. I have to head back to the surveyors."

"Wait a minute," Erin called, bouncing out of her chair. She caught him just outside. "You're just going to leave?" she hissed, hoping the other four weren't listening at the windows.

"This is your group now, E. You'll do great. Give me a call when you're through the agenda. We'll talk."

He turned.

"Wait. There's something else."

He raised his eyebrows. "Don't flake out on me now, Erin. I'm late."

"I have a condition for doing this," she rushed out. "Non-negotiable."

That stopped him, though he slowly smiled. "You have a condition? Would it involve a private dinner and candles?"

Erin ignored him. "This pilot race. I want to be in it."

"You're on the organising committee."

"No, I want to race. None of this office stuff is worth it for me if I can't be out on the water." She'd known that for sure the moment she'd described the course; she could already feel the salt water spray on her face, the adrenaline running hot through her body.

"You're expecting me to put up a boat and crew, too?"

"Nope," she said. "My yacht, my crew."

"What crew? And that yacht of yours isn't racing material."

Erin bristled. "She is. And the crew's my affair."

Tristan narrowed his eyes. "How are we supposed to run things on the day if my Racing Director is out on the water?"

"That's your problem," she shot back. And suddenly, this seemed as familiar as all those years ago, when they'd fought, and often ended up in bed afterwards. The way Tristan was staring at her now, all heat in his eyes, she wondered if that was what he was thinking, too.

"All right," he said slowly, "I'll let you race, but you owe me a dinner. Agreed?"

"After the pilot race."

He slowly shook his head, a smile growing on his face. "And you think you're not cut out for business. You're a woman of surprises, Erin Jacobs."

With that, he winked and pushed through the gate, leaving Erin to bring her breath under control before she went back to the meeting. The idea of sailing had gotten her blood pumping, it was true, but it was also Tristan. That was what she remembered from when they'd been together: he'd always had power, even before he owned this huge company, and that was exciting — like a twenty-five knot wind pushing in the sails, flying across the water.

Right against the edge of falling over.

Travers' cabin was dark later when she walked up the front steps, and she would have assumed he was out, but for the front door being cracked open. She stuck her head inside and found the place empty.

"Hello?"

"Up here," he called.

She tipped her head back and finally found him three-quarters of the way up the nearest coconut palm. "What in merry hell are you doing?"

"What do you think. Attempting to get a coconut. One fell down yesterday and it was great after a night in my fridge."

"So you were after more?"

"As you see."

"Why aren't you moving then?"

"Can't," he said shortly. "Seems I'm good enough to climb this far, but no further. It's pretty hard, you know."

Erin, who had climbed the palms plenty as a kid, knew how difficult it was and was impressed such a big man had made it so far. "Can't get down, can you?" she called.

"That part will take care of itself one way or another."

She laughed. "You want me to call the fire volunteers? They have a ladder."

"Hell, no. But you might need to call Alex after I break my neck. Now, move off the soft sand and turn your back."

"What?"

"I said, *turn your back.*"

Erin complied, still laughing, and after a good deal of swearing, grunting, and finally a *thud* that scattered sand up the backs of her legs, she turned around to find Travers dusting himself off.

"Any damage?"

"Skinned hand, mild ankle sprain and deep wound to pride. Might need stitches," he said. "Want a beer?"

Erin accepted, figuring it was the best way to put Travers in a receptive mood, and pulled herself onto his porch railing. Travers retrieved her a beer, but for himself pulled a roll of strapping tape from the huge medical kit stowed by his front door.

"Really looks like you know what you're doing," she said, watching him loop a strip down the outside of his leg, around his heel and back up the same side.

"I have bad joints," he said. "Had surgery on my ankle, a

knee and a shoulder. Strapping tape and me are mighty familiar."

"Alex said you were in the army," she said, easing towards her objective.

"Corporal in the infantry for ten years," Travers said, chucking away the tape roll and reaching for the Dettol. "Then a medic for five more after that."

"No experience on yachts, then?"

"Not unless you want me to shoot at one." He looked up suddenly, a new idea on his face. "Should have thought of that for the coconuts."

"Gus sells hooked poles for coconuts. I'll buy you one," Erin said. "But back to yachts: do you know which end is the bow and which is the stern?"

He narrowed his eyes. "What do you want, Erin Jacobs?"

Erin sipped her beer. "Looking for some crew."

He laughed heartily, until he dripped neat Dettol onto his hand and winced. "Me, on a yacht? I said army, not navy. Besides, I thought you were leaving the island."

"Maybe I'm not, just yet."

He shook his head, but she saw the interested glint in his eye. "You heard me mention my lousy joints?"

"Duly noted."

"Does it pay anything?"

She smiled sweetly. "If we win."

Travers got up and limped into the cabin, returning with his own beer. "Who else is going to be on this boat? Not that dick, Tristan?"

Erin frowned. "What'd he do to you?"

Travers shrugged. "I like this place the way it is. He's a developer. Some things shouldn't change."

"Most of the island would disagree," she said. "But no, actually. I was going to persuade Skye."

She watched for his reaction. And there it was, that little dip of his eyes. So, she hadn't been seeing things at the dance.

"She probably hasn't been on a boat in years," Erin said slowly, calculating. "She might need help. Or, and this is probably likely, she'll take over schooling you like the good teacher she is."

Travers gave her a hard look. "Yeah, okay. I'm in."

By the time Alex had finished the patient list the next day, another bank of cloud had rushed across the sky, and it was dark enough for dusk. Surprised to find it was only two in the afternoon, Alex went down to the dunes with the island map in his hand. Sandy had tried to convince him to come down to the hall, where the village committee was organising events to coincide with the pilot race, but Alex had a more pressing destination in mind. Besides — and he wouldn't have admitted this to anyone — he knew Erin would not be at the hall. She was down at the old resort every day, working long hours for Tristan apparently. Patient gossip had brought that news, and it was stirring an envious finger in his gut.

He stopped at the store to buy sunglasses, then struck out along the main beach, one eye trained on the tip of Bella's Leap. There was no one there today, but ever since he'd had that imagined glimpse of her, he felt the lure of the rock, as it had obviously lured Helmut.

At the end of the main beach, instead of turning inland to the pathways, Alex climbed across the rocky shore that ringed the base of the cliff. The tide was still way out, leaving pools of clear water and darting fish. Beyond that was the oyster line, the purple shells wet and glistening.

He picked his way across the large boulders, hugging the coast. He breathed air wet with salt and the freshness of the approaching storm, enjoying the pure rush of freedom. Around the headland peak, the rocks became flat mesas. Alex looked up. The cliff face was pale like bone. He was right under the Leap here, the very top grey as the clouds. But still, he didn't see Bella. He really must have imagined her last time. The mind was so suggestible.

He went on, through a miniature bay of white sand, and around the next headland, after which a longer beach went on and on to a distant rocky point. At the start of that beach was where he found the path, beaten down the hillside.

He climbed, and before half-way up, caught sight of an iron rooftop, level with the trees on the ledge above. Ten minutes later, his nose raw from the salty air, Alex burst from the trees beside a hexagonal hut, its huge windows facing out to sea.

Helmut appeared in the open doorway, paintbrush in hand. "Dr Alex," he said, beckoning, as though expecting Alex all along.

Inside the studio, the walls were three-deep in canvases, and others rested on easels, placed around the rotunda at different angles to the sea. Many paintings reflected those angles, but the greatest number were of Bella's Leap. Alex recognised the view instantly as the same one from the painting at the hospital's charity auction. From here, the real Leap was a striking, window-filling headland, framed with the sea, the sky, and the distant smaller islets. Helmut had a fresh canvas out, the primer still shining, and a beaten box of brushes and paint tubes on a low table alongside.

"You choose a good time for painting," Helmut said, rubbing his hands and nodding towards the Leap, which was luminous under the dark clouds. Alex was struck by the weirdness of the light, the way the heavy sky fought the afternoon sun, washing the whiteness of the cliff face into pale lemon yellow.

"You paint this view so often," Alex said, coming to watch as the artist chose a brush and began blocking the cliff's shadows in pale grey strokes.

"She is my muse," Helmut said, with a flourish towards the cliff. "No one else would live up here with the storms. But I never want to be far from her."

"*Who's* your muse?" came a woman's voice.

Alex turned to find Stella, as flamboyant as she had been on the plane, leaning in a doorway between the stacks of canvases. She had a cocktail glass pinched between two fingers, her other hand playing with the drape of her filmy yellow kaftan.

"We have a visitor," Helmut said, not pausing between brushstrokes.

"Ah, the dashing Dr Bell," she said with a dazzling smile. "I've been hoping you'd visit us. I'm Helmut's *other* muse. Not that he'll admit it." She winked, seeming utterly unoffended with Helmut's preoccupation. "Now, you're looking much better than when I last saw you. White as a sheet, he was, Helmut. I thought he was going to bring up his lunch all over the aisle of the plane."

"I do not like the flying either," Helmut put in, his attention still on the painting. "Planes, they are no good. Better to be on the sea."

Or on land, Alex thought, as Stella squeezed his arm.

"Now, come with me darling. He's going to be working a while. I'll fix you a drink and we can watch at a safe distance. He thinks he's going to see her today."

"Who?"

"Isabella. Now, come."

Goosebumps prickled Alex's arms as he followed Stella into the kitchen at the back of the rotunda, a partition wall separating it from the studio.

"You must have seen Bella before," Alex said, as Stella drew unlabelled bottles out of the freezer and filled a fresh glass with clinking ice.

"Once," she said. "I think. But that might have been the gin talking."

More ice and clear liquid splashed into a cocktail shaker, followed by a good slug of juice that smelled of passionfruit.

"Can you tell me Bella's story?"

Stella's hand paused on the way to the glass. "Oh, we don't talk about that. It's bad luck."

Alex was soon back out in the gallery, where Stella installed them both in deck chairs, to the side of Helmet's workspace where they could see, but not impede the artist's view. From here, the floor to ceiling glass made Alex feel he was sitting on the edge of the cliff, nothing to prevent a fall but the thin floor beneath. Surreptitiously, he inched his chair back.

"Helmut paints best when the weather is coming in," Stella whispered. "He says 'beauty is what is seen in the tempest'."

"This is true," Helmut murmured. "And also, the light is better. See, I show you."

He put down his brush and paced to the shelves, where he pulled a finished canvas from the rack. It was a picture of a yacht, red-hulled, sailing under blue skies on a perfect blue ocean, tiny white caps on the waves, the crew proud and carefree as they manned their stations. Every line was immaculate, the work of a master. "Yes, you see it?"

"Yes. Wonderful."

Helmut shook his head, and held up a finger. The canvas disappeared and another took its place. It was the same boat, though Alex didn't realise that at first because the palate was muted, the red hull a dark streak of blood in the midst of a black storm. The sky was a mass of clouds, the waves towering, the rain driving down from sunless heavens. And now, the crew were hunkered in their shining oilskins, soaked and desperate. A sail was torn, another about to tear free, a sailor's hand reaching for its rope, forever captured a moment too late. Another man crouched too close to the railing as a wave rose from behind, ready to wash him overboard. Alex felt the dread punch him in the chest like the blow from a heavyweight. These sailors were fighting for their lives.

"Yes, you see," Helmut said. "This is where the work of life is. In the storm, in the broken and desperate times. That is where there is strength, and transformation."

Alex blinked, and then the canvas was gone, and Helmut was back at the easel, working as before.

Stella smiled and took Alex's arm. Alex was caught between watching Helmut — the tension in his arms as he laid paint down, the picture emerging from nothing — and the gathering darkness outside. The storm was a clean band of ink black cloud now, which had covered the daylight and was raising white peaks far out on the sea. And then he saw the sails.

"Someone's out there," he said, as Helmut's strokes became more furious.

"Ah, Erin," Stella said. "You see that Helmut? Just like old times."

The painter grunted, dragging his brush through a puddle of Prussian blue. Alex peered down at the yacht, its sails tight with stormy air. He could see a single figure on the deck, behind the wheel. Definitely Erin. Alex took a slug of his drink to quench his dry mouth, trying to estimate how far she was from the rain front.

"God, that's strong," he said, coughing as the fiery fruit mix burned across his tongue.

Stella patted his arm. "Sorry love, but what's the point of being up here if you can't make a decent drink. It's not like we have to go anywhere. And it helps with the worldly cares."

"How fast will that storm come in?" he asked, as memories of kissing Erin on the resort roof dragged themselves before him.

"Oh, she'll make it back, don't worry," Stella said. "The front's a while out and Erin's first home was always out there. Probably needs to blow off some steam now she's working for Tristan Drummond. Can you believe it?"

Stella's eyes sparkled, as if this was the juiciest piece of gossip for a long while.

"Erin knows this water better than anyone," Helmut said, as the yacht slipped out of view.

Despite Alex's thundering heart, the drink did seem to help. By the time he was half-way down the glass, he'd shuffled his chair as close to the window as his knees would allow, watching the waves crashing into the rocks under Bella's Leap with increasing power. Erin had long disappeared into the main bay. Outside, the trees were bending under the wind gusts, the whine of it howling around the hut. The first drops that splattered into the glass sounded like pebbles. Alex glanced at Helmut and found the artist had stilled, his body tense as he stared towards the headland. Before him, the picture glistened.

"What's he doing?" Alex asked.

"Waiting for her."

It must have been the drink, because Alex found himself watching too. The closer the storm came, the more the cliff became its own place, like a tower divorced from the island, a pinnacle of land in the boiling sea and sky.

When the storm finally broke, the rain lashed down in great waves against the glass. Helmut continued to work, though Alex had no idea what the painter was seeing through the deluge. Alex finished his glass; or he thought he did. When he next picked it up, he found it full again. Time seemed fluid and slippery.

Finally, the storm began to pass over them, leaving a tail of cloud that shifted from grey to apricot, leaving a washed sunset behind. Water dripped from the eaves, and he could hear it still rushing through the gutters, more drops showering down as the wind tossed the trees dry. The air smelled of clean loam.

Helmut was cleaning brushes, muttering to himself, the canvas still incomplete, especially the detail atop the cliff.

"He doesn't finish if he doesn't see her," Stella whispered, collecting the empty glass.

Alex tried to stand and abruptly realised he was very drunk. He had to put a hand out to the chair to avoid toppling over.

"Best storm in a long while," Helmut said, finally glancing at Alex. "But maybe she doesn't like visitors."

"I'm sorry to deter the muse," Alex said, but Helmut waved it away.

"No, she comes when she comes. I wait, I wait."

"And I should go," Alex said, then he realised he really had no idea how to find his way back, especially half-cut. The inland paths were completely unlit, and there was no way he should be climbing over the rocks in his current state. He'd never be heard from again.

"You could always stay here," Stella said.

"Patients in the morning," he said, squinting out into the night.

Stella grabbed a lantern. "That's what I thought you'd say. I'll show you the way back to the main beach."

So Alex followed into the gloomy bush, all sound hushed after the storm, water still dripping into his hair. He had no idea how Stella was navigating; the lantern only lit a puddle a few metres wide. But after fifteen minutes heading gently downhill, he heard waves lapping, and she brought him out at the end of the main beach. The old resort crouched just to the north, hidden in the darkness, while the lights of the village invited him at the far end of the sand.

"You'll be fine from here?" she asked. "Remember, no swimming. Very bad idea."

"Got it," Alex said, his drunk focus looking back up the cliff. "Will you be okay getting back?"

She laughed. "I've walked this track so many times. And don't worry, the ghost never bothers me."

"How long's Helmut been watching her?"

"I've only been here ten years, but all that time, and probably another ten or twenty before."

Alex whistled. "That's quite an obsession."

"She's the mistress of the storm." Resignation in her voice, and fondness too.

Alex stuffed his hands in his pockets, not knowing whether

he should hug her goodbye or not.

"Oh, I almost forgot," he said, drawing out his earlier purchase and handing her a small oblong bag. "Sunglasses for Helmet. Tell him it helps with the radiation, for his eyes."

"Ah, yes. Thankyou Dr Alex." She gave him a grin, and leaned in to kiss him on the cheek.

As Alex stumbled back along the sand, he turned to wave and saw Stella climbing the path, her form disappearing and reappearing between the tree trunks, her pale hair and kaftan flowing colourless behind her. And he had to blink, and tell himself that she was a woman flesh and blood, and not an apparition. Time to go home and sleep it off.

Chapter 10

Three days later, Erin had spent most of her time scrambling to keep up in meetings by day, and hastily rejigging *Fair Winds'* hardware by night. Finally ready, she turned up unannounced at her sister's door at six in the morning.

"Just tell me what's going on," Skye said for the tenth time, as they creaked onto the wooden jetty boards five minutes later.

"You'll see when we get to the boat."

"I have a class in three hours. However important you think this is, it can wait. I have important things to do, too."

Erin paused, hearing the hurt in Skye's voice. It was plain that Skye wasn't happy about Erin working for Tristan. Whether that was because of jealousy, or general resentment of Erin, Erin couldn't pick apart. But she needed Skye. The biggest problem Tristan had in his regatta plan was attracting more entries, and bringing on a major sponsor for the future regatta. Erin had called ex-crew mates and captains, and hadn't gotten anywhere. Everyone was in the thick of training for the Sydney to Hobart. At least, that's what she told Tristan. She didn't mention the number who had hung up on her. She hadn't made many friends in the last year. So if she was going to deliver, she would need another reason to convince them to stop over in Great Haven for the pilot race on their way north to the Hamilton Race Week. Erin could only think of one thing to do, and she needed Skye.

"This is getting-the-island-back-on-its-feet important," Erin said, forcing herself to keep walking.

Skye muttered, but followed, until they reached the *Fair Winds* and Travers stuck his head out of the hatch.

"About time you came back," he said. "Hey, where's my pie?"

"What the hell is this?" said Skye, eyeing Travers. Then, her gaze fell on the yacht. "Wait a minute …"

Skye ran her eye suspiciously over the rigging. "You're set up for racing," she said. "And not one-handed anymore."

"Look," Erin said, knowing she'd have to talk fast. "The pilot races are coming up in two weeks, and Tristan agreed we can enter."

"*We?*"

"Three is the best number of crew on *Fair Winds* for the handicap class. Travers is on bow. I need you on mast and winches."

"You can't be serious." Skye spun in a circle, her arms over her head, as if appealing to some unseen gods. "Erin, I haven't crewed a boat in five years. And you *know* I hate it. Ask that new doctor with his muscles and suntanned legs, and leave me out of it."

"He's not here half the time, and he'll have to be on-call on race day," Erin argued, although not without a fizz of nerves at the mere mention of Alex. The longer that went since she'd last seen him, the worse it got.

Skye folded her arms. "And what, pray, does this have to do with helping the island."

"It's … promotion. Come on, Skye. It's one race."

"Plus training."

"Of course plus training. We've only got two weeks, and I'm working, too."

"Oh, you're *working*. Well, I have a class to run. I have responsibilities to fifteen kids that I can't just push off onto someone else. I can't just come in and out like you can, or *him* who just goes diving all day."

"I'm hurt," Travers said, now lounging against the cabin. But Erin saw how much he was enjoying watching Skye's fireworks.

Erin drew Skye aside and dropped her voice. "Four afternoons of training," Erin said. "Then the race and we're done. And I'm not pushing anything onto someone else."

Skye heaved a sigh, and looked out to sea. Erin suddenly saw her eyes shining, and realised her sister was trying to hold back tears.

"How do I know this isn't just your way of ducking out on Tristan?" Skye asked. "You said you'd do this important job for him, for all of us, and now you're just finding a way to do what you want."

"It's not like that," Erin said quickly, wounded. "This is trying to help the races succeed. Skye, please. I know you're good, even if you hate it. I don't want anyone else on my boat."

"What about *him*?" she said, jerking her chin towards Travers.

Erin made a so-so motion with her hand.

"Hey, I'm *right here*," Travers said.

Skye unfolded her arms, scratched her forehead, and folded them again. But Erin had seen a ghost of a smile. "Fine. Four training runs and one race, and that's it. I'm only doing this because you're going to need someone to teach him."

Travers gave Erin a mutinous eye. "I'm going to regret this, aren't I?"

But he was whistling as Erin started the motor and he went to release the bow line. Soon, they were motoring towards the mouth of the bay, the breeze picking up as they approached the headland.

"Listen up," Erin said, calling both of them to order. "I'm not even going to touch the spinnaker today. Main and jib only. Tacks and gybes only. We'll run down to half-mile island and back. Yeah?"

Skye gave a curt nod, then gave Travers her attention for the first time. "You worked bow before?"

"Nope."

"Well, then," she said brightly. "Be prepared to take a few hits to the head. Fortunately it looks like your skull can handle it. Come on, I'll run through hoisting the mainsail."

Erin breathed out. This was why she wanted Skye. Her sister might claim not to enjoy sailing, but she was a gifted teacher, and Travers would need that to come up to speed.

"Skye," she called, then dropped her voice as her sister padded back, sure-footed despite the rolling deck. "You look good together."

"Gimme a break."

"Skye, just remember he's got a busted shoulder, okay?"

"Scraping the barrel for crew here, Erin."

But she went off with her teacher's zeal, and ten minutes later, the main was hoisted and Erin killed the motor. The only sound then was the tinking of the rigging, and the rush of the water under the hull. She turned them out of the wind, and the breeze filled the mainsail. *Fair Winds* tugged at her hands, and then the yacht was leaning over, grabbing the wind and hauling them south.

Erin's whole body lifted. The breeze was in her hair and

inside her veins as Skye and Travers came back to the cabin winches.

"Right, unfurl the jib," she called. The foresail spun out, and then they were really moving, sleek and sure. Travers and Skye sat with their legs hanging over the side, adding their weight to keep them more level, Skye earnestly pointing and talking. Then Erin would see her pause, making Travers repeat something she'd said. From the rapt expression on Travers' face, he was in real trouble when it came to Skye.

Erin leaned back and flicked on the camera she'd mounted to the rear railing, and prayed this plan was going to work.

"Okay, let's get ready to tack," she called.

"Erin, where are you going?" Skye said a moment later. Erin glanced over to see her sister examining their heading, suspicion pinching her eyes.

"Just a little training run," Erin said.

"You are *not* going where I think you're going."

"Ready to tack, please," Erin yelled, her eyes trained on the narrow rocky mouth off the port side.

Two hours later, when they motored back into port, Skye looked even more thunderous than when they'd gone out. She barely said a word as they deployed the fenders and re-docked at the jetty.

Travers climbed down as though someone had been beating him for an hour with a wooden plank.

"What the hell were you playing at?" Skye hissed, once he was out of earshot. "You didn't say you were taking us down The Gauntlet. On the first ever run! How stupid are you?"

The Gauntlet was the narrow strip of water between half-way island and its sister to the north, which funnelled air currents, requiring sharp precise tacks to navigate up, and careful down-wind running to come back. Erin had proposed it as part of the pilot race course, and it was the only part Tristan's team were still arguing about.

"You both managed just fine, and you know I've done it dozens of times. I did it two days ago to be sure, and that was when the storm was coming in."

"Yeah, but *he* hasn't. You put him off the first time you go out, he might not come back."

Erin glanced over to where Travers was stiffly bending to wind the bow line onto a cleat. He'd done a heap of work, winding winches, trimming sails. He'd probably run several k's up and down the deck. But despite the exhaustion, he kept working now, whistling again as he went to fetch the hose for the water tanks.

"He look like a man who gets scared off easily?" Erin asked.

Skye narrowed her eyes. "He did seem to be taking perverse pleasure in the hard stuff. Thought it might be a put-on."

"He's ex-military, Skye. Maybe he's just like that."

Skye grunted. "All right. I'm leaving for class. And *you*," she called to Travers. "You come to the classroom at three-thirty when the kids are gone. I'm going to run you through some theory."

"Skye," Erin said, stopping her sister before she took off. "Thanks."

"You owe me a massive favour, you do realise that?"

"I do," Erin said, even as she felt a qualm about what Skye might ask. "But actually … I also need one more thing."

"Oh, god, what now?"

"I need to use your computer."

As the sea was sinking into its final indigo later that night, Alex sat on the porch of Travers' cabin, downing the last of a beer and listening to the muttered complaints as Travers fetched another round from the fridge.

"You right there?" he asked, as the big man emerged and creaked down onto the cabin steps.

"Nothing alcohol can't fix," Travers said, knocking the head off the new beer and passing it over. "I'm sore from hair to heels. The woman's a slavedriver."

"Erin?"

"Skye. Oh, you think she'll be sweet with all that petite teacher stuff, and next thing you're following orders. She would have done well in the army."

Alex scrutinised Travers. "I'd never have picked her for sweet – she's more a crusader. Do you remember how many raffle tickets she sold me? But I think you knew that. And you like her for it."

"Well, shit," Travers muttered, drawing the beer. "Can't be a good thing, though."

"How so?"

"Been on a bad run with women these last years. I used to have my head together. Then one woman gets around the fence, suddenly I'm the one being walked out on."

"That's rough. How long are you planning on crewing for Erin, then?"

"As long as she wants I guess. It's good, you know? Never interested in sailing before – I just liked boats with big engines. Now I understand why people do it. Lot more work though. Haven't used some of these muscles in a long time. You should come out on the weekend run with us, maybe, if Erin's cool with that."

Alex swallowed the panic that rose in him at the idea, focusing his attention on the tiny waves breaking on the low-tide shore. "Can't. I'm back to the mainland tomorrow morning. It's my fortnightly four nights straight in emergency."

"Commiserations," Travers said. "That's something I don't miss – all the ED chaos. Most of the time, it was nothing cases – guys looking for a chit because they had a runny nose. Then there'd be one come out of nowhere that sent you scrambling. Much like being a soldier, really."

"Ninety-nine percent boredom, one percent pure terror?" Alex said.

"Exactly."

Talking about the hospital shifts reminded Alex of the last one, when Tristan Drummond had showed up with his offer. Now that Erin was working for him, Alex was wondering what to do about it.

"Travers, what do you know about Erin and Tristan Drummond? Any history there?"

"That cocksucker?" Travers asked.

Alex raised his eyebrows. "Not a fan, huh?"

"I'm not a local, I don't have to like him. You know, he nearly ran me over once in that stupid super yacht of his, when I was out on a dive," Travers said, scratching the back of his neck. "But yeah, I heard they used to be a thing, years back. Don't know any details though."

"Really," Alex said.

"Yep."

"They seemed close at the town meeting," Alex said, unable to leave the idea alone. "And he came to the hospital last time I was on the mainland. Big boss attitude. Think he was trying to get my measure, though I've no idea why."

"Half the sergeants I worked under were like that. I took comfort in the fact that I was the one with the high-powered rifle. Never seemed to bother me when I remembered that."

Alex laughed, shaking his head. "If I didn't know better, I'd say you're a dangerous kind of man, Travers."

"Only for the right cause, my friend."

"What the hell you were thinking?"

Erin had barely made it into the planning office on Monday morning before Troy – or was it Benny? – confronted her.

"What do you mean?" she asked sweetly, though one glance at his monitor, currently open to the video clip she'd posted on YouTube, told her exactly what he meant.

"This video. It's all over the forums, Facebook, Instagram, not to mention YouTube. I wouldn't be surprised if Mel and Kochie ran it on *Sunrise* this morning!"

"Well, that would be a good thing, wouldn't it?"

"No, it bloody wouldn't! It's unprofessional. It's amateur! Its completely not in line with the image we are trying to sculpt for this—"

At that moment, Tristan appeared in the office door, unusually casual in a pale blue polo and caramel shorts, which showed his tanned thigh muscles as he stepped into the tension of the meeting. "I hear excitement. Is this good news?"

"No, it's not," fumed Troy, returning the monitor and hitting play for Tristan's benefit.

The video began with the funky opening bars of an indie song, then the video jumped to a view along the deck of the *Fair Winds*, her sails framing the characteristic cliffs of Great Haven in the distance. Erin was centred in the shot at the helm, giving the camera a cheeky wink and a thumbs-up before the boat roared into The Gauntlet. The music put a pulse in every action, as the camera's low angle emphasised the proximity of the rocks, the hard tack, and Travers' muscled arm working the winch. Erin steered one-handed, calling instructions as they made the turn, Skye swearing at Erin without a single bleep. Two more tacks followed in a run time of less than two minutes, all washing machine drama. The action was fantastic. Only now, watching in company, did Erin realised how much her bare legs were in shot. Or, more to the point, the too-short sawn-off hem of her shorts. And that at the end, when she turned to the camera and said, "I'm getting wet at the Great Haven Race Day – what about you?", how suggestive it sounded. She bit her lip as the music strummed to a close.

Troy's head was in his hands. "This is a disaster."

Tristan's face was impassive, and Erin's confidence wobbled for the first time.

"Was that The Gauntlet?" he asked, and when she nodded, he turned to Troy. "What exactly are you objections?"

"It's completely unprofessional," he burst out. "There's no editing, the sound is terrible. Whoever the band is will sue us for copyright. We're trying to put together a multi-million dollar event and you've made us look like hicks with some sleezy promo girl doing our marketing."

Tristan's head snapped up. "You watch your mouth. That's your Racing Director you're talking about."

Troy turned away muttering.

"If that's true, then why have two skippers signed on since last night?" Erin shot back.

"Probably hicks as well!"

"If you want to call Quentin Beaumont and Antonio Ferrua,

hicks, then yeah, I suppose so."

That shut Troy up. Tristan started laughing. "I'll be damned, I knew I hired the right woman," he said. "Even if Beaumont is a thorn in my side, I'm happy to take his money. Both of them are A-grade. Serious boats, serious cash."

"We still have to pull it," Troy pressed, belligerently.

"Now, Troy," Tristan said, his voice dangerously soft. "Don't be dirty you got outflanked here. You might see shaky GoPro footage and low-end production, but the owners see a sexy woman, a little innuendo and a challenging course. Am I right?"

Erin smiled weakly. Her intent had been to show the course challenge for sure. The sexy woman and innuendo part hadn't been the plan. But the job was done, so she wouldn't quibble.

"I think," Tristan went on, "this actually solves a bunch of problems for us. One, we definitely put The Gauntlet into the course, maybe as a riskier short-cut. There'll be a longer option out through some buoys, so it will introduce an interesting strategy choice. Everyone's signing away liability, and they'll be fully informed. Two, I think we just found our official theme song. Find the band and apologise for the clip usage, and offer them a licensing deal. Hell, see if they're interesting in playing in the VIP tent. That's win-win. And three, now we know our biggest drawcard."

"What?" Erin said.

"You. I want you front and centre. You're already racing, but I want you as the spokesperson, too. Interviews. Sponsorship negotiations. This is going to be great."

Erin swallowed, as the high from having done something well was crushed under more responsibility. But she hardly had time to dwell; the meeting pushed on another two hours, ironing out the details, assigning tasks. When they broke for late-morning coffee, Tristan pulled Erin outside and into the shade of a large pandanus.

"Erin, that video was a stroke of genius. Just next time – run these things past me, okay?"

"I thought you liked it."

"Oh I did, but you'll give Troy heart failure. He's got contacts I can't afford to lose."

Erin made a face. "He's doing heart failure to himself, the number of Danishes he eats."

Tristan grinned and tapped a finger before he said, "Speaking of problems, what do you know about this new doctor?"

He asked the question so casually Erin was taken completely off-guard. What shot into her mind was that night with Alex, up on the old resort roof, making out under the stars. It was a little over a week ago, but between Alex's hospital work, and Erin's new job, they'd not seen each other since. After that amount of time, it seemed uncertain if the moment between them had meant anything. And Erin knew that all of this showed on her face before she could remember to be cautious around Tristan.

She shrugged. "He's okay I guess."

"People have seen him on your boat," Tristan said.

"People are nosy."

"Just watch yourself. This guy has a record, Erin. Not a nice one."

Erin frowned, thinking of the rumours Gus had told her about Alex. She wanted to see him again, but she knew this was absolutely not something she should share with Tristan. She glanced towards the meeting room, suddenly eager to get back to fighting it out with Troy and Benny. "Come on, are we planning a race or what?"

Tristan caught her arm. "Seriously, Erin."

Erin shook him off, a little too roughly. "Geez, come on Tristan," she said, trying to soften the blow, her heart pounding. "People probably still talk about us, you know."

Tristan smiled. "Well, *that* I don't mind a bit. But let's be serious for a minute. About the spokesperson role. I have a potential sponsor I want you to meet. Work your magic on."

"I'm not good in the boardrooms, Tristan. As you can see."

"Who said anything about boardrooms? I'm talking about a private dinner, on the water. Just us and the sponsor. No pressure."

"Who is it?"

Tristan shook his head, gently teasing. "I'll tell you after the pilot race. *If* he's still interested."

"No pressure," Erin muttered.

Chapter 11

The two weeks to the pilot race sped past, Erin feeling the whole time that she barely had time to breathe. On race morning, Great Haven was surrounded with boats. The early arrivals had moored in the main bay, and others had filled the sheltered western side of the island. The A-listers who had camped in the marina on the mainland sailed in all morning for the midday start.

Erin had planned to spend the morning in final preparations on *Fair Winds*, but she found herself waylaid from dawn, occupied with the lead-in events. First were the sailboards, like windblown butterflies as they streaked out in a short course race just out of the main bay; then came the small catamaran class. Both events had been designed to entertain the growing crowd on the beach, who flocked around a fleet of mobile food trucks. Sandy had been vocal in her displeasure, but had to concede Tristan's point: the crowds were far too large for the bakery and cafe to handle alone.

The cable TV crew had set up in the old ocean-view bar in the resort, the producer waxing lyrical to Erin how the degraded industrial space created such an atmosphere to the proceedings. The pre-race interview with the commentators delayed Erin another twenty minutes. As she finally put the last check through her list, it was past ten-thirty, cutting it fine to make it back to the yacht and out ready for the start.

"Wait, Erin," Tristan called as she tried to exit the war room, which was what Tristan had dubbed the main organising office for the day. "Here – earpiece and transmitter. We'll have up-to-the-minute tide and wind forecasting for you throughout."

Erin didn't think she'd need it, but took it anyway, desperate to get moving. Out of breath by the time she reached the jetty, she found a stony-faced Travers waiting with the tender, all yachts having been prohibited from tying up for the week.

"You are in trouble," he said as she piled into the dingy.

"Let's just get out there."

But Skye said nothing about her being late. Maybe it was the joy of seeing Haven once again so alive with boats. As they motored out towards the rest of the fleet, the sky was a blinding blue, the air full of conversation, and the ocean rippling with coloured sails. Travers was quickly talent spotting, awed as *Wild Oats* muscled past, clunking through a turn.

"Why does it sound like a steamship?" he asked.

"Everything's motorised," Erin explained. "Winches, the whole lot."

"So I'm clearly on the wrong boat."

The earpiece cracked. *"Erin, how's it looking?"*

"You're not going to be in my head the whole time are you? I'm taking it off if you are."

Tristan laughed. *"Just doing a test. Your on-board camera feed is perfect, and we've got drone eyes in the sky for the whole race too. We'll only come on the mike if there's something we think you need."*

"Who are you talking to?" Skye asked.

"Tristan in mission control," Erin muttered, pointing to her ear. "Now let's get the sails up."

The start was a jostle, every yacht trying to be in the perfect position as they timed the last minute from the warning gun. Erin's heart was pumping for a different reason entirely. She'd been on shore far too long. While the training runs had been good, nothing compared to being in the thick of the other hulls, the sails snapping tight in the breeze, the course ahead. She felt like the horses she saw on television, lining up for a big race, wound high with energy and ready to run. She caught Skye's eye in the last seconds, and her sister actually gave her a grin. They were ten metres from the line; Travers threw her a worried glance lest they cross before the gun. Then the klaxon rang out, and they were flying.

The column of yachts sped away south. Even over the rush of wind and water, Erin could hear the cheers from the beach. The wind was perfect across the beam, the biggest yachts in a class above easily pulling away.

Erin didn't care. They were in a handicap class, and doing well. The *Fair Winds* wasn't the fastest yacht, but she could hold her own, and they had an advantage through The Gauntlet, which would slow many of the boats down.

"Looking good, Erin. You might want to come out to the west a bit more, avoid falling in the sail shadows."

"We're okay here," Erin snapped back. "We'll be around the first marker soon, and better placed for the next turn."

A pause. *"Okay."*

By the time they'd turned tight into the wind around the first mark, then back south around the next, Erin thought they'd gained some ground. She hugged close to a small islet, looking for the next mark that would turn them east for the run towards The Gauntlet.

"Erin, you're a bit close to the island."

"The tide's running west now," she answered. "Everyone

further out is fighting it."

"*But there's more wind pressure—*"

Erin pulled the earpiece out and passed it to Skye. "Here, you take it. Let me know if they say anything interesting."

As she suspected, The Gauntlet knocked everyone off pace. A few boats screamed in too confident and found they had to drop sails to make the turns, and others had to hang back to avoid a pile-up. Almost no one had elected for the safer, long run out to the buoys, but probably a few wished they had. Erin saw more than one circling around to come at the entry again, having muffed it the first time. She saw a gap and took it, roaring into the mouth of The Gauntlet, maintaining the pace that Travers and Skye had practiced over and over in their training runs. They whipped back and forth through the tacking turns, outpacing other boats that were taking more care. And then, they were out the other end and tacking a huge turn around the next mark, Skye and Travers flawless in dropping the jib and hoisting the spinnaker. Their biggest sail was blue, like the sky itself, and they flew down-wind under its pull.

"Control says there's only one handicap boat in front now," Skye said.

Erin could see them, their bright red spinnaker covered in corporate logos impossible to miss. Only a short dog-leg around two marks was left before the turn for the big run back into the bay. She turned her face into the breeze, scanned the water and clouds ahead. The dog-leg took them around the end of one of the small islets, the last turn right off its point. Erin called Travers and Skye in.

"Change of plan. We're dropping the kite at the next turn, and we won't put it back up for the short down-wind leg."

"Control room says we can't possibly win that way," Skye

relayed. "We don't have the speed without the spinnaker."

The mark was coming up fast.

"That boat ahead will lose time changing their sails twice, and we won't," Erin argued. "Plus, around that last mark, the pressure's going to come roaring around the island point. We'll be catching that before they've even got their jib up again."

Skye made a face, and held out the earpiece. "He wants to talk to you."

Erin had had enough. She grabbed the earpiece. "Stop racing for me," she yelled at it, and chucked it in the ocean.

Travers laughed, but then they were on the mark, and everyone had to focus. Erin steered them tight and smooth, the spinnaker collapsing down and the jib unfurling again as though Skye and Travers had been working together for a year. By the next mark, they'd maintained position, and as the boat ahead re-hoisted their spinnaker at the next turn, Erin gained, so that by the final turn, the *Fair Winds'* nose was right on their stern. This was where it would all happen. Erin couldn't hope to hold them in a straight line race. The whole margin would be decided in the next turn.

As they gybed around, she cut them tight on the inside, inches to spare between the two hulls. The roaring wind off the tip of the island caught *Fair Winds'* sails. The competitor's boat was not only in the middle of changing sails, they fell directly in the *Fair Winds'* wind shadow.

Erin watched the other boat's sails droop, momentarily dead in the water. They'd never recover their loss of speed. Instead, it was the *Fair Winds* flying towards home and the finish line. The A-listers had come in already, several of them lining the way like an honour guard. Erin was screaming encouragement, one hand firm on the wheel, the other holding the main sheet as Skye and

Travers maintained the foresail trim.

The boat behind was gaining, their momentary lull over, their streamlined form making up the error. As the finish line zoomed into view, their bow was level with the *Fair Winds'* stern. But it was too late. Erin crossed the line half a length ahead, the guns sounding with a huge cheer from the crowd.

Erin soared on the high of that moment, at one with the world around her. The ocean had never smelled so clean, the temperature had never been so perfect. She was overcome with a calm, easing the *Fair Winds* around to head into shore, even while Skye and Travers were fist-pumping and waving. Erin could see the size of the monitors that were currently showing her hands on the wheel. It all seemed so surreal. Slowly, she let the power out of the mainsail and turned for a lap along the beach.

Before she knew what she was doing, she was looking for her father in the crowd, and then the pain of remembering he was gone cut her down. She swiped away the tears, the moment tarnished. She sucked some breaths, avoiding Skye who would notice something was wrong. And by the time they were under motor again and heading back to moor, she'd recovered enough to gather her team and thank them. It was then she noticed the blood running down Travers' neck.

"What happened to you?" she asked, as Skye turned white and rushed to find the first-aid box.

"Oh, nothing," he said, examining his red fingers in amazement. "Just copped a hit from the spinnaker pole in the last turn. What a rush. I didn't even realise."

Alex had watched the whole race from the shore, on one of the large screens positioned not far from the community ambulance station.

Before the race, he'd been professionally occupied, ensuring the ambulances had let air out of their tyres, to cope with the sandy road down to the clinic, and then making some noise in the office to get the marshals to keep a path clear of umbrellas in case they had to use it. After that had come a case of heat stress and a few minor injuries.

None of it compared to watching Erin race. They'd allocated more than a fair share of the screen coverage to footage from on-board cameras, in between zoom-outs over the course with all the boats marked with their relative positions and classes. Alex had been impatient, even when several boats came to grief in The Gauntlet, for them to return to Erin's boat. Then, they did, through those final magical turns, where she'd pulled away and won.

Alex had known she must be good, but the command of her on the boat, the assurance and confidence, the skill ... he felt magnetised, and he'd cheered louder than anyone when she'd crossed first for her division. He wanted nothing more than to find her.

Which of course was when he'd seen one of the volunteers running towards him.

"Doc, we've got someone needs you," she panted. "Took a bad fall out on course. They're bringing him up now."

"Head injury?" Alex asked.

"Not sure."

"Bleeding?"

"Yeah."

"Straight to the clinic then."

They brought him in on a stretcher, the man softly moaning, still wearing his crew's racing colours. His leg was at an angle Alex instantly knew was bad news.

Alex pushed all but the crewman's captain and the paramedics – who were rapidly quoting vitals – out the door. The crewman wasn't making much sense.

"Talk to me about what happened," Alex said, as he motioned to the paramedic to start a drip line. The crewman's breathing was rapid, but as yet uncompromised.

"We were turning at the mark and got broadsided with a big wave, just a freak one. Spencer fell. He was wearing a tether, but he slid down the deck, and hit the winch pretty hard. We all heard the crack."

Alex grabbed the scissors and slit Spencer's fitted racing skins from ankle to waist. What he found was a deep purple bruise, running from the man's hip right over his thigh.

"He hit his head at any point? Or pass out?"

"No, he was screaming the whole way back."

Alex grabbed a morphine vial and drew the drug. "Sandy!" he called.

"She's still down at the race," said the captain.

"Well, then—" And that was when Alex noticed Anna Jacobs standing in the doorway, one hand on the jamb, as if she'd tried to leave many times and yet hadn't been able to move her feet. Alex didn't really know Anna; they'd only met at the dance. But patients talked about her. Mostly about how she'd never be able to rest, not knowing what had happened to her husband. Or how dreadfully unlucky she'd been – no, they'd *all* been – to lose Dr Jacobs. That they could understand how she'd buried herself in her book projects, nursing her broken heart. But among all of that, people also said that she'd run his medical practice. Right now, Alex needed the help.

He beckoned her over as he checked the morphine and pushed it into the drip. She came, haltingly, standing off to the side, an older version of Skye.

"Anna, you know how to call an evac?"

"Yes." She recited the number as if it was in an internal speed dial.

"Do that, please? Tell them we've got a mid-twenties man with likely pelvic and femur fractures for priority one. Might be spinal involvement, too."

Anna moved with surprising speed. If Alex had any doubt as to her capability, it was wiped out as he heard the call go through out in reception. Anna then stood in the door of the room with the phone to her ear, waiting in case he had other information to add.

Alex worked as fast as possible to splint Spencer's leg for transport. He made sure they had two drip lines, that oxygen saturation was high. Blood pressure was holding.

"What's happening?" asked the captain, as the paramedics disappeared to ensure the road to the airstrip was clear.

"Spencer needs to fly to the mainland," Alex explained. "We're organising it now. You can probably go along if you want. Is there any family we can call?"

Half an hour later, Alex had just returned from passing Spencer over to the flying doctor when he heard the clinic door chimes again. Thinking it must be Anna coming back, he stopped short when he found Erin in the waiting area, looking windblown but utterly wonderful. She had Travers' shirtsleeve twisted into a knot, the big man pressing a bloodstained towel to his head.

"Caught him trying to sneak home," Erin said. "He took a

hit from the spinnaker pole. I think it needs stitches."

"I wasn't sneaking home," Travers argued. "Just *someone* here – not mentioning names – won't do a field dressing. I've got all the kit at home. I don't need to trouble Alex."

Erin rolled her eyes. Alex grinned, feeling an intense relief after the Spencer drama, and more than a little jubilation. Erin was the best thing that could have walked in the door. He knew he was staring, but after admiring her on the screens during the race, having her standing here in front of him was shorting something in his brain. All that was in his mind was kissing her on the roof top. He had to focus on the blood to remember his job.

"In there, big guy," he said finally.

Travers hauled himself onto the exam couch, muttering.

"Busy day in here?" Erin asked, stopping to look at the mess through the doorway of the second room, which Alex hadn't yet cleaned up.

"Someone was just evacced. Had an argument with a winch block in the race," he said, sounding more casual about it than he felt.

Erin winced. "That's awful. Is he going to be okay? Which team?"

Alex told her, and that it might be a long recovery. Erin said she'd make sure the race committee followed up on it.

Then she said, "Listen, I have to head back. There's the awards presentation and stupid official stuff." But she hesitated. "Sandy said you're not heading back to the mainland until tomorrow."

Her smile hit him like an electric shock. "My usual shifts got pushed back a day, because of the race," he said.

"Well, I might see you later, then."

Chapter 12

Tristan caught Erin in a bear hug the moment she reappeared at the race headquarters.

"There you are, woman of the moment!" he said, loud enough for everyone to hear. He drew her across to the stairs up to the TV crew's area. There, he dropped his voice to an insistent whisper. "Where the hell have you been?"

"Travers needed his head stitched."

"They've been waiting for you. Come on, you can't just dive off into the small stuff." Affectionately, he plonked a cap embroidered with *Great Haven Regatta* on her head.

Five minutes later, Erin was sitting in an interview chair. The cable sports anchors had both shaken her hand and congratulated her, and they were just waiting for the count-down to the live cross. Both of them were in network polo shirts and smart trousers. Erin pulled off the cap and stuck it across her knee instead. She tried to stop her foot from jogging on the floor. She'd been expecting any interviews to be outside, on the sand, or on the boat. Not here under glaring lights where she could feel the sand on her legs falling onto the carpet.

"Welcome back to the Great Haven Pilot Race," the first anchor began. "Where it's been a day of high excitement and spills to keep any armchair sports fan on the edge of their seat. We've already heard glowing reports from the supermaxis and with us now in the studio is the winner of the handicap division, and local island girl, Erin Jacobs. Welcome, Erin."

Both the anchors grinned at her. Erin found she couldn't look at the camera, so she tried looking over the anchor's shoulder. "Thanks for having me," she managed over her thundering heart.

Across the floor, she saw Tristan give her a thumbs-up.

"We all saw that fantastic finish in the final legs today," said the anchor. "That decision to change sails – was that always the plan?"

Erin relaxed, and smiled. Easy question. She could do this. "It was a little on the fly, seeing the conditions coming off the point. It's a challenging place to sail and you have to be ready to make changes."

"And didn't it pay off! We're just playing the footage again for our viewers. Will you take us through it step by step?" One of them pointed to a monitor so she could follow.

So Erin took them through it, haltingly at first, but then with the excitement she'd felt out on the course. The two anchors nodded along, encouraging.

"That's amazing stuff. But as you say, it's a challenging place and two boats came to grief through The Gauntlet. Do you have any regrets including it in the course?"

Erin could see the cloud descend on Tristan's face, but they'd gone over it so often in the meetings, she was ready.

"Not at all. Yacht racing is a game of high skills, and Great Haven's well known for difficult sailing. I've sailed all over the world and this is a test only the best are worthy of."

The anchors chuckled indulgently, as if enjoying her moxie. "Of course, we understand you've spent several years crewing in races from the Caribbean to the Seychelles. How does that experience compare to Great Haven?"

"International experience is the reality of professional sailing and I've loved seeing and racing in all those places." Erin paused as unexpected memories flooded through her – the blue sea of the beaches in Bermuda, a sunset in the Canaries, the smell of rum and salt. "But Great Haven's challenges are right up there with the world's best – and we're running new technologies to make it a better experience for viewers too – that all makes winning sweeter." She gave them a dazzling smile, beginning to enjoy herself. The anchors smiled back with their very white teeth.

"Well, you're certainly in that sweet spot today. Of course, your own father was a great yachtsman and tragically killed four years ago. Did you feel he was with you today, racing in your home territory?"

A silence fell as Erin blinked, the question cutting her voice from her throat. She knew they were waiting for an answer, but all she could hear was the rush of waves in her ears. Tristan was making some gesture, but she couldn't focus on him. She shook herself, feeling stripped to her skin.

"Uh, sorry I didn't catch that," she managed, kneading the cap in her hands.

"Were you thinking of your father today?"

"He was a great sailor," she said softly, and glanced away, wrestling for control. Please, no, she was not going to cry on television.

"Well, we wish you the best with the regatta next year," said the anchor smoothly, as some flurry went through the crew, and the monitor showed them cutting the camera angle. "Will you be celebrating?"

"Oh yes," Erin said, forcing a smile over the hollow feeling in her heart. Her voice was flat. "We know how to party on Great Haven."

When the light blinked red, the anchor leaned over. "Well done, that was great. Sorry about that last question. Producer put it in the mix."

Erin smiled weakly, jamming the cap back on to hide her eyes. The interview might be over, but she couldn't help feeling her guilt had been broadcast. She wondered how long it would be before someone else would ask the same questions. Tristan was pulling her up into a hug, his face jubilant.

"Well done, E. You are brilliant." He kissed her cheek, smelling strongly of another expensive cologne she associated with a wealthy owner from Florida. "Let's keep moving, lots more to do."

On the stairs, Erin shook him off. "Tristan, I don't feel like it. I'm just going to skip out."

"What's wrong?" Unexpected tenderness.

She couldn't say the words.

"This about the last question?" Tristan asked, and when she nodded, he took her gently by the shoulders. "Erin, I know it must have come out of the blue, but it added dimensions."

"I don't want more dimensions. It ... still hurts."

"There won't be any more questions. No one's going to care today except about that magic last turn. Now, we've got interviews with the local news downstairs, then the sponsor's party. I'll be beside you the whole time. You'll be safe – trust me. And we've landed that dinner with the potential big fish sponsor. We've done the hard part, now we have to follow through – show these guys we mean business. Get the main regatta off the ground."

So Erin went. The local interviews were easy, Tristan

standing by her shoulder, and then the sponsors all shook her hand in the big party marquee, and she held her own through the talks about the next race, about the big regatta, what events could be added. Then later, after she'd had a few rums, someone put a phone in her hand.

"Miss Erin, I see you on the television," said a familiar man on the line.

Erin paused, trying to place the accented voice. "Ivan?"

"That's right. The owner you left without his best tactician. Now, I see where you ended up! Well done, my friend. When you have finished the party, you call me back, yes?"

Quickly, he was gone. Erin shook her head. Ivan was a shipping billionaire whose boat she'd crewed for six months, the only owner she'd considered calling for work and hadn't. He'd been generous with his time and the crew had loved him, but she'd found him difficult – always wanting to get too close. He'd been trying to hire her again ever since, but so far, she had kept clear. Something in her just couldn't settle in that team.

Then Tristan was introducing her to the local member, who'd come over for the day. Evidentially ecstatic that the island's prospects had made an abrupt upswing, the member was keen to hear all the details for the new development – how plans and permissions were progressing, when the construction would start. How she could help. Tristan answered most of the questions, and Erin paid as much attention as she could through the haze of rum and cheering. As the sun was going down, someone got the finish feed back on the TV inside the tent, and made a bunch of noisy toasts to everyone. Erin looked around; even the crews of the supermaxis had stayed for the party – unusual at a small event. They would often have pushed on from here, leaving the organisers to post their trophies. It seemed a great success.

Sometime after dark, Erin escaped outside the tent and stumbled down to the ocean. A glassy expanse now, under a clear sky. None of the fabled Great Haven storms were brewing tonight. Bella's Leap was a slap of darkness against the indigo sky.

And all she could think of was her father, a memory brighter than her others, like the evening star.

As the heavens made full dark, Alex scrutinised the same sky from the front steps of Travers' cabin, following a blipping marker on his phone screen.

"What are you doing with that anyway?" asked Travers, who was propped in a newly acquired lounge chair, an ice pack on his head.

"Satellite tracking," Alex answered, finding the point, down in the west, probably too low to see with the island in the way. Using his vantage in the old resort was out of the question with all the people still hanging around.

"Into that sort of stuff, then?"

"Not in a serious way," Alex said, sliding the phone away. "But it passes the time. Always liked the night sky. But speaking of seeing stars, how's the pain?"

"Better, I think," Travers said, scowling at the lemonade in his hand. "I'll be fine you know, you don't have to hang out here."

"When you were a medic, did you ever see anyone who took a head injury and then came back later with a bad bleed?"

"No."

"Yeah, well, I've seen a few. We don't have CT scanners

here. I don't anticipate with your thick skull you'll have a problem," he said. "But if you do, the only signs will be neurological deficits. That's why I don't want you drinking. And why I'm quite happy to sit here a few more hours. Beats you sitting in the surgery."

Travers grunted. "Fair enough. So, show me this satellite thing."

Alex chucked his phone over and let the big man play around with the app for a while. Without the distraction, Alex found himself thinking of Erin, and then sometimes, less pleasantly, of Erin and Tristan on the TV screens earlier in the day. He knew she was still at the sponsors party.

"So, you used to sail, right?" Travers asked eventually.

"Who said that?"

"Gathered as much from something Erin said."

Alex leaned back against the stair railing. "Yeah. Used to. Past tense."

"You enjoy it?"

"Absolutely."

"But you don't go out on the water now. I'm not trying to be nosy, Doc. Just you've been here a couple of weeks, and most people – they do something. Take out a kayak, a surf ski, something like that. Not you."

"Maybe I did and didn't tell you." Alex leaned back and glanced in Travers' direction. "No, haven't been out. Haven't sailed in a few years now. Work's been busy."

Travers made a considering face, and handed the phone back. "Well, when you want to go out on the water again, you let me know. Just don't go with Skye, for Chrissakes."

Alex grinned. "And where is the fair Skye tonight? I'd thought she'd be here, tending your wounds."

"Hardly," said Travers, rolling his eyes. Then he winced. "Ow, shit. I have to remember not to do that. Anyway. She's at the backpacker shindig. They were full to capacity in all the accommodation tonight, so they were putting on a big communal dinner. Something about community – I wasn't paying attention."

"Too enraptured?"

"Hey, what do you want from me? I've got a head wound here."

Alex laughed.

Travers' eye shifted sideways. "Someone's coming."

Alex followed his gaze and saw a shadow coming up the path, a little unsteady. But even with the small stumble, his heart beat double-time in his chest. A second later, Erin came in reach of the porch light.

"Well, well. Here she is," said Travers, in mock disdain. "All over the news taking credit. How come us crew weren't in on the interviews?"

"Mostly because you need to learn to duck," she said.

Travers grinned. "I'm hurt."

"I came to make sure you weren't passed out or dead or something."

"The Doc's looking after me. Looks like a long recovery," he said, stretching out.

Next thing, Erin had pulled herself onto the top step next to Alex. He could smell the faint sweetness of rum on her clothes, the familiar smell of a yacht racing after-party.

"How's the guy you sent back to the mainland?" she asked.

"In surgery. I called them an hour ago and he's having a pin put in his leg. I'll take a while to knit, but he should recover."

"Good. I'm glad. Well, I suppose I'd better go."

She was half-way down the path before Alex realised he'd stood, staring after her.

"Go on, then," Travers said. "I'll still be injured later."

Alex caught up with her at the turn where sand-covered stairs led down to the beach. "Erin, wait a sec."

"Yeah?"

"Great race today," he said. "I watched the whole thing from the beach. Never seen anything like it."

"Thanks," she said, but he heard the tired note in her voice. People must have been congratulating her all day. Or was it that she'd been hoping he'd say something else?

"Well, I'll let you get back," he said, feeling the loss of her already. "I'm guessing the party is still going."

"It's okay," she said, surprising him. She pushed herself up onto the flat spot at the top of the stair rail. "I'm not going back to the party. How long do you need to keep tabs on Travers?"

"Just another hour or so, enough to make sure he doesn't drink tonight."

She smiled, as though knowing he'd have his work cut out, then she looked down at the sand. "I saw my mother in the clinic today. Did you ask her to come in?"

"She turned up at just the right time when I needed someone to call the evac."

"I'm glad." She paused. "I don't think she's set foot in the clinic in a long time. We … don't exactly get along, but she's just changed. She's so thin. Skye says she goes walking a lot."

Alex, who'd seen the interview on the cable channel in the clinic waiting room while waiting on news about Spencer, sensed the connection leading back to Dr Jacob's death.

"Grief can take a long time to resolve," he said carefully. "Are you worried?"

"Not exactly, no ..."

"Do you think she would take her old job back?"

Erin looked away. "I don't know. Sandy said they offered it before and she said no." She straightened. "I'm going back to the boat, and you're going back to the mainland."

"I know," he said. "And here I was, hoping for another night on a rooftop."

She ghosted a smile, and he saw again how tired she was.

"How about dinner one night, when I get back next week?"

She paused, and he thought she was going to refuse. Then she said, "You cook?"

"I do, but I don't have a kitchen. That sink in the back of the surgery doesn't count. How about the cafe?"

She laughed. "Okay, then. What night?"

"How about Thursday, when I'm back? Not traditional, but displaying all my overeager qualities."

She groaned. "I can't. I have to schmooze a sponsor that night. Tristan thinks I can convince them."

Alex didn't enjoy the mention of Tristan, but she hadn't said no. "How about Saturday, then, the classic date night?"

"Saturday it is."

"Next week, then." It seemed an age away. But then, she reached a hand to clasp his, and they stood like that for a few heartbeats, fingers laced, the waves softly hissing into the sand. Alex could have lived in that moment.

When she finally disappeared into the dark down the stairs, he was sure he would feel her touch pulling him back here, all the way from across the ocean.

Two hours later, having left Travers watching a beaten VHS

copy of *Survive the Savage Sea*, Alex cleaned up the second consulting room, not wanting to leave a mess for the day he was off-island.

Fortunately, most of the mess was open packets on the floor, and the disposable liners on the bed. It didn't take too long to put all that into the bin, wipe down with steriliser and run a mop over the floor. Sandy would probably have come in to do it tomorrow, but he didn't want to go and lie in bed with his thoughts just yet.

When he finished cleaning, he found himself staring at the shelves of patient files in the nook behind reception. The tiny practice had nothing electronic, so everything was old-school, with coloured stickers on the edges of the folders.

Alex trailed his fingers over the files, until he arrived at *Jacobs*. With Erin's concerns in mind, he pulled out Anna's file and flipped past the blood results in the front, to the clinical notes.

It was a slim file, but then maybe Anna would have had a GP on the mainland instead of seeing her husband. In any case, the entries were more than six years old, the last for some stitches in her knee. The others were check-ups – two-yearly bloods for cholesterol and liver function. Certainly nothing noted about a history of depression or background problems like that to worry about.

As Alex went to replace the file, two loose sheets slipped out. Picking them up, he noted they were pathology results, the text faded as though they'd been left in the sun. One was a blood count, the other a plasma glucose. The blood count was normal, but for mild anaemia. The plasma glucose was a little elevated.

Alex frowned, looking at the dates. These were from five years ago, but there were no associated clinical notes. Could Anna have developed diabetes? If it wasn't being treated, that was a problem. Then again, anaemia was very common, and one abnormal blood glucose didn't prove anything. His mind raced into the possibilities. He wanted to understand this. Maybe he could …

Alex stopped. Could what, exactly? Go poking around, overstepping the bounds of his duty?

He slotted the old results into the front of the file and put it back on the shelf. Anna was an adult. Unless she turned up here as a patient, he couldn't just go and start asking questions.

Chapter 13

"You're not going to wear that, I hope?"

Skye stood in the doorway of her cottage the following Thursday, scrutinising the contents of a dry-cleaning packet that Erin was holding up to keep it out of the sand.

"Why, what's wrong with it?"

"You're having dinner with a potential huge sponsor, and you're going to wear pants?"

"They're my black dress pants, cleaned fresh and everything. And the top has sequins, look."

Erin tugged the plastic up so that Skye could see the halter-neck brimming with deep-blue sequins at the throat, then fading to pale azure down the front. It tied at the neck and waist, leaving much of her back bare. She'd picked it up in a boutique somewhere in the Caribbean.

"It looks like a stripper outfit," Skye said.

"No it doesn't! Pants are practical. What if I need to do something on the boat?"

"Like what? Climb the mast? It's dinner on a superyacht. We have to fix this," Skye said, pulling Erin inside. "I'm sure I have something you can borrow. There's the costumes from last year's play if nothing else."

"Oh. My. God. Skye, this is not what I had in mind when I asked to use your bathroom mirror."

"Yes, well, you're new at playing nice. What's the deal, anyway? Tristan wouldn't tell me anything about this guy. He so rich he has to fly under the radar?"

"No idea," Erin admitted, allowing Skye to hang her packet on a door lintel. "All I know is that it's very important. Not really looking forward to it. Big money can be tricky."

"Tricky how?" Skye asked, with uncommon interest.

Erin shrugged, thinking of a dozen pushy owners she'd met in the last few years. "Expect you to say yes to everything they want."

"Well, I don't know how you can't look forward to Tristan's yacht. It's divine."

"Oh yeah? How do you know?"

"I've seen it," Skye said, drawing Erin into the spare room, where the cupboard rail was bowed under the weight of costumes.

"I'm not wearing some hideous play dress," Erin said.

"They're not all costumes. I go to vintage stores on the mainland sometimes. Here, try this," she said, passing over a slinky dress in fire-engine red, fitted to the ankle but with unfortunate capped sleeves.

Erin set her jaw. "No."

In the end, Skye found a simple elegant black skirt – hiding under a hideous ruffled overskirt from *Oklahoma*. Paired with Erin's sequinned top it looked dramatic and sophisticated. Skye trained Erin's hair into a French twist, and Erin toned down the choice of lipstick. When she finally left the house, carrying a strappy pair of black heels, Skye pronounced her acceptable.

"What's the point of the shoes? It's dinner on a yacht," Erin grumbled, throwing Skye's words back at her.

"It's a look," Skye snapped, then took a deep breath. "Erin, are you … really not interested in Tristan again?"

"Nope."

A pause. "But you understand how important this all is to me. To us."

Erin turned to look at Skye, whose carefully shaped brows were clamped together. She sensed that undercurrent from Skye again, the vibe that said Erin wasn't part of the island anymore, that she wasn't entirely welcome.

"I lived here my whole life. Of course I do."

"And you remember you owe me a favour."

"I'm wearing this, aren't I?"

Skye ignored her. "So you can put in a good word for me with Tristan."

Erin blinked. "A good word?"

"You know what I mean."

Erin paused, trying to pick apart the look on Skye's face, and what this was all about. For the first time, she worried about Skye being interested in Tristan.

"Don't look at me like that," Skye said, breaking the silence. "You said you weren't interested."

"I'm not," Erin said, but her chest whirlpooled with conflict. She didn't want to put in any kind of word with Tristan, didn't want to be caught in the middle. "But isn't this all about the future of the island?"

Skye looked away briefly, then said, "So go convince that sponsor."

It took a good long while for Erin to pick her way down the sun-warmed sand to the beach. She checked the watch she'd hidden from Skye in the skirt's waistband. At least she was on time, and it couldn't have been a more beautiful night. The western horizon was a wash of gold and orange, streaks of cloud catching the colour and reflecting it back into the sky. To the east, the deeper indigo of the coming night was showing the stars. The breeze hummed through the sheoaks behind the beach path, the air fresh but touched with delicate cooking scents – pepper, cardamom and citrus. Probably Sandy was experimenting in her kitchen, buoyed by the success of the pilot race and the extra income.

And there, down on the beach in the gently-lapping waves, Tristan was waiting with the dingy.

"Wow, look at you," he said, kissing her on both cheeks. He was wearing a dark suit, albeit with no shoes and the pants rolled up, his tie undone. "You look amazing."

Erin managed to climb into the boat without ending up in the water, and Tristan expertly pushed off, barely wetting his feet. Then, they were cutting a slim wake towards the splendour of his corporate yacht, the *Seven Seas*.

"I had it brought out just before the race last week," he explained. "Had Gus do a few fixes."

Erin admired the *Seven Seas* as they pulled up at the folding rear platform. She was a massive superyacht, over one-hundred and forty feet. The deck was pale wood, probably oak, a theme that carried through into what Erin could see of the internal cabin space and cockpit. In the sumptuous rear seating area, the end of a long table was set for two.

"You're not just going to abandon me to Mr Moneybags, are you?" Erin said, feeling a qualm.

"Actually," he said. "I thought it would be more fun with just the two of us."

Alex had arrived back on the morning ferry after five nights at the mainland hospital, feeling as though he'd been flattened by one of the resort's construction steamrollers – the ones with the toothed wheels. He'd gone straight to bed, only emerging on dark when his satellite tracking app sounded an alarm. The ISS was passing over again tonight, and Jupiter and Saturn were in good places to view.

That was how he ended up at the top of the sand dunes, binoculars in hand, when Erin had appeared, picking her way over the sand.

For a long moment, Alex thought he was seeing things. She was dressed like she was going to a ball – in a black skirt that shifted like midnight water and sparkling top, her hair smooth and strappy shoes in her hand. She looked ... incredible. And that was when he realised who the man was, waiting with the tender on the far side of the jetty.

Tristan Drummond.

Alex squeezed a fist full of sand, until the grains burst through his fingers. They worked together, he knew that. But they also had a history. And some primal drive within him didn't like it.

Didn't like Tristan.

He imagined striding down the beach and stopping them. Punching Tristan in that sculpted face.

Grimly, he noted his thoughts going through these turns. For all the rules of society, everyone was such an animal underneath. At least tonight was business. Still, he watched the dingy leave the beach, knowing he wanted to be the one she was spending the evening with.

"I don't understand, I thought we were meeting with a big

sponsor," Erin said, as Tristan poured from a bottle of champagne with an expensive looking label. She rubbed her arms. "You didn't tell me that just to get me here, did you?"

He racked the bottle into the bucket with a crash of ice. "Of course not. Patrick had some crisis with the board and had to cancel. I didn't want to waste the food. Flown in fresh just a few hours ago, and we need to celebrate your win properly."

He drew her towards the table, where a seafood feast was spread on a silver platter: plump oysters, enormous prawns, and lobster tails with delectably delicate white flesh. Erin slid in front of the food, salivating, the champagne dulling her unease. She felt only mildly traitorous when there was amazing local shellfish that could have come straight from the island, not to mention the warm bread and butter that Tristan produced from the galley kitchen, fresh from a bakery in Sydney that morning, and not from Sandy's oven. But Tristan was right – it would be a tragedy to waste it.

"So this Patrick," she said, as Tristan took a prawn and expertly beheaded it. "You don't mean Patrick Donnelly, the mining guy?"

"Mining magnate I think is the term," Tristan said with a grin. "And yes, but you have to keep that quiet. He's been a silent partner in a maxi-yacht for a few years now – loves sailing. But he wants something bigger, and sponsoring the regatta here is what I'm hoping he'll do. Great exposure for his company, and he's starting a philanthropic foundation, and an Australian adventure challenge series. He's just what we need."

"What about him being in court last year? That stuff his wife was saying about his business?" *And their relationship*, she didn't say. Mrs Donnelly had been doing the rounds of the tabloids, spilling her heart on how Patrick's various mistresses has broken her heart.

"Just a bad divorce. She was hurt, and she tried to make things up as a cheap parting shot. You could tell by how fast it disappeared from the news."

"Oh, okay," Erin said, feeling uneasy as she speared a piece of smoked salmon with her fork. "Why does he even want to meet me? Not looking for a new wife, I hope."

Tristan laughed with a sparkle in his eyes. "No, I think he's shy of all that for a while. Besides, I don't like to share." He gave her a wink, which Erin ignored. "But it's a long-term commitment we're asking for – five years of sponsorship at least, so he needs to feel comfortable."

Erin laughed. "And you think that's what I'm good at? Come on, Tristan. Skye complains about my lack of social skills."

"I've never felt that. I think you're very, very good at it, actually."

Erin swallowed. The salmon was silky and smooth, but it didn't taste of anything. He was doing it again; trying to make her remember when they'd been together, and forget how long had passed. To forget that she was the one who'd ended it, and especially why. And this time, she found herself thinking of Alex. That night on the rooftop had held the kind of promise she'd never had with Tristan. She would much rather have been having dinner with him.

When she looked up, she found Tristan watching her, his eyes crinkled in fondness, but she was no longer touched by him. "You don't like the food?"

"It's amazing," she said, forcing herself to take a lobster half and pull out the delicate meat. The next second, Tristan's hand covered hers.

"It's fine, I'm nervous too," he said. Then, before she could say anything, he'd topped up her glass and disappeared inside. A moment later, soft guitar music spilled from the speakers.

"That's better," Tristan said, as he returned. "I thought something was missing. Now, shall we talk about the next race?"

"The next race?"

"Sure. The pilot went so well, we're offering a re-match, just as everyone's heading south again after the Hamilton meet. We should get a bunch of interest."

"But everyone will be preparing for Sydney to Hobart," she argued.

"What's one more stop? And they'll want to be here with the money we're putting up. But we need to top last time – new course, new challenge. It can't be a carbon copy. Then next year for the regatta, we'll roll both type of events together – maybe the opening and closing races. I'm thinking of naming the trophy the *Erin Jacobs Cup*."

Erin choked on her wine. "Don't do that." But she tapped a finger on the table, sliding naturally into strategy. "If you want something new, what about a circumnavigation of the island?"

"Is there enough drama in that? We need something no one else has done."

Erin frowned, thinking hard, even as the evening air slipped gently over her bare back. The waters around Great Haven had many challenges, but they weren't always sporting for a race. The Gauntlet had been reasonable – the channel was deep, even if it was narrow. But in many parts around the smaller islands, there were hidden rocks and reefs, some that weren't marked. She didn't want to send any boats over those. Someone like Patrick Donnelly would no doubt think it was unsporting, too.

Stuck, she got up and paced to the edge of the deck, leaning on the railing. Could they do something in two parts, maybe? Allow the crews to map their route first in a tender, then sail it later? No, that wouldn't play on TV. Maybe she could plot a course, but send Travers out to dive the worst parts, ensure it was free of obstacles.

Erin glanced over her shoulder. Tristan lounged in his chair, wine glass nearly empty, watching her like a big cat.

"What?" she asked.

"I like watching you think. And that shirt looks best from behind."

She turned back to the table, ready to tell him that she couldn't think straight, that she'd have to come back to it later. Then a different thought occurred. She leaned her hands on the back of her chair.

"Patrick Donnelly – you mentioned he's starting some kind of adventure series?"

"Yep. Endurance racing, all across Australia. Showcasing the natural beauty with physical challenges, something like that. Kind of like *The Amazing Race*. Raising money for Legacy I think."

"Legacy? Is he ex-military?"

"His father and grandfather."

"And he's Irish?"

Tristan gave her a funny look. "What are you doing in that head of yours, Erin?"

She grinned. "How about a dual race – land and sea at the same time?"

"Go on," he said, leaning forward.

Erin pointed off towards the darkness of the island. "The island can be circumnavigated on land – in theory," she said. "There's parts that are difficult – rock-hopping and having to cut inland around the cliff points, but definitely doable. What if we set a course around the island on the water as well as on land – we'd have to send the yachts on a long bend up north to make it a long race – but the team who has both their land team and sea team cross in the least total time, wins."

For a long pause, Tristan said nothing. Erin tried to read his face with the blood thrumming in her chest and failed. Finally, he pushed back his chair.

"You know, you might actually be a genius," he said, disappearing inside the cabin to retrieve his phone. Then he was dialling, setting up meetings in the morning with the team, then interrupting people's dinner in Sydney and Melbourne to put them on the task. As Erin watched him, she couldn't help but admire his decisiveness, the resources at his disposal. And then it dawned on her that all this was being set in motion because of a few sentences that she'd just thrown out with less than a minute's thought. Was he crazy? A peal of nerves shot through her – what if it was a bad idea?

"I love it," he said finally as he put the phone down. "But we need to put the foot down. We'll have to be advertising in a few days. The event's only four weeks away."

"Isn't that awfully tight?" After the pilot race, Erin had a new appreciation for everything that had to happen behind the scenes – insurance, advertising, coordinating the sponsors and the equipment, contracts.

"Absolutely," Tristan said, guiding her back to her chair and encouraging her to eat more. "Remember all the background work's been happening for a while, we'll just have to tweak the plans. My philosophy has always been to dive in, then swim like crazy. Now, tell me more."

Erin managed to eat most of what was on her plate as they

threw ideas back and forth, but still felt bad when the platter went back to the fridge half-finished. Tristan then produced two crème brûlée, dusting them with sugar and flaming them with a small blowtorch right at the table. The smell of burnt sugar made Erin's mouth water, and she cut-off midsentence.

"You did do this deliberately, didn't you?" she asked. She could never go past crème brûlée. Once, after a particularly rough trans-Atlantic crossing, she'd walked off the boat in southern France and gone straight to the nearest restaurant and eaten three.

"I do everything deliberately," he said. A quick caress of his eyes, and then they were back to business, talking potential strategy, even long after the finished ramekins were pushed away. Tristan told her at one point she was a natural; Erin blushed, pinkly enjoying herself. She didn't really enjoy overpraise, or this business stuff, but she did want Great Haven out there in the world, being promoted. It would bring better times for her mother, Skye, Sandy and everyone in the village.

Finally, Tristan leaned back in his chair. "I think that's enough shop talk tonight. But we'll need to map the island course quickly. I noticed the old trails are a bit overgrown. Who can we get to plot a GPS path, that kind of thing?"

"I'll do it," Erin said. Actually, she planned on asking Travers for help. If anyone would be good at it, she figured he would. Maybe even Skye. She smiled to herself at the thought of the two of them striking sparks off each other.

"What's that smile for?" Tristan asked softly.

"Oh, nothing."

He stood, and offered his hand. "Come on."

"Where are we going?"

"Not far," he said, then as the song changed, he drew her in close. "Care to dance?"

After all the wine, Erin found herself leaning against him, his hands warm on her bare skin, tiny shivers running up her back and across her shoulders. He was wearing that expensive cologne again: she could smell it on his neck and shirt. And that was when Erin realised she'd let her head fall against his shoulder as they slowly danced around the deck. The small part of her mind that wasn't drunk wondered what the hell she was doing. But it was a quiet protest. The boat barely moved under them, the cabin lights buttery splashes that made the rest of the world fade into darkness. All she could see past Tristan's shoulder was a slip of moon peeking above Bella's Leap, a sliver that looked for a moment like a thin woman, standing on the cliff.

Erin jerked her head up, and the image disappeared. She blinked, thinking it was time to go home. Tristan leaned in close. "Isn't this nice?"

"Mmm."

Erin realised what was about to happen a moment before it did. Tristan's lips covered hers, with a demand of long-restrained longing. He pulled her closer, until his body was full against her. But there was nothing familiar about him. Their relationship had been so long ago, he felt like a different man, and as she tried to kiss him back, the fact was only underscored; nothing about this was magical. She didn't want it. Didn't want him anymore.

She pushed away, her hands on his chest, her head spinning. "Tristan, stop."

He let his hands slip to her elbows. "Too much wine?"

"It's not that." She pulled him over to the couches, giving herself time to think. Even drunk, she knew to tread carefully.

"I really don't want to do this," she said. "We work together. I want to keep things professional. I think what you're doing on the island is amazing," she rushed on, seeing him about to speak, "but it's years since we were together and you move in a different world to me, now. I hope you can understand that."

It was far short of the *hell, no* she wanted to say.

Tristan rubbed his face. She saw the flints of annoyance in his eyes. "You can't blame me for trying, though, right? I mean, that shirt. I'm just human." He squinted out into the night. "There isn't someone else, is there? Maybe that nosy diver on your crew?"

Erin eased further away from him. "Travers is just a ... well, I'm not sure if friend is the right word. But he's just that. And anyway, he's got his eye on Skye. Besides, I'm too busy for a relationship."

Oh, man, he had her stumbling now.

Tristan smiled, but it only moved the corners of his mouth. She expected that he'd be hurt; no one liked rejection. But he had a rage in him, and she glimpsed it in the way he held his body.

She shivered. The soft music was still spilling from the speakers. "I know this isn't what you wanted to hear," she said, before he could ask about Alex, too. "And I'm sorry. I think it's best if I go now."

He nodded. All trace of the rage was gone as they climbed back into the tender; or, at least, he was hiding it well. They said nothing as he took her back to the shore. As she climbed out, she was afraid he was going to tell her that she was fired.

Instead, he said, "There's one thing I want to know."

"What?"

"Why did you ask if Patrick was Irish?"

Erin glanced at the Leap, a chill running over her skin. "Because of the homestead. I thought we could put it on the course."

"What does that have to do with anything?"

"Bella was Irish."

Chapter 14

The next day, Alex was on hold on the surgery phone, watching the path outside the window in case Erin walked past. He was waiting to speak with Luke Hurley, who Alex had known since medical school. They'd drunk beers together at hospital keg parties, but all that seemed a long time ago now as he came off hold for the second time.

"Sorry," Luke said briskly. "Now, you said it's just the one patient?"

"One definite — he's a famous painter. You'd like a celebrity patient, wouldn't you?" Alex said, picking at the vinyl on the edge of his desk calendar and trying not to let his dark mood over Erin and Tristan leak into the conversation.

"Oh? Who's that?"

"Helmut Meyer. He paints seascapes. You haven't heard of *The Woman on the Cliff?*"

"Can't say I have. I like art, Alex, but I leave the buying of it to my wife."

Alex tried another angle, feeling his temper rising. "It's a postcard-perfect tropical island — bound to be heaps of cataracts and pterygia. I could fill your card for a whole Friday and then you could drink cocktails on the beach all weekend. For any patients who need surgery we can book the theatre on the mainland for the Monday morning. What do you say?"

A long silence. "My schedule's pretty full."

"Come on, Luke. You play golf three mornings a week. How about trading one of those and throw your old drinking buddy a break up here. We're isolated and we need your skills."

"It's not as simple as that," Luke said, sounding wounded and haughty. "I've got a wife to clear it with, and I'll have you know I do plenty of regional work."

Alex sighed silently. He knew Luke's wife was no impediment when Luke was jetting off to overseas conferences, and that the regional work probably consisted of a few days in Longreach last year, but saying so wouldn't do any good.

"Well, bring her along," he tried. "They're starting a yacht racing festival up here. Chance to peruse the real estate before the market leaps." Alex pressed a thumb into his right eyeball. He must be desperate to be invoking Tristan's plans. "At least tell me you'll think about it?"

A sigh. "I'll think about it." Then he paused delicately. "I did hear talk about your troubles. Everything going better for you now? You're back in practice obviously."

"Things are great," Alex said automatically, though his heart kicked into a loud drumming beat. He put down the phone feeling oddly exposed. He hadn't expected the medical grapevine to stretch all the way to Luke's fancy offices in the capital. Maybe that was how Tristan had heard about his past. His thoughts were interrupted as Sandy appeared with a steaming mug, which she set carefully on his desk. To Alex, it smelled like dirt.

"What's this?"

"It's camomile tea," she said. "You sounded as if you were having a rough day."

"Fine, thank you," he snapped. Then he caught himself.

"Sorry, Sandy."

"That's fine. Must be terrible coming back after all those night shifts over on the mainland. Shortens your life, you know. Bet you hardly slept last night."

"Something like that."

He wouldn't admit to anyone that his poor sleep had been less about his schedule and more because of wild thoughts about Erin on Tristan's boat. Or that he'd then had a rare but intense nightmare about the accident. He'd woken in a tangled sweat, momentarily convinced the white sheets were foaming water. That he could hear helicopter blades beating in the distance.

"Well," Sandy said, eyeing him like a head nurse. "You drink that up, and I'll fetch you a pie for lunch. There's no more appointments. Maybe some fresh air would be a good idea? You must have been inside for a week. Go get some sunshine and reset your body clock."

So that was how Alex ended up hiking up the hillside behind the village, over the ridge that separated it from the rest of the island, scouting for a new vantage for sky viewing, now that the resort had been taken over by Tristan's workforce.

Once the beach was out of view, it was easy to forget he was on an island – the bushland looked the same as on the mainland. Dry, dusty, with eroded gullies. The island might enjoy regular storms and significant rainfall, but up on the hill under the baking sun it made little difference. The trees were thin and scraggly along the ridge, and at the highest point, he spotted an old rotunda.

The place was neglected, each wooden board swollen and

warped, but the roof was still intact, and it offered a sheltered position with a good view from the cleared ground around it. He could see all the way out to the smaller southern Haven islands, and to the north, he could see the vast bowl of the island's interior.

Down there, it was truly green with a creek glittering between folds in the wooded fields, its mouth spilling out into a marsh at the western shore. And tucked down in the middle of the fields, he saw a roof.

Pulling out the island's map, he realised it could only be one place: Bella's homestead. He checked his watch; still hours before dark. He found the trail and set off.

The journey was much longer than it looked. Alex kept thinking that around the next bend, or the next, he would find the place, but the bush kept on, the cicadas deafening. The trail was wide as a road and took him across a dry creek bed and through the open gate of a tumble-down fence. Just when he thought he'd taken a wrong turn and should head back, the trees gave way to open grass, and the homestead appeared.

Close up, he could clearly see the peeling boards, the rusting roof that had fallen in at one corner, the slump of the frame on its foundations. Then Alex's senses lurched: someone was standing under the giant pine tree that spread its boughs over the house.

Erin.

The last time he'd seen her, she'd been dressed up and heading to Tristan's boat. Now, she wore ragged boat shorts and singlet. She had a notebook in her hand, her head bent as she worked the pen against the paper. Trying not to scare her, he cleared his throat.

"Don't worry, I saw you five minutes ago," she said without

looking up. "You were making a lot of noise coming down the hill."

Alex squinted over his shoulder at the distant ridge, the rotunda now a miniature against the sky. There'd been loose rocks and sand on the path down. "I wouldn't have thought you could hear this far away."

Erin smiled. "It's an amphitheatre in here – you can hear the echoes bouncing down from the hills. Listen."

Alex stood still. At first he heard nothing, then he tuned into the subtle sounds. A tiny loose of pebbles rushing down a hill. The crack of a dry stick. The shush of the wind driving through the grassland. Each sound came with a trail of miniature echoes, so he couldn't place where any of it came from. It began to make him feel dizzy.

"Creepy," he said, feeling goosebumps erupt over his skin. The pine's lower limbs were skeletal fingers, the breeze whining somewhere further to the north, where the sheoaks reclaimed the fields and the hills rose up again. He couldn't imagine living here, but the house bore witness to someone's long-ago life in its empty window eyes. Erin seemed immune to the eeriness, until he saw her arms were prickled too. She finished scribbling and caught his eye.

"Yeah, I know. It's a bit ghostly, being Bella's place and all," she said. "Travers tell you I was here?"

"I saw the homestead from up on the hill. Why are you here?"

"Planning for the next race."

When he frowned, she quickly explained the dual land-sea concept, and that Travers and Skye had struck out in the opposite direction down the main beach, in an attempt to cover more ground, mapping the route with GPS.

"We're thinking of sending the land race straight through here," she said. "The homestead's the most visible part of the island's history. At least, recent history. There's middens on the eastern coast that go back thousands of years, but Tristan will say they won't play well on TV. Do you want to see inside?"

"Inside here?"

"Yeah, come on. The side door's not locked. Unless, of course, you're scared."

"Scared, no," he said, following her, eyeing the house's lean, the stain of water damage in the corner with the fallen roof. The timbers were probably rotten through. "Pragmatic, yes."

Inside, the place proved more sad than ghostly. The raw wooden floorboards were covered in dust, cobwebs hanging thickly in every corner. Deep shadows fell everywhere, thanks to the pine tree's shade. A constant buzz emanated from two wasp's nests growing from window lintels. The air smelled of damp and possum piss, with droppings scattered over the floor. A rusting stove sat in an antechamber at the slumped end of the main room. Through another doorway was a second room, same as the first, but attached to a slim verandah.

"Hmph," Erin said, poking her head into the antechamber. "Can't believe no one fixed the roof."

"How long since anyone's lived here?" Alex asked, picking his way across the droppings and unsticking the verandah door. A gust of fresh air displaced some of the possum reek.

Erin stepped past him, sitting on the edge of the verandah outside. Alex followed, after checking for wasps. From here, the overgrown field sloped downhill to the creek, its water shining silver in the sunlight.

"A while I guess. Bella died in 1908," she said. "After that, the place was abandoned until after the first world war, when someone else took over the pastoral lease."

"It was a farm?" he said, sitting beside her.

"Yeah, sheep. Hence the fences, and the cleared fields. So various people came through after that, from the 20s through to the 50s. No one stayed longer than a year or two though. Everyone said the place was cursed. The house changed over that time. We don't really know how much of it was Bella's."

"How long was she here?"

"Twenty years, more or less. She came with her husband in the late 1880s. He died pretty soon after, but she stayed and ran the place herself."

"Must have been lonely," said Alex, as Erin shifted herself closer to him, rubbing her shoulders. Alex moved his arm naturally around her.

"She was a tough woman," Erin said. "She'd only have seen the shearers when they came in once a year, and the Indigenous folk of course."

She was so close; he could smell a faint trace of apple shampoo, and feel the smooth perfection of her tanned skin, warm against him.

"I didn't know there were Aboriginal people on the island."

"Used to be."

And then her eyes were fixed on his, and he dropped his gaze to the delicate curve of her mouth. She slid her arm underneath his, turning towards him, one hand resting lightly on his chest. Then he was kissing her, the force of their attraction as intense as it had been that night in the old resort. Alex floated on the freedom of how he felt with her, and drowned in the possibilities. He hadn't had feelings like this for someone in a long time. Finally, when they broke for air, he pressed his forehead to hers.

"Erin, are you with Tristan?"

She pulled back, a frown knitting her brows. "No. Why?"

"I saw you the other night, going to his yacht."

"Oh. And I was hoping no one would see me in that get-up."

"You looked incredible."

It just tumbled out. Erin stopped, a suspicious expression putting lines around her eyes. "Right."

"I mean it." He ran his thumbs over her cheeks. "I was madly jealous. I know you had a work dinner, but I couldn't help it."

She took a breath, as though she might say something difficult, then she said, "Skye made me wear the skirt. But the evening didn't go so well anyway."

"Oh," he said, the scenario changing slowly in his mind, like a freighter making a turn. "It's just I know you and Tristan have a history—"

"People shouldn't talk so much," she said, standing up. And then, the moment broke again. Whatever that magic that led to the passionate kissing, it was gone again now. She held her notebook and GPS to her chest. "I need to try to make it to the north-west beach before I head back."

Alex followed her out of the house, watching as she closed the door again with care. "I could come with you."

"Worried I'll get eaten by The Beast?"

"What Beast?"

"No one told you about the Great Haven Beast?" She beckoned him to follow as she swished through the grass towards the creek. "I'm surprised. Usually that's the first one the locals try. It's a legendary animal that's supposed to live in the northern hills. It's what the older kids scare the little ones with every time they find a dead possum near the village. *Must have been The Beast.*"

"Oh right. Sandy did try that, but I was preoccupied at the time. So, it's like a dog?"

"Or a big cat. Or an old ram, gone wild. Just stories. Every small place has a story like that."

"Not really," Alex said, as they arrived at the creek edge, a series of flat rocks making a path across the shallow water. "I've worked out west, in Queensland and down south and I've never been anywhere with so many stories."

"I suppose," Erin said, hopping across with sure steps. "But on the mainland people can drive away. It's more cooped here. Breeds a good tale."

"Well, what others are there, then?" Alex asked, just managing to avoid wetting his shoes as the last rock moved under his feet.

"That's it really. Just The Beast. And the wreck. Oh, and the waterhole."

"I've seen both of those marked on Skye's map."

Erin laughed. "You remember I told you Skye drew that when she was a kid. The wreck's real enough. It's an old ship that went down off the east coast, near the point rocks. Supposed to be full of Spanish gold. It's pretty much collapsed though, so not many divers bother. Travers might have been down there. The waterhole, though, that one's a mystery. It's meant to be somewhere in the northern hills, which is why Skye put it on the map. Big enough to swim in, supposedly, but no one's ever found it."

"So you think it's just made up?"

They were approaching the end of the field now, where the sheoak grove whispered like the distant sound of the sea. Erin stopped to take a waypoint on the GPS.

"It's not impossible. We have springs, as you can see from this creek. The northern hills have some deep gullies, and difficult terrain. But it's an island after all – there's only so much land. If it was there, you'd think it would have been found years ago."

"I wonder why the story hasn't died then."

"Nothing to wonder about there. There's actual records."

"What sort of records?"

She stopped again, just inside the cool shadow of the sheoaks where the dappled light draped her skin in a pale lattice. She turned away from him, staring down the path. Without turning around, she said, "Bella wrote about the waterhole. In her letters."

Alex shivered in the cool shade. "Let me guess – The Beast is also supposed to be her dog, or her ram, something like that?"

A nod. "It all comes back to Bella around here."

They pushed on through the whispering sheoaks, the smell of shellfish and seaweed growing steadily stronger.

"Will you tell me her story?"

"I'd really rather not right now, okay? Besides, no one really knows what happened to her."

Her tone surprised him. It was the same reluctance Stella had had, as though talking about it made them uncomfortable without knowing why. He let it go.

"Okay, then. Let's go back to the race. Where does the trail go from here?"

She grinned. "Don't tell me you'll be looking to join a team, Dr Bell?"

"I'm thinking about how many broken ankles we'll have."

"Hmm," she said, as if the idea hadn't occurred to her. "Maybe we should bring you on as a consultant."

And that was how they passed the rest of the day. After a scramble up a short headland, then down the other side, they came to the stretch of the north-west beach, a wilder shore than the main bay, the beach deserted but for seagulls. The mainland was still visible across the sea, though, and the waves were lazy. Erin pointed out where they were on Alex's map, their conversation now all about the race and the various medical travesties Alex could foresee happening on the way. What was their plan for emergency evac? How many water stations would they have, and where? Erin adjusted her plans accordingly, pulling the route away from inland to keep to the beaches so that any emergency help could come in from the sea. She avoided the northern hills, except where the route must cut across headlands not navigable around the rocks.

They drifted together, fingers touching here and there. Alex might have been frustrated about what they were to each other, except that Erin fascinated him too much. Just being in her company enraptured him.

As they retraced their steps back to the village, she was saying, "The new route will work better for the coverage, too. If we keep people out of the trees, they'll be able to use drone cameras, and if we need a rescue we'll be faster by boat off a beach." Then she caught herself. "God, I sound like Troy. I wonder how far Travers and Skye got."

"Second base?" Alex said, feeling relaxed and happy as they made the crest at the top of the ridge.

Erin laughed. "You noticed too, huh?"

But as they reached the village again, when Alex was about to suggest they move their dinner to tonight, he spotted Sandy waving from the path to the surgery.

"Patient for you," she said.

"I better go," Erin said quickly, turning to go.

"Wait, Erin," he said, but then he found he couldn't say anything because Sandy was hovering. "Don't forget to check for ticks. That grass was pretty long," he said, feeling like a lame idiot.

Sandy popped her eyebrows at him as Erin left. "Where have you two been, then?"

"Patient in the surgery?"

"Oh, yes, but that can wait. Tell me all about your exploring."

Annoyed, Alex paced back ahead of her, hoping the waiting patient wasn't urgent. If he walked in to find someone bleeding, Sandy was going to get an earful.

"Out by the homestead," he said finally, when she didn't let up. "Erin's making a route for the next race."

"Oh, that's so exciting, isn't it? We all heard this morning and everyone's already preparing. We're going to put on a concert, hopefully encourage people to stay the night."

Alex glanced around the empty waiting room. No one was in the consult room, either, or the second room. Sandy was still rabbiting.

"Sandy. Sandy?"

"Yes, what?" she asked, finally breaking the flow about event plans and foreign yachts.

"Where's the patient?"

"Oh, around the back. It's Monster again. Tim says he ran away on his own for a while, and can you look at something in his eye, please?"

Chapter 15

Tristan, Erin reflected, was in the foulest of moods. They'd been in this meeting since nine, yesterday's exploring of the island a dim memory in the white room where tension seemed to be coming out of the air-conditioner. No one could meet Tristan's gaze as he hammered them about all the things they hadn't done.

"Come on, now people. Where are we with the banners? Hamilton Race Week starts in two days and we need our advertising there and visible."

"I've been on the phone, Tristan," one of the team bravely said. "They're trying to rush it, but it's tight. It's not like getting things done in Sydney."

"I think it will be *Mr Drummond* today," Tristan said in a low tone. "Are you telling me it could be done faster if we just pay to fly it up from Sydney? Why the hell wasn't that the first thing you said."

"Tristan," Erin said.

"What?" he barked.

Erin was through with this. She'd seen enough captains take frustrations out on their crews and there was no faster way to screw morale. She might have begun this process as an outsider, and the team still wore expensive shirts while she wore cut-off denim, but they'd all worked hard on the successful pilot race.

She stood and forced herself to speak calmly.

"Tristan, can I talk to you outside please?"

Out under the pandanus, he put his hands on his hips. "You going to waste my time, too?"

Intuition kept Erin from quipping back at him, like she might with a worked-up captain, or as she might have years ago. She'd learned since then, and wondered if this was all about the other night, but she would never ask him that directly.

"Is there something going on I don't know about? Did Patrick pull out or something?"

For a second, she thought he was going to lose it. Then he huffed a breath. "No. Everything is fine. Or it would be if the team would do their jobs."

"You under a lot of pressure?"

"That shouldn't be surprising." But he seemed to be calming.

"Look, I can't imagine what stress it is to be CEO. But I know crews, and this lot is going to work harder if they aren't being reamed at every step. Can you maybe tone it back a bit? We can make this happen."

"Then let's stop screwing around."

He stalked back to the meeting, leaving Erin with a black feeling inside. It *was* about the other night. Not all of it, perhaps, but some of it. Was this how it was going to be? She would quit on the spot, but for the people around the table inside that meeting room who'd all worked hard. And she'd be quitting on Skye and her mother and the rest of the village. Again. She couldn't do that. Even if she didn't plan to stay long-term, she wanted them to have a better next five years than the last five had been.

So she went back to the meeting, and kept working. Tristan didn't change into Mr Sunny, but he didn't explode again.

Eventually, he stalked back to his office, saying he had business to take care of in Sydney.

Benny blew out a breath as everyone packed away their materials. "Don't worry, Erin, he gets like this sometimes."

"Oh, yeah," Shelly agreed. "When that merger was going on and he caught that manager out? It was ugly like this for a week. No, two."

The others murmured their agreement.

"What'd he catch the manager doing?" Erin asked.

Kit grinned. "Having a good time in the stationery cupboard with the project admin assistant. Everyone thought it was kind of funny … but Tristan didn't. He went nuclear. They were both off the team after that."

Erin was glad the rest of them seemed unfazed, but Tristan's mood made her nervous. She was glad to get away from him. Dinner with Alex was just what she needed. But, later in the afternoon, when she called in on Skye to combine their maps and discuss the northern join-up for the race, Skye said,

"And can you stop past the store on your way to the jetty and get some butter? I want to make bread tonight."

"Whatever for?" Erin asked. "Sandy's bakery is right around the corner."

"I want to make it personally. It'll be nice with Tristan coming for dinner."

Erin felt the dark feeling return, twisting between the memories of the morning's meeting, and the time much longer-ago. "Since when?"

"He called earlier and I invited him."

"I don't think that's a good idea, Skye."

"Why? You're coming too."

Erin imagined being in the same room with Tristan after this morning – let alone the other night – and how awkward that would be with Skye and their mother trying to do pleasant chit-chat, and then Skye wanting to know what was wrong. Erin couldn't pull it off, not today.

"Tristan's under a lot of pressure," she said. "He was in a foul mood today. I just don't think we should add to it with dinner as well."

"What, so you get to see him all day at work, but we can't have him for dinner?"

"I can't."

"Why not? You're always off doing your own thing. For once you can come and have dinner with Mum and me. Family's very important to him."

Around the mountain of guilt, Erin groped for words that she had other plans, without having to tell Skye those plans involved Alex, and staying as far from Tristan as possible. Skye would see only selfishness. Instead, she hastily said she would get the butter, but her stomach was rolling on storm swell. At the beach road, she had to stop and suck a breath, just as Travers appeared with a dripping pair of fins and snorkel in his hands.

"You sick?" he asked.

"Think I might be coming down with a migraine," Erin lied, the excuse bringing instant relief, even if it meant she would be standing Alex up. She handed Travers the butter. "Can you take this to Skye and tell her I won't make it? I'm going to go lie somewhere dark and quiet."

Two hours later, when the whole world had turned to night, Erin was in the front cabin, curled around a wrinkled Jilly

Cooper novel with a map light clipped to the pages. An hour ago, the jetty had been alive as a fishing boat offloaded part of its catch. Now, there was nothing but the gentle liquid tinkling of the waves, and the growling of Erin's stomach.

Shoving an old chandlery receipt into the book, Erin threw the two balled-up chip packets she'd already emptied towards the bin and prowled back to the pantry. She kept the light off, but she didn't need it. The contents were the same as ten minutes ago when she'd last checked – half a packet of stock cubes, a jar of satay sauce, and an open packet of biscuits that were stale, because she'd never sealed them properly. She'd been lax in provisioning, eating too many dinners during the long work days with Troy, Benny, Kit and Shelly on Tristan's account. She couldn't go up to the cafe now; she'd be spotted, and that would get back to Skye and Tristan.

She pulled down the satay sauce, which had expired in 2016. She'd eaten some bad stuff over the years on long sailing journeys, but this was a new low. She was just contemplating pulling out her fishing gear when she heard creaking footsteps on the jetty. She put an eye to the port window. A dark shape stood beside the boat. She hadn't even heard them coming. Only Skye was that sneaky.

"Hello? Erin?" Alex called.

Relieved, she mounted the cabin stairs and stuck her head out the hatch. He was wearing a pair of cut-off track pants and a t-shirt with a ripped collar, completely at odds with the dark leather bag in his hand.

"What are you doing here?" she hissed.

"Well I exhausted the courtesy bread at the cafe and I'm here to exact my revenge as the stood-up date," he said, in good humour. "Seriously, Travers said you had a migraine. Came to see if you needed anything." He lifted the bag and shook it.

Erin hesitated for a bare second. "Hurry up and come in here before someone sees you."

Erin gripped her hands on the tiny galley sink as Alex climbed down the cabin stairs. Even in the dim reflected jetty light, she could see the frown pulling at his brows. Looking around the dark cabin, he said, "You have photophobia?"

"What's that?"

"The light hurts your eyes."

"Oh, no. I'm not really sick."

"Oh, so you did stand me up." A pause. "I didn't wake you, did I?"

"No ... I'm avoiding Skye. She was having dinner with—it doesn't matter. I didn't want to go, so here I am, pretending a migraine like someone in a bad movie."

Alex slid the doctor's bag onto her table and sank into a couch seat with a chuckle. "Seems a bit extreme."

"You don't know Skye. She is a force of nature. This is easier, believe me. What do you have in there, anyway?"

Alex ran a hand fondly over the bag. "Oh, all the good stuff. Tramadol. Morphine."

"Pizza?"

He opened the bag and tipped it forward. Erin grabbed a flashlight from the wall mount and shone it in. Bandages, syringes, vials in a clear-topped box, a yellow sharps container, and a bunch of other unidentifiable packets. Much as her father's visiting bag had been.

"Dammit," she whispered. "Would it kill you to keep two minute noodles in there?"

"Wait a second," Alex said, taking her light and digging around in the bottom. "Oh, yes. Here."

He threw a tiny packet, which Erin managed to catch. Lumpy. Taking back the torch, she let out a grateful moan.

"Oh yes! Jelly beans!" She tore into the packet, devouring half of them before she offered him one, which he refused, an amused expression pulling his lips. Even in the dim light leaking in from the jetty lights, she could see only kindness in his eyes.

"You do realise," he said. "You're eating my stock of bribes."

"I'll replace it," she said, popping the last one in her mouth and chewing.

"That's really not a suitable dinner. Would you like a lecture on diabetes?"

"Don't start. I don't have any food in the pantry – well, not edible food. Before you got here, I was about to go fishing. That's where I'm at."

"I can't think of anything better than sitting on a dark boat fishing with you. But …"

Then he closed the bag and stood.

Erin pushed up off the sink. "You're leaving?"

"Yeah. I need to if I'm going to bring back some real food. You've never seen me fish; we'd starve first. So that means back to Plan A – me cooking."

Erin's lips tingled with anticipation. In the dark, close cabin, he was a warm presence, reminding her of the kisses they'd shared on the resort roof, and at the homestead. Both those times, memories had intruded, but tonight those thoughts seemed at a safe distance.

"Don't take too long," she said.

Chapter 16

Forty minutes later, Erin licked her fork and half-stood to peer at the stove.

"No, it's all gone," Alex answered, from the other end of the half-moon table. "But you can have the rest of mine if you want."

Erin eyed his plate. "No, I'm not really hungry anymore. It's just so good."

"It's ten-minute pasta, bacon and beer," he said, with a laugh. "You must have been starving."

"I cite my previously mentioned fishing plans as evidence to the fact. I'm impressed you had the makings of a fine dinner in your room. No man I ever knew could have brought more than the beer. Mind you, I can hardly talk with my pantry."

"You don't have much room in here for provisions," Alex said, collecting their plates and edging out the tight space around the table to put them in the sink. "Especially with being cut down for racing. Every live-aboard racing sailor I ever saw ate in the bars."

"Oh? Racing where?" she asked, interested. Both their eyes had long ago adjusted to the dim lighting, Alex taking up the challenge of cooking by torch and jetty light, so as not to scuttle Erin's migraine story. He slid back into the other side of the table, stretching out. And while he hesitated, his previous reluctance seemed to slide away.

"Mostly small meets, up and down the east coast. But I was at Kiel Week, once," he said, his voice soft like a confession.

"Really?" Erin edged around the bench seat towards him. Kiel Week was the largest regatta in the world, held in Germany and attracting thousands of boats. Despite the places Erin had crewed and raced, Kiel had always eluded her. She'd been on a crew to go one year, and then the owner's business had ended up in some trouble and the whole trip was cancelled. "Tell me what it was like."

"Massive," Alex said. "I couldn't believe how many people turned out."

She listened while he described the sails filling the horizon, the crowds and the spirit of the week, the fireworks on the last night. How he'd found himself treating injuries, mostly sprains and strains but occasionally something serious – a degloved finger (Erin made a gagging noise) and a broken arm.

"You are handy to have around. How did you manage to score that gig?"

"Someone I used to know had family who were professional racers in Europe. They organised it."

The way he said *someone I used to know* told Erin that his person was either an ex, or a friend he'd fallen out with. But the way he talked about the boats – the colours and the smells and the spectacle – she found herself itching to be back on the water. If it hadn't been night, she'd have taken the boat out immediately, at risk of taking off across the water for Fiji and beyond. She edged around further and put her hand up to crack the port window, wanting to smell the sea. The window refused to budge, and the next moment, the seat shifted and Alex reached up behind her, giving the pane a shove.

It opened, flooding them with a rush of cool night air, even as Erin felt the warmth of him beside her. She sank down slowly, her body fitting beside him. She looked up and he met her eyes, a smile on his lips. He looked lazily and deliciously mysterious.

"Sure puts our tiny plans in perspective," Erin said, her blood warming.

His lips curved as he ran a finger down her cheek. "I don't know, I hear there's some big guns signing up for the next one." But his eyes said he didn't give a fig about the race. He wanted her, and all she had to do was give him a reason to take her to the cabin. The atmosphere was pure liquid heat, and she could barely think of anything but pulling his clothes off and putting her lips to his skin.

"Go on," he whispered.

She stretched up and kissed him. A groan escaped him, and his hands gripped her ribs, the heat of his hands moving as his kiss became a naked demand. In response, Erin turned, splitting her thighs around him so she could face him and brush her tongue inside his mouth. The table creaked as he moved, his hands sliding over the curve of her butt. His head dropped to her neck, his lips brushing along her collarbone and sending shivers down her back. She tugged at his shirt. When it came away over his head, she ran her hand over the smooth muscle, the soft hair trailing down to the waistband of his pants. He unbuttoned her shirt and pushed it off her shoulders. Erin, braless, had the cool night air run over her flesh before the warmth of his mouth replaced it. She arched her back, sliding her hands under his waistband as he pulled her down to his mouth again.

"Bed," he said in her ear. "Right now."

Later, they lay in the bunk's twisted sheets, listening to the gentle wash of swell against the jetty piles. Erin's fingers were still twined in Alex's, her head against his shoulder. She'd half-expected him to be searching for his pants, making fast work of getting off the boat. That had often been her experience, sleeping with men she didn't know so well, no matter what port she'd been in, no matter how amazing the experience.

But Alex didn't seem to be going anywhere. And when he did finally say something, it wasn't anything close to what she expected.

"How long have you had this boat?"

Erin laughed. "A few years."

"Looks like it's done a few miles."

She softly snorted. "Yeah, a few. Across the Pacific four times, who knows how many trips from here to Sydney. Auckland, too. I've lived on it, except when I had to fly somewhere."

"Nice," he said, simply.

"Dad helped me pick it out," she said. "She was run down, and the interior was a mess. The whole thing smelled like weed and garbage. She was part of some divorce dispute – been sitting in a marina rotting away while the lawyers fought it out. Some local kids were using it as a hang out. But it had good bones, and I'd never have afforded anything better. We stripped it out and fixed her up. You'd never know now."

Alex moved a warm hand to her waist. "You don't talk much about your Dad. Everyone says they loved him. And now, I'm working out of his office. Does it upset you?"

Erin shifted onto her side away from him, so the pressure in her chest could drain itself in tears, without having to show him her face. He slid his arms around her. "I'm sorry," he said softly. "Insensitive question. Talk about something else."

"Like what?"

"You ever done the Sydney to Hobart?"

"Sure, a few times," she said, sucking back the emotion into its proper hidden place. But it was still pushing at the edges of her soul, and so she found herself telling him something she hadn't mentioned in many, many years.

"My first Sydney to Hobart was in 1998," she said. "When that huge storm hit the fleet. We'd had a bad start, so we were lagging well back in the field. Dad saw the weather reports coming in, saw other people pushing ahead, but he kept looking at the horizon and saying he didn't like it. It got rougher and rougher. I remember being cold and soaked through, and we weren't even in the worst of it. Dad pulled us out and turned back. I was so disappointed at the time. We only found out later about what happened to everyone else. Six people died. Five boats sank. One of our crew never went out on the water again. They never got over it."

She stopped, feeling the tension that had developed in Alex's body, his chest like a brace of steel cables. She turned back over, stroking his skin, until he let out a long breath. "Jesus, Erin. You can't have been very old."

"Sixteen," she answered. "After that year, they changed the rules. Made the minimum eighteen. Required everyone to do survival training, and a bunch of other stuff. It didn't put me off sailing. But I did get a lesson in who's in control out there. And it's not us. Up until then, I trusted my Dad could handle anything – Haven has weird storms as I'm sure you've heard, and we'd been out in them before. But after that race, I realised that I had to be smarter than thinking I would always be safe. I don't love it any less but there's a time to turn back."

He made a sound, deep in his chest, pushing himself up on his elbow. "This is going to sound stupid ... but I hate the idea of you out in something like that."

"That's because you just slept with me," Erin teased. "It's caveman brain. You'll get over it."

"I would never stop you," he said, bending his head to kiss the bare skin along her collarbone, his voice gruff. "But I like you here much better."

"Better make use of me, then," she whispered, pulling him close.

Much later, as Alex slept softly beside her, Erin lay awake with memories of her father rushing through her mind. The ninety-eight Sydney to Hobart was a distant memory now, fogged in time. She'd been young; almost too young to trust her own memories of it. But more recent events were very clear. Too clear. A different night, a different storm. And she'd been alone to face that one. So newly alone.

She was glad Alex was asleep, because the pressure of those secrets wanted relief. Here in the quiet with him, she almost felt she could tell him if she wanted to.

The idea was so frightening she dug her fingernails into her palm until they bled.

He left just after dawn, kissing her goodbye all the way to the cabin stairs. Erin stared after him as he sauntered down the jetty like a satisfied man, having no idea what this all meant. She was used to moving from port to port. And for all she knew, so did he. He was a blow-in from the mainland, maybe as intense as a Haven storm, but over just as quickly. But she liked the idea he was here now, and she was already thinking about the next time, about wordlessly undressing him right in the middle of the main cabin. She smiled at the thought even before he was out of sight.

Alex went back to bed at the clinic, sleeping late, and still had a smile on his face when he eventually grabbed a coffee from the bakery around lunch time.

"You're awfully happy today," Sandy commented, clearly suspicious.

"It's Sunday," he said. "Sun's out, slept in, what's not to be happy about?"

"I hear Erin's gone over the other side of the island again, plotting the course for the race. That Travers took her round there couple of hours ago in his boat."

Sandy was clearly fishing with the surest bait she had. Alex rubbed the back of his head as if confused. "Oh yeah, she might have mentioned that."

Alex could tell Sandy wasn't buying it; she was convinced *something* was going on. She was focused on him so intently, she was going to burn the milk. But there was no way Alex was giving up any of the delicious details. If anyone had asked directly, he'd tell them he'd given her a shot for her migraine. Awful things, migraines. No one needed to know it was Erin who'd given him the shot. He hadn't felt this alive in years.

"I'll come by in half an hour and do the appointment book for tomorrow," Sandy said, as she dumped the milk into his coffee.

"Nah, enjoy your Sunday," Alex said. "I'll do it myself. And I'll water the plants."

He left Sandy in a cloud of voyeuristic frustration and let himself back into the surgery through his room in the back.

Courtesy of the wide awnings, the air inside was cool. Alex sipped the coffee, sliding into the front desk chair to dig in the drawer for the appointment book, even as he wondered when Erin and Travers would be done with mapping today. The computer was right in front of him.

He found himself googling Dr Jacobs. Alex knew next to nothing about the man who had used these rooms before him, but Erin had cracked the window open, just barely, and now he wanted to see what was beyond it. He knew Dr Jacobs' first name had been Bryan – Sandy had hastily removed the name plate from the desk on Alex's first day. It was still in a storage box that lived in the bottom filing drawer.

Most of the pages Alex turned up were for other Dr Bryan Jacobs. Seemed there were quite a few – an obstetrician in Brisbane, a max-facs surgeon in Melbourne, a dozen others. So he started adding Great Haven to the search, and then he found a scatter of stories from local papers – Dr Jacobs sponsoring renovation work in the children's ward at the mainland hospital. Dr Jacobs posing with his family on the main beach on Great Haven.

Alex leaned forward to squint at the photo – it was old and pixelated, a black-and-white scan. Anna was young and carefree in the photo, her hair dark and long, her arms around her husband. Skye and Erin came barely to their father's chest. Skye was a young copy of Anna, Erin so like her father in the slope of her shoulders, the expression on her face – a careful smile, but at the same time, fiercely determined. And there, over Dr Jacobs' shoulder was Bella's Leap against the white backdrop of the sky.

Alex closed the page and moved on, but there wasn't much else to find. Many of the tiny regional papers hadn't put their back-catalogues up online, if they were still in business. He found brief mentions – regattas and race meets at yacht clubs where B. Jacobs was listed among the winners, or on the organising committee. He had been a community man, through and through. Accomplished in his career, and in his sport. So why wasn't what had happened to him reported?

It wasn't until Alex began searching specifically for his death that a story from a yachting quarterly surfaced, and then two others. Dr Bryan Jacobs and his oldest daughter had been sailing across the Pacific when they were caught in a storm. A line had snapped and Dr Jacobs had gone out onto the deck to try to cut away the sail, which had been dragging in the water. His oldest daughter then said that he had been lost overboard, and despite frantic searching in the waves, had lost contact with him. Dr Jacobs' body had never been recovered. He hadn't been wearing a harness at the time, or a life jacket, which was highly out of character.

Alex flicked through the different accounts of the accident, all the same. The journalists had obviously taken the information from the same place. A few pictures accompanied the items – old stock photos of Dr Jacobs racing, for when the stories described him as an experienced sailor. Erin reportedly limped the boat into Fiji, and had disappeared without comment. Without compelling pictures, Alex supposed perhaps it hadn't made much splash in the Australian news. He certainly never remembered hearing about it. But it was odd that such an upstanding member of the local community could depart this world with so little fanfare.

He found only two further sources – one, an item from the mainland paper listing a vale for Dr Jacobs, with interviews with the mainland hospital administration and nurses, all lauding him as a talented doctor and family man. And another, just a few lines in a side bar, saying that the investigation into his death had concluded that he had likely drowned after being lost at sea. And there, the trail seemed to end.

Alex sat back in his chair, mulling. After what Erin had said about the Sydney to Hobart, and her father being cautious and well-prepared, it didn't make much sense. They must have been unlucky. Lost overboard in a storm. Five simple words that denied the calamity of the sea. And Erin had been there in the middle of it. Frantic, scared, alone.

The idea wrapped him in knots. Because he knew exactly what that was like.

Chapter 17

Monday's meeting was the flip side of Saturday's. Erin and the others worked through issues and planning, taking two conference calls with printers and promoters in Sydney and Cairns, all while Tristan sat in the corner, barely saying a word. Erin watched him from the corner of her eye as he nursed a coffee in one of those fancy reusable cups, but didn't drink it. His attention seemed somewhere else. Erin found this quiet, brooding Tristan more unnerving than the fiery, argumentative one of the last meeting.

Because he wasn't distracted, not really.

She was almost sure he was angry.

She could feel him radiating displeasure, so intense it almost made the air shimmer around him like a mirage. The others had noticed too; Troy and Benny had dropped their voices, and Kit, who tended to be the comedian, loosening up the suppliers with jokes, had lost her sense of humour. All of them made a quick exit when Erin called a lunch break, leaving Erin and Tristan alone in the meeting room.

The ticking of laptops shutting down was the only noise for three long minutes. Erin wasn't keen to stand in front of whatever speeding truck of frustration Tristan had going on; maybe it was about a short piece in the news yesterday about some merger Drummond Industries was involved in, and it being held up or subject to government oversight, or *something*. But they were too short on time. With less than four weeks to race day, they couldn't afford impediments, especially in the form of the company's short-tempered CEO.

"Want to clue me in on what's bothering you?" she asked.

He raised an eyebrow. "I would have thought that was obvious."

She pulled her chair around to face him, wondering if he was offended that she'd skipped out on the dinner with Skye. "Sorry, my mind-reading's on the blink today."

"How's the migraine?" he asked, with a very direct stare.

So it *was* about the dinner.

"Look, Tristan, I didn't know Skye had invited you. I just didn't want to spend an evening with her questions."

Tristan stood up, pacing to the window where he squinted out into the overgrown garden, which had once lined the resort's western-most pool. He hadn't removed his suit jacket today, the slate designer grey just like the Haven thunderclouds.

"You know what I can't stand?" he said. "When people lie to me. I don't care when people don't agree with me, but lying is a weakness. It's the easy way out. And if someone's lying, I can't trust them. So I have to ask myself, why am I trusting you?"

Erin's stomach clenched and her skin tightened across the back of her neck. "I don't know what you're saying."

"Four days ago, you told me you weren't interested in a relationship. That there wasn't anyone else. Did you really expect someone wouldn't see? I was quite off the money, wasn't I, asking you about the diver boy. No, you're screwing a real genuine doctor instead."

Erin stared into Tristan's angry eyes, her cheeks burning. "That's none of your business."

"Oh, isn't it? I'd say it's my business when someone I've employed demonstrates their casual disregard for the truth."

Erin tried not to remember the last time they'd been in a real argument, but she couldn't help that day coming to mind. Years ago, on the mainland, when she'd been about to leave for a competition and he'd still been an up-and-comer, far from the high-powered business man he was today. But it was the same look in his eye, the same rage on his tongue. She couldn't even remember how that argument had started back then, but she remembered exactly the way it had ended. In the years since she'd doubted how she'd acted, then.

She didn't now.

She stood and gathered her notes, very carefully to disguise the shaking. "I'm not working for someone who can't respect the difference between my work and my private life. And I'm not going to ever be in *that* situation with you again, Tristan." She met his eyes. "Never again."

"I have no idea what you're—"

"*Never* again," she said, and walked out. Onto the parched grass crackling under her boat shoes, across the sand-covered pavers and through the construction fence. *Shit*, she thought, over and over. *Shit, shit, shit.* She'd been stupid to work with him. Shit, there went the whole deal to help the village.

He caught up with her just before the main beach.

"Erin, wait."

She kept walking.

"Just stop, will you."

She turned. "What?"

He was puffing, for once looking out of place, no longer the man in control of his world. He tried to step closer and she stepped back.

"Look, I probably deserve that," he said.

"Probably?"

"Okay, I do."

Erin huffed a breath, looking down at the sand. "You asked me before why we broke up years ago. Well you know exactly why, so don't pretend." Erin pushed the words out around the blockage in her chest. She could taste blood in her mouth again, like the night she'd walked out on him. Blood from where he'd hit her.

"I meant it when I said I don't care if you don't agree with me. You don't want to be with me, fine. But not with this guy, Erin. You don't know him."

"What's that supposed to mean?" His apparent concern had her wrongfooted.

"I mean that, as I would for any employee, I did my due diligence. I might not be the perfect white knight, but I don't want to see you with *him*."

"Crap, Tristan. You wouldn't have hired him if you thought that." But she couldn't help think of the rumours Gus had heard, about Alex being thrown out of a club. The things he kept to himself.

"He seems a reasonable doctor, I'm not denying that. Just, think about what you're doing."

"Are you done?" she managed, though she was no longer sure of herself.

"No, I'm not. I don't want to lose you from the team. Everyone's working really well and we're on a tight schedule. This all has to come together."

Erin squinted down the beach path, thinking about all their work, the role she was playing in the group. They'd never replace her at this short notice. And then what would the village say? That she'd run out on them all again. She rubbed her arms, hating the thought.

"Not to mention," Tristan said, more softly, as though he didn't really want to say this. "It would go a long way to quashing any misgivings anyone has about you around here. I know how hurtful it is when—"

"Yes, thank you," she said, curtly.

He didn't say anything for a second, then he carefully put a hand on her arm. Erin had to steel herself not to flinch. "I think the world of you, Erin. I don't care what anyone says. That's why I don't want to see you make any mistakes. Are you still in?"

Erin pulled back, feeling a thousand miles away from this place she used to call home. "Fine," she said, knowing that she couldn't walk away, except in this one moment.

Erin spent the remainder of the day numbly restocking her on-board pantry and cleaning inside the yacht cabin. Her mood, which normally improved with the fading light at sunset, remained stony. Her mother had come by for another awkward round of tea at the cabin table, which along with Tristan's warnings, had set her on edge. She wondering what time she would hear Alex's footsteps on the jetty. Last night, it had been around eight. After the long day trekking through the overgrown paths in the north of the island, he had been perfect. She hadn't wanted to talk. She wasn't sure how it was possible that today felt so much different.

She remembered other things, too. Like how last night, she'd noticed the tension within him. At the time, she thought it could be the wanting-to-know-what-we-are talk, or the I-think-we-should-remember-this-is-casual talk. Now, she didn't know what to make of him at all.

She heard him earlier than expected around seven-thirty, and didn't know what to say to him. His familiar movements climbing down the cabin stairs, even his smile, seemed odd and unfamiliar.

"What's wrong?" he said as soon as he saw her face. He pulled her into an embrace. She ducked her head. "What?" he asked again, his lips against her neck, those large warm hands caressing her back.

"Bad day," she croaked eventually, those hands melting her apprehensions. "Tristan was on the war path."

He grunted in response. "Not surprised, really. Attitude like his."

She looked up at him. "Did he say something to you, too?

"Sure, came to stick his oar in on the mainland. Not that different to any high-and-mighty management really."

Erin frowned. "Wait, when was this?"

"Weeks back. I suspect he likes to know where he can put pressure on people."

Erin breathed out. So he *wasn't* talking about today. Then she took in what he'd said.

"What sort of pressure?" she asked.

"Hang on, what did you mean, *too*?" Alex said at the same time. "What did he say to you?"

Erin tried to make light of it. "Someone must have seen you coming and going from here, that's all. That information made it back to the boardroom. He made a comment."

"I hope you told him where to stick his comments."

Erin might have smiled to herself, if the memory of Tristan's anger wasn't so fresh.

"Hey, what's the frown for?" Alex asked softly.

Erin relaxed her face. "Nothing."

"Are you worried about people knowing about this?" he said, his fingers moving across the bare skin of her back.

"Not exactly …" she answered, running her hand in turn over his chest, her doubts fluttering away to the edges of the present. "Are you?"

"I've had my share of gossip. So believe me when I say that I don't care about people talking about us."

"That right?" she asked, but she was grinning stupidly. Whatever Tristan's warnings, she liked that he didn't want it to be a secret.

"Yes," he said, walking her towards the cabin mattress, his mouth coming down warm on her lips and throat.

"Be prepared," she warned. "Your patients will be quizzing you next."

"You mean they haven't started yet?"

She laughed but he stopped kissing her, and lay down in the bunk beside her and took a breath. Erin suddenly realised he was about to say whatever it was he'd been thinking about last night.

"The other day when you were talking about your father … after that I walked around the surgery, wondering about him. I mean, he's the last doctor to use the place, and it's his handwriting in all the files. Will you tell me about him?"

Erin's limbs froze. She forced herself to relax, first her arms, then the large muscles in her legs. Of all the things she thought he was going to ask, that wasn't it. She'd started out apprehensive about who he really was, been reassured, and now he had her back at these questions.

"What do you want to know?"

"Anything. How he ran the practice. What you remember. Anything."

"Sandy could tell you that."

"I don't want to ask Sandy."

Erin shook her head. "I can't tell you much about his work. I only went to the surgery to steal jelly beans."

Alex chuckled. "Okay, forget that. What's the earliest thing you remember?"

Erin took a breath. That long-ago time was safe relative to the near-present.

"We lived in Sydney before we came up here, but I don't remember much about that. We had a pretty big house, but he was working all the time at the practice, and he didn't smile much. One year we came up here for a holiday. The resort was open then. We spent the afternoons racing around the harbour on the catamarans. Dad was a sailor, but he'd never had the time in Sydney, or that's what Mum said. I remember one day coming for a walk with Dad, down from the resort to the village. When we went home, we were only there a few weeks before he told us we were moving here. I think Mum was relieved. She was tired of Sydney."

"What did Skye think?"

"She was always happy if Mum was happy. And she liked school being two houses down. Dad set up the surgery here. He'd still go to the mainland for training or work, but we grew up here. We had Miss Rupert as our teacher for primary school, then I boarded for high school on the mainland. Mum didn't like that, but there wasn't much choice, and Dad said it was better for me. He was probably right."

Erin didn't mention that Tristan had been boarding at the same time, that their romance had begun there.

"Dad sometimes brought the boat across on weekends, and we'd go racing at the clubs up and down the coast. Those were the best times. He was happiest out on the water."

Next to her, Alex shifted. "Erin, what happened when he died?"

Erin recoiled as if a boom had just come flying towards her head. "He was lost at sea," she said softly. But the truth of that night was a painful pressure against the lie. She knew Alex sensed it.

"Do you want to talk about it?"

Erin pulled her arms around herself. "No."

"It must have been terrible," he said, soothingly, in a tone she'd heard before.

"Don't use that encouraging doctor technique on me," she snapped. "I don't want to talk about it, so back off."

In the silence that followed, Erin bit her lip. He didn't say anything more, but her anger hung between them, a signpost that her version of the events that night were not the whole truth. And now here was this man who she barely knew trying to dig into it all, while at the same time being coy about his own past. Who Tristan had cautioned her about. In that moment, Erin wondered who the hell it was she'd invited willingly into her bed.

She slid out of the bunk. "I think you'd better go."

"I'm sorry, Erin. I just didn't want the rumours. I wanted to know him like you did."

"Now," she said, turning cold. No one would know her father as she had done.

Alex tried to apologise again, but Erin couldn't hear a word he said. And then finally, she was alone on the yacht, just as she'd been that night off Fiji. Alone without her father, knowing she would never see him again.

Angry, she punched the mattress still warm from Alex's body, feeling her heart crack down the middle. She'd fallen for Alex more quickly than she'd realised, and now look what had happened. She'd let him get in under her defences. Maybe Tristan had been right.

Matters did not improve two days later when Erin returned from the team meeting to find her mother waiting at the end of the jetty.

"I'll make the tea," Erin said automatically.

"No, not today. This will only take a minute. What happened between you and Tristan?"

Her mother's firm tone was so unexpected, Erin stumbled before she said, "Nothing."

"Erin, don't do that." Her mother's voice was soft, but a steel sheet lay underneath it. "I'm not stupid, despite appearances. He was at the house having dinner on Saturday, and he's been calling Skye from the mainland. She's whipping around like a flag in a storm trying to work him out, and you're tense whenever he's mentioned. I know something's happened."

Erin felt the guilt that normally tore at her in her mother's company bury itself under these observations. Suddenly it seemed ten years ago, when they'd all been happy, and conversations like this had been a weekly occurrence.

"He wanted to get back together and I didn't," she answered finally. "He was in a mood about it."

Her mother made a noise in her throat. "Skye's saying the resort has problems in the approval process. And that Tristan's been in meetings for two days about it."

"I honestly don't know. I haven't heard anything about problems, and I think one of the team would have said something if there was."

"Skye also says she's going to some dinner with a potential sponsor on the mainland this Friday."

Erin's stomach dipped, as if cresting a rollercoaster. "Why?"

"Something about the sponsor wanting to meet a local teacher."

Erin mulled. Patrick Donnelly's mother had been a teacher; she'd seen it in the bio pack they had on him in the office. Aside from his love of endurance racing, he supported many local schools in remote communities. "Is he thinking of donating money to the school here, or something?"

"You'd have to ask Skye," said her mother. Then a veil dropped over her features, as though the effort of this conversation had become too much. Her skin paled.

"Mum?" Erin asked, dodging around the galley so fast she caught her hip on the table.

Anna pressed her hand into her temple, veins standing out against the lean fingers. She was sucking slow breaths and staring at the ground through half-lidded eyes. Erin stuck her head out towards the jetty, hoping to see someone around. But no one was.

She turned back and helped her mother sit on the bench seat.

"Mum? Mum! What's going on?"

Her mother shook her head faintly. Then Erin heard a bark down on the beach, and saw a black shape bounding after a ball. Monster. Erin stuck her head out again and yelled.

"Tim! Tim, where are you?"

The boy appeared guiltily from under the jetty, a slimy ball in his fist. His school shirt was askew, his bag slipping off his shoulder. Clearly late returning to class after lunch. "I was just—"

"Run to the surgery and fetch Alex," Erin said. "Right now."

Tim took off, calling to Monster. The minutes seemed so long passing; all Erin could do was rub her mother's back, tell her not to worry, that help was coming, until she finally heard Alex's familiar footsteps running down the jetty.

Chapter 18

Half an hour later, Erin sat chewing her nails in the surgery's waiting room, trying not to let memories crowd out the present problems. She hadn't been in the surgery since she'd come back, but almost nothing had changed. Same chairs. Same mark on the wall, the result of chasing Skye one afternoon. Erin had almost been grateful when Alex had asked her to wait a few minutes, so she didn't have to go into the consulting room.

"You feeling all right, honey?" Sandy asked, leaning on the reception desk.

Erin nodded, and continued chewing her nail.

"Can I get you anything? Cup of tea?"

"No."

After that, Sandy went instead to make herself a cup, mumbling she'd make one for Dr Bell too, for when he was finished. She'd just brought the two mugs back to reception when the consulting room door opened and Alex appeared.

"Sandy, could you come in and sit with Mrs Jacobs for a moment?"

Sandy cast a furtive glance between Alex and Erin but she took the two mugs and disappeared inside the room. Erin hardly noticed. Her heart was stretched in so many directions, her stomach flipping with worry. Alex seemed sombre; she dreaded how bad this would be. She searched him, looking for clues, but he was collected and professional, far from the man she'd thrown out of her bed. He pulled a chair in opposite her and sat down.

"She's fine for now," he began. "I think she probably fainted. She said there wasn't any pain, and the ECG is clear. I'm happy saying this was nothing to do with her heart or brain."

Erin blew out a breath. "What, then?"

"Her blood pressure's very low, which is usually a good thing. But she might be prone to fainting, especially if she stands up quickly."

"She was sitting down when this happened."

He nodded. "She's also pale on the inside of her eyelids, so she might be anaemic, too. And I don't know her, but I'm wondering if she's lost weight recently."

"I think so. I don't think she's eating well. She never drinks her tea," Erin said faintly. This was all horribly familiar.

He nodded again. "I'm going to send some blood away to check it's nothing else. I'll check out her nutritional status, a few other things too. If it's just anaemia, it's probably an iron deficiency, and we can address that pretty easily."

Erin rubbed her arms. "Can I see her now?"

"Of course."

Before she could move, Skye burst in the surgery door. "Where is she?"

"She's okay," Alex said, pointing to the consulting room. "Go ahead." Skye disappeared, leaving Alex and Erin alone in the waiting room.

"You're not going in?" he asked.

"I'll give them a minute," Erin said.

She didn't mention that at this moment, she felt she didn't have the right to be here. That she was a stranger to both of them and all because of events that had started right here where she was standing. Alex lingered nearby, another painful reminder. Only two nights ago, he'd been lying beside her.

"Erin, about the other night, I'm sorry—"

"Don't," she said. She couldn't go there now. Her mind was still reeling with her mother's sudden turn, and the possibility the resort plan might be crumbling behind closed doors. She still had a job to do, but for how long would that matter? And even if she did well, the island would never be home again. Everything was falling apart, all over again. And all these fears, she turned on Alex.

"I need you to leave me alone."

At least he didn't argue. And an hour later, when she was satisfied her mother really was fine, and insisting on returning home, Erin marched back down to the old resort. Tristan's office was empty, the door closed against the encroaching sand and sneaky nighttime possums, but she found Troy in the meeting room, packing up.

"Where's Tristan?" she asked.

"Sydney, I think," he answered.

"When's he due back?"

Troy shrugged. "Supposed to be here tomorrow for the morning meeting, but not confirmed yet."

Erin took out her phone. At least here she was right under the mobile tower and reception was excellent. Still, her call went to voicemail three times before she sent a text, telling him it was urgent. An assistant with a bouncy voice then called her back and asked her to hold. Two minutes became five, then ten, as Erin's patience ground to a nub. Sweat gathered under her hair, even in the shade of the pandanus.

Eventually, he answered, and the weariness in his voice

blunted all the barbs she might have thrown at him.

"Erin?"

"Are you coming back out tomorrow?" she asked, hating the desperation she felt.

"We're trying to resolve a few things here."

Erin detected doubt. She'd never heard him like this before.

"Tristan – is the resort in trouble?"

A long pause. "We have hit a few snags, but sometimes this happens. It's not over yet."

Erin bit her lip. She needed his reassurance. "I want to make sure it isn't. Just tell me what I need to do."

By Friday afternoon, Alex had the results of Anna's bloodwork. Just as he suspected, she looked to have garden variety anaemia, an iron deficiency. Anna looked much better when Alex dropped around to talk to her about it.

"Anaemia can sneak up," he said. "And there's a couple of tests I'd like to do to make sure there's nothing sinister going on."

"Like bowel cancer?"

Alex ghosted a smile. "Of course. I shouldn't forget how many years you worked in the surgery. But yes, I'd like to rule that out. And we should talk about your diet."

Anna sighed. "I've been a vegetarian for a long time. I suppose with the way food supply is on the island, that might be some of the problem."

"Can't be helping. Has iron deficiency been a problem for you before?"

"Never. Barely needed a doctor my whole life."

Alex made a note, resisting the urge to ask Anna about Erin.

He was still ripping himself for how he'd behaved the other night, and desperate to apologise. But he needed to remain professional, and something about Anna still concerned him.

"Mrs Jacobs, I don't know how to say this delicately, but I know your husband's passing must have been incredibly hard. And now my being here and opening the practice again, it might be dragging up memories. It's not uncommon to feel depressed, even years afterward. I know Skye and Erin are worried."

Anna glanced out the window and Alex saw the tears shine in her eyes, before she blinked and faced him again. "They're good girls. Even if they are very different. I thank you for your concern, Dr Bell. But things are as they are. Now, I imagine you'd like me to take a supplement?"

It wasn't until Alex returned to the clinic to file Anna's test results that he remembered the blood work reports he'd found two weeks ago. They showed anaemia, too.

He frowned. Anna had been adamant she'd never had this issue before. Surely she wouldn't have forgotten? He scanned over the header, printed in faded dot-matrix ink. All it gave was Dr Jacobs's details, no patient.

Then with a jolt, Alex realised the doctor's name was printed in the patient box.

So, these weren't Anna's results. These were Dr Jacobs's blood tests. Anaemia, and elevated blood glucose.

Alex was still mulling on this the next morning as he wandered down the main beach. The day was bright, Bella's Leap a clear outline against a sky stuffed with white clouds, a stiff breeze announcing good sailing weather. To cement the fact, two new boats had appeared, and he spotted a racing crew in matching shirts at the end of the jetty, downing coffees and laughing. Alex, who'd been hoping to run into Erin, or chance another visit to her yacht to apologise, noting that her boat was moored further out, unreachable unless he dragged a kayak down from the old water sports hut. In its place at the jetty was a forty-foot racing yacht, blazoned with Drummond Industries logos on the hull.

Alex abruptly realised the crew at the end of the jetty were Tristan's, and a moment too late he realised the man himself was there among them, one foot up on the railing, an expensive weather-beater vest over his racing skins.

"It's the fine doctor," declared Tristan, jumping down and jogging over. The man seemed in high spirits, but Alex hadn't forgotten his visit to the mainland hospital, or Travers' opinion, or Erin's distress.

"Mr Drummond," he said carefully, accepting the handshake, which Tristan held a fraction too long.

"Out for a walk?" he asked, the question pointed, something glittering in his eyes. "Come and meet my crew."

Alex found himself being introduced around the group of men, clearly all professional sailors, who likely staffed Tristan's racer year-round, delivering it wherever he wanted it. Alex had known plenty of sailors like them when he'd been in the club scene. Easy-going, until the competition was hot, and then they became ruthless with a tendency to hard drinking. Among them, Tristan stood out like Bella's Leap against the sky.

"We're just heading out for a light training run around the island," Tristan was now saying. "You should join us, Doctor. Best way to see the place."

The others mostly smiled at him at this point, even as Alex's stomach was diving into the waves near their feet. *Screw you, Tristan.* Alex hadn't been on a moving sailing vessel in years. Tristan couldn't have known that, but he did know Alex's history. And clearly, he was getting just the reaction he'd wanted.

"Oh, no thanks," Alex said quickly. "I'm just on my way to breakfast."

"Well, no problems there," Tristan said, pointing at one of the crew, who found a spare breakfast pie from Sandy's. "We've got you sorted. And you'll love it. You used to race up north, right?"

Tristan's carefully constructed comment plucked the nerve it was no doubt meant to. The man knew what had happened up north.

"That was a long time ago," he said. Some small voice inside him said that he could just walk away, that he could say he had to be on the ferry back to the mainland in a few hours, ready for his five days of night shifts. But Alex knew the hot current that was burning in him now wouldn't allow him to walk away. Not from this man who'd once been with Erin. Someone then put a coffee flavoured milk in Alex's hand. He glanced at the label; he was pretty sure it was a company Tristan had some kind of stake in: certainly it wasn't a brand that Sandy usually stocked.

"Not intimidated are you?" Tristan asked, pausing for just a second, before he said, "Because I know we've got a mean reputation, but there's really nothing to be worried about."

And there, in this stupid schoolyard situation in front of men he didn't even know, Alex found himself cracking the milk, and slamming it back. It was cold, just like the fear coating his heart. He didn't want to feel that way any more.

"Lead on, then," he said.

They broke the edge of the bay fifteen minutes later, running under two sails, the wind across their beam. Alex took one sidelong look at Bella's Leap, pulled on a life vest, then focused his attention back on the boat. At first, Tristan had tried to send him forward to the mast, but even the crew recognised that Alex's lack of familiarity with the boat was hardly helpful. So Alex came back to the pit, manning a winch, which put him right under Tristan's scrutiny from behind the helm.

"Going to wear that pansy life jacket the whole time?" asked Tristan jovially at one point. Alex ignored him.

He was probably imagining things, but Tristan seemed to put them through harder tacks than necessary, delighting in the spray, flirting with the danger marker that stood of the end of Bella's Leap.

Delighting, perhaps, in Alex's discomfort.

Alex kept himself very quiet, focusing all his attention on what was in front of him. He knew his face was white and that he was unable to respond to the questions or banter the other crew tried to start up with him. Instead, he watched the jib, trimming it each time they corrected course, or the wind shifted, so that even Tristan had nothing to complain about. Two of the crew patted him on the shoulder.

So, it really was like riding a bike.

Except it wasn't, not really. He might know the moves, but the feel of the boat provoked such polar emotions in him, from remorse to longing. He'd never imagined that his first time back on the water would be like this, so exhilarating and yet so poisoned. The only thing holding him together was pure, belligerent machoism. He wouldn't give Tristan the satisfaction.

What seemed an endless time later, Alex only conscious of the way the sun had shifted around them, they pulled within the bay's shelter and the crew were up and madly dropping the sails.

"How was that then?" Tristan asked, still looking like a cologne commercial at the helm.

Alex shrugged. "Maybe next time we'll get a decent wind."

He hoped that Tristan couldn't see how much the nonchalance had cost him.

They were almost to the jetty when Tristan shifted position, pretending to adjust the motor revs. "And how was Erin last night?"

Alex met Tristan's eyes the implication crackling between them like blue fire. "Anna's doing fine, now," Alex said. "Anything more is private."

Tristan straightened. "No such thing on the island," he said. "But I've been meaning to say, that change in position we spoke about a while back isn't available anymore. I figured since I hadn't heard, you weren't interested in being here full-time."

Alex had no intention of changing the arrangement, especially not with this man. He clamped his molars. "That's fine."

"Pity," Tristan said, as they pulled into the dock. "So many better things on the island. You take care, Dr Bell."

In another time and place, Alex would have dropped the guy in the ocean. At school, he'd been a boxer, and he'd never lost the slug in his right hook. But he'd done too much work these last years to forget there would be no satisfaction in doing it in front of the crew, and much as it killed him, Erin was far from his to fight over.

"You too, Tristan."

Sunday afternoon, Erin stretched her aching back as Travers and Skye flaked the mainsail, both of them subdued after their three-hour training run.

"That's it, I'm out," Skye declared, the moment the sail cover was on.

"You can't go yet – we still have to plan the next one."

"Erin, I need to prepare classes for tomorrow. So unless you're going to start paying, you can drop by later and tell me the plan. I'm already in this beyond what I agreed."

"Fine," muttered Erin, as Skye's long legs made an exit along the jetty, Travers watching her go.

"Hey, no slacking off," Erin snapped at him, knowing she was being unfair.

"Give it a rest, E. Even you have to admit that was a hard run."

Erin relented. Around the north of the island the wind had been screaming in at twenty knots, the waves white-tipped. They'd all had to work hard to stay on course, to keep the yacht level as they smashed through the swell. They'd managed, but Erin worried about the actual race when Travers would be completing the land-leg and it would just be Skye and Erin on the water. That would be tough if the conditions were like today.

That wasn't the only concern. Erin glanced at Travers, who was now slinging the jib sheets into tidy bundles and looping them over the hatch winches. She had no doubts after their time mapping the course that he had skills in navigation, but he was also damaged in his joints, which even he admitted was a disadvantage.

"What?" he asked, glancing up at her from his last rope. Erin stopped staring and reached for the instrument covers. She should only be proud of what they'd pulled together in so short a time, in no small part because Travers didn't do things by halves. When she looked back, he had taken up a piece of old rope and was practicing knots. Erin went below and dug two beers out of her ice box.

"Still working?" she asked him, sitting beside him against the cabin and offering the beer. Travers took it, but set it aside as he finished the loop of a bowline.

"Skye said there's going to be a test tomorrow," he said with a grin.

"You know she's kidding about that."

Travers leaned back, retrieving the beer. "She really isn't. She set me an exam in points of sail yesterday."

"Spending some time together, then?"

Travers tipped his beer at her, but said nothing. Instead, he squinted across the bay to where Tristan's pleasure yacht and racing yacht were anchored alongside each other.

"How's things in the evil empire?" Travers asked.

Erin detected that same simmering resentment again.

"What'd he do to you, Travers?"

A pause. "Nothing personal. It's the island, the resort. The whole thing is one big dodge. What, don't tell me you didn't know?" he added, when Erin frowned.

"I don't have anything to do with the resort development," she said.

"But surely there's talk?"

Erin shrugged. "We've been on tight schedules. Tristan has all the meetings about the development and most of them are back on the mainland. I've really no idea. Why, what do you know?"

Travers' mouth was working now, as though his beer suddenly tasted sour. He flicked his eyes from Tristan's boats to Erin.

"There still something between you and Tristan?"

"No."

"I mean, loyalty-wise. You still on his side about all this stuff?"

"Travers, what do you know?"

He tipped his head to the side. "How familiar are you with the reefs around the island?"

The question took Erin by surprise. She'd been a sailor all her life; reefs were underwater hazards, like rocks, but beyond that she'd never had any interest. She'd been snorkelling a few times as a kid, but never dived. She'd always been too ready to get back under sail.

"I know not to run into them," she admitted.

Travers shook his head. "Thought as much. There's fifteen different reefs around the island, not including the one on the wreck off the east point. I did a bunch of surveys for a university study earlier this year. They are some of the most brilliant hard coral formations I've ever seen, and the marine life ... there's some species here that the academics are excited about. Things they haven't seen before."

"If that's true, how come we're not inundated with diving tourists?"

"Probably because the island does a shit job of marketing itself. Well, that and the diving's hard like the sailing is. The currents are tricky. You need light to see the colours, because the reefs are fairly deep. Did you know you lose colours of light as you dive down?"

"Really?"

"Yeah. Progressively up the rainbow. Red disappears first. So if you cut yourself deep under, blood looks green. Cool huh?"

Erin swallowed. "I guess."

Travers grinned, but it quickly disappeared. "You ever wonder why the previous owners of the resort never developed it like Tristan's trying to?"

"Island businesses always have problems making the economics work."

Travers snorted. "That's not it. All of them had problems getting approval. Everyone wants to build a huge resort, put a marina in, things like that. And that means pollution, run-off. It all ends up out in the water. So why, suddenly, does Tristan get around that? I'm no bleeding heart hippy, Erin, but there's something dodgy going on when three previous plans all got shut down for environmental concerns, and Tristan's goes through."

"Maybe he's done other things to compensate. Recycling or something."

Travers raised his eyebrows. "Yeah, maybe."

They sat in silence drinking beers as the light faded to blue, and the first scent of fish and chips cooking came down on the breeze. Erin's stomach growled, but her attention was on the resort as it faded through sunset into the island's green. The old restaurant wing with its roof terrace was just visible against the darkening hills. It seemed an age since she'd been up there with Alex.

As if Travers could hear her thought, he said, "So what happened with the doctor?"

"What are we doing next, brushing each other's hair?"

Travers laughed. "It could do with a cut actually, if you're offering. But the guy goes off yesterday with hardly a word after moping around for a week. Not too many things put a man in that frame of mind. Believe me, I've had some experience."

"What did he say?" Erin said, annoyed Alex might have confided in Travers.

"He's not one to talk. But it's hard to hide a man walking

down a jetty in the morning back to his own house."

Erin punched him in the arm, her cheeks burning. She stood. "Come on, then. Help me move back off the jetty."

"Nope," Travers said. "First, I'm going to buy you dinner. That chip smell is driving me nuts, and we need to talk about the race plan. You'll have the perfect opportunity to start a new rumour."

"Oh, don't worry, the rumour about you and me's already done the rounds," Erin said, thinking of Tristan's comments a few weeks ago. "Though I do admire your work ethic."

"It's not entirely altruistic," Travers said, climbing over the railing and down onto the jetty. "You have a bad habit of waking me up early in the morning for this stuff. I'm just trying to avoid that tomorrow."

As she went to bed later that night, Erin couldn't help staring out at the ocean surface, glassy and starlit in the night. She'd never thought much about what was under it before, or about the resort redevelopment. It wasn't her department. But she had seen the reality of what went into to organising a regatta – the iceberg of work and plans and workarounds that stretched under the visible tip. And now, she wondered what the resort was hiding beneath its glossy-brochure surface.

Chapter 19

By Wednesday, Tristan had rejoined the meetings, and seemed in a much better mood. Skye had returned from the potential sponsor's dinner the night before in great excitement over details she couldn't talk about. So it was clear that while Erin had been moved from the inner circle, whatever calamity had been bearing on Tristan's mind last week seemed to have passed. He was back to the Tristan who'd come to the town meeting: confident, reassuring, ready to conquer the world. The whole racing team played off his energy, and they soon had achievements to celebrate. Two more high-profile teams had signed on for the land-sea race, the cable channel was keen to broadcast again, and a chandlery had taken up one of the lower tier sponsorships.

"Not a Rolex-level deal, but that's progress," Tristan said.

Erin shifted in her seat, uneasy. A week ago, he'd have chastised them for not upselling. His change of mood made no sense to her, but no one else seemed to notice. Maybe she was imagining it.

Or maybe it was just that Alex was due back tomorrow, and she couldn't think straight after their argument.

"We have less than two weeks," Tristan said, finishing up. "Our courses are set down, and we have a good long-range weather forecast. Patrick Donnelly's on board to sponsor this time around, but we need to convince him to commit for the long-haul. Now his divorce is behind him, he's looking for distraction and he has the time, so let's make sure we don't give him any reason to doubt the future of this place. Okay, that's it. Work hard, and I'll see you all tomorrow."

Buoyed on Tristan's praise, the team stuck around to cover off on a number of items they wanted sorted. Erin asked them to excuse her for a minute and ducked out, following Tristan back to his office in the resort's old reception area.

While most of the old furniture had been cleared out, a damp smell persisted that not even strong espresso could compete with. There were roots growing from a hallway ceiling in the back. Stacks of paper had grown around the desk since Erin had last come in here, mostly large architectural plans marked in highlighter and red pen. Tristan went straight to the coffee machine.

"Tristan," Erin said, pausing at the door. "Can I have a word?"

"Just one?"

She perched on the edge of the visitor's chair beside his desk, thinking about how to begin.

"The dinner went well," he said. "You know, your sister really is quite a woman. Patrick was extremely impressed with her work at the school. I think he signed up on the spot."

Erin's heart twisted, just a little. She would be the first to admit Skye was the better person to cajole sponsors, if her work with the village events was anything to go by. But she couldn't help feel rejected, replaced.

"It's not about that," she managed. "It's about the resort, and the development."

"Oh?"

"I heard that the last three owners had plans rejected because of an environmental impact problem. I was wondering how you managed to pass it through the regulators."

Tristan extracted his cup from the machine. "It was an effort," he said, after just the barest pause. "There's marine park areas out there, and we can't get around the fact that more people means more potential for pollution. Run-off, litter, emissions, all that stuff. We're putting in a solar farm and a black-water system to keep all the waste out of the bay."

"What about the marina?"

Tristan gave a slight lift of his shoulders. "We won't allow dumping, and we're finding other ways to combat the water quality degradation. I'm confident."

"So it isn't actually approved yet?"

She saw the flicker of irritation in his face. "It will be. We've worked very hard to ensure the plans will pass. You don't have to worry about that."

"I'm not worried."

He popped his eyebrows playfully, and Erin relaxed. She'd been dreading asking him these questions, but he didn't seem fazed. Travers must have it all wrong.

"Where's this all coming from?" Tristan asked.

"I love the island, that's all. Thought I had to ask."

"I grew up here too, you know," he said, setting his mug down on the desk.

"Of course, I know that—"

"Maybe you should spend less time with people who didn't."

Erin paused, all her caution flags flying up again. "I'd better go."

"Would you like to see the plans? Would that satisfy you?" he said. "They're right here."

"Maybe another time."

"Erin," he said, so sharply she stopped at the door. "Remember what your job is. Land me a big sponsor. If not Patrick, then someone else. I mean it."

Erin went back to work with her heart thumping in her chest. What had just happened? Tristan was playing the calm-sailing boss in meetings, but something else was bringing his barbs out. Or maybe it was that jealous streak again. He clearly didn't like Travers, and had probably guessed that was where Erin had heard rumours. She bit her lip, knowing the only thing she controlled was whether the next race went ahead and the regatta in the long term. Tristan was right: they needed that sponsor.

When she got back to the yacht, she dug in the old ice-cream container she kept under the radio. At the bottom, among the bits of chord, fishing sinkers, pegs, and screws was Ivan's business card. The personal mobile number scrawled on the back was still legible. Erin played with the card. Ivan was the kind of sponsor Tristan would salivate over, and since he'd called her after the pilot race win, she knew he didn't hold her leaving his crew against her.

She took her phone out and dialled.

While Erin was dialling, Alex was near the end of a punishing five days of work on the mainland. To start with, Karen – the regular doctor – had dashed home to Cairns to her sick mother, leaving Alex and Wendy plugging the roster with a handful of locums. Short-staffed, they'd been faced with a nasty car wreck at two am one morning, needing three seriously injured patients evacuated to the big hospital in Townsville. Alex had worked flat-out trying to stabilise the victims, who were little older than teenagers. By the time the last had left on the chopper and all the paperwork complete, it was ten in the morning. So wired he'd been unable to sleep, he then had to be back at work at five in the evening.

The thing that had kept him going through all of it was a resolve to see Erin when he got back to the island. But circumstance conspired against him from the moment his toes hit the Haven sand. Several land-sea race teams had sent scouts ahead to reconnoitre the land course, and a good number of interested spectators had done the same. So his waiting room was full of sprained ankles and oyster shell cuts, and travellers with gyppy belly from drinking the untreated island water.

The village was buzzing with excitement for the upcoming race. Accommodation was filling up and the bakery and cafe were enjoying full tables at night. A concert had been planned for the evening of the race, and rumours were flying that celebrities would be making an appearance — *Hugh Jackman*, whispered Sandy, as if the full power of her voice would shatter the possibility. Alex couldn't begrudge anyone the much needed revenue, even when the village's boon had added to an already overworked week.

But all this activity meant that Erin had been elusive. Travers had been out on training runs with her over the weekend while Alex was stuck in the clinic, and her evenings were full of meetings. Her yacht — still moored inaccessibly off the jetty — had still been dark when his last patient had left. More than once, Alex had walked down the main beach under the stars, Bella's Leap backlit in the full moon, hoping to run into her returning from the old resort. It hadn't happened.

Now it was Friday and he had only a day until returning to

the mainland again. The moon had waned to a fat quarter, throwing silvery light across the sand and the piers of the jetty. Alex trudged along the waterline, wondering whether to call in on Travers. Then, he spotted someone sitting half-way along the jetty, and his heart stopped.

Erin.

She had an open packet of fish and chips, a bottle of ginger beer open alongside. His palms prickled as he climbed the jetty and she glanced around. Even in her bad books, she made him absolutely giddy. She frowned when she saw him, but there were tired circles under her eyes.

"Can I sit down?" he asked.

"Only if you can eat a kilo of chips. I think they thought I was feeding Travers again."

He felt a glimmer of hope. Erin had crossed her arms, but she wasn't telling him to piss off either.

"Beautiful night," Alex said as he sat. Out of the jetty lights, the bay was black glass, the breeze lazy. "Thought Haven had a reputation for bad weather."

"Unexpected weather," Erin said. "When it's quiet like this, you can bet it's brewing something. See the way the water's breaking on the point? That swirl?"

Alex peered through the darkness, but all he could make out was the occasional silent plume of spray catching the moonlight. He could never read signs in the darkness.

"Erin, I've been wanting to talk to you all week."

"I've been busy." She crammed another few chips in her mouth, wiping salt across her knee.

"To apologise."

"For what?" she asked, around her mouthful.

Alex plucked a chip from the packet and squeezed its soft

sides. "For being an insensitive ass."

"And?"

He smiled. "And … anything else I did to upset you."

Erin flicked a glance at him, and he saw the possibility of forgiveness. "You kinda suck at apologies," she said.

He was taking a breath to make a joke, to build more in this wall of repair when his phone rang. Alex pulled it out, and saw the clinic number. "Let this not be another I-can't-leave-the-toilet call," he muttered, and was rewarded to see Erin smile.

But Sandy's voice sobered him immediately. "It's Helmut," she said down the line. "Stella called. He's having trouble breathing."

A chill ran down Alex's arms. He was on his feet in an instant. "He's still at the hut?"

"Yes. She didn't think he could move. She sounded terrified."

Alex pinched the bridge of his nose, his thoughts turning together like well-oiled gears. "Sandy, grab my bag from the surgery and come down to the jetty. After that, find Travers and tell him bring the portable stretcher up to Helmut's. Then I need you to stay at the surgery by the phone. Got it? Now *run*."

He then had to turn to Erin, who had scrambled up, her brow furrowed in concern. "What's going on?"

"Do you know your way up to Helmut's hut in the dark? I need you to show me. He's sick."

Erin ran to the jetty's end and grabbed two torches from the courtesy box. Then they were running together, across the sand, meeting Sandy huffing under the weight of the mobile medical kit. Alex grabbed the case, then he was sprinting after Erin, down the long arc of beach and towards the dark headland.

He had no idea how Erin navigated through the bush. To

Alex, it seemed an endless uphill climb in bobbing torchlight over no discernible path, his feet and head crashing against rocks and branches. By the time they reached the hut, he was soaked in sweat, his lungs painful with each breath. But the scene he found inside threw an icy bucket of water over him.

"Thank god," Stella exclaimed as she pulled them inside. Her mascara had run, her face pale and panicked. "He only had a sniffle this afternoon."

Helmut sat in a chair in the main gallery, his arms propped on his knees, his wiry hair damp. Through the collar of his shirt, Alex could see all the accessory muscles struggling to pull in each breath.

"Helmut, it's Alex," he said, kneeling by the chair. "How long has it been like this?"

Helmut tried to speak, but he sounded like his mouth was full of marbles. A string of drool escaped his lips and smacked the floor. Alex felt a cold dread.

"It's been maybe forty minutes now," Stella said, her voice wobbling. "He said it was just a sore throat!"

"Do you need me?" Erin asked quickly, and when Alex shook his head, "Then I'll run back and meet Travers."

A second later, Alex was alone with Helmut and Stella. With rapid movements, he took pulse and counted the respirations, then felt over Helmut's throat, which made the artist jump like he'd been branded. Alex pulled his bag open, acutely aware that he was a long way from a hospital.

"Stella, he allergic to anything? Or complain of being bitten by anything?"

"No, nothing."

"Call the clinic again. Tell Sandy to organise an evac right now."

Alex heard a rumble come into Helmut's breaths, an audible noise on the inhale. Stridor. That was not good. Not good.

Alex could see where this was going. Helmut was finding each breath harder and harder, his airway clearly obstructed. Left much longer, he might not be able to breathe at all. As Stella spoke to Sandy, he began pulling out packets, hoping with all the good luck he had that Travers was nearly here.

He motioned for Stella to give him the phone. "Sandy, this is a cat one emergency. Get them here asap. Stella will stay on the phone."

"What's happening?" Stella begged.

The artist's eyes flickered over Alex, full of fear. "I think this is epiglottitis. That's when the flap that keeps your food pipe separate from your airway swells up. Kids get it a lot, but in an adult it's really serious. That noise you're making means your airway's closing up. We've got a plane coming, so my job is to keep you breathing until we get you to hospital."

He squeezed Helmut's hand. "I am absolutely going to get you through this, but I need to make you a new airway – like on the movies, a tube into your throat, do you understand?"

Helmut's eyes flashed to Stella, then he nodded. At that moment, Alex heard heavy footsteps crashing towards the hut. Erin and Travers appeared, the medic hauling another medical kit like a bandolier and a collapsed mobile stretcher on his back. Travers was sweating, but his eyes were calm as he took in the situation.

"What are we doing, doc?"

"Emergency cric, then we need to transfer down to the airstrip."

"Right." In ten seconds flat, Travers had assembled the stretcher, and was back helping Alex prepare.

"Don't suppose you've got a tracheostomy tube in that bag?" Alex asked.

"Nah, but I've got a fourteen gauge cannula. You got a bag?"

In no time, they had helped Helmut to the stretcher. Alex knew he would have to work fast; the stridor was worse, and Helmut found breathing even harder on his back. Travers had snapped on gloves and was wiping Helmut's throat with antiseptic, and handing across the cannula, attached to a syringe of saline. Alex quickly numbed the area with local anaesthetic, then palpated the cartilages with his left hand, looking for the membrane between.

There.

Angling down, he slipped the needle through the membrane, withdrawing the plunger until he saw air bubbles in the syringe. "Yep, got it," he said, pushing the cannula down and removing the core. Travers was ready with a syringe connector and the bag. The cannula was narrow, so they had to help Helmut breathe, but the stridor was gone.

They heard the evac plane land when they were almost down the hill. Travers insisted on taking the heavy head end of the stretcher, while Stella, Erin and Alex rotated carrying the other two handles. By the time they were half-way past the old resort, they saw Sandy and two paramedics rushing towards them and soon, the weight was gone and Helmut was loaded into the plane. Stella climbed in, then Alex followed, knowing he could help and that he would be on shift at the mainland hospital tomorrow anyway.

As the door closed, he caught sight of Erin, so small next to Travers on the edge of the runway. Her hair and skin were pale in the lone light post, just like the woman he'd imagined on Bella's Leap those weeks ago. Then the plane lifted towards the mainland, and he left her behind.

The next morning, Alex dropped by the hospital early where Stella wrapped him in a grateful hug. She was much more collected this morning, fresh in a borrowed set of scrubs, her hair plaited in a rope down her back.

"Thank you so much, Dr Alex. You are a miracle," she said, rubbing his back.

"How is he?" Alex asked.

"Still on the tube, but the doctor says he's responding well to the antibiotics, and they should be able to remove it soon. I can't tell you how grateful I was that you were there. You must take a job permanently – this just proves that we can't be without you."

"I'm glad I was there," he said, knowing that Helmut could easily have died if it had happened just a day later, when Alex had been back on the mainland. He kept that to himself and allowed Stella to draw him down to the hospital canteen, where she insisted on paying for breakfast. They sat in the window seat, where they could see the ocean. The sea was a grey slab today, the sky thick with clouds that promised humidity, but no relief in rain. Great Haven was not even visible over the horizon.

"I've told him before how dangerous it is living up on that cliff at our age," Stella was saying. "But he won't leave. 'The muse is too strong,' he says."

"It is a beautiful spot," Alex said carefully. "If a little ... macabre."

"Oh yes, I mean, what could be more macabre than a murder? No wonder he's so obsessed with her. When I first came to the island, I wondered if Bella would be the death of him. I'm just glad it wasn't this time."

Alex paused with his coffee half-way to his lips. "Did you say murder?"

Stella nodded sagely. "Of course. What, you didn't think Bella threw herself off the cliff, did you?"

"Well, I just assumed … Bella's Leap and all."

"Just a name. I suppose they might have thought it was suicide after everything that had happened to her, but it just doesn't make any sense. Think about it. She comes out to the island with her husband. He dies early, but she stays on running the place, isolated, only dogs for company. Builds it into a prosperous place, good relationship with the Elders, even after all that earlier trouble and the people who'd failed before her. Then suddenly, at the end, she kills herself? No, that's not Bella. She met a foul end. And that's why she's still here."

Stella crossed herself.

Alex rotated the cup in his hands. "Why are you telling me this? Is it like the Masons? I've saved the life of a local, so I get the real story?"

Stella's laugh tinkled like crystal. "Oh, there's lots of versions of Bella's story. Helmut says he knows what really happened. But then, he does paint ghosts. Maybe in another ten years, he'll tell me too and confirm my suspicions. All I know is that she didn't kill herself. It all feels more sinister than that."

All this secrecy was still turning in Alex's mind later, even after he'd been to the visiting doctor's flat to sleep, and after he'd dealt with the first cases of the evening. Unresolved questions always niggled him. So, in a quiet early hour in the ED – when he should have been sleeping – he found himself opening the hospital records catalogue.

Bryan Jacobs, he typed.

Only one record came back on the search, and the birth date was correct. But when he opened the record, it appeared to be empty. No clinical notes, just a few blood tests.

"Hey, Wendy, why would a patient's records be blank?"

The triage nurse wandered over with a yawn, stirring sugar into her third black tea since midnight. She peered at the screen. "They only digitised the files a few years ago. Maybe they missed this one."

"Why's there blood results in it, then?"

"Bloods went digital earlier. If you want the file, you'll have to go down to the stacks."

So that was how Alex found himself in the dusty basement, trolling through curling folders in a room that smelled like an old gym sock. After ten minutes, he had to admit the file wasn't there. Ten other *Jacobs*, but none for Bryan.

"Couldn't find it," he explained, when he returned empty handed.

"These bloods are interesting, though," Wendy said, clicking through the screens. "Low albumin, elevated lipase, liver function's a bit off, too."

Alex leaned in and flipped through the screen. "CA's up too," he said grimly.

"That's a tumour marker, isn't it?"

"Yeah."

Wendy glanced at the top of the screen. "This the same Jacobs you were asking about a few weeks back?"

Alex closed the file down and made a non-committal sound. Fortunately Wendy shrugged and went back to her tea. But Alex knew he had stumbled onto something. Dr Jacobs had been sick before his mysterious accident at sea. Where her father was concerned, he knew Erin didn't want to talk, and Alex had crossed the line: he'd used his position to get information she hadn't volunteered. Maybe she hadn't even known.

Alex sighed. Either way, it wouldn't help make things right with her.

Chapter 20

The week of the big race arrived with disturbing speed. For Erin, the shift in focus was a relief after six days of the whole village talking about what had happened with Helmut. Even absent on the mainland, Alex was the hero of the hour. Some in the village had started a petition to offer Alex a full-time position, and some kind of role for Travers, too. They might complain that Helmut was aloof, but the village knew how important he was to the island, and the incident had reminded everyone of their own mortality. No one liked to think of something similar happening again when the doctor was away.

Erin quietly watched these developments with some alarm, because Tristan was irritated by the constant focus on someone other than him. At the same time, she dearly wanted to know how Alex was.

After his abrupt and dramatic departure with Helmut, she'd received only second-hand information from Sandy. She wanted Alex to call her, to hear his voice, to take up from where they'd left off at the jetty. She kept looking at her phone all through the long meetings. The reception was fantastic, but he didn't call. Maybe their tentative reconnection had been too brief. So she had no choice but to bury herself in the frantic work of the last week.

She did have one piece of good news – Ivan, as a potential

mega sponsor, had agreed to meet her after the race was over. For the moment, she kept it to herself. Meetings weren't meetings until they happened.

On the Friday evening, the team closed out the last check before the big day. The island had been steadily filling with people, as it had before the last race. Space in the bay was scarce, with many yachts seeking out vantages in the other protected bays around the island, then zipping into the jetty in their tenders for supplies.

Cut adrift with nothing to do, Erin wandered up the beach towards Travers' cabin, seeing the jetty and beach covered in tinnies, the owners either eating in the cafe or taking advantage of the store's extended trading hours. She hoped for another smooth success.

She found Travers on his porch, gear spread out before him and a frown in his face.

"What's up?" she asked.

"Have a look at this. Tell me what you think," he said, handing over a regulator assembly from his dive gear.

Erin turned it over in her hands. It resembled a giant, black, four-legged spider. "What am I looking at?"

"The tube, down at the regulator end."

Erin peered, seeing tiny splits in the hose. "It's perished?"

"Nope," Travers said. "That reg was new this year, and I take very good care of my gear. Someone did that deliberately. I've also got a cut weight belt here. Two of my tanks have been bled dry, and they murdered the shoes I was going to wear for the land-leg."

"They got your *shoes*?"

In response, Travers held up an expensive pair of trainers, which had been slashed from the tongue to toe.

"I think someone's trying to knobble us."

"People aren't *that* competitive," Erin said. This behaviour didn't fit with the sailing world she knew. "Anything else damaged?"

"One of my walking poles was snapped. And do you want to know where all this stuff was, Erin?"

"Where?"

"In my goddamn house."

Erin didn't know what to say after that. Crime on the island was unheard of. It made sense that if someone had done this, it might be someone coming in for the race. But she still couldn't believe someone would do it maliciously.

"Maybe it was just some kids, mucking around."

Travers made a dismissive noise, then took the gear back inside, muttering about installing cameras. Erin steered him to Gus's, where they were able to replace his shoes, and find an aluminium tube section to replace the broken pole. After that, Travers pulled Erin towards the jetty. "And we're going to check everything on your boat, too."

An hour later, satisfied that all the safety gear, ropes and sails were intact, they sat on the deck eating another round of fish and chips from the cafe.

"I'll sleep on the deck tonight," Travers said finally, as he polished off his ginger beer. "Can't be too careful."

"What? No you won't," she argued. "This has gone far enough. Go home and sleep in your bed. We need you in top condition tomorrow, not bleary-eyed from squashing your man-frame onto a deck cushion."

Travers just shredded some of the chip paper. Erin peered at him, wondering. Travers was always intense, but not jumpy. "What's this really about? You have a fight with Skye or something?"

He grunted. "You say that like I was in with a chance to begin with."

"Oh," she said softly, realising that Travers must have had his heart handed back to him, and in quite a battered state. "I'm sorry Travers. I thought she really liked you."

"Yeah, me too. But that was before poncy boy started inviting her to meetings again. It's hard to compete with a millionaire."

"Tristan?"

"Unless you know any other millionaires around here."

Erin's stomach dived. So Skye was still pursuing Tristan.

"Dammit, I hoped that was done," she said, her chest feeling as if she was pinned to the bottom of the ocean.

"I have to tell you, Erin, I've done this before and it doesn't get any easier. I'm just glad I'm not on the boat with her tomorrow. I don't think I can keep a civil tongue in my head. I'm not a gentleman, in case you hadn't noticed."

To Erin, the land-sea race had a different atmosphere to the pilot event: more intensity, less fun. The pilot race had set expectations for success and big prize money was on offer. So despite the short notice, the field was huge.

Travers went off to the land-race briefing in an old army shirt and compression leggings, his mouth a tight line, a three-litre water pack on his back. Erin and Skye headed out to the start line well ahead of time. Skye complained the whole way out, and didn't let up as they had to sit waiting, the only boat to have come out so early.

"Quit whining," Erin snapped. "It's not like there was

anything else to do. And I wanted to see what the wind pressure was doing out here."

"Same as what it is in the bay. I could have gone down to the sponsor's tent for another half an hour. Tristan—"

"Wow, just to moon over Tristan for a few more minutes?"

Skye gave her a dirty look. "Don't get stuck into me about that. You had your chance."

Erin stared into the water. The ocean rolled under the yacht, the sky an open and endless blue. Her sister was leaving herself open for hurt, but Erin held her frustration tight, so she wouldn't say anything worse, not when they were about to race. She went below and pulled two cans of soft drink from the cooler.

"I'm sorry about what I said," she said, when she re-emerged, handing across Skye's favourite passionfruit flavour. "It's just ... Skye, you and Tristan, is it serious?"

"What if it is?"

Erin closed her eyes, feeling a stab of worry. Skye's eyes were shining, her smile pure and sunny. She didn't know what Erin did.

"Skye ... Tristan might not be the kind of person you think he is."

"And what's that supposed to mean?"

"Just be careful, okay?"

Skye stood. "Oh, I see. You can't have him, so I can't either?"

"That's not what I'm saying!" Erin screwed her hands into fists, focusing on the green blob of Great Haven, the golden strip of sand capped with crowds. "Look, Skye, I've never told anyone the reason that Tristan and I broke up, but I think you should know."

She glanced up to see Skye had perched on the cabin edge, her long brown legs disappearing into her boat shorts, her drink balanced between her feet. Listening.

Erin puffed a breath. Out under the sun, the sounds of the rigging wire tinking against the mast, she was too exposed to speak of these things. But if she didn't now, perhaps she never would.

"I won't deny we used to fight a lot," she began. In fact, that had probably been part of the attraction. Tristan liked sparring with her. At least, when he was in a good mood. "We had some bad arguments. Once, I locked him out of the hotel for an hour. But when I let him back in, he was laughing. That was how it used to go. Fight first, then he'd laugh and say how much he'd enjoyed it."

"So what?"

"Something changed, that first year he was starting his business. He wasn't in such a good mood anymore. Pickier too. The arguments we'd always had used to start over small things, but then nothing particularly would start it. And then he began finding reasons to kick off a fight. If I'd left a race shirt on the bath, or eaten the last biscuit."

"This story going somewhere?"

Erin looked her sister in the eye. "He hit me, Skye."

Skye jerked. "When?"

"One night, when I left a tea bag in the sink. I'd never seen him that mad. That was over six years ago." Erin rubbed the centre of her chest, remembering what that moment had felt like. The shock and dismay of seeing Tristan as someone she didn't know. "He tried to apologise, but I knew that was the end. Dad always said—"

She cut herself off. Her father had given her strong

convictions about how men were supposed to behave. The moment Tristan crossed that line, she'd known they were done.

She glanced at Skye. " I just don't want you to have the same experience. That's all I wanted to say."

Erin saw the flash of doubt in Skye's expression before it hardened. "I can look after myself, thanks very much."

Skye prowled up to the bow to check the spinnaker pole. Erin sighed. Just as it was with her mother, it seemed so many years since she and her sister had felt a bond. And now, Erin knew she'd poisoned their sail.

Skye entered brooding mode, every action executed with unnecessary vigour, not speaking unless it was necessary. Even as the number of yachts grew, and began to circle the start line. No matter what Erin said, she couldn't recover the collegiate tone they'd had in training runs. Without Travers, there was no buffer between them, no one to lighten the mood with stupid jokes. So when the starting guns finally fired, the cheer from the shore sounded hollow.

They made a reasonable start. Erin knew the round-island racers would be starting up the hill climb past Bella's Leap, then across past the Helmut's studio. Poor Helmut — he'd only just come back to the island, but would probably have a canvas out ready to capture the boats hurling around the headland. As they rounded the artist's point, Erin caught a glimpse of runners on the island trail, just flashes of red and orange and pink.

"Doing pretty well. We think you'll find extra pressure ahead," came the strategist in her ear. After the last race, the guys on shore had backed off with their advice. Erin could already see the darkening surface of the water ahead. They were in for a blustery race.

Blustery became gruelling. The moment they were out of the

island's shadow, the wind roared across the beam, until Erin could barely hear the voice in her ear. By the time they were turning at the next mark, both she and Skye were salt crusted, their arms aching, the good position they'd fought for beginning to slip.

"Keep it tight on the next turn," Skye yelled.

Erin tried, but another yacht was chasing them on the inside, putting them in a wind shadow. Desperation set in when the strategist crackled in to say that Travers was pacing well on the land race, keeping in touch with the top ten. But Erin couldn't avoid the fact that they weren't as fast as the boat alongside, who streaked into the tighter turn, the name *Gale Abandon* scrawled down her hull. Erin had to round the mark wider, losing momentum, and she fumbled the mainsail trim while Skye was working on the headsail.

"Chrissakes focus!" Skye yelled.

Then, just when the wind snapped back, the *Fair Winds* lurched. The stern dug in, then she pitched forward, sending Skye and Erin both sprawling. Erin watched the rear winch rush up into her face. A heavy *thunk* stopped her, and she tasted blood. Her mouth was numb. Dazed, Erin scrambled to her knees knowing something was badly wrong, fumbling for the wheel to maintain control. Pain came pounding into her cheek as she tried to regain footing. The mainsail dropped down. What was Skye doing?

But Skye was screaming, "The halyard! We lost the halyard!"

Erin looked up and saw the top of the mainsail slipping down the mast, ragged end of its rope was whipping like a cut snake. Worse, the foresail's halyard was also gone, its canvas crumpling to the deck, too.

Erin let the wheel go as she registered what had happened.

There was nothing to do now but come around into the wind and drop what was left of the sails. They'd just lost the race.

They limped back into shore hours later, after the motor had failed to start and they'd had to radio for a tow. Skye had wordlessly tried to patch up her face, but Erin shook her off. The swelling was tight and painful, but it wasn't bleeding. She'd deal with it later.

By the time they'd managed to moor and find a lift back to the jetty, the prize ceremony was already under way. Still, a few reporters were waiting, and Erin found herself with fluffy microphones under her chin.

"Disappointing result, Erin. Any words about the race?"

"Looks like you copped quite a hit. Can you tell us what happened?"

Erin fended them off, mumbling that it was the nature of racing. But speaking pulled painfully at her cheek and her words slurred, making her sound drunk. As a featured entrant, she didn't think it could be worse than not finishing, but this was.

Tristan said as much as soon as they reached the marshalling tent. "This never would have happened if you'd done what I asked and raced one of the corporate boats. At least their gear is in working order."

"It was just bad luck, Tristan. Come on, when do two halyards break at once?"

But she couldn't look him in the eye. She could feel other people's attention on her like the scorching sun, fingers pointing at her face.

"For god's sake go and get cleaned up. We need you back at the sponsor's party."

Erin couldn't face it. Instead, she slipped away, desperate to find Travers and apologise for letting him down.

"Like I care about winning," he said, when she eventually found him drinking beer in the public section of the beach, an ice pack on his knee. He gently took her elbow and stiffly steered her away from the crowd, towards the old water sports hut, which had been roped off. Ignoring the cordon, he pulled her into the shade of the awning. "Let me look at your face."

She stood still, wincing while he gently probed her cheek.

"You didn't knock out any teeth?"

"No, thank crud."

"You going back down to the party?"

She shook her head.

"Well, put some ice on your face. Alex is tied up with a guy who had a heart attack on the beach. You can watch while I sort out your yacht, but you need to show him your face after that. You might have broken something."

"Watch, hey?"

"Supervise. Give orders, if you must. I know how these things go."

Erin looked down the beach, a tiny thread of goodwill stitching itself back into her attitude. The crowd at least seemed to be having a good time. People were swimming, inhaling Dagwood dogs and fairy floss, and a frozen slushie cart Sandy had hired was doing spectacular trade. She turned back to Travers.

"How good are you at going up a mast?"

"You remember finding me up a coconut tree, right?" He looked down at himself. "Erin, I weigh close to a hundred kilos. I've seen the guys they winch up to the top. They're air on bones."

"Then we're just going to have to get creative."

In the end, Erin was the one who went up the mast, hoisted on a spinnaker rope. She wanted to see if the halyards had frayed on something sharp at the mast top. The view from up there was spectacular and dizzying. Erin felt as though she were flying, and could glide right across to Bella's Leap on a wingbeat. It would have been nice to escape her problems so easily; she could find no issues with the mast. Nothing that could explain the gear breakage, especially on the main halyard, which had been brand new.

"You realise you're being held up there by the same kind of rope that you broke today?" was all Travers said.

As the sun was going down, Travers left, hauling the torn jib with him to Gus's. The two broken halyards had been looped onto the deck. A late mainland transit boat was just leaving the jetty, packed to the railings with spectators. Erin turned away. Her cheek was painful now, a pulse snapping in her skin with each heartbeat. It made her feel sick. She'd never be able to sleep like this. Besides, she'd promised Travers she'd get it checked.

On dark, she trekked up the beach and towards the surgery. The sand was still a sunlit warm, the cicadas drumming. From deeper in the village came the rumble of a crowd and piped music. The concert must be about to start.

The lights were all off in the surgery. She peered in the windows and found it empty, so she walked around the back. Pink Floyd's "Comfortably Numb" played softly through the window, a song she'd last heard in Bermuda. She could only wish for the sentiment of the lyrics.

With hesitation, she knocked.

The music turned down, and the door swung open. Alex looked like he'd just gotten up, his hair ruffled, shirt creased.

"Sorry, I didn't mean to wake you."

"Wait a sec," he said, catching her hand so she couldn't take off. "Come here."

He pulled her inside out of the blues and greys of the night and into the soft lemon light from his bedside lamp. Erin tried to stop herself looking around, but she couldn't help it. The small room was nearly filled with the double bed. Three shirts hung in the open closet, a suitcase underneath. A book was on the bedside table, a receipt stuck in to mark the page.

He tipped her chin gently, his gaze intent on her face. She knew he must just be being professional, but Erin was suddenly wondered how hideous she was. Was she going to be black and blue in two days when she met Ivan? Would that even go ahead now?

"Is it bad?" she asked. "I haven't dared look."

"Do you want to see?"

She shook her head, but he pulled her over to the mirror on the wall, his hands gentle. A bruise ran from the corner of her mouth and over the swell of her cheek, where the skin was red and mottled. Her lip had split, the spot scabbed over.

"See?" he said. "Not so bad. Just early for Halloween."

Erin put her hands up to her face, shaking her head, the upset of the day and the pain worming under her eyelids and threatening tears. Alex's hands guided her to the bed and sat her down.

"Hurting?"

She nodded.

"Let me make sure there's no serious damage, ok?"

He didn't ask her to come through into the clinic, simply sat alongside her on the bed, his hands sure as he tested each of the nerves in her face. Then, when he was fairly sure nothing was broken, he went to find her tablets for the pain. All the time, Pink Floyd played in the background, reminding Erin of summers on the island – crisp chips and tomato sauce, hot sand and cool fruity ice blocks.

"I wouldn't have picked you for a Floyd fan," she said when he returned from the surgery. "Though this is the only song I can think of that's about both medicine and sailing."

"I found the CD in the cupboard. Listen Erin, I want to apologise for what I said to you last time. Your father is none of my business. I was out of line. Way out."

He sat beside her again, the mattress shifting her towards him. "I don't want something like that to be the reason this never went anywhere. I want you to still be here tomorrow morning." He was looking down at the floor, putting it all out there.

Erin sucked a breath. She was tired and sore but something inside her responded. After the hellish week and the disappointments of the race, he was safe harbour. She wanted to believe that it could work.

She licked her sore lip, remembering the last time he'd been on her boat. Her fingers reached out to undo his top button, a smile suddenly tugging the sore parts of her face.

"Why doctor, are you going to take advantage of your patient?" she whispered.

His eyes were serious as he skimmed his thumbs along her jaw. "I'm not your doctor," he said. "I'm your lover."

Chapter 21

Erin surfaced from sleep some hours later, lingering in the soft warmth of the covers. As she rose closer to fully awake, her body knew something was different. The world was still; not a ripple moved the boat beneath her, almost as if she were on shore.

She cracked an eyelid. Alex lay beside her, his chest gently rising and falling, the sheets twisted around them both. It wasn't her cabin. A proper room with a lofting roof, the walls covered with familiar green wallpaper. The bookcase lining the opposite wall. Erin had slept in here once when her father had been working late one night, watching over Gus when he'd had his heart problems. This night was like that again, a weight of atmosphere sitting heavily on her shoulders. Rain was coming.

Erin pushed her feet to the carpet and stood. Alex never stirred, as though he wasn't really here. He was a shadow, an echo of the day world. Maybe, if Erin just glided down the hall to the consulting room, she would find her father there again.

The hall tiles were cold, sending shivers across her skin. She crept towards the waiting area, all exactly as it had been the last time she'd dared come in here. The same blue plastic chairs, the same desk, the same tub of worn wooden toys. All shadowed in midnight blues, the smallest sliver of moon hanging outside the window.

She ran her fingers along the smooth edge of the desk, watching the black space beyond the open consulting room door creep towards her. She half-expected her father to emerge, to put his hand on her shoulder, kiss her hand and guide her back to bed as he had that night. But he didn't. She stood in the doorway of his room, the contents resolving slowly, like ships raised from a gloomy sea floor. The pale examination couch, the hard edge of the sink. Her father would never be here again. She had lost him. And the secret of how burned in the back of her brain, bundled in shame and grief so thick she wished it could be a dream.

Then she did hear a footstep. A warm hand stroked her arm, and a kiss fell on her shoulder.

"Couldn't sleep?" Alex asked softly, as he drew her back into his embrace. His skin was a furnace against hers. "Erin, you're freezing."

Soon he had led her back to bed, pulling her under the covers. Erin lay awake, the pressure of her secret pushing forward onto her tongue.

"Did you have a bad dream?" he asked softly.

"Why do you ask?"

"Sometimes you talk in your sleep."

Erin felt a bolt of fear. "What do I say?"

The sheets shifted as he shook his head. "Nothing that makes sense. Something about the sea, and once you said, 'Dad, please'."

Erin let this wash through her. Alex didn't push. In fact, she could sense him pulling away, as if a tide was running out in the space between them. As if he was far away, under a different sky.

Then he said, "I have bad dreams sometimes, too."

Alex didn't know what it was about tonight, but he knew he had to tell her. He didn't reopen these memories willingly. But he also wanted his relationship with Erin to go somewhere, and he knew that couldn't happen without the truth.

"Six years ago," he began. "I was flying between islands over in Hawaii. There were five of us – a mate of mine, one of his friends, my fiancée Nikki, and the pilot. We'd all been sailing off one of the outer islands, and we were coming back for a wedding the next day. Sun was going down. I remember what it looked like on the water, all rippling gold."

Alex opened his eyes, focusing on the white ceiling, on the feel of his body against the bed. Anything to remind himself he was here, not back then. Erin was motionless beside him, only her breath telling him that she was listening to every word.

"We lost engine power. It was one of those small, single prop planes. I remember the pilot being so calm about telling us we'd have to ditch in the water. Nikki had hold of my hand really tight, but none of us said anything. I think we didn't believe it was happening. Even when we hit the water, I was still waiting for it all to not be real."

Alex blew out a breath, keen to get past this part. "It didn't take long to sink. My mate was stuck in his seat, trying to get out of his belt. I don't know how Nikki got out, to be honest. I just remember still being in the cabin, trying to get Trent's belt undone for him when the whole thing went under."

The memory of the black water came at him, as if it was happening again. The pressure of it squeezing his chest. He focused on his breath, in, out … in, out, until he could breathe around the choking feeling.

"We did make it out, though," he croaked. "Obviously. By

the time I broke the surface, my lungs were on fire. I thought that was the worst over. I mean, we were alive, right? But we were in the water. I could see land, but a long way off and the sun was nearly down. The water was black. We were pretty sure the pilot had a broken arm, and Trent was bleeding from a cut on his face. The only good thing was that it was summer, and the water was warm. So we started to swim."

"How far was it?" Erin asked, her voice barely a whisper.

Alex shrugged. "No idea. A few k's maybe? But the light faded fast and it was hard to see anything then. There weren't any lights, or even a moon. Just stars, and all that black ocean. We didn't know if anyone was looking for us. The pilot had made a distress call out, but we didn't know if anyone had heard it. And anyway, how would they see us at night? It was maybe an hour before we'd all worked that out. That's when we started to have problems. Nikki went into a panic, saying that we'd never make it. And then Trent said he didn't want to swim anymore. The defeat was contagious – once one person gave up, it spread. Trent's friend was falling further behind. I remember he was wearing this orange shirt, but I'd look back and barely be able to see him. The pilot, too."

"Did you feel like that, too?" Erin asked softly.

Alex shook his head against the pillow, not because he hadn't felt the same desperation, but because to this day, he didn't know why he'd reacted the way he had. He remembered the fear as black as the sea. Remembered how everyone's will to go on was unravelling, that they could easily give up and drown. And how that had made him angry.

"Something in me snapped," he said. "I managed to get everyone back into a group. The pilot was bleeding from his head, too, and we hadn't even noticed. We patched that up as best we could, then I told Nikki we weren't giving up. We were all going to stick together. I'd make sure of it. I pointed at a star over where I hoped the island was, and I told them we had to keep swimming towards it.

"My pep talk worked for about an hour. But everyone was tired, and cramping up. Nikki asked me to hold her up, just for a while. And I couldn't – I was exhausted too. But she leaned her weight on me, and I panicked that she'd push me under. So I shoved her off. I meant to tell her she could keep going, but all the positive stuff wasn't working any more. We probably had sharks circling us. So, I said … other things."

Alex could still feel those words he'd said, so harsh they'd cut his salt-swollen tongue. That he couldn't believe she'd just give up. How weak she was. That she mustn't really love him. That if she really wanted to be a mother, what kind of mother wouldn't want to keep swimming? That had been the worst one. They'd both wanted children, and Nikki was particularly keen to start, even before they got married. Alex had wanted the wedding first, but he'd never questioned Nikki's dedication to their future children. Never used it as a weapon on her like he had then.

It didn't matter that it seemed to have worked; that they'd kept swimming for the island even as the inky night deepened around them. That his taunts had given her the energy she needed. The shame of the memory never faded, and now he told this all to Erin.

"I don't know how many hours it was before we heard the first chopper go over. But they couldn't see us. Trent started yelling anyway that we were there, or trying to. He had no voice left. We could only listen to the engines fading away, then sometimes coming back, only to leave again. And then there was only stars, until dawn finally came.

"The pilot had disappeared by then. I swam back to look for him, but I couldn't find him. I tried to bunch us together, but the others weren't cooperating. Land seemed so much closer, so I tried to pull Nikki with me and make for the shore. It was only a few hundred metres. But she wouldn't come, so … I left her behind."

Alex drew in a breath. He smelled only the trace of apple scented detergent on the sheets, and the clean salty edge of Haven's bay. Erin's body was tense beside him.

"Did she … make it?" Erin asked.

"I didn't know for a while. I pulled myself up on the beach about twenty minutes later and collapsed. I don't know how long I was there on the sand. Eventually, someone was shaking my shoulder and hauling me up. I was put on a boat and ended up in the hospital on the big island. Nikki and the others were picked up in rescue boats, which had been out since first light. That was the funny thing – the searchers found them first, even the pilot, who I was sure must have drowned. I saw them finding me last as another sign of what a monster I'd been."

"I can't believe you went through all that," Erin said. "I can understand why you didn't want to sail anymore."

Alex gave her a bitter laugh. "It wasn't the accident that did that. That happened in the two years afterwards, and it was all me. Small planes? Now those I have definite pause about. But sailing's something different." Abruptly, he rolled towards her so that he could see her face, needing to know that she could understand what he was about to say next, because this, *this* was truly the point of the story.

"The accident wasn't the worst part of what happened," he said. "Yeah, I had dreams about it – still do – but the real damage was what it did to me and Nikki. After what happened in the water, those things I'd said to her? And leaving her behind? I couldn't take that back. She never trusted me again. Our relationship was broken. Of course, we tried to pretend, to go on with our lives. We did get married, but she didn't talk about having kids anymore. I wasn't the same man to her after the accident, even though I never meant any of the things I said. And I *was* changed. I couldn't control my temper. I'd never been a hothead before, but I couldn't suffer fools after that. One of the members at our racing club nearly collided with my boat at a race start one weekend, then later in the bar he made some stupid joke – chauvinistic, stupid blokey joke – and I knocked his head off for it. They threw me out after that. There'd been too many other problems before."

"So that was true," Erin said.

Alex allowed himself a dark smile towards the ceiling. Most of the rumours about him were true; the only thing people didn't know was the story behind it all.

"Did the rumour mill also say I'd had my medical registration suspended?"

Erin made a noise in her throat. "I was sure that one wasn't true."

"Well, it was." Alex sighed. "As I said, I had a lot of trouble controlling my temper. A patient of mine was being abused by her husband. Textbook case. She'd had many untreated injuries. They were all over the x-rays. The guy had the hide to front up to take her home, making lame excuses about how clumsy she was. I knocked him out cold. Not exactly how a hospital wants its doctors to behave."

Alex rubbed his forehead ruefully. As inappropriate as it had been, he'd never been so satisfied in his life. Even the police who'd read him the riot act seemed sympathetic.

"Of course, the guy was vocal about the police pressing charges. And that gave other colleagues of mine permission to raise their concerns about me. The charges ended up dropped but I was put on report while I worked my problems out. Nikki left after that. To be honest, I was surprised it wasn't sooner. We'd long stopped talking by then."

There was a long silence. Finally, Erin said, "How did you work things out?"

"A lot of therapy, a lot of meditation," Alex said. "The accident and how it affected me … that doesn't go away. I learned how to live with it. I don't sail anymore because it puts my blood up, but it's not a never-again thing. I … just thought you should know."

"About the sailing, or the whole thing?" Erin asked.

Alex gave a soft laugh. "Both seem pretty important when you're falling in love with a sailor."

She buried her face in his neck, her arms stretched around him.

"I'm so sorry all that happened to you," she said eventually. "It's amazing you survived. They should have given you some kind of bravery award."

"They tried."

"What?"

He gave a bitter laugh. "Right after Nikki left, I was nominated for one. Apparently Trent would've drowned in the crash if I hadn't helped pull him out, and maybe the others wouldn't have made it either. But I told them I didn't want it."

"Why?"

He shrugged. "I didn't feel like a hero, Erin. I felt despicable after what I said to Nikki. I didn't know I was capable of that, even under pressure. No way was I going to collect some award for it. What got me back on my feet was my job. And good therapy. I can't go back to how I was before the accident, but I won't settle for the man I was afterwards, either."

"Well, I like the man you are," she said softly. "I've never felt unsafe with you."

Alex had to reflect that he'd never met anyone in his life who could accept everything he'd just told her without their estimation of him changing. He'd confided the story in one girlfriend since (the relationship didn't last very long) and a colleague at another hospital, who had both seemed nervous afterwards. But Erin only tucked herself closer against him, as if the disclosure caused him to make more sense to her, not less.

For the first time since the accident, Alex found himself holding her close, hope so much more beautiful than the first light of day. Maybe this really could go somewhere. Maybe all his past mistakes could be absolved.

And just for tonight, he let himself push down the knowledge she was carrying some secret of her own that she hadn't shared. In a way, it made sense. In his experience, secrets weren't the things that hurt — well, except for yourself. It was when all the unspeakable acts were out in the open that they did the most harm.

Morning dawned with peach-streaked indigo clouds, and the sand was still cold under Erin's toes as she left the surgery. The pain tablets had worn off and her face was throbbing again. She wanted caffeine to clear her head, so she slipped over the short distance between the surgery and the bakery, picking her way down the path.

At the fork, she ran straight into Tristan.

He was walking barefoot down the main path towards the bakery. As he stopped and met her gaze, some instinct in Erin sounded a warning, and the moment for 'hello' slipped past her. She waited for him to speak, but he didn't. Just kept staring at her with hard eyes. Spooked, she kept walking into the shop, breathing in the aroma of freshly ground beans. But the caffeine wasn't the reason for her thudding heart and squirming stomach.

He was watching. He knew.

She ordered two takeaways, ignoring Sandy's clucking over her swollen face and attempts at chit-chat, expecting at any moment that Tristan would appear and she'd have to make excuses for not coming back to the sponsor's party yesterday. Maybe she could tell him about tomorrow's meeting with Ivan to placate him. But Tristan didn't come in. What was he doing out there?

Finally armed with the coffees, Erin emerged. And there he was, just off the path, leaning on a sign pole. Watching her.

Erin had the thought that she should walk straight down the main path, as if she was heading to Travers' cabin, or turn by the hall for Skye's. Anything to give the impression she'd bought the coffee for someone other than Alex.

But then, maybe Tristan was headed to Skye's, too, what did she know? And underneath that was the hard centre within her that couldn't abide being scared of him, even when she was. So, she looked away and swallowed the instinct to run, turned back down the path for the surgery.

So what if he knew she'd slept at the clinic. It was her business. It shouldn't matter. Didn't matter.

And by the time she eased the door closed behind her, and

Alex stirred at the scent of coffee, Tristan had faded from her mind like the early morning fog, burned away in the face of the sun.

Chapter 22

As the small island-hop plane angled for touchdown the following afternoon, Erin found herself squeezing the seat rest in a way she never normally did when flying. It wasn't anything to do with the plane, just that her collar was too tight. She tugged it down, straightened her lapels, smoothed her jacket. Formal business wear always sat on her like someone else's skin; she'd had to drag this suit out of the bottom of a storage bin on her boat last night, and spend an hour ironing it. All right, *she'd* spent five minutes attempting to iron in the backpackers' laundrette before Alex, clearly pained at watching her ineptitude, had taken over.

"I didn't even know the surgery had an iron," she said, watching him expertly steam a shirt cuff on the board he set up in his room.

"How does someone who's spent years living on millionaires' boats *not* know how to iron?"

Erin had shrugged. "Oh, they have other people for that. I stayed out of anything that smelled like needing my top button done up."

Except, now here she was, squirming around that top button. At least Alex had sent her off with good wishes and a kiss. Erin was as superstitious as any sailor, so their reconnection seemed fortuitous. As if the winds had finally shifted around in the right direction.

If only the jacket didn't feel like it had shrunk.

Then again, Ivan Borovich had that effect on people.

Erin still wasn't quite sure how she'd convinced him to come to the mainland for a meeting, so that in itself was encouraging. She hadn't told any of the race committee, because she didn't want any raised expectations. But the coverage for the dual race had been good, from the little she'd been able to bear watching.

On the other had, her fail-to-finish had been a very public debacle, and the bruise on her face had now come up in full glory. The preened front desk staff at *OceanRunner*, the swanky resort where Ivan was staying, were too polite to say anything, but Erin caught their eyes sliding over to look again. And now, with her fail-to-finish and beaten face, she was going to try to convince Ivan to sponsor the Haven Regatta. Sure, no problem. She'd have it done by lunchtime.

Erin smoothed down her jacket again, and tried to look like she belonged, but she wasn't at home in the resort's opulence. The big pavilion-roofed main building faced an infinity pool to the ocean, where staff bearing cocktail trays slid smoothly around the white lounge chairs. Mature palm trees framed an indoor lagoon, saving guests from going outside if they preferred not to. The bar staff wore bow-ties and waistcoats and called her ma'am.

Erin moved deeper into the lounge, still fifteen minutes early for her twelve o'clock with Ivan. When she'd worked for him, Ivan was always late. She would probably have a wait ahead.

She was surprised then to see him sitting in the lounge's sunken level, away from the windows in a private nook of two seats across a slim table. He was wearing an elegant white business shirt and black suit pants, his hair and beard more grey than she remembered. A tablet was propped before him on the table, and he occasionally swiped a finger across its screen, as though there was some smudge to remove. He looked up from under his shaggy eyebrows just as she reached the table.

"Ah," he said, rising immediately and kissing Erin on both cheeks. "Here is my defector, at last."

And while the cheek kissing always made Erin a little awkward, there was warmth in Ivan's voice, and the same enthusiasm she remembered. He summoned a waiter to take her drink order and gave her his full attention.

"You have an argument with the boom?" he said, pointing to her face.

"A winch block, actually. On the weekend."

Ivan nodded with sympathy. "I saw the race. You were unlucky, I think. But very exciting, this concept. Two races at the same time, land and sea. Brings a new dimension. Was it your idea?"

His gaze was intense, as if he already knew all the ins and outs of the race, and he was just looking for confirmation.

"Yes, I came up with it," she said quickly.

He sat back with a small, satisfied smile, saying nothing as the waiter put a short glass of clear liquor on ice down in front of him, and a lemonade in front of Erin. She cleared her throat.

"Thankyou for coming," she began stiffly, not knowing how to start. "I wanted to, I mean, I know this must have seemed sudden but—"

"What is this, Erin?" he asked with a sudden sharpness. He gestured to her jacket. "We know each other, but you sound like I just met you. Also, you are all dressed up. It doesn't suit you. I thought you would come in Bermudas and t-shirt, like our old meetings. Is this because you're working for Tristan

Drummond?"

Ivan twitched his lips, as if he'd tasted something unpleasant.

"Well, yes," said Erin a little defensively, but she was disarmed by him thinking she might have come in a t-shirt. He was being playful, the way he often was with his team, even though he was worth billions. "I have a serious business proposal for you. I didn't want to look like I was here to waste your time."

He flashed a quick smile. "I would never think that. You were my best tactician, and business is all tactics. Now, what is this proposal?"

"Sponsor the new Haven Regatta," she rushed out. "The pilot races have been successful, and we think it could be huge, bigger than Hamilton. Borovich could be the headline name on all of that. I can show you figures on the two pilot races ..."

Erin fumbled for her satchel, the sheaf of papers catching as she tried to tug them out. Ivan sat back in his chair, his expression impassive as she went through the sponsorship exposure from the two pilot races, the minutes of airtime, and the attendee survey results showing what they remembered of the sponsors. After ten minutes, she ran out of material and glanced at Ivan's face. Her heart sank. He was massaging his chin with one hand, the corners of his mouth pulled down. Distinctly unimpressed.

He leaned forward, one lean finger moving the papers around. "And these things ... these business things, you are enjoying them?"

Erin shrugged before she could catch herself. "I'll always love being out in the boat more," she said carefully. "But it has been interesting. I liked the idea for the land-sea race, and taking it from that idea to making it happen. Just a pity our team didn't do better."

"You were always a keen competitor," he said thoughtfully. "But I never considered you would like business before. I thought, she is too pragmatic. She would not want to sit in a boardroom. This is very interesting."

"But what do you think about sponsoring?"

Ivan narrowed his eyes. "You know, I sponsor many events already. Overseas, in America, in Europe. World-class events. Places that have been celebrated in books and movies and in legends. What makes Haven the next place? What is special?"

Erin sat back. She'd gone through it all already, hadn't she? She'd talked about how nowhere had the conditions Haven had – that it could become a great sailor's challenge, just like the Sydney to Hobart. That it had history and beauty. The only thing left was that it was home, and that was hardly relevant to Ivan. For the first time, she doubted her own conviction about the event. Was she just believing in it because she couldn't consider failing, and that Skye and her mother and all her childhood memories were there? That the best memories of her father were there?

"Haven has something nowhere else has," she said softly, not able to look him in the eye. "It might not translate into a glossy brochure or a two-sentence pitch, but it's unique. It has a gravity I've never experienced anywhere else."

"A *gravity*," he repeated. He rubbed his chin again. "I can tell you want this very badly, Erin. You want to see the resort reopen, like this one perhaps?" He gestured to the expansive bar around them.

"Well, maybe not quite like this one ..."

"Why not?"

"It's a bit ... flamboyant for Haven."

He grinned. "And yet, Tristan Drummond owns this hotel, too. Oh, you didn't know this?"

Erin frowned, looking around as though the beams in the ceiling might have changed colour. Tristan *owned* this place? It was very high-end, and she'd never heard of him being involved in the building of it.

"I will tell you another thing, Erin," Ivan said, wiping the condensation from his glass before he took a sip. "I will not sponsor anything Tristan Drummond is involved in. He is not my style."

"What does that mean?" Erin asked, bewildered. Ivan was in shipping, Tristan was a developer. How had they even crossed paths?

Ivan shook his head, indicating he would not be drawn on the subject. "What I want very much to know is when can I induce you to come and work for me again? My team misses you. My racing record also misses you, very dearly."

But Erin was still trying to process the blank refusal. "If I came to work for you, would you sponsor it then?"

"Ah, nice try," he said, indulgently. "But I am immune to bribes, even from you."

"Is that the only reason you agreed to meet with me?" she asked. "Because you thought I might come back to work for you?"

"Please, Erin. I have been in business a long time. I knew what you were going to ask. Tristan and his team have been very noisy about looking for sponsors. There are many onlookers circling."

"Then why?"

A kind smile, with something else colouring the kindness. Embarrassment? Sadness? "I want to see you. The team misses you. You always remind me of my daughter, god rest her soul. When you are done playing with Tristan, maybe I will look forward to hearing from you."

And with that, Ivan drained his drink, left a hundred dollar note on the table and smoothly left. Erin watched him walk out of the bar in his slacks and loose shirt, his demeanour telling the world he was both worth a packet, and had earned every cent. She admired him, but now what did she do?

She had to admit that somewhere in her more deluded thoughts, she'd imagined he would agree on the spot. That she would be able to go back to Tristan and the team and announce that she had saved the day. Having such a hopeful, even if outlandish, thought squashed left her empty.

She sat, her cheek throbbing, wondering what else she could do. Alex had said she could stay at his unit while she was on the mainland, but now Erin wondered if she should just find the quickest path back to the island. The two pilot races were over, now. She'd just played and lost her biggest hand when it came to industry people she knew. How was she supposed to land a sponsor now?

She looked out the floor to ceiling windows, past the grand pool and at the sky over the distant Haven islands. She could see the streak of grey clouds already there, a storm brewing up behind the misty mountains. Forces of nature, she could deal with. Why did these forces of human nature always seem so much more complex?

The next day, Alex finished the island clinic early and walked the winding path up the point to call on Helmut. The painter had been discharged back to the island after five days, the nearly deadly episode of epiglottitis resolved. Alex found Helmut propped in a day bed in his studio, a canvas and brushes within reach, and Stella hovering, trying to persuade him to eat.

"You must have a little. It's soup – very good for you," Alex heard her say. She looked relieved when she spotted him. "Ah, Dr Alex. Please tell this man he must eat to recover!"

"It is still sore inside," said Helmut, his voice raspy as he touched the white bandage over the tracheotomy site at his throat.

"Worse, the same or better?" Alex asked, sitting beside him.

"Better," Helmut acknowledged. "And I will eat more if you think it's good for me."

"Yes, but go slowly. Not too hot," Alex said, as Stella raised her eyes to heaven at Helmut's sudden acquiescence. Alex suspected she'd been trying the soup unsuccessfully for a while. Otherwise, Helmut seemed on the mend. The wound was healing well, and he'd already sketched the outline of the ocean and the headland in the painting.

"It is what I can paint from here," Helmut said when Alex's asked if he was hoping to paint Bella again. "But sometimes, days like today, I prefer to take the easel to the top of the next headland. From there, you can see to the misty mountains on the northern island. Watch the storms roll in. Can't you smell it?"

"Smell what?"

"*That*," Helmut insisted, flaring his nostrils to suck at the air.

All Alex could smell was paint and turps, and some kind of hearty broth, which must be the soup. Helmet jerked his head at Stella. "Take him outside and show him."

So Stella led Alex outside, into the fresh air. The breeze had a languid quality today, moving slow and thick over his skin. The sea was a luminous blue in the shallows near the rocks, and indigo elsewhere.

"Smell's not quite the right sense," Stella said, standing beside him. "But feel how the air prickles the inside of your nose. There's a bouquet to it, like a crushed gum leaf. Fresh and sharp. You feel it now?"

Alex inhaled deeply. And perhaps, yes, the thickness in the air did tingle his sinuses. But maybe he was imagining it. "So this means a storm later?"

Stella nodded. "A proper, Haven storm. The ones that come in over the northern island, squashing the wind up so it roars down into the ocean beyond us. Roughs up the sea and howls around the hut. It's not half-scary up here, I can tell you. Particularly when Helmut won't stand back from the windows. I'm always sure a tree branch is going to go through there. It would be much better down in the village. You know that's where the island got its name, right? One of those early explorers sheltered in the main bay. So it became Great Haven … the only place in the islands you can escape a storm. And now of course that's where the village and the resort are."

"What about at the homestead?"

Stella gave him a crooked grin. "Been thinking about Bella, too, huh? I don't know. But I think she'd have stuck through any storm, would Bella."

Alex was still thinking about it as he picked his way down the headland to the end of the main beach. Bella was a great mystery. What had possessed her to stay on at the homestead alone after her husband died, especially in this place with its unpredictable weather and isolation? Wasn't she lonely? Scared? Stella certainly didn't seem to think so, and the few articles he'd found about Bella seemed to think she was either half mad —

refusing the assistance of relatives who offered her places back on the mainland, or failing that, assistance with the farm – or that she wasn't alone after all, keeping the company of her dogs and the island's Indigenous people. But now all of them were gone. All that was left was the husk of the homestead, the ghost and an unfinished story.

Alex's feet hit the beach, retracing the prints he'd left on his way up. Erin was due back on the afternoon flight. He'd just have time to drop by Travers' place before she landed. Alex smiled to himself. There'd been a time when he preferred the part of his week on the mainland, with its freedom from scrutiny and memories. And now he found himself wanting those things, if they involved Erin.

He was lost enough in these thoughts that he'd almost reached the jetty before he realised someone was sitting there, watching him walk across the sand.

"Tristan," Alex said, as he approached. "I didn't expect to see you here."

Tristan looked a little off-colour. He had stubble on his chin, and his normally sleek hair had the look of being finger combed. An empty coffee cup dangled from his fingers, but his gaze was still intense, demanding respect.

"I was just thinking of taking a sail," Tristan said. "But the crew's all back on the mainland. How about it?"

"What, now?" Alex said, turning to look towards the north, where white clouds were already turning grey. He imagined the storm brewing up behind the northern island, all the things Stella had said. "Isn't there a storm coming?"

Tristan shrugged. "Maybe, maybe not. But that's the fun of it. When Erin and I were teenagers, we used to do it all the time. Take a boat out around to the north, and then race the storm back in. Exhilarating. Erin would be cheering her head off."

Tristan laughed, but he kept his eye on Alex, as if daring him to imagine the pair of them sailing together. Alex felt his stomach close like a fist, even aware Tristan might be goading him. He imagined the two of them in one small boat, Erin carefree and bold, her hair flying in the breeze, racing the storm.

"Those were the days," Tristan went on. "She's an amazing sailor, amazing woman. Don't you think?"

Now Alex knew Tristan was looking for a fight. That he was a cocky bastard, and in a moment he was going to find something really explosive to say, and hope that Alex threw the first punch. Alex could feel the familiar anger boiling up inside him, the kind that he'd had no control over after the accident. A few years back, Tristan would already have been on the ground with a broken jaw. And then Alex would soon be packing his bags off the island and probably heading to court.

That Alex was in the past, but the challenge couldn't go unanswered. Erin was in the middle. Alex knew that if he failed to face-off this time, Tristan wouldn't forget it.

Tristan gave him a sly smile. "Not afraid of a little storm, are you Dr Bell?"

Oh, that old nugget. It sounded so trite and ridiculous. And yet, Tristan's delivery – backed with all his power and influence – gave the schoolyard taunt new dimensions. It wasn't just about the sail and the storm. It was about Alex's career, and Erin, and what he was prepared to stand up for. Alex tamped down the rage just enough, so that he could feel it throbbing in his fingertips.

"Lead the way," he said, and followed Tristan up the jetty.

Chapter 23

An hour later, and Erin's flight would have been cancelled because of the storm. As she walked off the tarmac, the pilot was already taxiing the plane around at the end of the runway, about to push off back to the mainland before the weather could break. The north sky was a growing mass of thick cloud, the air heavy. Erin could smell it in the high parts of her nose: it was going to be a bad one.

She expected to see Alex waiting at the terminal hut, but no one was there. Ten minutes later when she knocked on the door of the clinic, she found it deserted. By then, the wind was whipping sand off the paths. It stung her legs as she turned the corner, and found Sandy pulling down the shutters at the bakery. She could hear Tim calling out for Monster somewhere behind the dunes.

"Going to be a wild one," Sandy called. "Your boat still tied on the jetty?"

"No, I moved it off yesterday," Erin said. "Have you seen Alex?"

"Went up the hill to see Helmut after the clinic. Thought he'd be back by now. Maybe he's staying up there for the storm."

"Okay." Erin swung to look towards Bella's Leap, frowning. Alex had said he'd meet her, but if he'd been checking on

Helmut, it made sense he might stay up there.

Just then, Tim burst out from the side of the bakery, fringe askew, a dog lead swinging from one hand. "Have you seen Monster?" he asked, and chewed his lip when they both said they hadn't. Tim cast his own look towards the Leap before dashing off across the path, still calling to the wayward dog.

"I guess I'll go down to the jetty, see if anyone needs help securing their boat," Erin said.

"Travers beat you to it," Sandy said. "He went down there a half-hour ago."

Erin went anyway. From the dunes, she could see all the boats had been moved away from the jetty, which would only become a smashing post in a storm. They were all huddled in the curve of the bay, tugging on anchor chains as the breeze whipped white caps over the water. A few had people still on the deck, tying down before they took the tenders back to shore. Only one boat was still moored at the jetty – the *Green Dream*. Squinting, Erin spotted Travers unravelling a line nearby.

She broke into a jog through the soft sand, her calves aching by the time she reached the dock. When she reached the end, Travers had the line untangled and was preparing to throw it into the boat.

"Leaving it a bit late aren't you?" she called.

Travers grinned. "Not at all. This is called perfect timing. Not a minute wasted."

"Were you planning to swim back?" Erin said, meaning once he'd anchored the boat, he'd be stuck. His boat was too small for a tender.

"Nope. Gus is picking me up." Travers nodded towards one of the forty-foot yachts, where the sailmaker was busy finishing his own tie-down.

Erin held the line for Travers as she ran her eyes again over all the boats in the harbour. Tristan's *Seven Seas* was there, more splendid than ever under the stormy sky, her hull gleaming clean. Wait.

Erin made another two sweeps through the crowd of masts.

"Hey Travers, where's *Rough House*, Tristan's racer? He take it back to the mainland?"

"It was there this morning," Travers said, scanning the boats. "You'd think he wouldn't risk it. Thing must be worth a couple of million."

Erin felt the skin between her eyes pull together, and she jumped in the boat, pushing them off the jetty. "Let's go ask Gus."

Travers shrugged and revved the engines, carving a lazy arc away from the pier and towards the anchored yachts. Gus was just climbing into his dingy, the wind tangling his white hair into a mop across his forehead.

"Erin!" he exclaimed at they pulled alongside. "I heard you went to the mainland, so I checked your yacht over myself, made sure she was all battened down. Travers, there's a good spot for yours in there." He pointed to a gap in the anchor chains.

"Where's Tristan's racer? He take it back to the mainland?"

Gus scratched his rough cheek. "Now there's a silly thing," he said. "I figure he must have."

"Wait, what's silly?"

Gus gave a dismissive wave. "I ran into him on the dock when I first came down to check my boat, couple of hours back. He had the racer pulled up to the jetty, said something about going out to race the storm. Now, I remember when you did it as teenagers, but surely you've grown out of it by now. He was laughing. Figured it was a joke.”

Erin felt her stomach turn.

“Anyway, next thing I look up, and there’s the racer heading out of the bay. I could only see the two of them, so they’re not crewed for racing. They have to have made a break for the coast. Maybe Tristan’s giving him a hitch back to the mainland.”

Erin looked up sharply. “Who?” she asked.

“The doc, Alex Bell.”

“Why the hell would Alex go out in this?” Travers asked. “Gus must be senile. He’s seeing things.”

But Travers didn’t look convinced and Erin had a very, very bad feeling. The air was almost thick enough to drink.

“He said he was going to meet me at the airstrip,” Erin said. “He didn’t show.”

“What’s this about racing the storm? Is that some kind of local tradition I don’t know about?”

“Hardly. It only happened a few times, and it was a stupid thing to do,” Erin snapped. “Tristan got the idea to go out and race the storm front back to the island. He claimed it was a rush, but he was terrified, too. Those fronts have winds at sixty knots, and the tide’s running straight into it, which creates a hell of a chop. It’s like sailing in a washing machine.”

She paused, her hand gripped on the wheel of Travers’ boat. She wouldn’t have believed Tristan was capable of such madness. Then again, she’d seen the look in his eyes when he’d watched her coming out of Alex’s room last week. She could certainly believe he was capable of doing it just to scare Alex. To assert his dominance as the bigger man of the island.

Shit.

"Hello, Erin?" Travers said. "Can I drop this anchor now or what?"

"Wait a sec."

She pulled out her phone, two bars of reception from the old resort's tower holding in the wide open bay, and called the marina on the mainland.

"We're preparing for a storm out here," she told the controller when she connected. "Someone saw the *Rough House* leave Haven about ninety minutes ago, have you got her there in the marina?"

"Nope," said the guy jovially. "It's at least a two hour trip in, but no one's radioed for a berth and we're full with Hamilton coming up."

Erin hung up, then she pushed the throttle and spun them out of the anchorage.

"You're not thinking of going out there I hope," Travers said. "I haven't owned this boat for two years yet. I'd prefer it didn't end up on the bottom."

Erin didn't answer, just rummaged in the console while she steered. Finally, her hand closed on a set of binoculars. She just wanted to look. She wasn't going out there. No bloody way. Especially as the further they went, the more the swell peaked and the wind lashed drops into the backs of their heads like tiny missiles, until the *Green Dream* was bouncing up waves and bursting through their crests. Finally, Erin cut the throttle at the edge of the bay, the boat settling into uncomfortable rolling. She squinted out past Bella's Leap and down the channel, where the last of the blue sky was disappearing before the roiling cloud. Towards the coast, the sky was clearer, but all that would end soon as the front swallowed them.

She knew in her marrow that Tristan hadn't gone back to the

mainland. He'd gone through the channel, out around Bella's Leap and the eastern headlands, and north towards the storm.

His timing had better be as lucky as it had been all those years ago.

"Hell," Travers yelled over the wind. "Why would anyone go out in this?"

"He can't leave it much longer to come back," she said. Tristan might be aggressive enough to do this, but Gus was right – his boat was worth a packet of money, and even Tristan didn't have a death wish.

The binoculars were useless in the swell; all she could see was a blur. Instead, she stood on the pilot seat and stared into the water, as the sky turned grey and green and the water turned to foam. Five minutes. Ten.

"Erin."

"Another minute."

"Erin, we need to go back in."

"Another—"

She saw it. There, right in the channel, almost invisible against the grey blur of the sea and sky. If it wasn't for the mast, making a hairline against the clouds, she'd have missed it.

"I see her!" she yelled, dragging Travers around to look, and finally he had to admit that it did look like a boat. Relief washed through Erin, bright and clean. They would make it back. Even fighting the tide, and even when Erin could clearly see they weren't sailing well. As the *Rough House* inched closer, she could see the flapping end of a torn sail, the spare spinnaker halyard that had been used to lash the boom, which looked to have snapped the pin holding it to the mast.

And finally, the boat was close enough to spot Tristan himself, grimly behind the wheel, who gave a frantic wave. Erin experienced a fresh wave of relief. Tristan appeared unharmed, and she couldn't see anyone else. Gus must have been imagining things. Alex was probably up the cliff at this moment, drinking coffee with Helmut.

She shook her head. Why the hell Tristan had even thought to take the boat out single-handed ... then she realised he was cupping his hand around his mouth, trying to yell over the wind and waves.

White-knuckled, Travers took the wheel inched the boat alongside, while Erin threw fenders over the edge so the hulls wouldn't crash together. Then, risking her neck, she timed the swell and stepped over the *Rough House* railing, the metal spar slipping under her fingers. She stumbled down to the wheel.

"What the bloody hell—" she began, but Tristan was yelling over her.

"I said get on the radio. Man overboard, for the fifth bloody time!"

Erin felt as though she'd run into a glass door. Stunned, she couldn't process what he'd said. "What?"

"Bell. Freak wave pitched us and turned the stern right into the wind. The main gybed round and he got smacked straight into the water. Can only hear static on the radio."

The stunned feeling morphed into a tight coil of anger and disbelief. "What the hell were you doing?" she yelled, smacking into him with her fists.

"Get off! He wanted to go. All taken with the idea of racing the storm like we used to."

"Bullshit!" she yelled. "And why aren't you looking for him? You just turn around and head back."

"Boat's disabled, Erin. Now help me get back in to shore and we'll call a search."

"Did you mark the waypoint where he went over? What position?" Then she saw that both life rings were still on their hooks behind the boat. He hadn't even thrown one in.

"The instruments are screwed, but it was somewhere around the east side, maybe two headlands over."

Erin had turned her back and was stumbling up towards the guy wires. Travers was still holding his position, two feet off the side of the racer. Erin didn't even wait this time; she climbed over the railing and threw herself back into his boat, landing heavily against the fibreglass side and smacking her shin. She found herself being hauled upright, one of Travers' meaty hands under her arm.

"What are you doing?" he demanded.

"He went into the sea," she rushed out, pointing crazily towards the east, something shaken loose inside her mind. "We have to, we have to ..."

She grabbed for the wheel, shoving Travers back and pushing the throttle and turning them away from Tristan's boat and towards the east headlands. She grabbed the radio and frantically made the call to the relay station on the shore. She had no idea if they'd heard her or not.

"Are you nuts? Erin! Turn around!"

She killed the throttle and dragged a life jacket out from the console. "You want to get off?" she asked, shaking it at him as the sea lurched beneath them. All she could think about was Alex, alone and in the water, in the menacing, heaving water. Again. After the story he'd told her, she could imagine his fear. Just like her own the night her father had died. The dark, despairing fear of facing a terror alone.

Travers must have seen something in her eyes, because he took the jacket and shoved it on. "This boat isn't designed for this," was all he yelled.

Then they were off, cutting into the raging swell outside the bay, waves dumping slosh over the sides, the bilge pump cutting in and out to deal with it. As they rounded Bella's Leap, Erin realised the enormity of the odds against Alex. She could no longer see the difference between the water and the sky. The rain was a grey sheet, the visibility ahead barely twenty metres in front of the bow. The waves created deep valleys where an entire boat could hide. How would they even spot him? Cloud fingers were rolling down over Bella's Leap, and Helmut's studio was invisible among the trees on the next headland. Wind was screaming down from the north.

"Where do you want to look?" yelled Travers, as he took the wheel and tried to steer the bow into the waves.

Erin mouthed helplessly. All she could think was to try the navigation line she'd have taken herself, to imagine how the tide might have carried Alex from there. The tide was running north-west now, but the wind was so savage it may well be reversed in the top water, and in any case large eddies formed all along the east coast of the island.

"That way." She guessed a direction, scanning every patch of ocean for a speck, anything that was different to the foaming water.

But as ten minutes dragged past, the conditions worsening, she had to begin to accept this was ludicrous. Even someone in a helicopter would be having an impossible time at the moment. They cut back and forth for another five minutes, until a large wave broadsided them and dumped a half-foot of water in the boat.

"Erin," Travers said with a quiet urgency she fully understood. They had to go back. But the idea turned her frantic. She was back on her empty yacht that night, her father gone, guilt and anger and grief replacing every other thought. In desperation, she spun back towards the island, rain stinging her eyes. If she could see a clear path back, they could stay out a little longer. It wasn't time to turn back.

And that was when she saw Bella.

At the crest of the Leap, like a wraith of clouds, a woman stood gazing out to sea, her body slowly turning, her misty dress lifting around her. Chills raced across Erin's scalp. The rare other times she'd seen Bella, they'd been mere glimpses, easily imagined away. Now, she could make out the dark dents of her eyes, the profile of her arms and body, enough to understand where she was looking. And she *was* looking. Bella's attention was somewhere under the cliffs, in the heaving water, just before it smashed onto the rocks of the next headland. Erin saw the ghostly hand lift, and point.

Erin followed the direction into that foaming swell, and saw a tiny wink. A light.

"What do you see?" Travers yelled.

Erin didn't answer, her eyes fixed on the tiny flash before a wave rose up and covered it.

"There!" She thrust her finger towards it, numb, as in the edge of her vision, the clouds were still swirling around Bella's Leap.

Travers swung the wheel, pointing them close in to the rocks.

"Hang on," he said, as the waves came on the stern and shoved them towards the coast.

It seemed to take hours to reach the spot, fighting the waves and current, and Erin was half terrified that her gaze had shifted. She only saw the point of light once more on the crest of a wave. But then, as the cliffs seemed to be looming right over them, and the rocks far too close, she saw a definite shape in the water. A mass with a flash of dull orange, and that single tiny point of light.

"Take the wheel," yelled Travers, fumbling for a grappling hook as the swell tilted the *Green Dream* on her side. Erin hooked a turn to point the bow up-swell and threw the motor in reverse, her hands slipping as the eddies tried to spin them.

Now, she could see Alex clearly, his head tipped back and to the side on the collar of his life jacket, his arms loose in the water, the jacket's light on his shoulder. He seemed still ten metres away until a wave picked them up and hurtled them towards the rocks, and suddenly, Alex was right off the stern.

"Got him!"

Travers was hanging off the rear deck, his leg hooked in a rope, the muscles in his arm bunching as he gripped the pole. Erin held their position as Travers hauled Alex aboard, his body limp inside his orange life jacket, and the rocks danced only metres away.

Alex didn't move. Erin stared in horror, looking for signs of life. Anything to tell her he was really okay. That this hadn't just happened.

"Erin, move it!" yelled Travers.

She snapped back in. Her hand was on the throttle, gunning the motors and sending them thudding back into the open sea. She had to watch the water ahead, steering them through the channel as the rain beat into her face. She could only hear Travers grunts and curses as he worked around Alex, but she had no idea what he was doing until they finally broke the line back into the bay and the swell diminished. Then she saw Travers had Alex flat on his back, his jacket and shirt torn away, his hands spread on his chest, elbows locked.

Her hand shook as she groped for the radio. "Great Haven, Great Haven, Great Haven," she began.

"Erin?" Sandy's voice crackled over the radio, distraught. "We thought you were—"

"Call an evac right now," Erin cut in, cold cutting in the spaces between her words. "We found him."

Chapter 24

It seemed the whole town were waiting at the jetty, half of them in raincoats, the others simply letting the storm soak them. The rain was falling steadily, but at least the wind was nothing like it was outside the bay.

Skye and Anna had pushed to the front of the crowd, and with Sandy they were shooing people to make room, and throwing spare fenders over the jetty edge to cushion the boat. Erin parked ungracefully, the inflatable fenders groaning as the sea shoved them into the wooden piles. Travers was barking instructions, his hair slicked with rain and sweat. Three men managed to transfer Alex onto a stretcher and then up onto the jetty while Travers kept up the CPR.

Erin hugged herself, numb with cold shock. She watched her mother slide in on the other side, keeping pace with Travers, then taking over to give him a rest. Then Travers was on the radio as other people formed a ring to hold a tarp over them all. But Alex still didn't move. Erin's body was unresponsive, too, stiff with disbelief. She had no idea what was going on. Anna had her head tilted over Alex's mouth, her fingers at his neck while Travers dug in a first-aid bag. Erin had seen Alex move like that himself, the night that Helmut had been sick. Her father, too, long ago, when someone was gravely ill. She felt she was back in those last hours with him on the Pacific Ocean, the sky so full of stars, being dragged unwilling through a night of unretractable change.

Finally, Skye's voice broke through, her sister's hand shaking her shoulder. "Erin. Travers thinks he has a heartbeat again. Erin?"

Erin finally snapped her gaze from Alex's blue lips to Skye's face, so oddly alive and warm.

"The evac plane has to wait for the storm to pass, but they'll be here as soon as they can. Are you going with them. Erin?"

The shake was harder this time. "Yes," Erin croaked. Her voice sounded as if it belonged to someone else. Desperate for a sign, she wrenched her eyes around to Bella's Leap, but no one was there now. Only the tendrils of mist over the rocks, and the foaming sea below.

Two hours passed before they reached the mainland hospital, by which time Erin was feeling the full horror of what had happened. A female doctor spoke to them for five minutes before disappearing back to Alex, and then Erin couldn't remember a word she'd said.

Skye put an arm around her. Her mother sat on her other side, a steady comfort, somehow knowing to say nothing. Travers collapsed in a chair across from them, his big hands tremoring as they held his head. The waiting room TV in the corner played the news with subtitles. Even the triage nurse seemed subdued. Everyone seemed to grasp the gravity of what had happened.

"What did she say again?" Erin whispered. "I was trying to listen but—"

A tear slicked down her cheek. Her body seemed outside her

control, crying and shaking without permission.

"He's in surgery," Anna said gently, rubbing warmth into Erin's arms. "He had a head injury, probably from the boom, and they need to relieve the pressure on his brain."

"After that, they'll take him to intensive care," Skye added.

"Is he going to die?"

Skye and Travers exchanged a look that said they were trying to think of what to say without admitting defeat.

"His heartbeat came back, Erin. And he was breathing on his own," Travers said. "Those are good signs. Plus, it was cold in the water. That can help."

But.

Erin heard the unsaid qualification. *But* none of that could matter. *But* no matter how much you want him to wake up, he won't. Her father was going to die tonight and it was her fault.

Erin shook herself, shooting up out of her seat, out of her mother's grasp. She rushed out of the waiting room, through the front doors and into the gathering night. The sky was still clouded over, not a star to be seen. Alex. She meant Alex. Not her father. That night was done with. But she felt the despair of knowing it would never leave her, nor would the guilt of keeping it from Skye and her mother.

The next moment, a blanket came around her shoulders, heavy and warm, and the triage nurse appeared. Erin's eyes dropped to her name tag: Wendy.

"There, now, you're frozen," Wendy said. "And you're still wet through. I'm going to show you where the showers are and find you some dry clothes."

Erin allowed herself to be led, as Wendy kept talking. "We're all amazed at what you did. Alex is ... well, we all want him to recover. We're all scared."

None of the fussing touched the well of grief inside Erin, but it seemed to keep her moving. Soon she was in the shower, mechanistically warming in the spray, then drying and putting on the offered hospital scrubs. When she re-emerged, Travers had also changed, the small group in its huddle. Erin didn't want to rejoin them, but then the female doctor appeared again. Erin finally remembered her name. Karen Bailey.

"He's come through the surgery," she told them, "and he's in intensive care now where we can closely monitor his progress. We're keeping him asleep for now with medication, until we're sure that it's safe to wake him up. We'll also be doing scans to check there's no more bleeding."

"Can we see him?" Skye asked.

"It can be a bit cramped for room, and there's lots of machines. It can be a bit confronting," Dr Bailey said. "So it would be best if it's just family and very close friends for now."

All eyes turned to Erin.

Travers and Skye came with her. All the way to the door, she floated in a weird in-between of now and then. It wasn't until she crossed into the intensive care space, with its ring of three curtained beds and the orderly central station, that she could push aside the long-ago images in her head. Of her father, appearing as though he was simply asleep and might wake at any moment, a cruel illusion when she knew he would never stir again.

Alex was nothing like that. He was swaddled in hospital blankets and diminished by the equipment around him – a tube in his mouth, ECG leads running to his chest, monitors showing his heart beat and blood pressure. A thick white bandage around his head. She sank into the hard chair beside the bed and sucked a breath of air that smelled of nothing at all.

His fingers were cold. Erin tried to remember what they'd felt like when they were warm. When he'd been part of her future. She feared she had to let him go, but she wasn't ready. Just like she hadn't been ready before.

And so she sat, hunched and unprepared, as the minutes became hours, as the nurses came to take observations and asked gentle questions to which she shook her head. Nothing else could reach her now, because she knew how this would end. History repeating itself, just as it had for Alex.

He'd survived the sea once, but he wouldn't again. And Erin was sure she would see two men die before their time.

The night deepened and the shift changed, but no one asked her to leave. The clock's hands closed on midnight, then spread apart as morning began, and all the while Erin felt time retreating.

I'm ready, Erin.

She heard her father's voice, waking her in the hour before dawn, as he had many times to go sailing. But this would be the last morning. They pulled up the anchor and left the bay, the only sounds from the gathering wind and waves.

It was that hour before dawn again now. Alex lay unchanged, maybe it would be the last dawn for him, too. Erin wanted to tell him before he went. She looked around. The station nurse was in the office with a large stack of charts. The other beds were empty.

"Alex," she whispered. "I have to tell you something."

Not a flicker. She didn't know if he could hear, but suddenly it seemed only to matter that she was speaking. A tiny crack had formed in the walls around that last night, and words were flowing through it like water, widening and widening, until everything behind would be seen.

"My father was sick, Alex, but no one knew. He didn't tell Mum or Skye. But he told me. He had pancreatic cancer. That's the one that celebrities tell everyone they're fighting, and that they're going to beat, but they always die anyway. I was angry at him, because he didn't want treatment. He said it was pointless. His cancer had already spread, and he would only have a few months. He didn't want to spend them in hospitals."

She paused, remembering the bizarreness of that time; their conversations late at night on the main beach, or on the boat, or in the surgery, but never in the house where someone could overhear. Erin hadn't understood why he wouldn't tell Skye, and he'd tried to explain what he'd seen on cancer wards in his work. That he didn't want to be a patient after a lifetime of helping them. That he wanted freedom from the other side of the table, from pain and suffering. Erin had loved him deeply, and that love had forced her to respect his wishes, however much she disagreed with them. She tried to explain this to Alex.

"I don't know if you would agree with him. Maybe you would," she said softly. "But the hardest thing was when he told me he wanted to die. Not just wait for the cancer, but beat it to the punch. That's how he put it."

The tears were back again, fat drops that streaked down her cheeks.

"He knew all about the technical side of it. He had bottles and vials – I have no idea what they were. And he knew what he wanted – to be on the boat, somewhere the horizon was an unbroken circle around him. He called it the primordial ring, which was a bit of a joke, but not completely. The ocean was his first love and he was returning to it. That was the only part I understood at first."

Erin remembered it, that calm stretch of water, the sky just lightening. The stars still sparkling in the sky. *It's time, Erin.*

"Otherwise, at first I was horrified. He said he didn't blame me, but that I should try to understand him. So I tried. He was already in pain. He'd watched so many patients die, I figured he should know more about it than me. He didn't exactly ask me to help, but I realised that if I didn't, I'd wake up one morning and find him gone. Then maybe we'd find the boat drifting somewhere without him, and never know what had really happened. Never be sure. If he'd been scared, or lonely, or ..." She swallowed. "So I said I would go with him."

"He tried to make me change my mind. It wasn't legal to help, and he thought it was risky for me. But I told him he would need someone to help sail, and I didn't want him to be alone. So we went on a long trip east into the Pacific, the last one ever. He was in a lot of pain by that point, and having trouble hiding it, but he'd wanted to wait for the right season. I could see how relieved he was as soon as we'd left the jetty – he didn't have to pretend anymore. He'd told everyone he was doing some kind of shake diet because of all the weight he'd lost. But as we sailed down the channel, I remember him just lying back on the deck, watching the Leap, like he was trying to fix the island in his mind. And he was calm in a way he hadn't been before then.

"Anyway, as we sailed, he waited for the right forecast: the possibility of storms. And on that last morning, the weather was finally right. He lay on the couch up on the back deck with the line stuck in his arm, watching the sun come up through the clouds. And then ..."

And then he was gone. Erin put her hands over her face, remembering. There had been a fog across her reality until that moment, as if she were acting out a part. Doing her job. But as soon as he was gone, the fantasy crumbled. Grief had come down on her like a house in an earthquake. Then had come anger, at him and herself, at a world that would make *this* the way things had to happen. And then, the loneliness. The great void that her father had left in her life.

Now, she sensed the void that Alex would leave, too. She kept talking, as if the words could keep that moment from arriving.

"He had planned everything, and I did what he had asked. I sailed towards a storm and a let him slip into the water. The storm was a bad one. I tore the sail coming back, surprised I didn't lose the mast, too. I told the police in Fiji that he'd fallen over the side when we were in the middle of it. They searched, of course. I always expected that they'd find him. But they didn't, and eventually the search was called off.

"I came home, but not for long. Mum's face ... I couldn't bear it. And I hated lying, even though Dad made me promise. So I left. I went as far away as I could and tried to forget. But the world isn't big enough for that."

Erin was aware she'd made a warm patch on Alex's hand. She had a moment of hope, before she heard a squeak behind her. A shoe shifting on the floor. Erin whipped her hand around and pushed back the curtain. Skye stood there, her face frozen, two coffees forgotten in her hands.

"Skye—"

"How dare you," she whispered.

"Skye—"

"Don't!" she hissed, and she turned and ran, the coffees sloshing from their cups. Erin stared after her with eyes of sandy tears. Through the hall window, the sun was just breaking the horizon, a pastel streak of pale pink, promising a new and lovely day. But Erin couldn't see how that was possible. Skye had heard what she had said, and now the secret was out.

Chapter 25

Erin caught up with Skye in the long hall that ran past the hospital's cafeteria, its roller door still closed. At the end of the hall was the rear exit that led to the car park. A fluoro light flickered overhead.

"Skye, wait."

Erin didn't know what she would say if Skye actually stopped. Ask her to keep her mouth shut? Ask for understanding? She knew she could ask for neither.

So when her sister did stop, right under that flickering light, Erin was utterly speechless.

Skye stared at her, furious, her toe tapping. "So, nothing to say?"

Erin flinched. Skye's tone cut like a flying guy-wire.

"I *knew* something was wrong," Skye went on. "I *knew* it. I even asked you if Dad was all right, and you! You told me you had no idea what I was talking about!"

"That was what he wanted—"

"Bullshit! That's not normal, Erin. Families are supposed to stick *together*. He must have been depressed. You should have told us!"

"He wasn't depressed," Erin said softly.

"He can't have been thinking straight—"

"He knew exactly what he was doing, Skye." Erin's voice had

found its own edge, like the icy wind of a winter's squall. For the first time since it had all happened, she could accept she was responsible for what she hadn't told. But *she'd* been there. She'd known her father, maybe better than anyone. She wouldn't have Skye projecting her own idea of what happened.

"He knew exactly," she repeated. "He'd seen a specialist on the mainland. There was no option for surgery, no chance of a cure. He'd seen enough other people go through it. He didn't want to die in a hospital!"

"You are deluded," Skye spat. In the flickering light, her face was grey and pinched. She stabbed her finger into Erin's shoulder. "You are *not* my sister."

"Where are you going?" Erin called after her, terrified Skye would go straight to their mother without any thought for the consequences.

"To find someone who knows what family's about," Skye yelled back.

Erin found Travers still in the waiting area, half-asleep, wedged uncomfortably into a hard chair. Her mother was nowhere to be seen.

"What's news?" he asked, cracking an eyelid.

Erin hardly heard him, searching around in her panic. Where was her mother?

Travers was fully awake in an instant. "What's happened?"

Erin's voice shook. "Skye's stormed off mad and I don't know where Mum is, and, and ..."

"Erin, stop," he said gently. "She just went down to the bathroom." He pulled Erin into a chair and tried to persuade her to tell him what had happened with Skye. Erin clamped her lips shut. She'd dared to speak it once, and look what had happened. She shoved her hands between her knees, and stared fixedly at the mute television in the corner, which was just starting up a vacuous morning show.

"Skye said she was going to find someone who knows what family's about," she said finally.

At this, Travers sighed. "Then she'll be going straight to Mr Moneybags, you know that, right?"

"Tristan? After what he bloody did!"

"I don't think anyone could convince her he's not a nice person. I couldn't, and my powers of persuasion used to be good." He tried to smile. "I'm getting quite good at surviving this kind of thing. I'll tell you the story of Katie some time."

Erin ran her eyes over the bulk of him, with his muscled shoulders and the strength of his hands and realised none of it mattered. The heart only seemed to come in one easily-breakable size.

"I need to find Mum," she said.

But Travers wasn't paying attention. "What the ..."

Erin followed his gaze to the television, where the news bulletin was now showing jerky pictures of a choppy sea. Some people were on a boat, bouncing through the waves, the sheer face of a cliff rising perilously close beside them. Erin's stomach dived; god, had other people had been caught in the storm?

Then slowly, she realised the footage was of her and Travers. That the cliff was the reach between Bella's Leap and the next headland. The footage had now reached the point where Travers was hauling Alex into the boat. Most of the action was off the far left of the camera, but it was unmistakable. Travers was fiddling with the volume buttons on the TV, while Erin covered her mouth with her hands. It wasn't as she remembered; the cliff hadn't been that close, had it?

"*... incredible pictures show just how perilous the rescue was. And again, as we understand, the people in the boat are Erin Jacobs, who recently found some fame as part of the revitalised Great Haven Regatta, and Darren Travers, an ex-army salvage diver who crews on Erin's boat. At the current time, we understand Dr Bell remains in a critical condition in the Port Hospital. In a few minutes, we'll speak to coastal search and rescue experts about the extraordinary footage. Meanwhile, the federal government is debating the future of Medicare ...*"

Travers shut off the volume again as the picture cut back to the studio anchor, fixing Erin with an apologetic look. "Shit."

"How is that even possible?" she asked.

"There's a GoPro on the side rail of my boat," Travers said. "I started running it when we were going in to the bay to anchor. I thought it would make some good footage, all the boats there, the storm coming in. I forgot to turn it off. But someone obviously noticed it and swiped it. Bloody hell."

He rubbed his mouth, as if trying to decide something important.

"What?" Erin asked.

"I'm just thinking I should get going. The journalists will turn up, if they aren't here already."

"You're leaving?"

He nodded reluctantly, but his eyes couldn't quite meet hers. He was up to something. "Yeah, I need to take care of things back there. Secure my ruddy property for a start."

He was at the door before Erin could comprehend what was happening. "Wait, Travers."

She was about to say *don't leave me*, but it would have been the wrong sentiment. Erin knew she had no right to expect anyone here with her. But he came back anyway, putting his two big hands on her shoulders. "I'll keep in touch," he said. And he gave her a rough kiss on the forehead, and squeezed her arms before he left. Erin rocked back in surprise.

She slipped out into the hall, creeping back towards the ICU. It seemed to take an age to reach Alex's bed again, another age to take his hand in hers. Still cold, so cold. The only evidence of life were the trace lines on the monitors. She had to feel for the pulse in his wrist before she would believe he was still alive.

But for how much longer?

She could see the day staff congregating in the nurses' station, about to start the ward round. Perhaps they would have something to say, but more likely it would be more waiting, more room for hope to grow and be shattered. She didn't realise she'd put her head down on her arm until someone tapped her on the shoulder.

"Erin?"

Erin pulled her eyes up to find Wendy, the triage nurse.

"Would you come down to the ED? Your mother's had a little turn."

Chapter 26

Erin hurried all the way with panic-laden footsteps, despite Wendy's assurances that she didn't need to rush. All Erin could think was *not her mother, too*. Had Skye told her after all?

Anna was lying on a bed on one of the emergency bays, another nurse just finishing an ECG trace.

"I'm really fine," she was protesting. "It's just my low blood pressure. Oh, Erin."

Erin gripped the blanket at the foot of the bed as the nurse scrutinised the ECG. Her mother seemed so thin and frail against the sheets, a smudge of blue paint on her index finger too close to the shade of her skin. Erin smelled nothing in the cool hospital air, which was completely wrong. Her mother should smell of warm paper, oil paints and blooming flowers.

"What happened?" Erin asked.

"I fainted just outside. I was sitting on the bench and all these news vans turned up. I stood up too fast, that's all."

"Does this happen a lot?" the nurse asked, slapping a blood pressure cuff on Anna's arm again and pumping it up as she plugged the stethoscope ends into her ears.

"All the time," Anna said. "Well, now and then."

The nurse nodded, pressing the stethoscope into her mother's elbow. The cuff hissed as she let off the pressure.

"I didn't know that," Erin said, guilt pumping through her

heart.

"It's not a big deal," Anna said firmly. "Low blood pressure is a good thing, right?"

"Generally, yes," said the nurse. "And the ECG does look normal. We should just make sure that there's nothing else to find. I'll be back with some other tests."

Anna watched her go. "It's all the walking," she said, then glanced at Erin. "I started just for the book research. But then parts of the island I'd never seen before. I enjoy finding new things every time I go out. I think half the village has never gone beyond the main beach."

"You should tell someone where you're going," Erin said. "What if you fainted out there, or twisted your ankle or something? Phones don't work on half the island!"

"I'm *fine*," Anna said emphatically. "Most the time, I don't know where I'm going anyway. Sometimes I find myself at the homestead, or in the hills, thinking about Bella. Looking for the waterhole. But I've never found it. Sometimes I think it's not meant to be found."

"Or it doesn't exist."

"Of course it *exists*."

Erin looked up with a jerk. That fierce tone was something she hadn't heard in a long time. Her mother almost looked surprised herself, then her expression drifted, her mouth corners tugging down. She looked at Erin sadly. "You don't know the whole story, do you?"

And suddenly, Erin couldn't bear her secret. She hated that her mother must have pined for her lost husband, knowing only that Erin had been the last to see him, and hadn't been able to save him. That her mother had buried herself in a research project that was now affecting her own health.

"Mum, I need to tell you something." The words fell from her mouth, outstripping the apprehension.

But her mother held up a finger. "Not here. They're going to let me go."

They found a tiny garden courtyard in the centre of the hospital. The tiny space was hung with fern baskets and decorated with a trickling water feature shaped like a green tree frog. Even so, Erin couldn't relax. She was strung as tight as mast wire in a forty-knot wind.

They sat on the bench, but Erin couldn't start. So finally, her mother spoke. "Do you want to know all of Bella's story?"

Erin shook her head, terrified of losing her chance. Her father had sworn her to secrecy, but Skye already knew, so Erin had to push every word past her fear.

"Mum ... I need to tell you what happened ... with Dad."

A long silence.

"What really happened, I mean."

The water feature gurgled, and a fern pot spun lazily. Erin snuck a glance at her mother, who was looking down at her hands, a frown of concentration between her brows. She prepared to be hated for what she had to say.

"Do you think I don't know?" Anna said finally.

Erin gritted her teeth. "I don't mean about the storm, about the police report, I mean what really happened. See he was—"

"I know about the cancer."

Erin stopped, dumbfounded. Anna glanced across. Her eyes were red, but there was no malice in her expression.

"I knew about the cancer," she said softly. "I knew what he was planning to do. At first, I was aghast. I didn't understand why he'd turn his back on the system he'd worked in all his life. I wanted to help him, but not what he wanted to do. And then, one day he sailed away with you and didn't come back. I loved him, but I never forgave him for asking you to help, and for keeping that from me. He shouldn't have put that on you."

Erin took a breath to speak, but her mother ploughed on, with a trace of bitterness. "He told me that the two of you were just going on a last trip so I thought there was still time. And then came the news reports, and I knew it wasn't an accident."

"Mum …"

Anna smiled sadly. "I thought you and I would end up talking about it. But everything was in such a mess afterwards, and then you left. I wondered if I was wrong for a while. Some days I'd convince myself it really was an accident, and then I didn't know which way was up. I must have walked the island a thousand times thinking the same thoughts. But then you came back, and I saw how you're walking around with the weight of it on you. I never, ever wanted that for you."

"I had no idea," Erin mumbled, her shock too fresh to feel any relief.

Her mother's shoulders lifted. "I haven't known how to talk to you. I didn't know if I'd be making it worse to bring it all up again. Besides, we were never … close like that. So I kept coming to your boat, just to give you that chance to say it if you needed to. Some people don't."

Erin felt the gulf between her and her mother, as though her toes were on the edge of a cliff. "I'm sorry," she whispered, guilty and sad.

"No, don't be," Anna said quickly.

"But your health," Erin said. "You look so unwell since I came back, and I know that has to be because of how it all happened."

Her mother took a deep breath. "Erin, I aged while you were

gone. A few more years than the four you were away, probably, but if it was anything, it was worrying about how you were. Yes, I've low blood pressure. But for most things you're concerned about … I've come to accept them for what they were. And I've enjoyed coming to know the island. I know it better now than I ever did the first decade we lived there. The only thing that gives me pain these days is seeing you not at peace. Do you regret what you did for him?"

"No," she said slowly. "I wished it could be different, but no."

"Then don't be sorry. It was a privilege to see how the two of you were together. No one would begrudge such closeness. I only regret that I couldn't have spared you however hard these years must have been, carrying around that secret."

"He didn't ask me to help," Erin said. "I don't want you to think that. I just couldn't let him sail off by himself."

Her mother sighed, as if a great weight had lifted. "Then you were braver than I was. Just like him. You really are the best of him, Erin."

Erin closed her eyes. "Skye knows," she said. "She overheard me telling Alex about what happened."

"Oh." Anna looked skywards, and sighed heavily. "And?"

Erin told her mother what Skye had said.

"Your sister has a firm sense of what's right, but she hasn't had to live outside the island. She should have a long time ago, spent some time broadening her horizons, learning to deal with people who don't agree with her. But she's also loyal and sensitive, underneath. She'll find her way round eventually," Anna said.

"But what if she tells—"

"Who? The village?"

"I was going to say, Tristan."

Anna frowned. "I don't think even Skye would do that. She might have a temper, but she also knows what's family business. I know because she kept your secrets when you were children."

Erin felt a smile tug her lips, thinking of all the things they'd gotten up to, and that Skye had always kept quiet about it, even when Erin had been the instigator, even when they'd both been in trouble. But abruptly, she realised how little any of it mattered. What did she care, when Alex was going to die?

Another fat tear slid down her cheek. Her mother's arm came around her. "How's he doing?"

Erin swiped the tears away. "No change."

"Then we'll go back up again," said Anna.

Alex was exactly as Erin had left him. The doctors' round had come and gone, but Karen Bailey came back to see them. Erin could tell from her expression that she was preparing them for bad news. Erin gripped the counter.

"We're concerned about ..." Dr Bailey began, and the list seemed not to end. Seizures. DVTs. Liver function. Electrolytes. Swelling.

Erin couldn't absorb any of the details, except that the outcome was still in jeopardy.

She went back to sit with him, anguished, hating everything she heard. The soft shush of the ventilator, reminding her that he wasn't breathing on his own; the electronic ticks and clicks of the machines that fed him fluids and medicines. She remembered her father being adamant he would never end up like this, and Erin could finally understand in a far too visceral way.

"I'll leave you," Anna said, softly.

"No, stay," said Erin, gripping her mother's hand in a way she never had in her life. She didn't want to be alone again. She and Alex hadn't had nearly enough time together, but she didn't want his last moments to be silent. She wanted to talk to him, to tell him something that would interest him, that he could take to wherever he was going. And she needed her mother to be here for that.

"Alex, I want to tell you Bella's story," she said. She glanced at Anna, who nodded once and then dragged a chair over.

"Bella came to Haven with her husband Thomas, and five hundred sheep," Erin continued. "No white men lived on the island then. No one had been game enough to take up the lease. The island was known as a devil's place – unpredictable weather. Treacherous waters. There were stories about men disappearing there, what with the savage Indigenous folk who were supposed to live there."

Anna made a disgruntled sound. Erin glanced across.

"Now of course those stories weren't true, Alex. But let's just say things were hard. Bella and Thomas had to build the homestead, and the shearing shed, and fences for the yards. Feed themselves and their dogs and horses. People thought they were mad, but they proved the doubters wrong. The herd grew, and with the shearing, they began to make money. But of course, it didn't last."

That was the way the story had always been told to Erin, but for the first time, she felt in her aching heart how those simple words could cover so much turmoil.

"Thomas died of a fever within three years. Bella was left on her own. Her family didn't want her to stay – they said it was madness for a woman to be running a sheep station, especially on some isolated island. But Bella refused their offers to go back to Sydney. Instead, she explored the island. She made notes about things she found, but not always exactly where. She wrote about caves in the northern hills, and a waterhole, though no one's ever found that one. Her family pressured her – both her brother and her brother-in-law visited, trying to convince her to leave. But she wouldn't go. She developed a very strong friendship with the local people. She wrote about how they nursed her once when she had a fever herself, and that they watched over her from the hills. By all accounts, she was a success, and so other people began to show an interest in the lease.

"She held onto it, through all the pressures. Her health was failing in the end – she had a cough that wouldn't shift, and arthritis from the heavy work, but she still resisted giving up the place. Until finally one day, she just disappeared. There's lots of stories about what happened to her. Some of them say that she walked up into the hills to live out her end in the caves, others that she did leave for Sydney after all, changing her name to avoid the stigma of being the crazy sheep lady from the Queensland Island. Or that she died in a shipwreck. No one knows the truth, except that she had a hard and amazing life—"

At another sound from her mother, Erin broke off.

"You must forgive her our Erin, Dr Alex," Anna said. "She doesn't know the real story. I wish it was such a fairytale. But Bella's life was nothing like that."

"You don't think she had an amazing life?" Erin asked.

"She was an amazing woman," Anna said. "But she lived through many hells, and what happened to her was a tragedy. Do you really want to know how it really goes?"

Erin nodded, her hand finding Alex's fingers again, which

held a faint trace of warmth.

Anna sighed. "Some of the details are right. She did come with her husband, and he did die, and so did she, but the story doesn't go the way you've just heard. Thomas, you see, was a violent man.

"These are things that I wish I never had to hear, or say. But from the moment they landed, Thomas was determined to make Haven his own island. He was ruthless. He hunted the Indigenous people, and Bella hated him for it. God knows how many he killed, but one sultry afternoon, with a storm blowing in, he'd cornered two boys by one of the sheds. He would have killed them cold, but for Bella. She felled him right there, with a branch, as I understand. He never woke again."

Anna leaned forward and pressed her hand to Alex's blanketed leg. "He was a bad sort of man, Alex. The sort who shouldn't wake up. So don't go taking any messages from that, you hear?"

She settled back. "So now, her husband's dead. And things are hard, yes. It took Bella a long time to establish trust with the local people. They saw her as part of Thomas. But eventually, they came to an understanding. Even an accord. Maybe, with one man in particular, even more. And that was where the trouble started. Erin is right – her family did want her to leave the island and go back to Sydney. They wanted her to marry again, and her brother-in-law was the one vying to take Thomas's place. That was his motivation in coming to the island. And I bet that Bella regretted having told her family so much about the place in her letters and piquing their interest.

"Because as she continually refused to leave, her brother-in-law formed the idea that she was living in sin with one of the local people, and not only that, that she had betrayed her husband. And so he tricked her. He said he would leave, if she would promise to wave him off from the lookout. That was how she came to be there, on another sultry afternoon, with a storm brewing. And that was where he pushed her into the ocean, as repayment for the disgrace he thought she'd brought on the family. And of course, so that he and her brother could take over the lease, prosperity at her expense. And that of the local people. Within a generation, you see, they were all gone from the island. The only reason the story survived is that one of them did, over on the mainland."

Erin listened, horrified, yet somehow she knew this was the truth. "That can't be what happened," she whispered.

"Why? Because it's not a happy ending?" asked Anna. She shook her head. "Bella's story is not about happy endings, nor even about extraordinary life. It's about injustice. That's why she watches us from the Leap – as a restless guardian. So, there you are Alex. Now you know. So you go ahead and work out how to wake up, because for certain this here is an injustice."

A silence settled. Alex's hand was warm where Erin held it, her body as rigid as his was limp. Nothing had changed, but the weight of Bella's story settled uncomfortably on her heart. If that was what had truly happened ... if someone as brave and unusual as Bella could fall to the forces against her, then what hope was there? Erin felt the woven pattern of the hospital blanket against her forehead. Anna's hand came against her shoulder, and she couldn't help feel her mother was really preparing her for the worst.

Erin woke with a jerk some time later, the blanket pattern now a painful score across her cheek. Around her, the ward was the same white, green and electronic blur. Alex slept on. She stumbled blearily out and stood in the long hall where a window overlooked the car park roof to a wedge of the shore and ocean. But seeing that expanse of blue couldn't temper the awful gloom growing inside her.

She went back to the bedside where a few minutes became an hour, and more, until darkness settled. She rose only for the evening ward round at seven, when the nurse encouraged her to get something to eat before the cafeteria closed, and showed her the way down the staff stairs so she could avoid the media hovering outside the front doors.

It was on the walk back upstairs, with a barely-touched cold toasted sandwich wrapped in foil, that Erin pulled her phone from her pocket and switched it on. Three messages from Travers had come through. Wearily, Erin leant against the wall next to the stair door to call him back.

"You might want to come back to the island," Travers said when the call connected.

"I'm not leaving here."

"It's important."

"Alex is still unconscious," Erin said, putting a hand to her forehead. "Besides I'm not responding to any more vague requests to come to the island. I did that for Skye, and look at how that turned out!"

"Fine. What about coming back to see what really happened on that boat?"

Erin suddenly felt very awake. "What are you talking about?"

"You remember weeks back, when I had my gear tampered with? Well, I'm not a trusting sort of person. I put cameras in my cabin, and a few other places. And there's something interesting here."

Erin sighed, her energy tank empty even of fumes. "Forget it, Travers."

"If you don't help me decide what to do, I'm calling the police," he said.

A jolt restarted Erin's heart. "Why?"

"Because I don't think what happened was an accident. Skye and Tristan are both back here. I know how important he is to the island. I don't want to be wrong about this."

But the island couldn't be further from Erin's cares, especially when she spotted her mother coming back down the hall. "I'll call you back," she told him, without any intention of doing so.

But as she approached the ICU, she nearly ran into the nurse coming the other way.

"Oh, Erin, I was just coming to find you."

Erin's skin tightened. *Here it comes.*

But the nurse smiled. "The doctor has decided to wake Alex up. He's breathing on his own now."

In disbelief, Erin followed the nurse back to the beside, standing back while the team removed the tube and carefully brought Alex round. He still didn't seem like himself, but the moment his fingers moved, Erin clapped her hand across her mouth. Oh my god, was he going to be all right?

The next moment, she had her hand in his. "Alex, it's Erin."

He made a low sound, his head turning towards her. He still seemed half-asleep but it was a miracle, more than she could ever have imagined. Dr Bailey pulled a chair in beside her.

"Now, it might be slow for a while," she said. "He's going to feel pretty awful, and we don't know yet how his body has been affected. Those things we'll work out gradually."

But all Erin cared about was that Alex had woken up. That

he could hold her hand. And even when he went back to sleep most of the night, she stayed where she was. The next morning, Erin woke cramped at the beside, and was surprised to find him looking down at her.

"You're awake," she said stupidly.

A tiny, lopsided smile. "I hear I've been ... sleeping a while," he said. His voice was rough, and he grimaced.

"They said your throat would be raw," Erin said, "so don't talk."

"I'll get used to it," he said slowly. That tiny grin again. He lifted a finger slowly to point at her. "You look funny."

Erin ran a hand over her face and again found the indentations of the blanket and sheets. Coupled with the fading bruises on her face, she could only imagine the stunning sight she must make. But it hardly mattered.

"I promise I'll go clean up when you're next asleep," she said, allowing herself to smile.

He shook his head. "Don't want to sleep yet. Need a shave. And coffee."

She laughed, relief making her giddy. "I think they call it designer stubble. And I don't think they're letting you near caffeine for a while."

Another ghosted smile on his face, then his expression turned serious. "Erin ... how did I get here?"

"To the hospital? You flew over in a helicopter."

Another shake of his head. "No. I mean. What happened?"

Erin glanced towards the nurse's station. "What did they tell you?"

"Accident. Nothing else."

Erin took a breath, thinking, careful. "What do you remember?" She squeezed his hand. Alex stared up at the ceiling, his eyelids red.

"Going to see Helmut. Then ... nothing."

"Nothing?"

A tiny shake of his head. "I start to think I remember, and then I ... get confused. I think about ... that other time."

"You'll get it straight, don't worry," Erin said, but the assurance she gave him she didn't feel in her heart.

She spoke Dr Bailey later, who was pleased with Alex's progress, but warned Erin again that there could be rough days ahead.

"His memory may recover, but it might not either. And he could have insomnia, or headaches. And of course there's always the risk of depression. It's not uncommon in people with a head injury, though Alex has several points that favour him avoiding it."

"Like what?"

"No problems with alcohol, his stable job before the accident, and his high level of education."

Erin chewed her lip. "Do you know about his other accident?"

When Dr Bailey's eyebrows lifted in question, Erin had to outline the crash that Alex had described in Hawaii, and how it had affected him afterwards.

"We didn't know about that," she said slowly, when Erin had finished. "Oh, man. How unlucky can you be? He always seemed so level and calm ... well, I never would have guessed. We'll be keeping a close eye on how he's doing."

Now the immediate danger seemed over, Erin was left with the consequences of the incident for everything else around her. From what the nurses told her, the media scrum was still outside, and at least one journalist had been ejected while trying to sneak into the hospital. Erin had been absent from work for several days now. Tristan would probably think the publicity was a good thing, but the idea made her ill. So did what Skye knew. And now, Travers was saying something about the incident.

Erin finally called him back.

"You'd better not be wasting my time," she said. "And it's going to be late afternoon before I can get on the shuttle."

"Don't even think about walking out the front doors of the hospital," Travers said. "It's a reporter madhouse. Get in a taxi out the back and head down to search and rescue. I've got a buddy there with a powerboat. He'll run you over, and I'll be waiting at the jetty."

Erin paused. "Not planning on taking over the world, are you Travers?"

"Not until Sunday."

Chapter 27

Travers was wearing a pair of dark glasses and leaning on the end of the jetty when the powerboat finally cut its engines. The owner, Charlie, was a jovial type who didn't seem in the least fazed to be taking a solo passenger at top, bone-jarring speed across to Haven. Erin expected a dozen questions, and then found he asked none. The engines and the wave shocks were too loud to talk over anyway.

Charlie didn't hang around. As soon as Erin's feet hit the dock, the power cruiser executed a neat circle and sped away. Travers already striding off, leaving Erin to follow.

"How's Alex?" Travers asked, when she caught up.

"You'd know if you'd stuck around," she fired back.

He compressed his lips. "It's not that I don't care. But this is important."

His tone was enough to keep Erin quiet until they reached his cabin. Inside, she found that his coffee table had been seconded as an electronics bench, the TV pulled in close with a tangle of wires connecting a number of different boxes.

Travers walked a circuit of the room, peering through each window before he sat down. Erin watched him with her eyes narrowed.

"Really? We playing secret agents now?"

"Pay me out all your want, Erin, but you have no idea what

sort of guy Tristan is and what resources he might have. It pays to be careful."

Erin threw up her hands. "I'm angry at him, too, Travers. It was a stupid thing he did, and I can't forgive him for it. But this is all ..."

She broke off as Travers pulled up pictures on the TV, grainy images of a room with a desk. It only took her a few minutes to recognise the location. "That's Tristan's office in the resort."

"Yes," Travers said, clicking on. Another view showed the inside of the portable meeting room. The next was another shot of the resort, though Erin had trouble working out where exactly. Then a view over the airstrip. Then a clear one of the main beach, looking down towards the resort and Bella's Leap – that one must be on the end of the jetty. Then two more of the jetty itself.

"Now, watch."

And so Erin did, while he played a sequence of videos. Alex coming down from the headland, walking along the beach. Talking with Tristan, their silent mouths moving. Alex turned his body, clear in his intent to leave, but then Tristan said something. Alex squared his shoulders. Then the two of them disappeared down the jetty, and onto Tristan's boat. Erin's skin prickled with goosebumps.

"Now, watch this from three hours earlier," Travers said.

Travers rewound and showed her Tristan sitting in his office, watching at the window. The time spinning in fast forward over hours, until Alex went past down the beach towards Helmut's. And then, Tristan going to the jetty, and waiting and waiting until Alex came back. Patiently. Calmly. Waiting.

Stalking.

"How did you even put a camera in Tristan's office?" Erin

said faintly.

"Let's just say before I was a medic, I did many other things for queen and country."

Travers paused the shot of Tristan on the jetty, just as Alex entered the frame again, and pushed his chair back. "I'm only sorry that I didn't wire his boat, too. Because there's no way what happened was an accident. I don't believe it. Tristan planned it. Very carefully."

"You expect me to believe that he *planned* Alex to go overboard?"

"You saw the tapes."

"They don't prove anything," she said.

"There's more. We need to go over to the clinic."

So Erin followed Travers to the clinic, which seemed dark until she walked in and found someone in a waiting-room chair.

"Helmut!" Erin exclaimed, as the old painter rose and kissed her on both cheeks, only the plaster on his throat evidence of his life-threatening illness.

"Erin," he said, kissing her on the cheek. But his eyes were grey and serious.

"Go ahead," Travers said. "Tell Erin what you saw."

Ten minutes later, Erin left the surgery with the glow of white rage lit behind her eyeballs.

"Erin, wait," Travers hissed as he dogged her heels. "I didn't clue you in so you could fly into a revenge spiral. At least think about what you're going to do."

Erin reached the edge of the old resort fence with Travers still jogging to keep up and snapped at him to stay put. She wasn't having someone standing behind her. Then she was through the fence, past the meeting room, and into the old overgrown courtyard.

The door of Tristan's office was slid half-open, and she heard voices inside. Slowing at the threshold, she saw Skye perched on the edge of Tristan's desk, a pencil stuck over her ear and a sheaf of papers in her hand. Tristan himself was on his feet, as though he'd been pacing, his face pinched. Both of them looked up as Erin tripped in the doorway.

Recovering, Erin caught Skye's scowl and Tristan's guarded expression.

"Can we help you?" Skye asked, icily.

"I need to talk to Tristan."

Erin could feel how wide her nostrils were, how she was drawing breath like a racehorse after The Cup. She caught her reflection in Tristan's television; she looked wild, a sea monster beached after a storm.

"Are you feeling all right?" Tristan asked. And for just a second, Erin's resolve faltered. The concern in his voice was so genuine. She could hardly imagine he was the same person in Travers' video, or in Helmut's description. It took a moment to remember how he'd turned on her once, too, and that Alex was still lying in his hospital bed. She sucked a breath, the air damp and smelling of stale coffee grounds from the machine.

"I just wondered," she said, "how you think you're going to get away with it."

"Erin, we're trying to work here," Skye interrupted.

"Is this more of that environmental bullshit from the nosy diver boy?" Tristan cut across Skye. "Do we have to go through it again?"

"Ignore her, Tristan," Skye said, putting a proprietary hand on his arm. "She doesn't care about the island. She doesn't care about anyone but herself."

Erin's gaze moved between the two of them. She saw the devotion in her sister's eyes and felt sick for her. Skye was smarter than this; she'd always been the one with the sharp observations and the cutting opinions.

"I'm not talking about *that*," Erin said.

Skye now tried to turn Tristan back to their work, shutting Erin out. "I think we should call Marcus again," she said. "Really try to hammer them."

Bad idea, Erin thought, just as Tristan shook Skye off, and not gently. He hated being pushed around.

"Stay out of this, will you Skye?" he said. "I can handle this myself. So take off and let me deal with it."

His anger was like a guard dog's snap: sudden and savage, before he jerked it back on some kind of control chain. Skye flinched. After a hurt pause, she pushed past Erin, but not before Erin could see the fear in her eyes. Maybe that was the first time she'd seen him this way.

Erin could only hope.

"What the hell are you going on about?" Tristan growled, when Skye had gone. "You're my Racing Director and you just take off for days. If this was a normal arrangement you'd be out the door."

Erin stepped across the room, keeping the desk between them, choosing her words. The idea of working for him again was so far from her mind. "How come you haven't asked me the most obvious question yet?"

Tristan seemed to take this as a reprieve. He smiled, clearly thinking she was playing. "What's the most obvious question?"

"'How's Alex?'"

"I'm hardly be interested in your boyfriend's health."

"No. I suppose not. Especially after you tried to murder him."

There was a pause, then Tristan actually laughed. A deep, hearty unbelieving laugh. He wiped at the corner of his eye with his knuckle. "Oh, wow, Erin. Haven't you been dreaming up some fantasies. I wish I could tell you that I cared so much that I tried to off the bastard, but he just can't sail for shit. You have to avoid the boom when you're running down-wind."

He was taking such a perverse pleasure in it, Erin felt her stomach bottom out, wondering how deeply this malevolent streak ran in him.

"The boom, yes. It's much harder to avoid a swinging grappling hook." She held his gaze, looking for some flicker that he was rattled. "Someone saw you, Tristan. They saw what really happened."

Tristan only laughed harder, but it sounded forced now. He leaned a hand casually on the desk, the other sliding into his pocket. "You're being taken in by a shyster, Erin. I would have thought you were smarter than that."

"Funny, I was just thinking the same thing about Skye. She doesn't know about your temper, does she?"

Tristan's smile flickered. "On the contrary, she has been very useful. Not much of a lay, though, I'd have to say. Nothing like you."

Erin gave a disgusted snort.

"Oh come on, Erin, you used to enjoy it. No need to be virtuously revolted after the fact."

"You are despicable."

Tristan's face hardened. "I rather think I'm the only person around here who's cared enough about this place to make a hard go of it. You won't find many allies around here. Erin —

the girl who mysteriously lost her father at sea, and then ran away for years? I think it's going to be you on the outside, and people talking about what really happened. Won't be long before rumours spread around. Besides, you haven't exactly done a stellar job for me, either. You've never brought in that big sponsor. If this whole show fell over, I know who I'd blame."

Erin's mouth parched.

"Now," he said, straightening. "Get your bony arse out of my office. You're fired."

Outside, the atmosphere was heavy. Sweat slicked between Erin's shoulders as she stalked back towards the village. The clouds were in the south this time, a storm gathering there, just to be different. She broke into a jog, reeling from what Tristan had said. She hadn't been thinking about what Tristan meant to the island when she'd walked into his office. He might be a crook and worse, but he was the village's last hope. If the races didn't succeed, then the village would be finished, and he would pin the blame for it on Erin. Any reconnection Erin had glimpsed with Skye would be finished, too.

She didn't think for a moment that Helmut's word would stand up against Tristan's, and if Alex didn't remember anything, then Helmut's word would be all there was. Helmut might be well known, but he was also an old man with failing eyesight who lived like a recluse and painted ghosts. Not exactly the most reliable witness. And what did that matter anyway, if the village was in ruins?

And then there was what Tristan might do if Skye had told him about her father. What Erin had done had been illegal. Her father had known it – that was the whole reason for the charade in the first place. Erin saw her only option to leave, and look for work in some distant port that wasn't home and never would be. The idea drove the parched feeling into her heart like a stake.

Travers was still waiting by the outer fence.

"Call your friend and tell him I want to go back," she told him.

"What about Tristan?"

"Not now, Travers."

By the time they were passing Sandy's bakery, Travers was onto his second attempt to contact Charlie.

"Can't get through. First time, someone picked up but the line was dead. Now, it's just not connecting."

"It's the mobile tower. Plays up," Erin said. "Especially when you need it."

At the stairs to Travers' cabin, she kicked off her sandy shoes and paced into the kitchen, where she drank a full glass of water from the tap. Travers was trying the call again.

"Nothing," he said a moment later.

"Can I take your boat, then?"

Travers narrowed his eyes. "And what am I supposed to do if I need to go out on the water?"

"You can have the tender from my yacht."

Travers snorted. "Take your own bloody boat."

"The motor on the yacht only does five knots if I'm lucky," she said. "I won't get back to the coast before dark at that rate."

"We're on an island with tons of boats. Go and find someone else to leech off."

Erin had just reached for the glass again when she heard stomping footsteps on the cabin stairs. The next second, Skye burst into the cabin.

"Are you happy now?" she yelled across the room. Her face was flushed from furious running, her chest heaving. Her angry eyes were fixed on Erin.

"What's—"

"He's *leaving*," she spat. "Pulling out, the whole deal. The resort is off. He's tearing up contracts. He says he'll move the workers onto other projects that will see a better return and he's not coming back."

At that moment, a helicopter thundered overhead, bound for the airstrip. That must be Tristan's ride. Skye's anger cracked, and tears spilled from her eyes. She swatted at her face.

"I wish I'd never asked you to come back," she hurled at Erin. "This is *all* your fault."

And then Skye was gone in a flurry of sundress.

Chapter 28

Travers and Erin both went after her, Erin's heart squeezing in her temples. It was obvious to Erin that whatever she and Tristan had had was over, too. However wrong Skye had been, she hated seeing her sister in so much pain. She could only imagine what he must have said.

Around the bend in the cabin path, before the main beach, Travers stopped, looking out over the dunes. Erin saw the beach was empty, the storm clouds now bunching tighter on the southern horizon.

"She didn't go that way," he said, backing up, searching the ground.

"We were right behind her."

Travers backed up ten metres, to a fork no one used anymore, that speared off through a narrow lane between two coconut palms, then a patch of deep sand before it joined the main path again.

They followed it, finding a fresh eruption of sand where Skye had pulled her feet out of the deep drift.

"Must be going home," Erin muttered, jogging down the path. But the house was dark. Unless she was hiding in a closet, she'd gone somewhere else.

"You looking for Miss Jacobs?" said a small voice.

Erin turned from looking in Skye's dining room window to

see Tim's face peering from a hibiscus bush. A moment later, Monster's huge black muzzle popped up next to him.

"Did you see her?" Erin asked.

"Yep," said Tim, extracting himself and dusting sticks and leaves off his knees. "She went that way, up the trail." He pointed to where the inland track joined the back of the village.

Erin groaned. If Skye had decided to take off inland, it could take hours to track her down. But Travers reached into his pocket. He pressed a boat key into Erin's hand.

"Just you be sure you bring her back in one piece," he said. "Leave Skye to me. And Tim? You and Monster show me the way."

Erin found Alex still in the ICU, with a nurse who was changing his drip.

"Good news. He's moving down to the ordinary ward later on. No more constant monitoring," she said, then paused. "Would you like some dry clothes?"

Erin realised that her shirt was still soaked in sea water, and she smelled like a ripe lobster pot. But Alex seemed so much brighter since just this morning. She changed into another set of borrowed scrubs, and sat with him, holding back what she'd learned from Helmut and Travers. She couldn't even begin to know what to do with that, and the loss of the resort project had filled her stomach with sinkers.

"You're quite the story," the nurse said at the next round of checks.

Alex raised his eyebrows.

"I guess you haven't been watching the TV," Erin said.

"I have had a few other things on my schedule," he said, with a small smile.

"Travers had a camera on the back of his boat. Someone got

a hold of the footage of us coming to get you."

The smile slipped, and Alex closed his eyes. "I still don't remember," he said. "Will you tell me what happened?"

Erin told him, as plainly and matter-of-factly as she could. When she was finished, he said nothing for a long time.

"I'm starting to think," he said finally. "That boats aren't particularly good for my health."

Erin laughed. "Uh oh, what does that say about your future with a sailor?"

She was trying to lighten the mood, but a deep crease formed between Alex's brows. He reached for her hand. "Thank god you were there," he said. His look said he hoped there was a future, after all. Only Erin couldn't share the hope.

When they moved him down to the ward in the early evening, the news carried the story about Tristan's departure from the resort project, including an official press release peppered with terms like "market conditions", "critical mass of interest" and "unfavourable sponsorship outcomes". All Erin could think of was the village's excitement at the announcement just a few months ago, and the jubilation when the pilot races had brought in so many people. The town would be shell-shocked now. Tristan wouldn't care; he would never have to set foot there again. With great sadness, Erin knew she would have to do the same.

But then someone tapped her shoulder just past eight in the evening, she turned to find Travers. Behind him was Skye, looking apprehensive in the ward doorway.

Skye seemed to have transformed since the confrontation earlier in the day. Her face was relaxed, but for a wrinkle high on her brow that told Erin she was nervous. She was wearing an old pair of cut-off shorts and a white singlet, as if she might be headed to the beach, except for the bandage on her right ankle and the pair of crutches under her arms.

"Can we talk?" she asked.

"What happened to you?" Erin asked, as Skye took off clumsily down the hall, her good foot encased in a sandal, the bandaged one swinging.

"I'll get to that." Skye paused at the stairwell door and after a moment trying to awkwardly open it herself, let Erin pull the handle.

"We should take the lift," Erin argued, but Skye shook her head and headed up, the crutches creaking on each step.

"Now where are you going?"

"Trust me," Skye panted. "The lift doesn't go up here."

Three long minutes later, Skye pushed open a door and Erin saw they were on the roof, the great blanket of evening sky stretching overhead. With the light from the mainland, the stars were nothing like they were on Haven, but the air was cool and quiet.

"One of the nurses said they come up here to take a break on night shift sometimes, and I saw the vans downstairs," Skye explained, hobbling across the roof to peer over the railing over the hospital's entry. "I thought this might be better."

"Unless they have a drone up there," Erin said.

Skye actually laughed. "You're not that interesting, Erin Jacobs."

Erin smiled back, feeling a tiny tendril of connection with Skye, as though they were teenagers again and up to no good. Erin leaned on the railing and narrowed her eyes at the vans. "I reckon I could spit on them from here."

"Yeah?" said Skye. "Who're you aiming at?"

"That one, there," she said, pointing out a man fiddling with a camera in the glow of an entryway light.

"Fifty bucks says you miss."

Erin let the idea widen her smile, but her mind was on other things. "I'm sorry about Tristan, Skye. And about what you heard the other day. I never meant for you to find out like that."

"I don't want to talk about it," Skye said quickly. "I can't even begin to think how to forgive you and I'm still as angry as hell." She blew out a breath. "But that's not why I'm here. You were right about Tristan. And I feel like an idiot."

"You don't have to—"

"No, let me finish. I wanted the resort back up and running very badly. We all do. But I let it blind me. I don't think he ever cared about me, Erin. Just what I could do for him, which I'm ashamed to say wasn't very responsible."

"What do you mean?"

"I know some politicians, and some lobbyists. Being on the island, we've had to fight for a lot of things over the years. For the school, for everyone. I've done my networking. So I made introductions, told Tristan who he needed to see to get around some of the … obstacles." She gave Erin a sidelong glance. "You might think I'm just a boring schoolteacher, but that's only for the children. I know people. And how to get things done."

"Wow, Skye," Erin said, realising how little she knew about Skye's life in the past few years. "You should run for office."

Skye gave her a considering look, then shrugged. "Maybe. But can you imagine if it came out I'd helped a development get around environmental protections? Travers was foul when he found out. I don't know if he's forgiven me yet. But I'm not proud of myself either. I never really wanted to do it, but Tristan made me believe it was the only way to make the resort happen. Then later I started to have doubts, and I wouldn't push for the last barrier he needed moved. That's really what happened. I kept thinking that we would be able to make it work legitimately, but he'd already started to lose interest. I should have seen that in the way he behaved after you came back, but I didn't want to see that at first. In a way I'm glad that he's pulling out. The resort might have brought a lot of people, but maybe it would have ruined the island. I don't know how I'd have felt in five years if it had all gone ahead in those circumstances. Of course if Tristan and I had been—"

Erin snorted.

"Yes, look I know. I can't believe I didn't see what he was like. I'm sorry I turned on you for trying to warn me."

"But now the island's back to square one," Erin said. "I've been trying to think of what we could do. The resort was a massive thing; I have no idea where to begin and Tristan's right – no one else wanted to touch it. But the races were successful. Maybe we could run events like that ourselves. It wouldn't be a resort, but there would be high points in the year with more business for everyone at least."

Secretly, Erin couldn't imagine how to cover all the publicity and marketing that Tristan's people had done, but in the hope of the moment, it seemed a small thing.

"I've been thinking about that, too," Skye admitted. "I want you to tell me about how those things were organised."

Without prompt, both of them left the railing and pulled up two folding chairs that were tucked against a silver vent. Skye slipped her crutches to the floor.

"Well, there was a big group of people behind it," Erin

began, then outlined all the people she'd met and their roles. "But a huge number of other people were in Sydney, inside Tristan's company or hired consultants – marketing and all that. I don't know how they did their jobs. And they were the ones who brought in the cable coverage. To be honest, I haven't the first clue on that. And I saw the budget sheets – they spent tens of thousands before any boat had even sent an entry form."

They both fell silent, feeling the enormity of the task and how out of place they were to take it on.

"It wouldn't be a novel event anymore, either," Skye said. "This year it was something new. That won't be the case next year."

But Erin had seen the glimmer of hope. Fixing her mind on that bright spot, she ploughed on, sounding like Tony at one of their planning meetings. "No, that's an advantage. We can point to past success. We might just have to find a hook each year, something new to add to the program, to keep a spark alive."

"But what about the marketing stuff? I might know some politicians, but I don't have the first clue about that."

Erin leant back in her chair, picking out the stars overhead. "Actually, I have an idea about that."

"What?"

"You'll have to leave it with me." If she told Skye, Skye would want to come, and that wouldn't be right.

"I don't like secrets," Skye said coldly.

"Tell me what you did to your ankle, then."

Skye's grin turned sheepish. "Well, I went for a walk after the whole thing this morning."

"More like a run, I would think."

Skye scowled. "Fine, yes, an *energetic* walk. And I fell down a gully didn't I? Then of course the storm came in, and I couldn't get out again. I think I hurt it worse trying to climb out."

"Bloody hell, Skye. That's why Mum always wanted to know where we were going!"

"Travers found me." That small smile again.

"Oh, now I see," Erin said, teasing.

"No need to sound like that. I'm not barrelling into something else, not after Tristan."

"But?"

"But, I suppose he seems a good man," Skye conceded, with more affection that Erin had ever heard her use for anything, except maybe the island itself. "He's talking about sending his surveillance tapes to Drummond Enterprises – anonymously of course. I think he loves the island as much as any of us. I treated him rather badly and he's not holding a grudge, so who knows. Besides, we had an interesting time after he found me."

Erin's eyebrows rose.

"Your mind is in the gutter, Erin Jacobs!" Skye exclaimed, slapping Erin on the arm.

Erin only grinned more. "Well, explain yourself then. Stop leaving room for innuendo."

"Fine. To be honest, we were a bit lost. I'd made it a long way inland before Travers caught up, all the way into the foothills of the north. I don't know if I've ever been that way before. I didn't think it was possible after all these years exploring."

"So?"

Skye paused, and whispered. "We found the waterhole, Erin."

"What?"

"Bella's waterhole."

Erin felt as though a wire inside her was plucked and

hummed, singing a note that was warm and wonderous. "Are you sure?" she asked, breathless.

Skye nodded, her eyes shining. And so Erin had to ask.

"Skye – did Mum tell you Bella's real story?"

Skye lost her smile. "A year ago."

"Mum told me yesterday," Erin said.

"What did you think?"

"I was angry," Erin admitted. "And I feel awful for her, like I can't do anything about it. And yet … grateful. Because if she wasn't still hanging out the island, then Alex wouldn't be here either."

She told Skye about seeing Bella on the point during Alex's rescue, and Skye didn't seem at all surprised.

"She'll always be part of the island," Skye said. "And Erin, the waterhole? It's a *really* special place. There are Aboriginal paintings on the overhanging rocks. Whatever happens to the island, it shouldn't be somewhere just anyone can go. We have to protect it. Talk to the right people about how to do that."

"Mum can help," Erin said. "She said at least one Elder survived on the mainland. Maybe there's descendants."

They nodded in silent agreement, the first thing that seemed truly solid and agreed between them in years. Finally, Erin said, "Does this mean we're okay again?"

"Not yet," Skye said, frank to the last. "I can't begin to process Dad. It's such a shock. But I know how close you were. How he trusted you. Much as that makes me jealous, he must have had his reasons. Maybe in time we can work on it."

Erin bit her lip. "Skye … did you tell Tristan?"

Skye gave her a look like Erin was mad. "Of course not. But I don't want any secrets in our family again. Deal?"

They shook, and then seemingly satisfied, Skye dragged her

crutches up off the floor. "Come on then. You have to fill me in on Alex. And I want to hear the moment your idea for the marketing stuff plays out."

Alex had another good night, and the next morning the hospital physiotherapist had him up and moving. It thrilled Erin that he was leaving the bed, but she gave him the privacy she knew he would have wanted. She had a meeting to make.

She dodged the lingering news vans and snuck away from the hospital towards *OceanRunner*, the fancy resort where Ivan had last handed her back her sponsorship proposal.

She was extremely lucky, especially dressed in borrowed jeans and a scrub top, that the reception staff remembered her. She supposed that anyone meeting with Ivan in an exclusive resort would probably be burned into the eyeballs of the staff, but maybe her collision with the winch block had helped after all. And that was how she came to be sitting in the near-empty sunken bar with an untouched glass of sparkling wine that the waiter had brought with the compliments of Mr Borovich.

Erin was about to give up waiting when she heard footsteps, and Ivan appeared out of the elevators, trailing a man and a woman in sharp suits who were both frantically tapping on mini tablets. Ivan shook both their hands as they exited the front doors, and came towards Erin, putting in a jog that surprised her.

"Erin, I am sorry to keep you. I had a meeting to finish."

"Thanks for seeing me. I'm sorry I didn't call first."

"Please, please," he said, sitting across from her. "You do not need appointments, even if you are my defector." He gave her a friendly wink. "Besides, you are all over the news. Tell me, how is the doctor?"

"Out of danger, now, thank you," Erin said, surprised Ivan had paid so much attention. She paused as an unexpected well of emotion choked her at his kindness. She cleared her throat. "I want to talk about Haven — not the sponsorship again, just for advice. I thought maybe you could point me in the right direction."

"Of course. Please." He gestured her to speak.

"Tristan's pulling out of the project, so the whole resort and regatta development is over. And that means the village is losing its future. It can't survive for another five years like it is now. But Skye and I have a plan." She paused.

"Go on," he said.

"We want to keep the races going, maybe as they were in the pilot events this year. I know a bit about how it was done, because I designed the courses and helped with the team, but there was a lot of background business I don't know how to do. Promotion, marketing. Getting the cable channels interested in covering it. Can you help me find people who I could learn from? I don't have much money—"

Ivan cut her off with a raised hand. "Before I talk of this, I need to ask some things. Who is involved in these new races?"

"Well, just my sister Skye and me, so far. Besides that, I'm hoping to rope in Travers — he was the one with me on the boat you might have seen on the news — and find other people in the village who can help. Keep it on the island, an all-in-the-family kind of thing."

"Yes, good, okay. And has anyone offered you money yet?"

Erin laughed. "No, why would they?"

Ivan's eyebrows shot up. "Erin, your rescue was very visible. My people showed me the video on the YouTube. It has more than one million hits. Did you not know this?"

"Um, no?"

Ivan sat back, his tongue between his front teeth, arms folded, as he did when considering something important. "Let us go for a walk. I have some thoughts for you," he said finally.

They stepped out of the big glass windows by the pool, and walked around the sparkling water until they could face out over the ocean, where Haven was barely visible in the smudge of haze on the horizon.

"I like your ideas, Erin," Ivan said. "But what I like more is passion, and I see that in your eyes. You are interested. You want to make this happen. It is important for your home, for your family. You feel this project fits with you, in here, yes?" He made a fist over his heart.

"That's right," Erin said.

"It was the same for me, when I started my business. My family was poor, very poor. In the beginning, they keep me going. Over time, I enjoyed the work more and more, but I remember the reason I started. I think it helped my success. So, yes, Erin, I will help you. But if you are going to do this, you must learn business, too. Negotiation. That part, also, I will teach you, if you are willing."

Erin stared at him, incredulous. "How would that work?"

"The island races will be your project, but I will keep it directly under me. If I see you need help, I will send you to other projects, have you sit in on meetings so you can see how it is done. You will have to work very hard," he warned. "But I think you could be very good at this."

"Why would you do that? I mean, that's more than I was asking."

Ivan shrugged. "There are not enough women in my

company. Besides, I want something from you also."

"What's that?"

Ivan shaded his eyes, squinting at the horizon. "I wish to see this Great Haven. I am interested after all the videos, and I like the work of this painter, Helmut, who lives on the cliff. I bought one of his pictures. I would like to meet him."

Erin laughed. "Well, that's fairly easy to arrange."

"Also, I wish to see the resort."

"You do?" Hope flared like a shooting star in Erin's mind.

"Perhaps it is not dead. Perhaps Tristan is simply not the man for it. Did you know this hotel, here, is for sale?"

"No ..."

Ivan looked back at the resort building, with its Pacific island thatched style roof and the sculpted gardens. "It is well built, for sure. But inefficient. There is no renewable energy here — unimaginable with all this sunshine! And it appeals to a very small market when it is so expensive. No, no, the model is not sound. Not sustainable. No wonder it is for sale."

Erin raised her eyebrows. "Ok, so …"

"So, I am saying there is opportunity. Come, you will learn. Oh, and one more thing. I am intrigued about this Bella in Helmut's paintings. There is a story, yes? You will tell me?"

All Erin could do was smile. Bella's real story would stay in her heart, part of the glue that bound her to the island. Inspiring her to make a better tomorrow.

Chapter 29

Alex returned to the island a week later, his body on the way back to normal, even if his mind wasn't quite recovered. He still remembered nothing of the accident. In the afternoons, he often wandered down to sit on the jetty and stare at Bella's Leap, as if waiting patiently would bring it all back. Sometimes, he thought he had a flash of memory: the sound of sails snapping in the wind, the crash of a pulley block switching sides, the thumps of waves … but it wasn't a complete picture. He wondered if he was just imaging from what Erin had told him.

He'd walked all over the headlands, and gone out with Travers into the channel, refamiliarising, searching for triggers that just didn't seem to be there. As if the sea had washed him clean.

As if making it safe for him to stay.

He was almost glad his memory had blocked it. One harrowing experience in the ocean was enough for a lifetime. But he thought a lot about Erin. He had dreams of her sitting by his bedside, but could never quite hear what she was saying.

He began seeing patients the next week, even though with Tristan's departure, his employment had technically been terminated. Sandy had kept the practice stocked, and no one else was claiming the surgery so he thought he should keep busy. In fact, his waiting room was full to bursting as everyone found ailments they needed checking in the wave of the now famous Dr Bell coming back to the island. Alex could only laugh. He was touched so many people were concerned for his safety. His room was stuffed with gifts, his calendar groaning with invitations to dinner. It gave him a warm sense of belonging.

But it was Erin who truly held his heart.

He finished in the clinic and came through to his room to find her perched on the bed, a stack of business documents fanned out around her, a pen behind her ear, one tanned leg tucked up underneath her. He found it startling and incongruous, like finding a surfer trading stocks on a laptop, but she and Skye were determined to make the races a success. Ivan was coming out later in the week.

"What time do we have to leave again?" he asked.

She looked up, her attention broken, blue eyes refocusing as she smiled. "It's island time, babe. No hurry."

They were going up to Helmut's for dinner, an invitation Alex looked forward to fulfilling. He sat down now beside Erin. "I decided something today."

"What's that?"

"I'm going to stay on in the clinic, set it up as a private practice. The island needs one."

"What about the financials? It was never solvent as a practice on its own."

Alex smiled to himself. Erin had become increasingly conscious of such things. He imagined in a few months, she'd have a pair of horn-rimmed glasses and a green lamp. Actually, the idea of her in glasses was sexy, like a naughty librarian. He had to swallow and redirect his thoughts before he got distracted.

"Well, yes you're right. Not enough patients, and the cost of supplying is higher. I'm still going to have to take some shifts at the base hospital. But I think you might be spending some time on the mainland, too, right?"

She nodded, slowly gathering her notes into a pile. Then she rose and put her arms around him, burying her face in his shoulder for just a moment.

"It's nice that you're going to keep the surgery open. Dad always worked on the mainland, too, for the same reason. And everyone will be over the moon you're staying. I don't think any of them expect that."

Alex hadn't expected it either. From a job that was supposed to be temporary, he had found a new direction. Karen Bailey, the doctor on the mainland, was talking about setting up a regional medical association, so all the doctors who worked remotely could have a group to discuss their practices with. In an isolated and demanding profession, Alex thought it was a brilliant idea, and it was something he could help run with some time on the mainland.

And then there was Erin. Brave and clever and fascinating, who made the days light up. He had never expected to find her, or anything like he felt for her again. She was part of the Haven paradise – a tempestuous, unpredictable paradise, perhaps, but that kept things interesting.

They ascended the headland just as the sun was sinking down over the water. The sky was clear tonight, the first stars showing through the darkening blue, a bare smudge of pink backlighting the horizon. Instead of taking the inland path, they cut to the top of Bella's Leap, pausing wordlessly near the summit to watch the last light fade. Erin was drawn here now more than ever, and every time she looked out on the ocean and the rocks below, she wanted to build some kind of cairn, or leave a lantern burning. Bella was part of the island, and regardless of whether she was real or a trick of the light, she had saved Alex's life.

Alex hadn't asked about Bella since the accident, but something about his stillness beside her now made Erin wonder if he'd heard every word she'd said while he was unconscious, and was now turning the knowledge over like a pebble, deep in his mind.

Finally, when the sky in the east was flat black and starlit, they broke out their lanterns and followed the path to Helmut's studio, the air thickening with a delicious scent of Stella's goulash. Then they laughed over food and wine deep into the night, Helmut telling stories of paintings and artists, Stella hugging Alex and Erin in gratitude of his rescue, in between tales of her years in the European bohemian scene.

"You can't tell me you don't miss Europe," Alex said at one stage, still wiping the tears from his eyes after a sordid story involving a drinking contest and a donkey.

"Well, yes," Stella admitted. "It's nothing like Australia. I don't want to *live* there again, but it does feel like home going back."

"Mmm," Erin agreed. "I'd put up with the awful showers for a few months. The Med is amazing in places. And the food, *my god*."

"I've never been, apart from for Kiel," Alex said, enjoying Erin's constant delight in eating.

"What? How could this be true?" Helmet said.

Erin caught Alex's eye. In that glance, she saw possibilities. Sailing with him in the clear waters off Turkey, or eating dinner together in a rustic restaurant on the Riviera. In response, a slow smile spread across his face. That was when she truly believed they could make a life together.

When dinner was over, Helmut produced a bottle of port, poured them glasses and ushered them into the studio. "I want you to see my latest work."

There, three canvases stood proudly on easels by the dark windows, only the moon casting glow over the calm evening sea below the cliffs outside.

Erin gasped.

The first canvas showed the boiling cloud of a storm, tearing down from the north, the sea whipped to froth and pummelling the headland. And there, dwarfed by all of it, was a sailboat racing the wind, two tiny figures visible on the deck. In the next, painted as though looking towards the island, a white boat came perilously close to the towering cliffs, its side just visible over a wave roll, two figures bent over the side. The third was a view of Bella's Leap itself, the storm now retreating into the south, the sky gone blue behind it. In each of the pictures, Bella appeared on the cliff. In the first she was an apparition, insubstance, part of the storm. In the second, she had solidified, a deity with a lantern shining mercy down from above. And in the last, she became part of the reborn day – calm and graceful, a mere wisp of cloud, a suggestion of a woman. Half memory, half dream.

"She appeared a long time that day," Helmet said. "I paint like a madman, thinking she is going to disappear. But no, she stays on. I think she stay so that you can, too, Dr Alex."

Erin watched for Alex's reaction. He was stroking his chin,

peering at the pictures with intensity.

"Even I saw her," Stella said, her voice wonderous. "Even if everyone's saying it was just Monster, I know what I saw."

"Monster?" Erin said.

Stella nodded. "Was lost all during the storm apparently. Tim was quite beside himself. The dog came back with his coat full of the burrs from those weeds that grow around the cliff top."

"No," Helmut said. "This was not what I saw."

"But you are going blind, darling," Stella said, and Helmut laughed.

"Two of the pictures already sell," Helmut said. "She is my patron saint, I think."

Much later, as they walked back towards the village in the lantern light, Alex paused at the top of the Leap again. He turned off the light, letting the moonlight paint the rocks in pale luminous grey. The waves shushed in and out below them. The world up here seemed so empty, a place between sky and sea, as it had been the day he and Erin had first met here.

"I dream about her sometimes," he said. "I feel like I knew she was there that day, even though I can't remember anything. I know sailors are a superstitious lot, but is that strange?"

Erin slid her hand into his. "No."

Alex chuckled. "Maybe it was Monster."

Erin shook her head, and didn't say anything for a long time. Most of the memories of that day were like wisps of fog, but her vision of Bella was a rock in a channel – the one fixed and undeniable reference.

"She showed me where you were, you know," Erin said. "I looked up onto the cliff top, and she pointed down into the waves. I'm not going to explain something I couldn't be more grateful for."

Alex let a deep breath go, as if something long held had torn free and it was easier to breathe without the weight.

Erin took another breath. "There's something else I want to tell you. About what happened when my father died."

He put an arm around her shoulders, warm against her skin. "I have a feeling," he said slowly, "that you may have already told me."

Erin leaned her head against him, knowing her time of running away was finally over.

"Let's go home," she said.

12 months later

The dance had been Skye's idea, a fitting end to the race weekend, and a reason to keep the crowds on the island for another night. The weather had been cooperative – twenty knots of wind that set the yachts flying, a small storm Friday night that had kept alive Haven's notoriety, and clear evening skies that lifted spirits as the music pumped from the new village square. Erin couldn't have hoped for better.

Except that she was exhausted. It was worse than any sailing race she'd been part of; she seemed to spend the whole weekend dashing around, a radio or phone constantly to her ear, having to be *nice* and diplomatic to people, and correcting last-minute disasters, like the near loss of the caterers suckling pig. Of all the things. All this was enough to turn her mad, if she hadn't been so deliriously satisfied.

Because, despite the problems, she was mostly on top of it. Ivan had been as good as his word, and his training had prepared her. She'd never worked so hard in her life as this last year, but it all seemed worth it. Two race weekends had brought a huge injection of cash to the island businesses, and rave reviews across the sailing and holiday world. Sponsors were now approaching them, interested in what they had in store next year, and rumours had already leaked about the planned music festival. And just down the main beach, work was just beginning on the new, re-visioned Great Haven resort.

"There you are," Erin exclaimed, as Alex appeared at the edge of the crowd, his sleeves rolled up. "I wondered where you'd escaped to."

"Glass in a foot, and another kid who burned himself on a lighter."

"I thought it would be duty calling."

Alex kissed her. "How about your duties?"

"Almost, done, I think. Nothing else to do but everyone to have a good time, but not so good the mainland cops have anything to do. I want them to come back next year."

Alex laughed. "I saw the police in the queue for the suckling pig earlier. People were whispering jokes, and Skye gave them all stern looks."

"I think she still has the local member bailed up now. She might retire at the next election, and I think Skye's trying to encourage her to stay on."

Erin scanned the crowed and pointed out Skye, in one of the corners away from the speakers, animated as she talked to an older woman. "Well, if she's relaxed enough to be shoring up future support, our work here must be done. Good. I'll get us some food and we can head down the beach."

They ate at the crest of the dunes, under the star-filled sky. Erin savoured the idea of a sleep-in tomorrow. Then it would be back to the project office, still under Ivan's guidance but increasingly being given independence.

Erin had been so busy in the last year she'd almost missed when the media first began reporting Tristan's business troubles – creditors accusing Drummond Enterprises of failing to pay accounts, then the company being placed in administration. At first, Tristan fronted the cameras himself, denying everything.

He only stopped when the first of two harassment and intimidation claims surfaced from former employees. That was when rumours also started up about incriminating footage. These were too circumstantial for the mainstream media, but the online sailing community buzzed with it for a while, though the footage itself never did come to light. Travers wouldn't be drawn about it, but he toasted the news anytime the a Drummond Enterprises story of woe was reported. Erin watched the empire crumbling, and couldn't help feel justice had come around to Tristan, too.

Ivan's style was very different to Tristan's – his business was vast, and he delegated to his trusted people. He insisted on doing things right the first time and never raised his voice. The resort plans had taken a long while to remodel, making it energy efficient and automated enough to bring costs way down, and including a resort-owned launch boat to strip the supply costs. Ivan's shipping business had been perfect to take that on, and they'd then included black-water processing and a water use strategy to minimise any damage to the local marine environment. It had taken time and money, which Ivan had rigorously taught Erin to take into account. All the effort had been worth it. The village was optimistic and the resort would be as good as they could make it. Now, they just needed it finished ... and for people to come.

"I'm really proud of you," Alex said. "Everyone said it couldn't be done, but you found a way. And you and Skye made these races a success."

"With a lot of help."

He shook his head. "We all do things with a lot of help. But leadership doesn't come around so often. That part was all you. And tomorrow, you get to be an actual star."

Erin groaned. "Don't remind me." A director was coming out to the island in the afternoon, keen to discuss a movie concept about the island, maybe about Bella, maybe about Erin and the village. Maybe about both.

"He doesn't even know what he wants," Erin said. "I'd be happier if it was never made. They won't get the story right anyway."

"Maybe not, but we'll know."

Erin leaned against him, solid and reassuring. They had begun to talk about what had happened that day in the storm, carefully, but both of them admitted there were parts of what happened they would never be sure of. When Erin looked up towards Bella's Leap, she did so without a trace of the story from her childhood. She saw Bella now as a survivor, a symbol of vigilant hope. Because Erin and Alex had both survived and found love. The island would go on, and they would call it home wherever the winds took them.

Thank You

I am immensely proud and grateful to have such a community of loyal readers, many of whom have been with me since my first novel was published in 2013. My career exists because of you all, and your support has allowed me to keep writing as publishing has changed around us.

Reviews help us writers immensely, so please do leave yours on your preferred platform if you can. It makes a huge difference in helping other readers discover books, and in making our careers viable. A recommendation is the highest form of praise.

You can find my other books through your local library and through ebook borrowing platforms, at online book retailers, or through my website, charlottenash.net. My social media links are at the front of this book, and I'm always happy to receive messages. Happy reading!

Charlotte
April 2020

Saving You

Three escaped pensioners
One single mother
A road trip across the USA

In their tiny green cottage under the trees, Mallory Cook and her five-year-old son, Harry, are a little family unit who weather the storms of life together. Money is tight after Harry's father, Duncan, abandoned them to expand his business in New York. So when Duncan fails to return Harry after a visit, Mallory boards a plane to bring her son home any way she can.

During the journey, a chance encounter with three retirees on the run from their care home leads Mallory on an unlikely group road trip across the United States. Zadie, Ernie and Jock each have their own reasons for making the journey and along the way the four of them will learn the lengths they will travel to save each other – and themselves.

An uplifting drama leavened by gentle humour, blossoming friendships and a good, old-fashioned romance — The Courier-Mail

Fans of The Unlikely Pilgrimage of Harold Fry and The Best Exotic Marigold Hotel will enjoy this tale of friendship, family and the road — The New Daily

The Horseman

Escape to the High Country in this passionate love story of a young doctor and a legendary horseman whose lives become inextricably linked.

It's been eleven years since Dr Peta Woodward, born into a horse-breeding dynasty, fled the family stud in the wake of a deadly tragedy that split her family apart. Carrying wounds that have never truly healed, Peta has focused on helping others. But when an injury during a solo trip through the Australian High Country leaves her stranded, the man who comes to her rescue is Craig Munroe, a born and bred high-country horseman, and the kind of man legends are written about.

Stuck in the tiny town of Yarraman Falls while she recovers, Peta is surrounded by prying eyes and heartbreaking reminders of all she has lost. But while she resolves to leave as soon as she can, fate has other ideas . . .

... features the kind of country town we all want to settle down in and the kind of man we'd pick to fall in love with — iBooks review

The Paris Wedding

Ten years ago, Rachael gave up the love of her life. Now, he's marrying someone else. In Paris. Would you go?

It's been ages since Rachael West has seen Mathew, the man she once believed she couldn't live without. Receiving his wedding invitation is bittersweet—while oddly touched he's asked her, she knows that facing him will be the hardest thing she's ever done. Because Rachael has never gotten over Matthew.

But her friends and family convince her to attend. After all, it's an all-expenses-paid trip to Paris! Surely she can get through that one day, and discover all the delights of that magical city.

So Rachael leaves her small town, setting off for the City of Lights with her best friend, two feuding neighbours, and a suitcase full of home-sewn couture in tow. She's determined to let Paris work its magic—and it does by way of a handsome photojournalist. And before her adventure is over, Rachael will be faced with yet another choice. But this time, hers isn't the only happiness at risk ...

A tale of loss, self-discovery and the depth of friendship ... Nash's spellbinding descriptions of Paris, the City of Love are a treat, as is that bittersweet idea of "the one that got away" — iBooks review

The Walker-Bell Saga

The bestselling, intertwined romance stories of the brothers in two families, and the women they love. The books can be read as stand-alones or as a series for a richer reading experience.

Ryders Ridge (Book 1)

Daniella Bell comes to town with an unspeakable secret ... then she meets Mark Walker. Will she be strong enough to face the past?

Iron Junction (Book 2)

Beth Harding runs away to a remote town at the same time Will Walker is running from his home. Can they love each other despite all that stands in their way?

Crystal Creek (Book 3)

Christina Price vowed to never go home, but when fate lands her back in the military town, she falls in love with Captain Aiden Bell, and nothing can be the same again.

A spirited heroine, a sexy farmer and a secret. Nash has created a dynamic debut novel that grabs you from the first page — Fleur McDonald

A skilful mix of rural charm and gripping medical drama — West Weekend Magazine

www.ingramcontent.com/pod-product-compliance
Lightning Source LLC
Chambersburg PA
CBHW061050190726
48286CB00006B/1684